MAR 2 2 2005

D0457750

THE
BARON HONOR

THE
BARON HONOR

JORY SHERMAN

A TOM DOHERTY ASSOCIATES BOOK
NEW YORK

This is a work of fiction. All the characters and events portrayed in this novel are either fictitious or are used fictitiously.

THE BARON HONOR

This book is printed on acid-free paper.

A Forge Book
Published by Tom Doherty Associates, LLC
175 Fifth Avenue
New York, NY 10010

www.tor.com

Forge® is a registered trademark of Tom Doherty Associates, LLC.

Library of Congress Cataloging-in-Publication Data

Sherman, Jory.
  The Baron honor / Jory Sherman.—1st ed.
    p.   cm.
  "A Tom Doherty Associates book."
  ISBN 0-312-86736-0 (acid-free paper)
  EAN 978-0312-86736-2
    1. Baron family (Fictitious characters)—Fiction.   2. Rio Grande Valley—Fiction.
  3. Ranch life—Fiction.   4. Texas—Fiction.   I. Title.

PS3569.H43B354   2005
813'.54—dc22

                                                                        2004056326

First Edition: March 2005

Printed in the United States of America

0 9 8 7 6 5 4 3 2 1

To Sandy and Bob St. John,
with respect and admiration

I am convinced that the world is not a mere bog in which men and women trample themselves and die. Something magnificent is taking place here amidst the cruelties and tragedies, and the supreme challenge to intelligence is that of making the noblest and best in our curious heritage prevail.

—C. A. Beard

Cast of Characters

Box B Ranch

MARTIN BARON — Texas Ranger
ANSON BARON — Martin's son
PEEBO ELVES — Anson's friend
SOCRATES — freed slave
FORREST REDMOND — architect
JULIO SIFUENTES — ranch hand
CARMEN SIFUENTES — Julio's wife
CARLOS QUINTANA — ranch hand
AUGUSTO MONTECITO — ranch hand
LUCIA MONTECITO — Augusto's wife

Townspeople

KEN RICHMAN — Martin Baron's friend
NANCY GRANT — Ken's girlfriend
PATRICK "DOC" PURVIS — town doctor
LORENE SISLER — Doc Purvis's niece
ED WALES — publisher, *The Baronsville Bugle*
JIM CALLAN — typesetter
MILLIE COLLINS — waitress, Longhorn Saloon

Rangers

ALLEN "AL" OLTMAN
DAN SHEPLEY
KENNY DARNELL — Anson's uncle (Caroline's brother)
JIM JOE CASEBOLT
PIERRE "DUBIOUS" DEBOIS
SGT. JAMES REASONER

Lazy K Ranch

ROY KILLIAN
URSULA (KILLIAN) WILHOIT — Roy's mother
DAVID WILHOIT — married Ursula
WANDA FANCHER — Roy's girlfriend

HATTIE FANCHER — Wanda's mother
FIDELIUS — freed slave
PETUNIA — Fidelius's wife

Rocking A Ranch

MATTEO AGUILAR
LUZ AGUILAR — Matteo's wife
JULIO AGUILAR — Matteo's son
LUCINDA — Luz's twin sister
CAUDILLO — Aguilar ranch hand
PEREZ — Aguilar ranch hand
DAGOBERTO SANTOS — ranch hand
EMILIO
NUNCIO ALICANTE — ranch hand
TOMAS LUCERO — ranch hand
ALLESANDRO GOMEZ — ranch hand
FIDEL RIOS — ranch hand
JORGE RIOS — brother of Fidel

Mescalero Band

CULEBRA "SNAKE" — Chief of Mescalero Band
OSO "BEAR"
TECOLATE
LOBITO
ABEJA

Others

MICKEY "MIGUEL" BONE
DAWN (MADRUGADA) BONE — Bone's wife
JUAN BONE — Bone's son
JULES REYNAUD — a Frenchman
SETH "CULLIE" CULBERTSON
BENDIGO VARGAS — curander (healer, witch doctor)
ROBERTO SAN JUAN — acting constable of Baronsville
VIEJO (Fidelio Antonio de Lopez y Santiago)
FRANCISCO SANTIAGO, "PACO" — Viejo's son

THE
BARON HONOR

THE GROUND REEKED of death and wood smoke. The dead lay in grotesque, unnatural positions all around the charred and smoldering ruins of La Loma de Sombra, the Baron house, on the Box B. The faces of the dead were brown Mexican faces, faces that revealed the Indian and Spanish bloodlines, gnarled now, as if from a sudden onset of old age, and frozen to rigid, leathery masks that resembled ancient pagan wood carvings.

The land around the burned house looked like a tableau of a battlefield, with the dead men strewn like dolls in the green grass, leaning against a tree, or lying beside the barn as if halted while going about their errands, their rifles beside them like some form of arcane punctuation.

Some lay with outstretched hands as if they had been grasping for something beyond their reach before they died; others lay scrunched up as if, in their last agonizing moments, they were trying to return to the womb from whence they came. One young Mexican lay facedown, his head twisted to one side, his cheek resting on an arm, and his face bore the linear, meandering tracks of his last tears. One side of his lips was caked with dirt and beneath his nose was visible the stippling of a moustache that now would never grow. His lips were slightly parted as if he had uttered a small prayer just before he took his last breath. His eyes were closed and would ever remain so on that earthly corpse.

A riderless horse stood next to the cornfield in the garden out back of where the house used to be, its reins dangling on the ground. Its dead rider lay against one of the furrows, his face striped by the shadows of the stalks and leaves playing across his features, so that he seemed almost alive. But his eyes were closed and the only movements were those wispy shadows shifting, shifting, like the ghostly arms and hands of wraiths, as if trying to reach inside his body and pluck out his soul.

Anson Baron stood there, all alone, as if entranced, his gaze sweeping the battlefield and noting the dead and their forlorn horses, their rifles and pistols lying on the ground like toys in an empty schoolyard. His nostrils burned from the smoke that drifted from the charred lumber that had once been his father's house and his own. It seemed to him that he had been raped by some unseen force and he felt soiled and empty, angry and forsaken.

Out of the corner of his eye, he saw his father walking toward him, his bootheels making him wobble slightly. And when Anson turned to look at him, his father seemed out of focus, unreal, like one of those dead men coming to life and walking his way. But it was only that his father was obscured by the pall of smoke that hung over the land like a mortician's shroud.

As Martin Baron drew closer, his son noticed the years his father was carrying and he was struck with a sudden pang of sadness. He had not noticed that his father was growing older, had hardly noticed any change in him at all.

"Pa," Anson said.

"You all right, son?"

Anson nodded. "You?"

"On the outside."

"I know what you mean. Well, you got him."

"Matteo? Yes. He's going to jail for what he did."

"You ought to hang him from one of those box elders yonder."

Martin reached in his pocket and pulled out something that

caught a glint of sun from somewhere beyond the pall of smoke.

"What's that?" Anson asked.

Martin handed it to him. Anson turned it over in his hands. It was light in weight but seemed to weigh a ton with something intangible that it carried. "You decided, then. Oltman talked you into joining the Texas Rangers."

"I—" Martin started, but he didn't finish what he was going to say.

"You're going away again."

"That's about it. Yes."

"When?"

"Today. Now."

"You're just going to walk away from all this. As if it never happened."

"The whole country's at war, Anson. I thought about this. I don't want to be cannon fodder for an army. With the Rangers, I can fight on my own terms."

"There's plenty of fighting right here, Pa."

"This fight is over. There's a bigger one waiting out there." Martin swept the air with his right arm.

"What if the war comes right here?"

"Maybe I'll be better able to help if I'm not tied down."

"What about me?"

"This is your ranch, Anson. Your ma gave it to you. You'll know what to do."

Anson felt something tighten inside him, as if a fist was knotting up in his stomach. It was like the feeling he'd had when his mother died, a feeling of abandonment, and more than a slight twinge of anger. He fought to keep his emotions under control. He wanted to strike his father and compel him to stay. He wanted to punish him for walking away from the Box B at such a crucial time.

"You always do this," Anson said.

"What?"

"Run away when things get rough."

"I'm not running away, son."

"Yes you are."

"Look, Oltman made me a good offer. And I can't just sit here and do nothing. Texas is part of the Confederacy and I'm not going to let others fight my battles for me. There's a lot at stake."

"There's a lot at stake *here*."

"You can handle it. You know how to run this ranch better than anyone."

"What if it was me going away?"

"What do you mean?"

"Would you stay and run the ranch?"

"I would hate to see you go. I would not like to send my only son off to war—off to a war he might not come back from."

"I guess it's in your blood, Pa."

"What?"

"The wanderlust. Seems like you're always running off somewhere, leavin' us to worry and wonder."

"Well, your ma's not worrying any more."

"No, I reckon not. Me, neither. You go on. I hope you come back someday."

"I hope so, too."

"The ranch'll be here and so will I, I reckon."

"I'll talk to Ken Richman in town, have him send out some men and lumber to help rebuild the house."

"Well, I reckon that's it, then," Anson said, his stomach muscles tightening like barrel straps.

"You take care of yourself, son."

"I'll do my best."

His father walked away, then, and Anson couldn't look at him. He turned and stumbled, almost unaware of where he was walking, but when he looked up, he saw the smoking ruins of the house and everything seemed to come down on him all at once, the whole weight of what had happened, the battle, the screaming, the fire, the dead Mexicans, his father saying goodbye.

At that moment, nothing seemed real. It was if he were stumbling through a dream and would wake up at any moment. Everything he saw blurred and he realized his eyes were wet. He wiped a hand across them and drew in a deep breath. He looked around for a familiar face and finally saw Peebo Elves standing on the slope of the hill to the right of where the house had stood, as if surveying the ravages of war from a high point. Peebo waved and Anson started toward him, picking up his feet and trying to control the emotions seething within him like writhing snakes.

"I hope the bastard never comes back," he said, and clenched his fists in a blind rage. "I hope the son of a bitch gets killed and don't never come round here no more."

2

───■───

GLASSY FIXED EYES stared up at the sun, the frosty pupils frozen like the hideous grin on the dead Mexican's face, which seemed to mock the onlookers with its rows of white teeth flecked with blood.

"Take a good look, you son of a bitch," Martin Baron said to Matteo Aguilar. "That's what you've done here."

"I did not kill that man," Matteo said.

"No, I killed him. But he was one of your soldiers and you sent him to his death when you brought war to my ranch."

Matteo forced himself to look at the grinning death mask again. He recognized the man now. His name was Cosimo Puentes and he was only twenty-two years old. He had a wife and daughter who would never see him again. There was a small black hole in his throat and he lay in a pool of his own blood, which was turning thick and hard in the sun.

"This is what happens in war," Matteo said, shrugging. "I wish that was you lying there dead."

"I ought to take you over to the nearest tree and hang you," Martin said, a thin muscle quivering along his jawline. "But these boys say you've got to stand trial."

"I have done nothing but try and reclaim my own family's land," Matteo said.

"I paid your family for this land and you know it. It is no longer your land. It never was."

"Martin, we'd better light a shuck," Allen Oltman said. "We've got a ride ahead of us and we're burning daylight."

"I just wanted this bastard to take a good long look at what he's done to the men who worked for him and trusted him."

"It ain't going to help none," Oltman said. "You lost just about everything and you need to testify against this man."

Martin looked up and turned his head toward the ruins of his home, still smoking, razed to ashes. He clenched his teeth and his jaw tightened so that the muscle stopped quivering.

"Yeah, let's go, Al. Maybe I'll see Matteo hang yet."

"Maybe," Oltman said. "But I'll see you sworn in as a Texas Ranger first."

Martin let out a breath. He had made his decision. If there was to be more fighting in Texas, he would wage war as a Texas Ranger, not as a Confederate soldier. If he was going to fight for something, it would not be for slavery, but for Texas, for his home.

"Yeah," Martin said. "Let's go. I can't stand looking at what this bastard has done anymore."

"One day, Martin," Matteo said, "I will piss on your grave, and where your house once stood, mine will stand. This is Aguilar land, gringo."

"No, you're wrong, Matteo," Martin said, with an even tone. "This is Baron land. And it always will be."

Oltman jerked on the reins of Matteo's horse and headed toward the road to Baronsville. He had seen the dark look in Martin's eyes and knew that Matteo was just a whisper away from death. Martin was ready to kill the Mexican with his bare hands, and if he did, it would be his sad duty to lead Martin off to the gallows, and he wanted him alive and wearing a Ranger badge.

When the Civil War crept toward Texas it was like a dark cloud hiding the sun and staining the land. For Anson Baron, the war started the day his father left to join the Texas Rangers, the same day that their home was burned to the ground by Matteo Aguilar.

The pall of smoke that hung in the sky over the ruins of the Baron home at La Loma de Sombra cast a shadow over the Box B that would linger for years, and no amount of rebuilding would ever completely drive away the shadow that had found its way into Anson Baron's heart as he watched his father ride away to join the Texas Rangers that same day, while the wood still smoldered and the embers winked and flared with the vagrant breezes of afternoon.

"Goodbye, son," Martin Baron called out to Anson. "You take care of the ranch, will you?"

"I always do."

Anson saw something flash in his father's eyes, and Martin's face took on a somber cast for a brief moment. But Martin said no more, and rode away with Al and the two other rangers, Dan Shepley and Kenny Darnell, Anson's uncle, who had Matteo Aguilar in custody. Anson stood there and watched them ride toward Baronsville until they turned into small specks on the horizon, then disappeared.

"Mighty tough," Peebo Elves said in the quiet that rose up like the smoke still pigtailing toward the sky from the burnt house.

"What's tough?" Anson asked.

"Your father leavin' and all."

"He's left before." Anson could not blanch the bitterness in his tone, or in his heart. His pa was always leaving, it seemed. The man grew no moss on his feet.

"But it's different this time. He's goin' off to war."

"What in hell do you think we just went through here with Aguilar?" At least this one was over with, he thought. His pa just didn't want to stay around to clean up the mess. Martin was a coward about some things. When it came to fixing family troubles, his pa just up and left.

"Well, it ain't exactly the same thing, Anson."

Anson frowned. "Ain't it? Matteo was our neighbor, for Christ's sake. Now, we're goin' to have Yankees swarming all over us like hornets. And Pa is going to be right in the thick of it. Maybe us, too."

"Shit, I never thought of it like that. I figured the Yankees would stay the hell out of Texas. I never figured we'd be fighting any war here."

"Well, war is just another word for robbery. Matteo wanted the

Box B and he declared war on us. The North wants to take over the South, steal every goddamn thing we have."

"I thought it was about slavery."

"That's just an excuse," Anson said. "The North means to rob us blind."

"Damn," Peebo said, and Anson could see that his friend was genuinely puzzled. Gone was that wide grin of his, the dazzle in his eye. He looked, Anson thought, like a man who had been punched in the stomach. But that was the way it was when a man's world started to overturn, when he felt the ground sinking beneath him and sensed a bottomless pit below. Anson had had that same feeling many times. When Mickey Bone left the ranch, when Juanito left, when his father went away to sea or to New Orleans. When his mother died. The world changed. All the time. And, there was no predicting the future, no correcting the past. What was done, was done, and what was to come was anybody's guess.

"It may not be so bad," Anson said, to bring Peebo back from where he had gone in his mind. "Maybe it'll be a quick war, and the Yankees will lose."

"Maybe shit ain't brown," Peebo said, and he flashed a shadow of that famous grin of his. It was brief and winking, and soon fled his face, as if a cloud had passed over it.

Anson looked at the smoking ruins of his home and saw Doc Purvis and his niece Lorene Sisler attending to the wounded. Some of his men were carrying wounded Mexicans, Matteo's men, over to one of the trees where the doctor had set up a kind of outdoor hospital. Other men walked around, looking dazed, and the tall Negro, Socrates, stood by the wagon beyond the house, looking at the cannon that sat atop its bed, the cannon Anson's father had not fired in this fight because Anson's dead mother, Caroline, had not wanted him to use the cannon. The cannon's brass barrel gleamed in the sun as if it were covered with bluebottle flies crawling over something dead and grisly.

"La Loma de Sombra," Anson breathed.

"Huh?" Peebo said.

"Shadow Hill. Where our home once stood. Aptly named, wouldn't you say?"

"Christ, Anson. What made you think of that at a time like this?"

"It was named because of the big live oaks that shaded us, but now it has a whole different meaning. The smoke just hangs up there in the sky, like a dark cloud. Gives me the willies."

"Hell, this whole thing has me spooked. I'm still tryin' to get it all straight in my mind. How Aguilar come at us with a damned small army and we nearly got skinned, the whole bunch of us."

"Where's Roy Killian?" Anson asked suddenly.

"I don't know. Over yonder with all his women, I reckon." Peebo pointed to the clump of trees that stood at what had once been the left side of the house.

"I don't see him there," Anson said, and turned away suddenly, a catch in his throat, tears filling his eyes.

"Smoke?" Peebo asked inanely.

"Damn, I can't look at it any more," Anson said.

"The house?"

"The ashes. It's like being raped, Peebo. If I had Matteo in my hands now, I'd wring his damned neck and keep squeezing until every last breath was out of his chest."

"You can bunk with me, you know. It ain't much, but I didn't get burned out."

"It's the books," Anson said.

"Huh?"

"All my books were in there. The ones Juanito Salazar gave me, and some I got on my own that he told me to read."

"Oh, books. You can always get more. Someplace, I reckon."

"Oh, Christ, Peebo. You don't understand. Those books were my friends, especially those Juanito gave me. When I read them, it was almost as if Juanito was still alive and I was talking to him."

"I reckon I don't understand. They're just a bunch of words to me."

"Well, those words came from some mighty fine minds and Juanito knew what they all meant."

"I reckon you still miss that Argentine cowboy. I'm sorry he got hisself killed."

Anson straightened up, sucked in a breath to calm himself. He remembered, then, something Juanito had said to him once. "When you travel with a man, you travel with him even after he is dead and gone from the world." Sometimes, he felt Juanito was still there, walking beside him. But he knew that Juanito was gone. Dead and gone, damn it all. "Where in hell is Roy?"

"Maybe he went to bring back Dave Wilhoit's body. I see Ursula's over yonder, still broken up."

"I'm sorry Dave got killed."

"I could put a ball in Aguilar's gut for that myself."

"There's a lot of burying to do," Anson said, an almost wistful tone to his voice.

"What do you want with Roy?" Peebo asked.

"I've got a favor to ask of him," Anson said, kicking the ground with the toe of his boot. He still could not look at the smoking house, but he looked everywhere else, at the dead bodies, a wounded Mexican being tended to by Doc Purvis and Lorene. While he was watching them, Lorene looked up, saw Anson staring at her.

"Uh-oh," Peebo said. "Here comes that gal what's sweet on you, Anson."

"Why don't you shut up, Peebo." Anson's face flushed, his skin turning a pale scarlet, a rosy hue that almost wiped out the tan.

Lorene walked toward them, her hips swaying like the leafy limbs of trees along the Gulf Coast. Peebo shuffled his feet. "Want me to go someplace else, Anson?"

"No. You stay right here unless you want to pick up a shovel and start digging holes in the ground for those dead men out there."

"I reckon I'll stay right here," Peebo said, grinning wide. "Just don't do nothin' I wouldn't do."

"Keep your big mouth shut."

"Well, son, I can do that."

Lorene came up. She looked haggard and was panting from climbing the gentle slope to where Anson and Peebo stood.

"I haven't had the chance to say how sorry I am, Anson," Lorene said. She was a beautiful young woman with dark hair and nut-brown eyes, hair soft as silk. The sun enhanced its sheen, like rays striking a raven's wing. She had smudges of dirt on her face and there were flecks of blood on her hands.

"Thanks," Anson said. "I'm sorry myself."

"You can stay in town with us," she said, brushing away a lock of hair that had fallen over her forehead. "I've already talked to my uncle."

"It's a long ride into town," Anson said. "And as you can see, I've got my hands full here."

"But you have no home," she said. "No place to sleep."

Peebo suppressed a snicker. Anson's lips stitched a thread of a smile over his teeth.

"I'll bunk with Peebo tonight, Lorene. But I've slept out in the open a time or two."

"Well, suit yourself, Anson," Lorene said.

"Don't be miffed."

"I'm not miffed. I just thought . . ."

"What?"

"That we could spend more time together if you stayed in town."

Peebo looked down at his feet. He shifted his weight from one foot to the other as if wishing he might sink into the ground and out of sight and earshot of Anson and Lorene.

Anson looked at Lorene, at the passion that swirled in her flashing brown eyes. He liked the way her black hair streamed down in little curlicue tendrils behind her ears. Her trailing hair set off her beautiful face and displayed its remarkable symmetry. He was tempted to take her up on her offer, and he knew if he didn't fight it, he would give in and lose sight of all that he must do now that his father was gone.

Anson cleared his throat, suddenly uncomfortable, consumed by feelings that swarmed up in him like clouds of moths winging around a naked tongue of fire. "Maybe you better get on out of here, Peebo. See if you can find Roy somewheres."

"I'll do 'er," Peebo said, almost too eagerly, as if he could feel the cord between Anson and Lorene tightening, thickening into something palpable. Peebo touched a finger to his hat and nodded to Lorene. Then he was gone.

"You sent him away," she said.

"Damn, Lorene."

"Are you swearing at me?" she mocked. Her lips curved in a thin smile, connecting her dimples.

"I got something to say," he said.

"Have something to say."

"I know the right words, it's just hard for me to say what I got— what I have to say."

"I won't bite."

"You might want to, when I tell you."

"So, go on and tell me. I still won't bite."

"Lorene, I like you a lot, and all," he floundered, "but I think you got the wrong idea."

"What idea is that?" she asked tightly.

"What happened between us the other day. Well, it just happened, is all."

"And it means nothing to you? Is that what you're saying? I was a virgin and I gave myself to you. I gave my body to you."

"I know. That's what makes it hard. I'm mighty grateful, but I . . . I . . ."

"But what?" Her eyes flickered dangerously, as if their dark depths concealed daggers.

"I think you've got a mind to get married and I'm just not ready yet, that's all."

Lorene's nostrils distended as she drew air through them. Her eyes flashed with a dark anger that flared up like a sudden heat from their depths. Anson stiffened as if to brace himself for a blow from her fist.

"Did I ever ask you to marry me, Anson Baron?"

"No, I reckon not."

"Then what makes you say something like that? Don't put words in my mouth. Don't put intentions in my mind. If I was of a mind to marry you, you'd sure know it."

"Well, I thought. I mean, you inviting me to stay with you in town."

"You mean like setting up housekeeping?"

"Yeah, something like that."

"Oh, you're the smug one, all right, Anson. How dare you? I was being kind and this is my reward."

Anson sighed with relief.

"I'm sorry," he said, "I guess I took it all wrong."

"You sure did. Now what's the real reason you turned my offer down? Is there another girl you like better than me?"

"No'm, it's just that I've got something to do."

"What? Rebuild your house?"

"No, I'll have Ken do that for me. I'm going away. With Peebo. I don't know when we'll be back."

"Going away where?" Her voice faltered, and trailed away as if her breath had left her.

"There's a white bull I've got to catch. I want him to sire my herd. This war we had took me away from that."

Lorene stepped back as if he had slapped her in the face. Her mouth dropped open and stayed slack until she drew herself up straight and regained her composure.

"I see," she said. "I see how important I am to you. I see how shallow and cheap you think I am. Well, let me tell you something, Mr. Anson Baron. You go on and chase after that damned white bull. But when you come back, I'll still be waiting for you and I am going to marry you, whether you like it or not. You just think about that while you and Peebo are running around out in the brush after that damned old bull."

Lorene's mouth tightened as she glared at him, before turning on her heel and running down the hill, her skirt whipping about her flashing legs, her tresses flying backward, streaming like a tattered black battle banner.

Anson stood there, frozen to the spot, staring after her. It was then that he felt a tug at his loins and a terrible emptiness in his stomach. And it seemed to him he felt a hand squeeze his heart until he was sure it had stopped dead still.

3

MICKEY BONE RODE up on Aguilar's Rocking A ranch just before the dawn broke, wary as a wolf sniffing a man's scent. Part Lipan Apache, part Kickapoo, he relied on his instincts and something told him to be careful. He did not trust Matteo Aguilar, not any more. Matteo had gone off to kill the Barons and reclaim Aguilar land that had been lawfully sold to Martin Baron, and Bone would have no part of it, so he had come back by himself to get his wife, Madrugada—Dawn—and their son, Juan, and find another place to live. Matteo was too treacherous; he was not a man to be trusted.

He circled the main house, keeping well away from all the buildings, walking his horse slow so that its shod hooves made little sound. Something was not right. He didn't know what bothered him at first, but as he circled again, he decided that the silence about the place was not natural. He smelled the familiar scents, the pungent aromas of the stable, the musty, cloying spoor emanating from the chicken house, the perfume of the blossoms in the orchard, the damp reek of old wood, the lingering smoke from the previous evening's cookfires. It smelled like home, to him, but he knew this was no longer his home. He knew that he had no home. Matteo had ordered him to leave, and now he had no place to go. His own tribe was decimated, the Lipan almost all dead now, or old, scattered like dead leaves, lost.

On the second circling, Bone saw the orange glow of a cigarette buried deep in the shadows of the livery stable, where the personal horses of Matteo, and his wife, Luz, were kept. Just a tiny pinpoint of light that could have been a firefly, but was not. The light did not flicker or wink on and off, but made an arc through the air, then disappeared for a few moments. Bone reined up his horse near a live oak, stood the animal still in the leaf shadows that blocked him from view. A man smoking a cigarette; that was all.

Bone peered into the darkness of the stable, his senses attuned for any movement, any sound. The silence pooled up like something leaden in the predawn stillness. The cigarette glowed once more, then fell to the ground, flicked there by a man's fingers. Something protruded beyond the wall of the barn, too small and too far away to identify, even with Bone's keen eyes.

But he knew what it was without seeing it clearly. The snout of a rifle barrel. Bone sucked in a breath, held it as his mind raced backward in time.

He and Matteo had argued over the killing of Martin and Anson Baron. Matteo had hired the Frenchman, Jules Reynaud, to assassinate the two Barons because Bone had refused. Bone had once worked for Martin Baron and he had grown to like Anson. They were friends, in a strange, distant way. He had told Matteo he would not kill either of the Barons and perhaps Matteo not only held a grudge, but felt betrayed and now wanted to kill him, as well.

Bone sniffed the air. There were no lamps lit in Matteo's house. He could not see the little houses of the hands, nor his own, where he lived with Dawn and little Juan. But someone should have arisen and begun to make coffee for Luz. There was still no light in the east, but the sky was beginning to pale and the stars were fading. The moon had set and he now began to feel a slight chill rising from the earth.

Bone waited, staring into the blackness of the barn, at that protrusion that he knew was the barrel of a rifle. He wondered who was holding it and why. Were they expecting Martin Baron, perhaps, to return and destroy the Rocking A rancho? He did not know, of course, if Matteo's raid on the Box B had been successful. Perhaps it had been, perhaps not.

A muffled sound arrested Bone's attention. He seemed to shrink inside himself as he listened with an intensity that would help him identify not only the sound, but where it came from. It had sounded like a cough, but the suddenness of it defied quick and certain analysis. It could just as well have been a footfall, or a horse scraping its hoof on the ground.

Then, he heard another sound and saw something move, a man, from the shape of it. A change in the texture of the darkness marking the movement more than the figure itself. As he waited, Bone saw the rifle barrel steady and withdraw from the opening of the barn.

"¿Caudillo?"

"¿Quien es?"

"Perez. ¿Que pasa?"

"Nada. 'Stoy cansado. Andale."

Bone knew both Perez and Caudillo. It was Perez walking toward the barn, probably to relieve Caudillo and take over his watch.

The two men met. Perez carried a rifle. Caudillo stepped outside the barn. Bone could not hear what they said, because they were now whispering, but he knew Caudillo was reporting what had occurred on his watch during the hours he had been hiding in the barn. After a few moments, Caudillo started to walk away, carrying his rifle.

"Do you think Bone will come?" Perez said, in Spanish.

"If he does, you know what to do. Shoot him."

"I hope he does not come."

"Hope that if he does come, he does not shoot you, Perez. Good night."

Perez didn't reply, and after a few minutes, he struck a match and lit a cigarette. Bone tapped his horse's flanks with his heels and moved off, meaning to follow Caudillo. He knew where Perez would be for the next few hours.

Bone was about to follow Caudillo, when he heard another sound, a distant one, and there was no mistaking what it was, or where it was coming from. He turned his horse and let it slip through the deep shadows of the trees bordering the house and back out onto the road that led from the Rocking A to the Box B. Someone was riding toward the Aguilar spread from the Baron ranch. Someone all alone.

4

MILLICENT COLLINS NEARLY dropped a tray full of soiled dishes
when she looked out the window of the Longhorn and saw the
riders approaching the hitching rail. She and Lonnie Viser were virtually the only ones still inside the restaurant. The street outside was
filled with people looking at the smoke in the sky over the distant
Box B Ranch. That's why she was surprised to see Martin Baron ride
up with the three Texas Rangers and a Mexican she did not know.
The Mexican's wrists were bound.

She set the tray down on an empty table and watched as Al Oltman and Martin helped the Mexican dismount.

"Lonnie," Millie called out.

Lonnie made a sound. "Yump."

"Go to the kitchen and tell Cookie to get ready. There'll be a
gang back in here any minute now."

"Shit," Lonnie said, looking out the window, before he shuffled
off to the kitchen, a place he hated thoroughly.

Millie watched as men and women swarmed toward Martin Baron
and the other men, crowding around them, all talking at once, asking
questions. She stood up, straightened her frock from hem to waist, a
powder blue dress with white piping starched to a fare-thee-well at

collar and hem. She patted her hair, replaced a dangling strand that had corkscrewed down the side of her face in front of her left ear.

"Lonnie," she called. "Take these dishes back to the kitchen."

"I was just out there," he said, coming back into the room.

"Hurry up."

"What are you so fired up about, Millie?"

"Never mind. Just do what you're told."

Lonnie started to pick up the tray Millie had set down, then looked out the window at the crowd of people.

"Oh, I see. Mr. Martin Baron. Your sweetie."

Millie's face flushed a rosy color. "Mind your mouth, Lonnie."

"Beg your pardon, ma'am." He jerked the tray up and waddled toward the kitchen, humming a love song that made Millie blush again. She scowled and turned back to the window and looked outside. She felt a squeezing tug at her heart as she looked at Martin Baron. He was taller than anyone in the crowd and she could see his face clearly. She drew in a deep breath to keep from sighing, but she sighed anyway when she let it back out.

The crowd started to move as Martin headed toward the front door of the Longhorn. The people parted as he forged ahead, the Rangers and their prisoner following in his wake.

Millie trotted to the batwing doors and pulled one of them back, holding it so the people could enter unhindered. Martin filled the doorway, nodded to her.

"Hello, Mr. Baron," Millie said, her voice low and dulcet toned.

"Thanks, Millie."

"I hope you're in town to stay a while."

"Nope," he said. "Just stopping for some lunch."

Before she could say anything more, he swept past her and she stood there, holding the door as the Rangers passed through with their Mexican prisoner. On their heels were Ed Wales, publisher of the *Baronsville Bugle,* Ken Richman, who owned the Longhorn, Nancy Grant, a schoolteacher and Ken's girlfriend, and others whose faces blurred as they streamed in. She let the door fall back and rushed over to the table Martin had taken in the center of the large room.

"Will you need a larger table?" she asked. "I can push some together."

Martin looked at those coming to sit with them and nodded. "I'll help you," he said. Al Oltman helped Martin and Millie push two other tables over and she arranged the chairs as everyone began to sit down.

"I've got to talk to you, in private," Millie whispered into Martin's ear. "If you have time."

"Now?"

"Before you leave."

"All right. We'll need grub for four men for three days, Millie. Can you fix us up?"

"Why, I surely can, Mr. Baron."

"Call me Martin, will you?"

Millie blushed and curtsied. She looked over and motioned to Lonnie, who came over carrying a slate and chalk. "Take their orders, Lonnie," she said. "I'll be in the kitchen."

"Yes'm." Lonnie nodded and stood next to the table, chalk poised over the slate.

Martin ordered for himself and Matteo. Al ordered for himself and the other two Rangers, all simple fare: beefsteaks, turnips, potatoes, beans, and biscuits. Ken and Ed ordered drinks from the bar, whiskies.

"It must have been quite a war," Ken said, after Lonnie had left. "We've been watching the smoke. I thought about sending some men out."

"Wouldn't have done any good, Ken," Martin said. "This bastard here burned down my house."

Ken swore. Ed Wales shook his head as if he was disconsolate. It was obvious that he and Ken had been drinking all morning, or for a good part of it.

"Where are you boys taking the Mex?" Wales asked.

"Up to Waco, likely," Oltman said quickly.

"To stand trial?" Wales asked.

"I reckon."

Wales snorted.

Martin looked at Wales, his eyebrows arching, his eyes widening. Richman also shot Wales a quizzical look.

"Let me know if he's found guilty or not," Wales said. "I'll put the notice in the paper."

"Fair enough," Oltman said. "I'll surely do that."

Martin would have sworn that there was a smirk on Ed Wales's face, but he let it pass. Aguilar said nothing, but looked around the large room as if sizing it up.

"Don't you get no ideas about goin' rabbit on me, Aguilar. Forget it," said Kenny Darnell, who, along with the other Ranger, Dan Shepley, flanked the prisoner.

Matteo said nothing, but continued to scout the room with hooded eyes.

The talk turned to war and other matters, as Ken Richman and Ed Wales drank their whiskies. When Lonnie served the food, everyone stopped to eat, with little conversation between bites and swallows.

"I've got your grub all ready," Millie told Martin. "Do you want to come out to the kitchen and see it before we pack it up?"

Martin started to say something, then caught the look Millie gave him. She cocked her head slightly in a beckoning motion, and he understood that she wanted to talk to him in private.

"I'll be right back," Martin said, scooting his chair away from the table.

The men nodded, all except Matteo, who scrubbed a piece of biscuit across his plate and stuffed it into his mouth.

Millie took Martin to a quiet corner of the kitchen and began to whisper to him.

"There's a stranger in town, Martin. Came in early this morning, ate breakfast, and left."

"A stranger?"

"I overhead him talking to another man I've never seen before, either."

"What about?"

"I don't know. But this one man was a Frenchman, and I heard the other man call him both Jules and Reynaud. Reynaud told the other man he knew you from New Orleans."

She waited as Martin mulled over what she had told him.

"I know him," he said. "Who was the other man?"

"Reynaud called him Cullie, that's all I know."

"Christ," Martin said. "I thought I ran him off for good."

"So you know both of these men."

"Yes, I do."

"Well, I think they're up to no good."

"That's likely."

"They didn't know I was listening, but I heard your name mentioned a lot."

"They should have better things on their minds."

"Martin, I'm worried. And scared."

"Why?"

"Just before they left the table, I heard Cullie tell Reynaud something you won't like to hear."

"Oh? What was that?"

"He said, this Cullie, that you were as good as dead. Then he asked Reynaud if he wanted the honor of killing you."

"And what did Reynaud say?"

"He said it didn't make any difference to him."

"Then they left, right?"

"I thought they left town, but they were both here when you rode in, standing out there in that crowd. Just before you got to the Longhorn, they got on their horses and left."

"So they must have seen that we have Matteo Aguilar in custody."

"I'm sure of it."

"Well, Millie, don't you worry your pretty little head about it. Those two are just common scoundrels. They aren't worth a tinker's damn, neither of them."

"They look dangerous to me."

"Well, they might look dangerous right up until the minute someone puts their lamps out."

Millie put her arms around Martin and squeezed him tightly. He could feel her tremble against him and could feel her legs shaking.

"Maybe you'd better show me that grub you've got set out for us," Martin said.

"Yes, yes, of course."

Millie showed him a table with all kinds of staples they would need on the trail: bacon, coffee, flour, beans, tortillas wrapped in a damp cloth, sugar, dried turnips, onions, and potatoes.

"I put some apples in a damp cloth for you, too," Millie said.

"That was nice of you, Millie."

"Martin."

"Yeah?"

"When you come back, I'll be waiting for you. I know it's a little soon after your wife's death, but . . ."

"You want to put your hat in the ring."

"Well, I never thought of it that way. Is there someone else?"

"No. It's just an expression. I feel kind of off kilter, you saying that to me."

"Don't be. I mean it. I love you, Martin."

"I don't know what to say."

"Maybe you'll think of me while you're gone. And maybe you'll come to love me, too. Or, at least to know that I can give you the love you need."

"That's fair enough."

He felt a swirling in his stomach as he looked into her eyes. Then a tug at his loins as he looked at her generous breasts. But he fought off the feeling. Millie was right. It was a little too soon.

When he looked at her, he saw Caroline. Not the way she had been the last few years, but the first time he ever saw her at the Darnells'. They were both young then, and Caroline was a rare beauty. No, he could not see himself with Millie. Not just yet.

5

BONE RODE HIS horse to a place near the road between the Rocking A and the Box B, where he could wait without being seen. The sound of hoofbeats grew louder, but the horse coming his way was not going fast. As he listened, he discerned that the horse was tired, so tired that it dragged its feet and stumbled.

Whoever was coming had ridden far, Bone reasoned. And the person on the horse was not worried about making noise. As the sounds grew louder, Bone listened more intently, trying to figure out if he knew the horse or its rider. Sometimes he could tell a horse by its gait, but this one was so tired, it did not move with its regular gait.

Then Bone heard the horse nicker as it came closer to the Rocking A headquarters. He knew that horse, and he knew who rode it. He edged closer to the road and laid his rifle across the pommel of his saddle, his finger inside the trigger guard. A moment later, he saw the shapes of horse and rider and that was all he needed to know. Still, he waited, until the man came within a dozen yards.

"Pedro," Bone said.

The rider reined up and his horse came to a halt.

"Bone? Is that you?" Pedro Castillo said, in Spanish. "You gave me much fear."

"Come here," Bone said, in the same tongue. "Tell me what you know."

Castillo clapped heels into his horse's flanks and rode toward Bone. Then he saw the rifle. "You are not going to shoot me are you, Mickey?"

"No, I am not going to shoot you. Where have you come from and what passes?"

"There was much shooting at the Baron rancho. Many vaqueros killed. Many friends dead now."

"What about Matteo?"

"Ah, Matteo. He is a prisoner. I saw men put rifles to his head and take him away. They have probably hanged him by now."

Bone showed no sign that he was struck by this news. But he felt a sense of satisfaction that Matteo had failed to take over the Baron rancho. Bone had warned him that he would be making a foolish mistake if he took up arms against Martin and Anson Baron. But Matteo was a stubborn, greedy man and he would not listen to reason.

"What will happen to the Rocking A?" Bone asked.

"I will speak to Matteo's wife. She will tell me what to do."

"You would run the ranch, Pedro?"

"If Luz wishes me to, I will work it."

"Do you think Matteo is dead?"

"I do not know. Maybe."

"I do not think Martin Baron would hang him."

"Why do you think Baron would not do that?"

"Because that is not his nature. He will punish Matteo, but he will not hang him."

"The men who captured Matteo were professionals."

"Professionals?"

"They looked like hunters of men. They were not men who worked the cows."

"How do you know this?"

"They looked like such men. They may be Texas Rangers, of whom I have heard much."

"I also have heard much of them. They are tough men. Killers."

It seemed to Bone that Castillo shuddered.

"Yes, that is why I think they will either shoot Matteo, or hang him from a tree."

"Why do you think you are the one to manage the Rocking A, Pedro?"

"Because . . . because Matteo, he put much trust in me."

"Did he tell you to kill me?" Bone asked.

This time, Bone was sure that Castillo shivered and shook a little. The light was edging into the sky and he could see his face, all but his black eyes which were sunk deep in his skull

"I do not know what you mean. Are we not friends, Mickey?"

"Did Matteo tell you to put my lamp out?" Bone asked again.

"I do not think he asked me to do that."

"I think he did. Matteo ran me off and I know he had much anger for me. If he wanted me dead, you are the one he would ask."

"Why?"

"Because he would always ask a friend to kill a friend. He asked me to kill Martin Baron and his son Anson. And they were my friends."

"But you did not do what Matteo asked. You told him you would not kill your friends."

"Did you tell Matteo you would not kill me?"

This time, Bone saw Castillo stiffen and he slid his finger closer to the trigger inside the trigger guard.

"He did not ask me to do that thing, I swear."

"Pedro, you are a liar," Bone said.

"I do not lie."

"Yes, you lie. You are lying now."

"Mickey, you do not know what happened. You were not there. Matteo and I did not talk about you."

"But now, you think you are going to take over the ranch and fill Matteo's boots."

"I am the one to do that, Mickey."

"Not me?"

Castillo hesitated and Bone saw him lick his dry lips.

"Matteo would never let you run the ranch," Castillo said.

"I ran a ranch in Mexico for him."

"That was not the same."

"It is the same," Bone said.

"We should not quarrel over this thing. It is of no import, Mickey."

"If Matteo is not here to make his wishes known, then it is of no import, Pedro."

"I will run the ranch. That is Matteo's wish, for certain. Besides, Matteo does not want you to live here any more."

"Did he tell you that?"

"I know he told you that before we left for the Baron ranch. He told me he told you to leave."

"Where are the others who went with you? Are they all dead?"

"I do not know. I think many are dead."

"So, who will know what Matteo told you, Pedro? Who will know what he now wishes?"

"I know."

"No, Pedro, you do not know anything."

Castillo's right hand moved as if he meant to reach for his pistol.

"Do not try it, Pedro."

"Let me pass, Mickey."

"In a minute," Bone said. "First, another question for you, *por favor.*"

"What do you want to ask me?"

"Matteo has men guarding the house all night. Do you know why he is doing this?"

Castillo coughed. "I do not know."

"Yes you do," Bone said. "They watch all night. They have never done this before."

"Perhaps it is because he worries over his wife and child while he is gone," Castillo said.

"I think these men are waiting for someone to come so they can shoot him."

"Who?"

"Maybe they wait for me, Pedro."

"I do not know."

"Matteo's wife does not need protection through the night. These guards are looking for someone. I think they are looking for me and I think they will shoot me when I ride up."

"You are very suspicious, Mickey."

"Yes, I have the suspicion," Bone said.

"I am sorry to hear this."

Bone rode up close to Castillo and swung his rifle around. He pushed the barrel into Castillo's belly and held it there. "Get off the horse," Bone said.

"Why do you do this, Mickey?"

"Be quiet. Just get off the horse and take off your shirt and hat."

Castillo handed Bone his pistol. Bone shoved it into his waistband. Castillo dismounted as Bone swung down from his horse, holding the rifle pointed at the vaquero's belly. "The shirt and hat, Pedro," Bone said.

Castillo took off his hat, then stripped off his shirt. He handed them to Bone. Bone let them fall to the ground. Then Bone unbuttoned his own shirt and handed it to Castillo. "Put the shirt on," Bone said, taking off his hat and holding it ready as Castillo donned Bone's shirt.

"Why do you do this, Mickey?"

"You are going to get on my horse and ride to the house of Matteo. I will be behind you. If you make a shout or call out, I will shoot you in the back."

"I do not want to do this," Castillo said.

Bone handed him his hat and Castillo put it on. Bone looked him over and then motioned with his rifle barrel for Castillo to climb up on Bone's horse.

"I—I have fear," Castillo said, as he climbed up into the saddle.

"Why? Do you think Matteo's men will shoot you?"

"I do not know."

"Well, we will find out, my friend." Bone climbed into the saddle of Castillo's horse and swung around until he was in back of Castillo.

"This is not funny, Mickey."

"I am not making a joke."

"Why do you not just shoot me?" Castillo asked.

"I want to see if you have been lying to me."

"I have not told lies to you."

"Let us see," Bone said, riding up close and prodding Castillo in the back. "Ride slow and keep your mouth shut."

Castillo kicked Bone's horse in the flanks and the horse moved down the road toward the Aguilar ranch house. Bone kept dropping back farther and farther as they drew closer to the house, after telling Castillo not to turn around.

A rooster crowed and Bone heard a scraping sound coming from the barn. Then, it grew very quiet as Castillo rode into the open area near the Aguilar house. Bone reined up the horse and watched as Castillo rode on.

Then Bone heard the sound of a hammer cocking. Castillo threw up one arm and shouted, "Do not shoot."

But he spoke too late. Rifles barked from two directions, cracking like bullwhips. Castillo's body jerked in the saddle and he twisted sideways with the impact of one bullet. His body jerked as a lead ball struck him in the chest. Bone saw him grab the saddle horn and try to hold on as two more shots rang out.

Bone put his rifle to his shoulder and waited, as his horse began to turn in circles until Castillo fell out of the saddle. His body hit the ground with a dull thud. The two men who had fired on Castillo emerged and started walking warily toward the body lying on the ground.

Bone smiled, cocked his rifle, and took aim at the nearest man who was looking at the ground where Castillo lay sprawled like a lifeless heap of rags.

6

Anson scuffed the dirt with the toe of his boot as if wishing to be someplace else, anywhere but where he was. There was a knot in his stomach, as if someone had buried a knife in it and was twisting it ever tighter.

"Roy was bringing his steppa's body back," Peebo was saying, "and now his ma's broken down with grief."

"So that's where Roy was," Anson said, knowing it was an inane thing to say even as the words came out of his mouth. "I forgot that David Wilhoit got killed."

"A lot of people got killed," Peebo said. "What do you want to do with all the dead Mexicans?"

"Are any of Matteo's men alive and still here?"

"There are two wounded and three what ain't got a scratch."

"Well, ask 'em if they want to tote those bodies back to the Rocking A."

"Not me, Anson. You ask 'em."

Anson looked up from the boot-scratched patch of earth he had worried with his foot. He seemed to have aged since the battle with the Rocking A hands. The furrows in his forehead seemed a little deeper, the frown lines at the corners of his mouth were etched a little sharper, and the frown on his face only made his brown eyes seem darker. The lock of sweat-soaked dark hair that fell over his forehead added to the look of worry and age on his weathered young face.

"Where have you got the Rocking A hands?" Anson asked.

"Over yonder, by the barn. That's where Roy is, too. They carried Wilhoit inside where the womenfolk can clean him up before buryin' him."

Anson started in that direction, Peebo following along in his wake. He knew that if they didn't start burying the dead pretty soon, there'd be a smell in the air worse than the smoke and the stench of burning wood.

The five Mexicans were sitting in the shade. They looked like beaten men, even the three who were not wounded. They looked up when Anson came near them. In their eyes, he could see a look of defeat and a forlorn pleading that, though wordless, spoke volumes about how they felt.

"You've got dead out there," Anson said, in Spanish. "I've got shovels in the barn. You can bury them here in that field behind here, or you can carry them back to the ranch."

"We will carry them back," one man said. He crossed himself, and the others there, even the wounded, followed suit. One of the Box B hands who was guarding the prisoners sneered and turned his head away in scornful disapproval.

"Do you know where your horses are?"

"No, we do not know."

Anson pointed to the man who was speaking. "You, find your horses. Bring them here and then pack up your dead companions and ride out of here."

"You are not going to shoot us?"

"No," Anson said. "There has been enough of that this day. Go. Go quickly."

The man spoke to his companions and rose from the ground. The two wounded men appeared to have lost some blood, but were not hurt badly. One had a bloody arm. The other had a ripped scalp where a lead ball had torn a furrow through his hair. Blood was caked on one side of his face. Two of Anson's hands, Mexicans as well, were

guarding the prisoners, and they stood there, puffing on rolled cigarettes, regarding Anson. Anson looked at them, and cracked a weak
smile.

"Help them," Anson said, speaking in Spanish. "They will fight
no more this day."

"They did not fight well this morning," one of the hands said.
"They are filth."

"They are men who obeyed the orders of Matteo. We have won.
We do not need to be cruel or show disrespect."

"Yes, *patrón,*" the man said, a sheepish look on his face.

Peebo and Anson entered the barn, which was already hot from
the morning sun. Shafts of sunlight streamed through openings,
and the beams danced with motes of dust that looked like swirling
insects.

Ursula knelt next to the body of her dead husband, David, her
face puffy from weeping, her cheeks streaked with hot wet tears. Her
son, Roy Killian, stood behind her, a comforting hand on her shoulder. Next to him, Wanda Fancher leaned against him, an arm
around his waist, while her mother, Hattie Fancher, stiff as a sentinel,
stood looking down at the dead man, her face devoid of emotion,
one fist clenched in silent anger.

"I'll wash him up," Hattie said. "Roy, you find a right nice spot for
him. Ursula, you go and help your boy find a good place for your
husband to rest in peace."

Ursula began to sob, her body shaking with the effort. Roy put
his arm around his mother's waist, drew her close to him. His lips
moved in a silent curse.

Wanda put both of her arms around Ursula and hugged her, and
she too began to weep, as if in sympathy with the woman she hoped
would soon become her mother-in-law.

"You go on with Roy, Ursula," Wanda said. "Mama and I will take
care of your husband."

"You're both so very sweet, Wanda. I—I want to help wash my
poor dear. You go on with Roy. I'm sure you both can pick out a good
resting place for my David."

Roy cleared his throat and shifted his weight from one foot to the
other.

A strange feeling come over Anson, as if he were in a funeral parlor staring at other mourners. He could almost smell the sweet cloying odor of fresh-picked flowers, and the light breeze moaning faintly through the rafters sounded almost like muted organ music. Where did such images and feelings come from? He had never been in a funeral parlor, but he had heard talk in town after Juanito had died that Baronsville ought to have one, and he had imagined what such a place would be like. He knew there would be floral wreaths and the wheeze and puff of a church organ playing a solemn dirge as people dressed in black stood in pews and murmured prayers for the dead and for the living. His skin prickled at the sharpness and clarity of the images, even though he had no idea from whence they had sprung.

The full impact of the war with Aguilar was beginning to sink in. Anson could feel the beginning of a trembling deep inside him unlike anything he had felt before.

War, he thought, wasn't in the faces of the dead, those who had been wiped off the face of the earth. Not entirely. War was in the faces of the women whose husbands had died; it was in their tears, in the dark tracks on their faces, in the blood that had drained from their faces as they grieved.

And this had been a war with Aguilar. He had attacked the Baron rancho with soldiers he had trained and outfitted. The ranch was a battlefield, strewn with the dead, the ground where he had lived now soaked with blood. It all made him sick inside and he had to take deep breaths to keep from retching. He held his breath until the queasiness passed and he could find his voice, bring it up and away from the scream of rage that lurked in his chest, as he looked at the women standing there over the body of David like mourners in a funeral parlor.

"Roy," Anson said, "Peebo and I'll walk out with you and the ladies. I'll have a word with you."

Roy turned and nodded. Wanda and Hattie looked at Anson as if he was an intruder. Anson smiled wanly at them and knew that it came out more as a grimace than a smile.

"I'm real sorry about David, Mrs. Wilhoit," Anson said. "We've got a cemetery if you want him to rest there."

"Thank you, Anson," Ursula said, but she did not take her eyes off her dead husband. .

Anson started walking toward the back doors of the barn. Peebo and Roy followed him. Wanda and Hattie gave Ursula one last hug and then left her alone to grieve for David as they slowly traipsed after the men.

"You know what you're doin', Anson?" Peebo said, when they were well away from the barn. He kept his voice low so that his words would not carry to those following them.

"I know what I'm doing, Peebo."

"Ye gods, Anson, these people are plumb caught up in their grief."

"Maybe what I have to ask of Roy will help some."

"What are you goin' to ask him?"

"It'll keep. Peebo, you're as curious as a damned cat."

"You got that look in your eye, Anson. I'm wonderin' if I ought to hear what you got to say to Roy."

"You'll want to hear it."

Anson walked wide of the burning house and out beyond the orchard to the hill that had become the Baron cemetery. This was where his mother, Caroline, was buried and where the grave of Juanito Salazar lay.

"This suit you, Roy?" Anson said after he stopped at the edge of the burial field. "Think your ma would like David to be buried here?"

"I was thinking of burying him on my land," Roy said.

"You don't have much land yet, Roy. You might not want to give up some of it for a cemetery."

"I got enough."

Wanda and her mother, Hattie, both looked at Anson with disapproving stares.

"David ought to be buried on Killian land," Hattie said. "Where his widow can visit and lay flowers when she wants."

"I've got a proposition for you, Roy," Anson said. "If you agree, I can add to your holdings some."

"More land?"

"Yes. I want you to do something for me."

"You be careful, Roy," Wanda said. "This isn't any time to talk business, with your mother freshly made a widow."

"I'll hear what Anson has to say, Wanda."

"I want you to find a man who can build my house back and I want you to help him build it. Not the way it was, but the way I want it to be."

"What kind of man are you looking for?" Roy asked.

"Someone who can lay it all out for you. You can deal with Ken Richman in town, have him get you and this feller what lumber and such you need. I want it built real quick so that I have a place to sleep when I get back."

"You leaving?" Roy asked.

"Peebo and I are going after that white bull. I want him to sire a herd of beef cattle for me."

"That's a wild-goose chase," Hattie said. "I've heard the Mexicans talk about that bull like it was a ghost or something."

"He's no ghost, Hattie. He's a big albino longhorn with a mean streak, that's all."

"I wouldn't have such," Hattie said with a disdainful snort from her nose. "The Mexes call it a white devil."

"They're superstitious, that's all. Well, Roy, can you find me a man to lay out a house the way I want it and give him a hand in building it? You can use any of my hands to help you."

"You're talking about an architect," Wanda said.

"I reckon." Anson looked at her with interest.

Hattie and Wanda exchanged knowing glances. Then Hattie smiled at Anson.

"We have a friend," Hattie said, "named Forrest Redmond. I have been writing him about our experiences in Texas and he wants to visit us. In fact, he's on his way here now. He's an architect and something of an amateur archaeologist."

"What's an arky whatchamacallit?" Peebo asked.

Wanda tittered. Hattie's face darkened into a scowl.

"An archaeologist, young man, is someone who digs up bones and studies the past. He looks at fossils and sees what kind of life was on earth millions of years ago. Do you know what a fossil is?"

Peebo shook his head.

"Did you ever see the impression of a leaf or a fish or some animal in a piece of rock?"

"Yeah, I reckon I've seen something like that once't or twice."

"Well, that's a fossil. Forrest is also a very good architect. He designs houses and buildings and bridges and such."

"Well, Roy," Anson said, "there's your answer. You and this Redmond can get together and put up a house to my liking. I'll pay the man, of course."

"Just what kind of house do you want us to build you?" Roy asked.

"One that can grow, like our ranches here, one that won't burn down easy and one that looks like it grew out of the land."

"That sounds like a tall order," Roy said.

"Forrest can do it," Hattie said. "You just leave everything to us, Anson."

"You really ought to be here, Anson," Roy said.

"I don't want to let that bull get away, and I don't want someone else to get him. I'll draw up what I want before we leave and you can show it to this Forrest feller."

"Don't you worry about a thing, Anson," Hattie said.

"I won't." But he could see from the look on Peebo's face that his friend thought he was crazy.

T HERE WERE TWO men he must kill and they were hidden from him. But Mickey Bone knew where they were and he knew how to wait. He was a patient man, and he was prudent, as well.

Mickey turned his horse quickly and rode back the way he and Castillo had come. He leaned low in the saddle. Rifles cracked behind him like snapping bullwhips and he heard the sizzle of bullets passing overhead. Soon, he was out of sight and out of range and he slowed the horse, then turned it to the right and headed into the mesquite that grew behind the house.

Bone dismounted, well into the trees, and ground-tied his horse. He slipped his rifle free of its scabbard and slunk to the back of the house, staying to the shadows and moving at careful intervals just in case someone was watching for him.

As Bone crept along the far side of the house, a lamp flickered on inside, splashing soft orange light through the side window. Bone peered inside and saw Luz, Matteo's wife, standing by the lamp, a smoking taper in her hand. She was wearing only a cotton nightgown, which gave her a ghostly appearance in that brief instant when he glimpsed her, before he moved past the window in a series of quick soft steps that brought him in the lee of the veranda, latticed on the side where he now stood.

He heard the pad of Luz's footsteps on the floor, the small squeal of the hinges as she opened the front door.

"*¿Quien es?*" she called.

Bone watched, his rifle at the ready. Two men emerged from the barn. They were still reloading their rifles, pushing their ramrods down the barrels to seat the lead balls atop the powder. He recognized them.

Caudillo and Perez. They replaced their ramrods before they approached the body of Pedro, sliding them back into place underneath the barrels.

"Who is that on the ground?" Luz asked, in Spanish. She stepped onto the porch, and Bone saw that she was holding an old shotgun, a double-barreled one with a worn stock and the bluing on the barrels faded to a dull pewter color.

"We do not know. We thought it was Bone," Perez said.

"Did you shoot him?"

"Yes, we shot him. Don Matteo told us to shoot Bone if he returned to the rancho."

"*Animales,*" Luz whispered. The two vaqueros could not hear her, but Bone could. He raised his rifle to his shoulder, took aim at the nearest man. He would have to kill the second one with his pistol.

"Is it Bone?" Luz asked, a trembling in her voice.

"Turn him over," Caudillo said. "Let us see his face."

Perez knelt down and felt the fallen man's neck. He looked up at Caudillo and then toward Luz. "It is not Bone," he said.

"*Hijo,*" Caudillo said. "It is Pedro." He crossed himself.

"Who?" Luz asked.

"It is Pedro," Perez said. "We thought it was Bone. Truly."

"You have shot Matteo's foreman," Luz said. "Is he dead?"

"He is dead," Caudillo said.

Bone lined up his sights on Caudillo, who was standing, and fired. White smoke and orange flame spewed from the muzzle of the rifle and Bone could not see through it. He knelt down and placed his rifle on the ground, then rushed forward at a crouch, beneath the smoke. He drew his pistol as Perez began to rise from his squatting position.

Perez swung his rifle toward Bone. He did not complete the swing.

Bone fired his pistol at Perez from ten yards away. Perez cried out as the ball struck him square in the center of his chest. The rifle fell from his hands. Perez made a last small sound and collapsed to the ground. His rifle clattered as it struck Caudillo's skull.

Bone wheeled and aimed his pistol at Luz, who stood transfixed on the porch, her hands gripping the shotgun with an intensity that frosted the knuckles of her hands.

"Put the shotgun down, Luz," Bone said, "or I will put a ball right between your pretty breasts."

"You bastard," Luz said, the words spewing out in Spanish on the air of an expelled breath.

"I do not want to shoot you."

"Where is Matteo?" Luz asked, still gripping the shotgun.

"Put the shotgun down. Now." Bone pushed the hammer on the single-action caplock pistol and it cocked with a loud click. In the silence, the sound was deafening, ominous. "Just stoop down and lay the gun down."

Luz hesitated, but she half knelt and laid the shotgun on the porch, then stood up again, tall and ghostly in the shimmering glow of the lamp that seeped through the open door.

Bone climbed the steps onto the porch and picked up the shotgun. Luz did not retreat, but stood her ground, her face a dark mask, without expression.

"Where is my husband?" she asked.

"I do not know. But Pedro told me that he had been captured by Martin Baron and two men that he thinks were Texas Rangers."

"Is Matteo alive?"

"I do not know. I was not there."

"Why are you here now?"

"Matteo told me that I would always have a home here on his rancho."

"But you just killed two men. Do you not have shame?"

"They were waiting to kill me. All three of them."

"Pedro, too? He was my husband's foreman."

"Matteo told him to kill me. But I did not kill him. Those two did. And they were hiding so that they could kill me when I returned."

"I don't believe you," she said.

"Did not Matteo tell you?"

"No. I thought you were his friend."

"I would not go with him to fight Martin Baron. That is why he wanted me dead. Matteo does not like people who disobey him."

"Matteo is not dead," she said, but there was no conviction in her voice. "I know he will return. And he will punish you for what you have done."

"Matteo will not return," Bone said. "They will probably shoot him, or hang him."

"I do not believe that," Luz said.

Bone shrugged. "Then he will go to the white man's jail. Either way, he will not be back. I will stay and run the ranch."

"You?"

"Yes. Matteo promised me I could live out my days here and this is where I will stay and raise the cattle."

"Matteo will kill you when he comes back."

Bone's face contorted into a mask of rage. He pushed Luz toward the door. She opened it and he shoved her inside.

"If he comes back," Bone said, "maybe I will kill him."

Luz drew away from Bone, but she did not show signs of fear. She stood there, defiant as a lioness, glaring at Bone as if her glance could wither him into a mass of desiccated flesh and bones.

"Get out of my house," she said.

Bone smiled. "I will go," he said. "But maybe I will come back sometime and see what Matteo's woman is like."

"I will die first before I let you touch me."

Bone laughed, and turned to go. Then he stopped and threw the shotgun at Luz. She jumped back as it struck the floor with a loud sound.

"You and I are partners, now, Luz," he said. "If you want to stay here in this house and wait for Matteo to return, you had better be good to me."

Luz said nothing. Bone left, and as he climbed down from the porch he could hear her sobs as she burst into tears.

He smiled. The Rocking A was his now, and there was nothing Luz could do about it.

8

MARTIN BARON BEGAN to feel uneasy when they were just a few miles out of Baronsville. He was riding drag, behind the two Texas Rangers, Al Oltman and Dan Shepley, who were bracing Matteo Aguilar who rode between them. Kenny Darnell rode point ahead of them all.

He wondered if it was because they were no longer on Baron land, or if it had anything to do with Millie Collins. No, it was something more than that, he thought. He had left the Box B many times before, on cattle drives, to go to sea again, to just get away from responsibilities.

But this time, it was different. He felt a strong pull from the land he was leaving behind, and, more than that, he felt a longing to be with Anson, his only son. He could still see the look on Anson's face when he told his son he was leaving.

But the burned house, the one he had built for Caroline, was a hideous sight, almost a sacrilege, and, in a cowardly way, he had known he could not look at its smoking remains another moment. All the memories it held for him had gone up in smoke. The house had been the last vestige of Caroline's spirit and, now, even that had been taken away from him. Perhaps Anson could rebuild it, but he could not. He felt as if Caroline's very grave had been desecrated when Aguilar's men set torch to it.

It was odd, but the image of the standing house, the way it had been when Caroline had been alive, was fading from memory, replaced by the eviscerated ruins smoldering like some vision from hell, all that was in it gone forever, all that it had been now only a smoking skeleton, its bones blackened and broken as if it had never existed.

Yet Martin felt a strong desire to go back and face the ugliness of the burned-down house, the destruction that Matteo and his men had caused to his home. But, all he could think of now was that he wanted to see Matteo hanging from a gallows up in San Antonio, or from a cottonwood tree somewhere along the way. The hatred inside of him was intense at that moment, and yet, he felt a strong sense of guilt about hating Matteo and wanting to kill him.

A fleeting thought crossed Martin's mind, unbidden, vagrant, from some unknown source. Yet the thought caught hold and worried him like a burr stuck to his trouser leg. It was something Juanito Salazar, the Argentine, had said to him once, something that had not stuck in his mind at the time, but now bloomed like a large flower on a barren hillside.

"If you are to live well," Juanito had said, "you must learn to forgive. You must forgive your wife; you must forgive your son. You must forgive your enemies."

"Why?" Martin had asked.

"Because, when you forgive, your hurting all goes away."

"Not from my enemy."

"Oh, yes, Martin, especially from your enemy. As long as you hate and do not forgive, your enemy has power over you. Once you forgive, once you give up the hate, that power disappears. It just goes away and you have all your power back."

"That doesn't make sense, Juanito," Martin had said.

And he remembered Juanito looking at him with those intense brown eyes of his and boring straight into his mind as if he could read it like a book. "Try it," Juanito had said. That was all. "Try it."

But he had never tried it. And now he realized that he still carried hate and anger around with him and it was a dead weight on his shoulders, as if he were lugging sacks of lead sash weights and climbing up a steep hill.

He had not forgiven Caroline for being raped. He had falsely accused Juanito of raping his wife and he had not forgiven the Apaches for raiding his ranch, nor had he forgiven Anson for growing up to be a man and taking over the ranch he had started.

There was something else Juanito had said, though, but it was just out of reach, right then. Yet he knew it was something important and he knew he should remember it. He thought about Juanito looking into his eyes and giving him that uneasy feeling that the Argentine could read his mind. He had felt skewered by his gaze and had squirmed inside as if he were turning on a spit over a flaming fire.

"I might try it," Martin remembered saying to Juanito.

And then Martin remembered what Juanito had said after that, and the truth of it struck him hard, like a fist slamming into his mouth.

"There is a way to begin," Juanito had said. "A way to begin to forgive all who ever wronged you."

"Yeah? How's that, Juanito?"

"First," Juanito had said, "you must forgive yourself."

And Juanito had said no more about it and Martin had forgotten about that part of it until now. *First, you must forgive yourself.*

For what? Martin wondered. And then he knew. He must forgive himself for all the hurts he had put on Caroline and his son, Anson. He had hurt Juanito. He had used the cannon on the Apache and Caroline had begged him to get rid of it, but he never had. He had hurt her a lot. He had hurt a lot of people. He had, he thought, even hurt himself.

But, he thought, how do I forgive myself? And who will know? He wished Juanito was still alive so that he could ask him these questions, and more. But, sadly, Juanito was dead and gone and only his words lived on in Martin's mind.

How do I forgive myself? Martin asked himself that question again and shook his head. He did not know, not then, not in that moment of reflection and introspection. Maybe it was impossible. Juanito had said a lot of strange things when he was alive and not a lot of what he had said made sense.

But somehow this remembrance did make sense and Martin thought there must be some reason for Juanito to have popped into his mind and taken it over against Martin's will. He could still see that wide bright smile of his and those dark wise eyes that seemed to mask so much knowledge for one so young.

The riders ahead of Martin were stopping. He saw Oltman turn and wave for him to ride up. Martin touched spurs to the big rangy gelding he called Omar because he had Arabian blood in him. Shepley was drinking from his canteen and Oltman was wiping his brow with the back of his hand when Martin caught up to them. Kenny Darnell had stopped, too. Matteo was scowling, but he seemed impervious to the heat.

"Ain't nary a speck of shade out here," Shepley grumbled.

"I'm going to ride point," Oltman said to Martin. "You want to stay back there and eat dust or die up here with Dan?"

"You expecting trouble?" Martin asked.

"Aguilar here kind of perked up the last couple of miles. There's a Mexican settlement up ahead where I reckon we could wash the dust out of our throats and get us some bunks for the night."

"Bandana," Martin said.

"That's the place. Aguilar have kin there?"

"I don't know," Martin said. "It's a Mexican settlement. Been there since God knows when. It's a watering place I've stopped at a time or two."

"Well, from what you tell me that waitress told you, some of Aguilar's cronies might be up ahead of us and I don't want any surprises."

Martin forced himself to look at Matteo. Aguilar stared back at him, his black agate eyes darker than a sinful man's heart. Martin wondered if he could forgive Matteo, ever. All the hatred for what he had done boiled up inside of him once again. He was tempted to draw his pistol and shoot Matteo out of the saddle right then and there.

"You have enemies," Matteo said, his voice soft and without emotion.

"You mean Reynaud," Martin said.

"Not only Reynaud."

"That the Frenchie from New Orleans?" Shepley asked.

"He's the dog Matteo here let loose on me," Martin said.

"You raped his sister," Matteo said.

"Reynaud is a liar. His own family kicked him out. He's a thief and a scoundrel."

Matteo smiled. "He says the same of you, Martin."

"Arguin' ain't goin' to put any proof in the puddin'," Shepley said. "You both got differences, but we got places to go. Move out, Aguilar. You so much as twitch and I'll blow a hole clean through your sorry Mexican ass."

Matteo scowled and clapped heels to his horse's flanks. Shepley held the reins to the animal and he rode slightly ahead of Matteo. Martin took the left flank so that Matteo couldn't escape if he wanted to. Darnell took up the rear.

Oltman had disappeared up ahead, and for the next few miles, the only life they saw was a roadrunner and an armadillo. The armadillo moved like a ponderous armored throwback to prehistoric times and the roadrunner had a small snake impaled on its beak. The snake was still wriggling, but the roadrunner seemed unperturbed by its movement.

Shepley studied the ground as he rode slightly ahead of Matteo, and Martin was looking at the various tracks every so often to break up the monotony of the endless plain that stretched out in all directions. The path they were taking was just one of many roads that ran, with a seeming aimlessness, through that part of the country. This one was not so rutted with wagon tracks as others, but it was well worn from travel.

"You see 'em, Baron?" Shepley asked, after a while.

"I see them," Martin said.

"Three horses, three men. Fairly fresh."

"Three, four hours," Martin said.

"Less than three, I reckon," Shepley said. "They ain't in no hurry, neither."

"In this heat, they'd better not be."

"I reckon Al's on it right smart. You keep your eyes peeled, just in case one of 'em decides to double back for a look-see."

"I'm watching," Martin said.

And he knew Matteo was right. Martin did have enemies. Not a lot, but enough for any man. Jules Reynaud had once been a friend, or at least his family had. But Reynaud was a treacherous sort, a gambler, and he had got into trouble in New Orleans, begun stealing from his family. Martin found out about it and told Jules's father, who had thrown his son out. Now, Jules had falsely accused Martin of sullying his sister, and had gone to Matteo, who had hired Reynaud to kill him.

Reynaud was dangerous, and if he had hooked up with those hard cases who had threatened Martin after he fired them, then they could all be after him. Martin had a hunch, though, that Reynaud would try and get Matteo free so that he could get more money out of him. And if Reynaud managed to carry out Matteo's order to assassinate Martin, then the Frenchman might be fixed for life.

He didn't tell any of this to Shepley, nor would he tell Oltman, either. They had enough to worry about as it was, with Matteo as their prisoner.

"You are thinking about Reynaud," Matteo said.

Martin had been deep in thought and Aguilar's words caught him by surprise. "What?" he asked.

"I recognize one of the horses' tracks. Reynaud is not far from us. He is probably waiting up ahead to kill you."

"Reynaud is just another mark against you, Matteo."

"You stole my black slaves. That is a mark against you, Martin."

"Slaves that Reynaud sold you."

"Legally."

"No, those men and women were smuggled into the country. You didn't have the right to own them. That is why I took them from you."

"I did not fight you over the slaves," Matteo said.

"No? I thought you wanted them back."

"I wanted the Aguilar land back."

"I paid for those lands. I own them legally."

"I did not sell them to you, Martin."

"No, but your relatives did. And they had the legal right to do so. The Box B lands are no longer yours."

"They are mine by right. You may have papers saying that you own them, but the Spanish gave those lands to my family, not to yours."

"You should have taken me to court, then, to try and prove your case. Instead, you attacked me and burned down my house."

"There is no law in Wild Horse Desert."

"You're wrong there, Matteo. These Rangers are the law as far as you're concerned. And the land is no longer Wild Horse Desert. The Box B is there to stay, in what I call the Rio Grande Valley."

Matteo let out a harsh, knifing laugh. "Where you squatted," he said, "the whites call it the Nueces Strip. Do you know the real name, the old name, of the place where you put your house?"

"I always heard it called Wild Horse Desert."

"That is not its old name, the name the Spaniards gave it."

"I don't give a damn what the Spaniards called it. They're dead and gone and they no longer have any say in any of this."

"Maybe not, but they gave the valley its true name, one you will soon learn still has meaning for you."

"Just shut up, Matteo," Martin said.

Matteo laughed again.

"The name the Spaniards gave it was *el Desierto de los Muertos.*"

Martin felt a rippling tingle in his spine. He thought about the dead men lying back there on the Box B, Matteo's men, but men no longer living, no longer breathing. Matteo was right. The Spaniards had named the place aptly.

The Desert of the Dead.

Matteo was still chuckling when Martin stiffened at the sound of a rifle shot. It had come from up ahead, where Oltman was riding point.

Then, there was more firing as a volley of shots cracked the air.

"Come on, Baron," Shepley said. "I think Al's in trouble. Shake a leg, Aguilar, and hold on to that apple."

With that, Shepley kicked his horse in the flanks and jerked the reins of Matteo's horse. Martin rode along with them, his own horse racing at a fast gallop. Darnell followed close behind.

And still, gunshots crackled like Chinese firecrackers somewhere up ahead of them.

9

―■―

O N FIRST SEEING him, Anson didn't think much of Forrest Redmond. Ken Richman had brought him out to the ranch, along
with a load of lumber for rebuilding the Baron house. Two of the
black slaves Anson had stolen from Matteo Aguilar sat atop the lumber, Pluto and Julius, their legs dangling off the back edges. They
grinned at Anson and he smiled back and nodded to them.

"He said he was a friend of the Fanchers," Ken explained. "One
thing. He knows lumber."

"Wanda and her mother mentioned you were coming, Redmond.
Can you build me a house?"

"I am a designer of houses and buildings," Redmond said. He
was a short man, slight of build, with large, piercing brown eyes and
a shock of unruly brown hair. He carried a leather satchel, but Anson would bet there were few clothes in it. Redmond was wearing an
old suit that had faded from weather and time, and it looked as if it
had been slept in for quite a long time. His small, battered hat was as
rumpled as his plain muslin shirt and seemed to match his worn-out
lace-up boots. The leather on his footware was scarred and the pol-
ish long since faded. The shoes were pocked with patches where the

smooth leather had been rubbed off, exposing the rough layer beneath.

"I'll design the house. I just want you to figure out what goes
where and how much lumber, nails, and such we need."

"I can do that, Mr. Baron," Redmond said. His voice was soft and
measured, as if it came from some deep quiet pool inside him. "I
can help you plan the flooring and match up the rooms to provide
the greatest comfort to you and your family."

Redmond glanced at the grim ruins of the Baron house. It no
longer smoldered, but the stench of burned wood still lingered in
the air. Peebo was walking through the rubble with a stick, poking
at the ashes, raising dust and burned flakes of wood and ash with
every step. Socrates, the tallest of the freed slaves, was helping some
of the Mexican hands load the wheelbarrows. He was shoveling debris into three of them. A steady stream of workers were cleaning up
the site, starting with the outer edges of the demolished house. All of
them were enveloped in dust and ash from the waist down. The
wooden wheelbarrows creaked as the Mexican hands pushed them
to a waiting wagon where men lifted them up into the bed and
dumped their contents. Two horses were hitched to the wagon and
stood there, switching their tails, slapping away flies on their rumps
and sides and legs.

"I want it built on that hill where the other house sat," Anson said.

"It's a fair spot," Redmond said.

"Where do you want this load of lumber, Anson?" Ken asked.

"I'll let Mr. Redmond here tell you that," Anson said. "He'll be
working with Roy Killian on the rebuilding."

"Where is Roy?" Ken asked.

"He'll be back tonight or tomorrow," Anson said. "He's got his
hands full with two women giving him orders."

Ken laughed.

"Call me Forrest," Redmond said when he climbed down from
the wagon. "I've never liked titles for myself."

"When I get to know you better, I might call you that," Anson
said. "For now, let's keep it at Redmond."

"Yes, that would put distance between us," Redmond said. "For-
malities were designed to distinguish the richer classes from the

poorer. I don't hold with that custom. One man may be better off than another, but, in the end, all men are pretty much equal in the eyes of God."

Ken's jaw dropped and Anson blinked, his eyes widening at the unexpected statement.

Anson liked Redmond a lot better after that.

"You aren't a preacher, are you, Redmond?" Anson asked.

Redmond grinned, a shy kind of grin that Anson found disarming.

"Nope. I'm not a philosopher, either. Just another example of *Homo Sapiens,* I'm afraid."

"What the hell is 'homo say whatever'?"

"That's Latin for 'thinking man.' I try to use my mind as much as my muscles, Mr. Baron."

"Well, that's what I want you to use, Redmond. I'll pay you bunk and board and thirty dollars a month for your services."

"That will be fine, Mr. Baron. Where is this bunk?"

"Peebo yonder will put you up in the bunkhouse with the hands. You just walk on down there and introduce yourself to that man poking around with the stick in his hand."

Redmond picked up his satchel and walked down to the ruins of the house.

"He's something, isn't he, Anson?" Ken wore a smile on his face. "He kept me entertained on the ride out here from Baronsville."

"I'll bet he did. What do you make of him?"

"He's a pretty smart feller," Ken said. "He and Ed Wales got into a lively palaver at lunch that was way over my head. Book talk, mostly, about some Greeks I've barely heard of, Plato, Aristotle, Socrates. But on the way out here, he and I talked mostly about the country. He's some kind of geologist or something like that. He can tell one kind of rock from another."

"So, he's full of useless information," Anson said.

Ken laughed. "I reckon you could say that. He doesn't know much about cows or horses, that's for sure."

"I just hope he knows something about building houses."

"He gave me some ideas on buildings I have planned to put up in Baronsville. I'll probably hire him on when you get through with him."

"Good. If he doesn't get snake-bit or die from the heat out here, he might like our town and want to stay on. Where'd he come from?"

"He said Missouri and Arkansas, but he didn't talk much about himself."

"That's in his favor," Anson said. Then, "I guess you can haul this lumber down and stack it under and around those trees in back of where the new house will be. Or you can ask Mr. Redmond where he wants you to put it."

"Want a ride?"

"No, thanks. I've got some horseflesh to take care of. Appreciate your bringing that lumber out. And that Redmond feller."

"Are you still planning to go after that white bull, the one the Mexes call the Diablo Blanco?"

"Yeah. Peebo and I are going to track him down and rope him, bring him back here and use him as a seed bull to build my herd."

"This may not be the best time for you to go, Anson."

"Yeah? Why not?"

"War's getting close. It's coming to Texas, mark my words."

"I just had a war, Ken. I don't need another."

"Ed Wales tells me he's getting news about the Union coming into Texas to take over all the Gulf ports. Galveston, Corpus Christi, Brownsville."

"Those are a long ways from here."

"There'll be fighting and soldiers in blue might be camped on your doorstep when you get back."

"I don't have a doorstep, Ken. Not yet."

"Well, I think you ought to stay and take care of what you have here. You can always go after that bull when the war's over."

"And I can go after him now, Ken. Or any damned time I please."

"Suit yourself, Anson. Someone will be out tomorrow with more of the same and I've got several kegs of nails due in tonight from Corpus Christi. They'll be in the wagon tomorrow, too. I'll leave Pluto and Julius here to help with the work. They said they don't like town much."

Anson nodded. "Be seeing you, Ken."

Ken pulled a whiskey flask out of his back pocket and took a pull. Then he offered the container to Anson. "Want a taste?"

Anson shook his head. "You've been hitting that pretty hard lately, don't you think?"

"Long days and long nights, Anson."

"You don't need it, Ken. Neither does Ed Wales."

Wales ran the *Baronsville Bugle*. He was an accomplished newspaperman, but Anson knew he was a heavy drinker, too.

"Ed and I are both in good health. I know when I've had too much and I stay well shy of that point."

Anson could see the tiny red spiders on Ken's cheekbones, the sure mark of a heavy drinker.

"You know what Juanito called whiskey?"

"No, I don't believe I do."

"He called it 'the widowmaker.' He said whiskey had brought down more good men than swords, arrows, knives, or guns."

"Like I said, Anson, I just use it for fortification on these long days."

"And nights."

"When the work's all done, a little taste brings me back down so I can get a good night's sleep."

"None of my business, Ken, but that flask is looking more and more like a crutch for a crippled man."

Ken reacted as if stung. He drew back, openmouthed, but no words escaped his lips. He stood there and pocketed the flask, then walked to the wagon and climbed up into the seat.

Anson walked off toward the barn. He glanced over at the ruins of the house and saw that Peebo and Redmond were engaged in conversation. A moment later, he saw Peebo leading Redmond toward the area where the bunkhouse was. Anson was anxious to leave, but there was so much to do before he and Peebo could chase after that white bull, and he knew he wouldn't get away for at least another day. Something Ken had said about Redmond gave him an idea. He had something to show Redmond and it was in the barn, still inside his saddlebag where he had left it after Bone had given it to him just before Matteo's attack on the ranch.

The barn gave Anson the shudders. He could still see David Wilhoit's body lying there on the dirty ground, could still smell the stench of death that seemed to have settled inside the gloomy darkness of the building. David had been buried late in the afternoon of the day before. It had been a simple ceremony, with Roy reading from the Good Book and saying a few words about his stepfather, Wanda and her mother, Hattie, consoling Ursula, the three of them weeping uncontrollably once the men had started shoveling dirt over the body. There had been no casket. Roy and his mother, Ursula, had wrapped David's body in heavy canvas.

But the barn still harbored David's ghost. As well as the ghosts of the Apaches who had died just outside the doors when his father had unloosed his four-pounder on them. They had charged down the slope, shrieking and screaming, until the cannon shredded them to pieces. Those ghosts were still there, too, and Anson now wished he had not come in here alone.

The horses in their stalls whickered as Anson walked to the back. He dipped a bucket into a barrel of oats and carried it with him to the stall where he kept his horse, Lancer. He went inside, pulling the door shut behind him. He poured the grain into the feed bin and reached up and took a currycomb from a nail on one of the posts. As Lancer began to feed on the oats, Anson began to curry the gelding's black coat.

"You ready to go, boy?" Anson said to the horse. "We've got a long ride ahead of us."

Anson finished currying Lancer, checked his hooves. He had been shod with new shoes less than a week and they were sound. The horse was only fifteen hands high, with small feet, quick, sturdy legs, a good bottom. He would be fine in the brush, Anson thought. He patted the horse's chest and rubbed his neck.

"Tomorrow, maybe," Anson said, as he left the stall. There were horses in the other stalls and he grained those, too. He and Peebo would each take an extra horse and these were being kept under cover in the barn. They would bring provisions to last them a month and live off the land while they hunted down the big white bull.

Anson finished feeding all the horses and closed the last stall door. He put the bucket back next to the oat barrel and went inside the small tack room. He lifted his saddlebags from a hook and reached inside the heaviest one. He sighed as he pulled out the strange stone that Bone had given him only a couple of days before. He put the saddlebags back on the hook and walked out of the tack room and out the back end of the barn, into the sunlight.

He was surprised to see a bunch of his men gathered outside, waiting for him. They stood there, leaning on shovels and hoes like dilapidated remnants of an army, their dark faces wrinkled with scowls. Even Socrates was there, standing to one side, looking oddly out of place. And hiding behind him were the two who had ridden on the wagon with Ken, Pluto and Julius, trying not to be noticed.

Julio Sifuentes and Carlos Quintana stood at the front of the group, scowling and squinting as if the sun had burned their eyes out. Anson figured they were the ones who had brought the others together and convinced them to go over to the barn as a group.

"Julio, what passes?" Anson asked Sifuentes in Spanish. "Did you finish your work?"

"No, we have not finish our work, Don Anson," Julio said in English. "We have come to talk to you."

"All of you?"

"We have talked together first and now we wish to talk to you."

"Spit it out," Anson said in English. "Whatever in hell you got in your craw."

"It is said that you are going to hunt the Diablo Blanco, the white bull."

"What of it?"

"We do not want you to do this, Don Anson."

"Well, I'm going."

Sifuentes shifted his weight and looked down at the ground for a moment. Then he lifted his head and looked straight at Anson. "Already, Don Martin has left the rancho. There is much work to do and we do not know what you want us to do."

"Roy Killian will manage the ranch while Peebo and I are gone."

"If you do this thing, Don Anson, then we will quit and go back home to Mexico."

Anson sucked in a breath and stiffened his spine as he drew up straight.

"What?"

"We will quit and go home if you are chasing the white bull. We do not want to work for a *patrón* who is never here. We do not want to work for Don Killian."

"I see," Anson said. He walked over to the group and looked in every man's face as if he were a general on the battlefield inspecting his troops. "So, you all will quit, huh? Just because I have work to do somewhere else on the Box B. Well, you're a sorry-assed bunch. My father brought you all here and gave you homes and jobs and now you want to go back to Mexico. Well, shit."

"We will go back today," Carlos Quintana said.

Anson looked at Socrates. "What about you? Do you want to go back to New Orleans? Be a damned slave?"

Socrates shrugged, but he did not lower his gaze.

"This is mutiny," Anson said.

"We wish you to stay and be our *patrón*," Quintana said. "You can chase the white bull some other time."

"What are you afraid of?" Anson asked.

"The two black boys told us there is going to be war here. Soldiers will come and kill us all. We are afraid of this war."

"Quintana, there isn't going to be a war here. We just had one, with Matteo Aguilar."

"No, there will be war. Don Richman, he say the same thing."

"Damn Ken," Anson muttered.

"He speaks the truth, I think," Quintana said.

Peebo and Redmond walked up behind the assembled group and stood there. Anson ignored them and kept his attention on Quintana and Sifuentes.

"I tell you," Anson said in Spanish, "I do not want you working for me. Go. Return to Mexico. You can draw your pay when you leave. I'll be in the bunkhouse."

The Mexican vaqueros all looked at each other and began murmuring among themselves. Socrates, Pluto, and Julius could not understand the words, which were in Spanish, and stood there, their faces devoid of emotion.

"Socrates, you take Julius and Plato and get back to work, or walk on back into town. These Mexicans are leaving."

"They will go to Mexico?" Socrates asked.

"I don't give a damn where they go. Just go on back to work."

The Mexicans glared at Anson, then turned away from him and started walking toward their little houses beyond the bunkhouse.

Peebo and Redmond walked over to Anson.

"What was that all about?" Peebo asked. "You're going to have a hell of a time without those vaqueros. Especially with us being gone and all."

"We're not going, Peebo. I've got to stay here and run the ranch."

"But ain't that what those boys wanted in the first place?"

"I'm not taking orders from those men."

"So what are you going to do for hands to work the ranch?"

"I'm giving that a hell of a lot of thought, Peebo."

"I bet you sure as hell are," Peebo said.

Redmond stood by in silence, but when Anson looked at him, he knew Forrest was doing some thinking, too.

10

B ONE'S WIFE, DAWN, was asleep when he entered his little house
on the Rocking A ranch. Matteo had given him the house for
his family, and he had been grateful at the time. He, Dawn, and their
son, Juan, had been sleeping on the hard ground, wandering up
from the mean mountains of Mexico, eating snakes and lizards and
jackrabbits, and the home had seemed like a haven to him. But now,
he realized it was a hovel, not much better than a crude *jacal,* such as
the poor Mexicans lived in. This one had a dirt floor, and was built
of adobe, and it had suited him, until now.

Their child was asleep in his mother's arms, and he was the first
to open his eyes. Bone stood there, gazing at his wife and child, the
weariness in him beginning to seep deep into his muscles. The sun
had still not risen and it was dark and airless inside the room, but the
sky to the east was paling, even so, and he could see the child's dark
eyes as he drew close to the bed.

"Madrugada," Bone whispered, as he touched his wife on her
bare shoulder. "Dawn, I am home."

Little Juan Bone gurgled, and Dawn's eyes fluttered slightly, but
did not open.

"Dawn," Bone said again. "I am home."

Dawn's eyes opened and Bone could see that she was still half-asleep, trying to focus on him.

"Mickey? Is that you?"

Bone laughed. "Did you think it was another?"

"Did you kill him?" she asked in a toneless voice.

"Who?"

"Martin Baron."

"No."

"I knew you would not. So did Matteo, I think."

"He knew I would not kill Martin or Anson. So he sent someone to kill me."

Dawn drew back in shock. Her eyes widened.

"Are you hurt?" she asked.

"No. Matteo will not return. I am going to run the ranch. We will not live here in this adobe any more."

"Where will we live?"

"In Matteo's house. Come. Put your clothes on. We will go there now."

"What about Luz?"

"She can live here if she wishes."

"You cannot do that to her, Mickey. That is cruel. I have been sleeping in the big house at night. I do work for her. We are friends."

"Then she can work for you, help you with the house and the garden."

Light began to seep in through the front window, spreading across the floor to the doorway of the bedroom. Dawn picked up Juan and held him to her breast. He suckled as she rocked back and forth.

"I do not know," she said.

"Matteo will not be back. They will hang him for what he did. He promised me a home here for as long as I live. I am taking his home. We will live there."

"I have fear," she said.

"I do not. When you are ready, we will walk to the big house and we will live there."

"Now?"

"Yes, now. I do not like this place. If I am going to do the work of a white man, I will live like a white man. Do you remember what you told me about how your people lived before the white man came to our country?"

"We lived," she said.

"Your people and mine lived in this place and we did not think of the land as something to be owned by one man or another."

"That is true."

"Our women dug in the anthills for the eggs so that we all could eat. We hunted and the women and children caught spiders and cooked them so that we did not have hunger."

"Yes, my old grandmother told me these things."

"And my grandfather told me these things, as well, and my father also remembered how it was to live here on the Desert of the Dead. We caught the fish in the tide pools and in the stinkwater of the brasada."

"Yes," she said, "and we left the fish in the sun to rot, so that the maggots would come, and we fed upon the rotten meat of the fish and ate the little white worms to fill our bellies."

"Yes, my grandfather told me that when the fish began to stink and to move with the maggots, then it was time to eat it."

"And when we had no good water to drink, we sucked out the juices of the nopal, and we ate the agave and made strong drink with its juices."

"If we go from here, Dawn, we may have to live as our grandmothers and grandfathers lived. Here, we have a chance to own the land and the cattle upon it and we do not have to drink the bad water or eat the stinking fish. Do you not see that we must not go back to where we came from, that we must learn to live like the white man and take those things the white man has so that we can live as he lives?"

"Mickey, you must think about this."

"I have thought about it all night and I have thought about it since I came back and two men tried to kill me. Did you not hear the shooting?"

"No, I heard nothing. I was asleep."

"I hope Matteo takes a long time to die. I hope he kicks and screams like a woman while he dangles at the end of a rope."

"You—you go to the house and talk to Luz. I—I will bring little Juan and meet you there. I want to think, too."

"Do not be long," Bone said.

"Be careful," she said. "Maybe Luz will want to kill you, too."

"I think she may want to kill me," Bone said, and laughed harshly as the sun rose above the horizon and streamed golden light into the adobe. All of his tiredness seemed to go away in that instant, as he turned to leave.

He had not touched his wife or held her and he was sorry about that. But if he had lain beside her, he would have wanted her and then he would have wanted to sleep and there was much to do.

He did not go to Matteo's house, but waited outside, watching the sun rise and flood the land with light. It felt good to be alive. It felt good to be moving to a new home. He would wait for Dawn and they would go to the Aguilar house together, as a family. Then Luz would see that he meant what he had said. He would be the master of the Rocking A. He would be a rich man.

He would find where Matteo kept his tobacco and he would smoke the pipe and roll the cigarette. He would sit on the porch in the evening and watch the land as the shadows grew and became black while it waited for the stars and moon to spread silver light over it.

As he sat there, Bone saw the men who had attacked the Baron ranch return, their heads drooping, their horses tired, trailed by dead men tied to their saddles like sacks. Some of the men were bloodied from wounds and others sat hunched over their saddles like men whipped within an inch of their lives, and stared at the ground as if hiding from the rising sun.

One rider looked up as he passed Bone, and his eyes widened as if he had suddenly been awakened. "I thought you were dead," he said to Bone.

"Why did you think that, Emilio?"

"So many of us died and I did not see you among those of us who are still alive."

"I am alive and I am the boss of this ranch."

"You are? Truly?"

"Truly, Emilio."

"Did you kill Caudillo and Perez?"

"Yes, I killed them."

"Why?"

"Because Matteo told them to kill me. He told Pedro to kill me, too."

"Did you also kill Pedro?"

"No, I did not kill him."

"Matteo is probably dead, too."

"Probably he too is dead."

"We should never have gone to the Baron ranch."

"No, that is true."

"Did Matteo give you his ranch, then?"

"I am taking it because of a promise he made to me."

"He promised to give you the ranch?"

"You ask too many questions. Bury the dead. Tomorrow we will go back to work."

"I will have to think about this, Mickey."

"If you think about this too long, you will join the others who are to be buried. Do you understand me?" Bone's right hand dropped down to the butt of the pistol hanging on his belt.

"Yes, I understand. I will help to bury the dead."

"I will be in the big house this day," Bone said. "I will live there."

"I understand, *patrón*."

"Good. Tell the others what I told you."

"I will tell them."

Bone watched the man ride away and join the others who were going to their dwellings. In a moment, he heard Dawn open the door and he turned around to look at her.

"I thought you would meet me at the big house," she said.

"I am here. Let us go."

"Oh," she said, "there are dead men." She held the boy tightly to her breast and pointed at the bodies draped over the saddles of horses.

"Yes. The soldiers have returned with their dead from the war." There was more than a trace of sarcasm in Bone's voice.

"Are you a coward that you did not fight with them? Is that why Matteo wanted to kill you?"

"What kind of a wife are you to ask me such a question?"

"I am a good wife who loves her husband. But I do not want to be married to a coward."

"I am not afraid to fight. I fought today, in my own way. But I did not want to fight Martin or Anson."

"They are white men. They are not of our blood. If you worked for Matteo and he wanted you to fight and kill those two white men, it would have brought great honor to you, and to me."

"And who would honor us? Your people are all in the spirit world or scattered like ashes on the wind. I could not wear a shirt of honor if I had to put it on over a shirt of shame."

"Shame? What shame?"

"Martin Baron gave me a home and a job and he never lied to me. His son Anson was like a brother to me. When I was on the Box B, Anson was my shadow and he would have ridden with me when I left the Baron ranch if his father would have let him. I do not see any good reason to kill either of these men."

"But they are white men. They took away all that our people held dear. They hunted us down like animals and cut us to pieces and threw our bones to the wild dogs."

"These white men are not of the same blood as those who did that to our people. These white men come from different ancestors."

"They are all the same," she said.

"You forget the Spaniards, with their missionaries and their greed. They were the white men who put their boots on the necks of our people."

"They are all the same," Dawn repeated.

"No, you are wrong, my dear one. Martin and Anson Baron are of a different breed."

"They take the land as their own, the same as the Spaniards."

"The Mexicans took the land from the Spaniards, and the Baron men bought the land from the Mexicans. They did not steal it."

"They bought something that was stolen from us, from our people."

"That is true, but they did not know that when they paid the money."

"It makes no difference, Miguel."

"Maybe it does not. And now I am taking this land from Matteo and it will be ours. Come, let us go to the big house, my love."

"I do not like this," she said.

But she followed Bone to the Aguilar house and up the stairs and through the open front door. Bone and Dawn called out Luz's name and they searched the house, but she was nowhere to be found and the baby was gone, as well.

"I wonder where she is?" Dawn said.

Bone smiled.

"She has gone to look for Matteo, I think," he said. "So now this house and all this land is ours."

"She will find Matteo and she will bring him back. And he will kill you."

"She will not find Matteo. I think she will only find his grave."

Dawn shuddered.

Bone spread his arms out and turned around in a circle in the front room.

"Welcome to your new home," he shouted, and his voice echoed through the empty house and the sounds faded away like the wind blowing through a hollow cave on some deserted Mexican mountain where they had once lived.

CULEBRA, WHO WAS called Snake in English, had listened, in silence, to what the scouts had told him and to the arguments among his men afterward. Now, he lit his pipe from one of the glowing faggots still smoldering in the dying fire at the center of his seated band of Mescaleros and Lipan. He let the smoke linger in his lungs until they warmed and then expelled the smoke into the still air of afternoon. He blew the smoke into the face of Oso, the one called Bear, who had been arguing more loudly than the others.

"Do you smell the smoke, Oso?" Culebra asked. "Do you see it?"

"I see it. I smell it."

"Did you see the smoke of the Baron house? Did you smell it?"

"I saw the smoke. I smelled it."

Culebra waited until the smoke spun into lacy wisps and evaporated.

"Do you see the smoke now, Oso?"

"No, it has become as the air I breathe," Oso said.

"Do you still smell it?"

"I smell it yet, Culebra. There is not much smell left."

"No, there is no more smoke in your nose and there is little smell. At the Baron rancho there is no more smoke and the dead have been returned to the earth. The white men with stars on their chests have taken Matteo Aguilar away. And the scouts say that Bone has returned to the Aguilar rancho. Is that not so?"

"It is so, my chieftain," Oso said.

"The son of Martin Baron is still alive and he has the big shining gun that shoots lead like the hail from the sky. He is very strong, like his father, Martin, the man who came from the big water. So we will not ride against the one called Anson. He is fierce like the white bull."

"I have no fear of Anson," Oso said.

"I have no fear also. But we are few and there are other signs our scouts have seen that make me want to stay away from the Baron rancho."

"What signs are these?" Oso asked.

"White soldiers ride into the Desert of the Dead. Tecolote has seen them. Lobito has seen them to the north and Abeja has seen them in the south. Along the big river, the Rio Bravo, the Mexicans say that the white men will war against each other and that the day of the red man is passing like the smoke that floats unseen between the earth and the sun."

"What will we do?" Oso asked, as the others grunted in assent to the words Culebra had spoken.

"We will wait and we will have the patience."

"What do we wait for?"

"We wait to see if the white soldiers come to this land."

"And what if they come, these soldiers?"

"We will see who they fight and ask them if they need scouts to be their eyes."

"Why do you speak of these things?" Oso asked.

"I speak of them because Abeja has spoken to the Mexicans in the south and they say the soldiers will come to the Rio Bravo and fight those who live there. They will want the boats that come and go along the river and they will want the cotton that they use to make the clothes they wear."

"What do the Mexicans know? They know nothing," Oso said.

"They have ears and eyes," Abeja said.

Tecolote was building another fire. They were at the bend of a small creek, and he made the fire under the live oak trees so that the smoke would not rise in the air and tell of their presence in that place.

Culebra stood up and walked over to the fire.

"Why do you make a fire, Tecolote?" he asked.

"Because I have hunger."

"We all have hunger. There is no meat."

"I hear some quail in the thicket beyond the bend in this creek."

"I do not hear the quail," Culebra said.

"Tell the others to get some rocks. I will take you there and we will kill some quail."

"If there are no quail there, they will throw their rocks at you."

"The quail are there," Tecolote said, fanning the small flames with one hand, urging them to grow. "I hear them chortling like women at their baths."

Culebra listened. He cupped a hand to his ear. But he heard nothing. He looked at Tecolote as if his friend had lost his senses. "You have been out in the sun too long, Tecolote. Stay in the shade for a time. The sounds will go away after a while."

"I am going to get two rocks and kill two quail, Culebra."

Tecolote put enough wood on the fire to keep it burning for a while. He walked along the bank and found two round pebbles. Culebra walked back and talked to the others. When they saw Tecolote walking toward the bend in the creek, they all got up and began searching for small stones. Even Culebra picked up two rocks and followed the others, who walked in single file without making a sound on the ground.

When Tecolote came to the thicket, he stopped and slowly sank to his haunches. The others, who came up behind him, all did the same. Like Tecolote, they listened.

It was very still and quiet, except for the faint lapping of the creek as it sloshed against the bank and burbled over smooth pebbles. In the silence all of the men heard the little chuckles and chortles of quail in the brambles. It sounded as if the quail were talking to each other and were not worried about anything that might be hunting them.

Tecolote turned and made spreading motions with his hands. In sign, he told the others to make a circle around the thicket and then to watch him with their eyes. The men did this, fanning out and circling the brush on silent moccasins. Culebra stayed close to Te-colote, but left room between their bodies so both could throw their stones.

When the other men were all in place and listening to the little coos and *chuck-chuck* sounds of the quail, Tecolote stood up and moved close to the thicket so that he could look down into it. The others did as he had done and they all looked down through the brambles and leaves and limbs of the plants growing there. They all saw the quail, and there were many of them, perhaps twenty or more.

Some of the quail were dusting themselves in a small wallow they had made. Others were walking around, taking tiny little steps but not going anywhere except in small circles. The quail looked like human people in a camp, walking around, talking, bathing in the dust that worried the mites on their backs.

Tecolote threw the first stone and it struck a quail, which fell over on its side and lay still. The other quail were not startled, and they kept doing what they were doing. Oso threw a stone and hit a quail's skull that was as soft and thin as the white man's paper. The quail's eyes blinked and stayed open, and it was dead.

Tecolote threw another stone and smashed the skull of still an-other bird, and then Culebra and the others all threw stones, taking their time, until many quail lay dead in the thicket while the other birds grew nervous and pecked at some of the dead ones, while oth-ers ran back and forth as if in disbelief.

The braves continued pelting the quail with stones until a dozen lay dead. Then, as if urged by some predetermined signal, the birds flushed out of the thicket in a whir of wings, scattering in all direc-tions like leaves blown before a sudden gust of wind.

Tecolote and the others stepped into the brush and began col-lecting the dead birds. They carried them back to the fire, twisted off their necks, gutted them, and began picking off their feathers.

"We thank you, our brothers," intoned Culebra, "for giving up your breaths so that we may eat. One day, we promise you that our bodies will return to the earth and feed your kind with the seeds that grow from our graves."

Oso and Tecolote got mud from the creek and packed the dressed quail, patting the mud down to form a solid casing. They placed the birds in the fire, and piled dirt on them and then more wood on top of the dirt, thus forming a primitive oven.

"I have been seeing pictures in my mind," Culebra said, while the quail were cooking in their little mud ovens, "and I see El Diablo Blanco, the big white bull that Anson wishes to capture for his herd of cattle."

"He did not catch the white bull," Oso said.

"No, he did not catch El Diablo," Culebra agreed. "That is why he will return to that place where the bull walks with the cows. He will chase the bull with his friend and try to catch him with ropes."

"I think he is afraid of the white bull," Tecolote said. "It is a devil bull. It has killed many men. It has killed many horses."

"This white man Anson is a brave man," Culebra said. "He is not afraid of El Diablo. He will come back to that place and hunt the white bull."

"And maybe he will be killed," Tecolote said.

"Maybe we will go there and find the white bull. Maybe we will wait until the two white men return and then we will kill them. Anson is like the head of the snake. If we cut it off, the snake will die. His father has gone to fight the white man's war and there will be no one to make the rancho work. Then the others will go away and leave us many cattle."

The others nodded as they thought about Culebra's words. He looked at each man and each man grunted in assent. They could smell the quail meat cooking and they looked into the smoke to see what they could see, for in smoke there were spirits and words that rose up to the sky and carried thoughts and prayers to the Great Spirit.

"I have seen these things in my mind," Culebra said, "and the smoke tells me where we should go. We will eat these quail and then we will find the white bull that young Baron wants. We will wait for him to come. We will live with the wild herd until he comes."

They all grunted as their hunger mounted with the aroma of the cooking meat.

"Yes, Culebra. That is so. We will follow you to that place where the white bull lives and we will roam with the wild cows until the young Baron comes to chase El Diablo. We will be like the quail in the thicket, but we will make no noise and we will not be seen. It is good."

When the wood had burned down and there were ashes thick upon the roasted quail, the men got sticks and scattered the coals. They dug out the birds and let the hot mud cool until they could peel it off like the shell from a pecan.

They ate without speaking, smearing their faces with grease and meat, chewing even the little bones and swallowing them so that they would be strong.

Culebra patted his belly when he was full and he rose up from where he was sitting and looked to the east where the white bull was lord over his herd of cows. He smiled, knowing that he had been shown the way to that place where he could kill his enemy, Anson Baron, and wear his scalp on his belt and brag to the women about his bravery and his wisdom.

"It is good," Culebra said. "We go to where the white bull lives."

And the others rose from their places and clucked to themselves in satisfaction. They walked to their horses, their bellies full and their hearts soaring like the hunting hawks that sailed on strong wings across the land and sky that belonged to them.

12

MILLIE SAT AT a table by the window, staring out at the empty main street of Baronsville. It was as empty as she felt inside. A lone tumbleweed blew down the middle of the dirt street, its dried skeleton so stark and bleak, so bereft of life, it made her sad, sad for its aimless, drifting life, sad for her own, which seemed at that moment just as bleak, just as lifeless.

She had cried most of the day, not in front of the customers, but back in the kitchen, and out back on her work breaks, when the apron she wore seemed like a coat of lead hanging from her neck, like a diabolical chastity belt that no man could pierce.

She missed Martin Baron as she had never missed any man and the hurt she felt at his absence went deep, deep into her heart and into her stomach, which burned as if she had swallowed hot coals, or crushed glass.

Ever since Martin had left that morning, she had been filled with a sense of dread, and she had not been able to shake it. Now that the restaurant was empty of customers, the sense of foreboding had returned, along with a large dosage of self-pity, self-administered, self-perpetuating.

She reached up and lifted the apron strap from around her neck, tore away the cloth and wadded it up, slammed it onto the table. It was stained and reeked with the foul odors of grease and fat and whiskey and beer and mustard and God knew what else. She pushed the wadded-up apron away from her, but could not elude its smell, nor its symbolism.

The apron reminded her of worse places, the taverns and fishy-smelling cafes in New Orleans with their drunks and pimps and whores and card-dealing Frenchmen with oily hair and lizard hands, the sailors and the pirates, the smugglers and the wharf rats, the stevedores and the pinch-faced thieves that lurked in the dark corners of the Quarter and along the docks where the seagulls screamed like the women behind the taverns and those being raped in their cribs above the alehouse.

The day had been bad ever since Martin left town, made worse because she suspected that someone, the Frenchman, Jules Reynaud, might be following Martin, tracking him down to kill him.

That fear made the knot in her stomach begin to harden and burn all over again. She had quarreled earlier with the barkeep, Biff Dubbins, and the cook, Willard Moody, whose sobriquet, for some unknown reason, was Skeeter. Biff had been busy at lunch and she had been slow, that was the truth of it, but he shouldn't have treated her like a damned field hand, ordering her to hurry up when he could see that she was distraught.

And Skeeter had berated her also, for being too slow in picking up the orders, as if he were some high-and-mighty chef from Delmonico's in New York, instead of a fry cook from Corpus Christi whose last job had been on a dilapidated freighter out of Biloxi, and before that, serving up grub from a chuck wagon somewhere down in Jalisco.

Millie heard the faint ringing of the school bell, its distant tolling sounding another sadness inside her as she recalled the little one-room schoolhouse in Blanchard, Louisiana, where she had gone until the sixth grade. They had moved there from Shreveport, which people still called Shreve's Port, so her daddy could sharecrop cotton on eighty acres.

She had loved going to school, loved walking barefoot in the summer and swimming in the pond they had in the tall pine woods, playing with the red clay of the fallow fields, watching the red-winged blackbirds wheel in the sky when she flushed them from the tall cat-tails down by the lake, where the turtles sunned on slick wet logs in the shallows and water moccasins slithered along the shore, silent and deadly. In the spring and fall, she would hear the geese calling from the sky, and for three days they would obscure the sun, their long vees trailing across the heavens for miles and miles, layer upon layer, ducks and geese heading for the Gulf to winter, or north to Canada and their nesting grounds in the spring.

She missed more than those times, she missed her girlhood, so suddenly gone, never to return, those days before her daddy died and her mother took them to Baton Rouge, away from the cotton fields and the sugarcane and the little bayous, and into the city with its filth and its crime and its blatant poverty matching their own, and New Orleans still worse with its mixture of races and tongues, its be-wildering maze of streets and languages.

The notes from the school bell faded and Millie sighed. Lorene would be stopping by soon, as she always did when school let out and she needed to talk to a grown person after spending a day teaching children. The school had gotten so big, Nancy Grant needed Lorene Sisler to help her teach the children. Today, Lorene was going to drop off a pamphlet her uncle, Doc Purvis, had received in the mail from a friend in New York. It was, Lorene had said, a remarkable col-lection of poems by a young man named Walt Whitman, and only published the year before, by the poet himself.

Lorene loved poetry and Millie shared her enthusiasm for the writ-ten word. She had just finished reading a translation of Dante's *Divine Comedy,* and returned the book to Lorene, along with a hundred ques-tions. She liked the music of the poetry, but did not always understand Dante's meaning. Lorene was a good teacher. She had explained a lot about the imagery and symbolism in Dante's long poem and Millie had begun to explore the mystery and the magic of words and lan-guage. That had helped put some color and light into her world, which would have otherwise been too dull and exhausting to bear.

She enjoyed waiting on people in the Longhorn, but sometimes they could be exasperating, and were often annoying as well. Still, it made her feel a part of the flow of life in Baronsville, and she loved listening to conversations as she passed the diners at breakfast, lunch, or supper, because that, too, also widened her small world and made her realize that there was more to life than working day after day in a restaurant with its food and whiskey smells, its dirty plates and floors that had to be swept and mopped, a short-tempered cook and a whiskey-breathed bartender, both men consumed with lewd thoughts and possessed of groping hands that she had to constantly swat away like flies.

Millie saw Lorene pass by the window and wave as she headed for the front door. She was smiling and she had her satchel with her, made out of carpet, a satchel that was full of her students' papers, schoolbooks, and the books she was reading.

Lorene came inside and walked over to the table, her silky black hair tousled from the breeze, her brown eyes sparkling with an inner radiance. Before she sat down, she opened the carpetbag and rummaged around in it until she found what she was looking for and brought it forth, laid it in front of Millie.

"That's the one Uncle Pat gave me," Lorene said. "I think you'll enjoy reading the poems. They're different."

"A lot easier to understand than Dante, you said."

"Oh, yes, but still full of beautiful thoughts and wonderful images."

Lorene placed the well worn little booklet on the table in front of Millie and sat down, setting her carpetbag on the floor next to her chair.

Millie looked at the title on the front cover.

" '*Leaves of Grass,*' " she said. " 'By Walt Whitman.' What a lovely title."

"Mr. Whitman does not use rhyme very much, but he has a unique rhythm to his language that is quite surprising and startling. He seems very American and you can see in your mind what he's talking about. He also seems very vain, but sure of himself. I think you'll like his poetry."

"I'm sure I will, Lorene. Thank you for the book. I'll read it tonight."

"And you'll want to read it again and again. We can talk about it when you're ready, if you like."

"Do you want something to drink, Lorene? Coffee, or I can make some tea. A glass of water?"

Lorene looked around at the empty room.

"Where's Biff?"

"He and Skeeter are out back having a smoke and telling dirty stories."

Lorene laughed. "I don't want anything, really. I was just anxious to give you this book my uncle gave me and see how you were."

"Tired, sad, lonely. Martin left this morning. He joined the Texas Rangers and he's taking Matteo Aguilar to jail."

"Oh, my. When will Martin be back?"

Millie shook her head. "I don't know. I just hope he doesn't get killed. All this war talk fills me with a sense of dread."

"Well, I'm glad Anson is not going into the Confederate Army. He's had enough of war with that despicable man, Aguilar. Good riddance, I say."

"Ken Richman thinks the war's going to last a long time," Millie said, a wistful expression on her face. "I don't know if I could stand Martin being away a long time. He might forget about me. And we've not really done anything, anyway. I mean . . ."

"I know what you mean, Millie. I get an ache in my stomach whenever I think about Anson. I want to just take him in my arms and never let him go. But he's not easy to catch. Sometimes I think men just care about cows and grass and fighting."

"They sure don't want to settle down, do they? The good ones are like quicksilver. They keep slipping away. If it's a long war, Martin might not come back, or he might meet someone else, some pretty little thing with her claws out, ready to grab him."

"This is a silly old war," Lorene said. "I don't see how it can last very long. Martin will be back before you know it."

Millie laughed, but there was no humor in it. It was instead a wry laugh, tinged with bitterness.

"From what I hear, Martin is a footloose man," Millie said. "He walks away from responsibility, according to Ken."

"Why do you want him, Millie? Surely there are better men, men who want to stay at home and raise a family."

"Why do you want Anson? He's from the same stock. The apple doesn't fall very far from the tree. He may turn out to be just like his father."

"I don't believe that. Anson is responsible. He doesn't like the way his father leaves the ranch every so often. Why, his father was away for years when Anson was growing up."

"Look at us, Lorene. We're heartbroken and lonesome and still we wait for men who probably don't care a whit about us."

Lorene reached across the table and put her hand atop Millie's.

"Martin cares about you. It's just that he's still broken up about his wife, Caroline."

"He didn't love her."

"How can you know that? He was married to her. They had a child, Anson."

"Oh, I think he loved her once, when they were young. I don't know what happened, but I think Caroline might have turned him against marriage, maybe even against women."

"Well, Millie, you can certainly change his mind. He's very attracted to you and I think he knows a good woman when he sees one."

"Do you think so? Really?"

Lorene withdrew her hand. "Yes, really." She sighed and sat back in her chair, a pensive look on her face. "I think," she said, "that both Martin and Anson are as wild as the land they own and are trying to tame. The best men have some wildness in them, and while they may not be easy to catch, they can be guided."

"Guided?"

"By a woman's wiles, by loving ways that they really can't do without."

Both women laughed.

"You're the wily one, Lorene. I'm pretty bold, I think."

"Well, maybe we can work together on this situation. I can borrow some of your boldness and you can use some of my wiliness."

"We're a couple of bitches," Millie said. "We should call ourselves 'the bitches of Baronsville.'"

Lorene laughed. "Yes, I think we should. We both want Baron men and we're a lot smarter than they are about such things."

At that moment, Skeeter came out of the kitchen, a scowl on his face. He stopped, saw the two women sitting up by the window, and walked over.

"Millie, dammit, you're sitting on your fat little ass when there's work to be done out in the kitchen. Somebody at the hotel wants some sandwiches and I need help makin' 'em up."

"Skeeter," Millie said, a smile on her face, "why don't you go back there and fuck your fist. Can't you see I'm busy? Besides, I'm on a break."

"I ain't takin' no sandwiches over to the hotel. That's your job."

"I'd better go," Lorene said. "I've got a lot of papers to grade."

"Don't go, Lorene, please," Millie said. She turned back to Skeeter. "Skeeter, I don't take sandwiches over to the hotel. That's Lonnie's job."

"Lonnie's not here. He had an errand to run."

"He can deliver the food when he gets back."

"Millie, you ain't nothin' but a hash-slingin' bitch, you know that?"

"Yes, Skeeter, I do. In fact, I'm one of the bitches of Baronsville and if you don't get out of here, I'll scratch your damned eyes out."

Skeeter fumed and turned on his heel. He winced when he heard the two women break out in laughter. He hesitated as if to return to the table, but thought better of it and continued walking back to the kitchen.

"Skeeter knows when he's outnumbered," Millie said.

"You were awful to him, Millie," Lorene said. Then she broke up again and both women began laughing until they had tears in their eyes.

"That's who we are, Lorene," Millie said. "The bitches of Baronsville."

"It feels good to be a bitch sometimes, doesn't it?" Lorene said.

Millie nodded and flashed a conspiratorial wink at Lorene. She felt better, truly, bitch or not.

13

J ULES REYNAUD WAS happy he had run into Seth Culbertson. He and Cullie shared a mutual goal, for different reasons. Both men wanted to kill Martin Baron. Cullie carried an old grudge. Reynaud wanted the money Miguel Aguilar would pay to have Martin killed.

Reynaud was a lean man, thin as a racing whippet, with a swarthy complexion that was more from his Gallic heritage than from the baking Texas sun. He was from New Orleans and his family had once befriended Martin Baron, accepting him as an adopted son, while casting Reynaud out of the household because of his nefarious deeds.

Reynaud plied the dark streets of New Orleans, gaining a reputation as a knife man who slit men's throats for pay and developing a temper that was like a poisonous weed. He'd had no conjunctions about concocting the tale that Martin had violated his little sister. He hated Martin and spread his own stories along with his poison and his hatred, until word got to Aguilar that he was a man who could be hired to slay his mortal enemy, Martin Baron, and never bat an eye.

Trouble was, Reynaud had explained to Cullie back in Baronsville, Aguilar had been arrested by those damned Texas Rangers and Baron was riding with them. As Reynaud had heard it, Martin was a Ranger himself, or soon to be.

"I know just the place to jump 'em," Cullie had said. "They won't be expectin' it, and we'll have a clear shot at Baron. If your Aguilar has any brains, he can run off from those Rangers."

"I'll pay you for your help, Cullie," Reynaud had said.

"I don't want no pay. I been carryin' a grudge against Martin Baron so long it's like a scab. I just want to rub that scab off me."

Culbertson was cut from a different bolt of cloth than Reynaud. He had grown up to become a wastrel, although he had worked from time to time, and had had some goodness in him. But that goodness had been burned out of him somewhere along the way. It was replaced by a treacherous, self-serving nature, and what he liked most about the West was its lawlessness. He too harbored a hatred for Martin Baron, but it was born of seeds blossoming in his own character that could not stand the light of Martin's eye shining on them, exposing him for what he was, an opportunist and a scoundrel, not fit for the company of men.

Cullie had none of the finesse of a killer like Reynaud. He was more rawhide than velvet, and if he schemed, it was with a small, bitter mind that was as narrow as it was uneducated and ignorant. Reynaud, at least, had once had a veneer of respectability, since he came from a good family. But Cullie came from hardscrabble farming folk who in their isolation cultivated mean-spiritedness and suspicion of others. They were a family with pinched faces and pinched minds who cursed the weather and the land with equal vehemence, and who read all the wrong passages from the Bible on Saturday night to justify their conviction that man was an evil creature who would one day be plunged into hellfire for foul deeds.

"I too carry a grudge. Martin sullied my sister in New Orleans."

"The hell you say. Well, that's reason enough, I reckon."

So the two men had ridden into a little Mexican settlement that Cullie knew about, a place called Bandana, north of Baronsville, and right in the path of the trail the Rangers and their prisoner, Miguel Aguilar, would take.

"This here Bandana is just a spot in the road, but them Rangers will stop there to water their horses and a man can hide most anyplace and pick 'em off like turtles sunnin' on a log."

Reynaud, when they first rode into Bandana, saw it as no more than a blemish on the earth, a tiny collection of adobes and *jacales*, inhabited by illiterate and filthy Mexicans who had no right to exist anyplace but there. But Cullie was right, the area did offer places of concealment, a watering trough in plain view, and a populace that was indifferent, lazy, and indigent, and would present no threat to them.

The settlement lay astride a maze of crossroads that, from Reynaud's perspective, all led nowhere, as if the Mexicans had settled there to perpetuate the joke on travelers who might believe that the place had a purpose, when, indeed, it had none. It was just a wart on the face of a harsh land of sun and wind, a place that collected tumbleweeds and rattlesnakes, teemed with starving dogs and a few scarred and mangy cats with stiffened and stained clumps of fur crawling with vermin.

"It is not much of a place," Reynaud said, sniffing the air with a look of distaste on his face as if he had smelled some foul odor.

"You just ain't used to places like this, Reynaud. If you been to enough border towns, this'un looks mite near respectable."

"If you ask me, Cullie, Texas is just one great big repository of border towns, each one filthier and more decrepit than the last."

"Them fancy words might work right well in New Orleans, but out here, you got to talk with the two-bit ones if you want anyone to savvy what you say."

Reynaud fixed Cullie with an open gaze that could have served as a warning, for his dark brown eyes glittered in the sun like the amber eyes of a viper. But the look was lost on Cullie, who was looking at a lone Mexican standing in a darkened doorway. The Mexican moved back inside, out of sight, and Cullie scanned the other adobe buildings to see if there was any threat from anyone.

"Looks good," Cullie said. "Now, there's a well just off the road in here. Did you notice?"

Reynaud nodded.

"They'll probably stop there to water their horses. Or at least the Ranger ridin' point will. Or he'll stop to check it, at least."

"So?"

"Come with me. We don't have no hell of a lot of time."

Cullie rode toward the watering trough at the southern entrance to the settlement. It too was constructed of adobe brick, and there was an old pump staring down into it that looked as dry as the rest of the town. However there was water in the trough and a thin patina of sand and tumbleweed cockleburs that had been blown in there by the wind.

Cullie stopped his horse and pointed to a little adobe over to the right.

"One of us can hide in that there adobe, and the other over yonder." He turned his horse and pointed to another adobe on the opposite side of the road. "Get 'em in our crossfire, slick as snot."

Reynaud winced at the reference, but said nothing.

He looked at both adobes. Neither was more than fifty yards from the watering trough. The angles were right. There was concealment for both men.

"We get our horses out of the way, on the other side of them adobes, and we can get to 'em real easy, 'case we have to light a shuck."

"I'll take the adobe on the right," Reynaud said. "But who's going to watch our backs?"

"You cut Matteo Aguilar loose and give him a gun, you won't need nobody to watch your back, Reynaud."

"Unless we drop them all, we will have lawmen chasing us across Texas. Of course, I have the guns for Matteo."

"I know you do. Let's just hope Matteo will know what to do. Reckon he can figure it out?"

"When the shooting starts," Reynaud said, "Matteo will know what to do."

Aguilar was like a coiled wire spring, Reynaud knew. He was primitive, cold, calculating. If anyone could manage to escape, Matteo was the man he would pick to get out of a tight spot. If they killed Martin Baron and at least one of the Rangers, he and Cullie, as well as Matteo, would have the advantage. They would outnumber the two Rangers left. Perhaps, he thought, they could kill all of them.

He wanted Martin dead more than Matteo did. He wanted to taste Martin's blood, dip his fingers in it and smear his dead face with it. That would give him as much satisfaction as counting the money Aguilar would pay for Baron's death and his own rescue from the law.

Reynaud turned to Cullie. "Let's wait until they all ride up to the watering trough before we open fire on them," he said. "I want to pick all of them off."

"It might work."

"It must work. I want to see Martin Baron fall out of the saddle and hit the ground with a bullet in his black heart."

"I'll wait until you shoot, Reynaud, before I cut loose."

"We had better take up our positions. It won't be long now."

"I reckon so," Cullie said. He turned his horse and rode toward the adobe where he would lie in wait for the Rangers he knew were coming. He liked Reynaud's plan. He had a score to settle with Baron himself, and it really didn't matter who dropped the son of a bitch.

Although if Reynaud's strategy worked, and they managed to kill all three Rangers and Baron, too, Cullie had made up his mind that he was going to turn his gun on Reynaud.

He did not trust the Frenchman, nor did he know anyone who did. Reynaud was well known for his treachery and he was pretty sure Reynaud would not share the money Matteo was going to give him for killing Baron. In fact, Cullie was pretty sure that, win or lose, when the fight was over, Reynaud would come gunning for him.

Cullie slid out of the saddle behind the adobe and loosely draped his reins around a homely hitching post a few yards away from the small building. He walked to the open door and looked inside, his rifle in his hands. He cocked it and stepped inside. The room was empty. It was as quiet inside as the settlement itself. It smelled musty and there were only a few boxes and feed sacks stored there. He walked to the window and looked out at the road coming in from the south.

He saw that Reynaud was gone, too, and that the surrounding land was deserted, baking in the sun. He heard the far-off screech of a hawk and looked at the few puffs of white clouds floating in the sky.

It was a beautiful day, Cullie thought, and as quiet as a man could want, with a light breeze stirring, picking up little tufts of dust and whirling sand and dirt from one place to another.

He laid his rifle against the windowsill and slipped his finger inside the trigger guard. He licked his dry lips and sighed.

"Now, Martin," he whispered to himself, "you just come on, man. You just come right on into the spider web, you son of a bitch."

The wind sighed inside the adobe and blew warm against his face. It made little whispers against the walls before it blew out the door behind him, as if telling him that the Rangers were coming, that they would be there soon and they would all die without ever knowing what hit them.

14

ANSON, HIS FACE devoid of expression, listened to Ken Richman as the two of them, along with Peebo, stood next to a pile of stacked lumber near the construction site of the new house.

"Anson," Ken said, "you'd better try and stop your Mexican hands from leaving. You'd better get down on your knees and start begging them to stay."

"I have no use for a damned one of them."

"Well, I damned sure do if I'm going to get this house built."

"How does my bank account stand?"

"There's money in it."

"Hire somebody from town to help you. And you've got Socrates over there."

Socrates sat in the shade, drawing in the dirt with a stick. Leaf shadows dappled the ground in front of him. His ebony face and shirtless torso glistened with a sheen of sweat and small beads of perspiration dewed up beneath his hairline and just above his thick black brows, some of the moisture seeping through the hairs to drip onto his cheeks like tears.

"I'd like to have a dozen more like Socks. The house would go up in no time."

"Ken, find some hands in town to help you here. I've got other things on my mind."

"You've got yourself a mutiny here. If you let those Mexicans desert your ship, you might sink."

"I won't put up with disloyalty, Ken." Anson's gaze hardened as he looked into Ken's eyes, boring into them like an agate dagger. "Those Mexes had a choice. I gave it to them. If they don't want to work for me, I don't want them on the Box B."

Peebo cleared his throat, but said nothing. He was plainly irritated with Anson, but he had just about talked himself out on the subject of the Mexican hands packing up to leave and he thought they had good reason. Anson was as stubborn as cold iron and would not bend one damned whit. Their horses were still saddled so Anson and he could ride off on a wild-goose chase after an elusive white longhorn bull the size of a small elephant.

"Loyalty," Ken said, "grows on both sides of the creek."

"That may be so, Ken, but in this case, I'm the damned creek. I won't have a man working for me who thinks he can run the Box B better'n I can."

"Those hands of yours know that, Anson. They just want you to run it, that's all. They look up to you as their leader. And when you go away, they don't trust anyone else to make the right decisions."

"I think you're giving those Mexicans more credit than they deserve, Ken. That's why I have a *segundo,* a foreman. If they don't know what I want done by now, they never will."

There was a silence, then, between the three men. Ken shook his head slowly and lifted his hands in the air as if in surrender. Peebo squinched up his face as if he had just tasted something sour, but he knew better than to jump into this argument between good friends, no matter how well-meaning he might be.

"What's the matter with you, Peebo?" Anson asked, after several seconds had passed. "You swallow a bee?"

Peebo shook his head.

"You got something to say, Peebo?"

"I reckon not."

"But you got something in your craw, don't you?" Anson was glaring at him as if he had found a new target now that Ken had given up the argument.

"Nothing but a little dust and maybe some of that smoke from your burned house," Peebo said softly.

"Are you trying to be smart, Peebo?"

Peebo smiled that wry twisted smile of his and walked a few feet away. Then he stopped and looked back at Anson. Anson stared at him and balled his fists.

"I know you ain't rightly mad at me, Anson, so I ain't talkin' back to you. You're mad at something, sure as hell has wheels. But I ain't done nothin' to you and neither has nobody else that's right close by. So if you want to pick on somebody else besides those poor Mexicans you fired, I guess it'll have to be Ken or Socks, 'cause I'm leavin'."

"Where you going?" Anson asked.

"Someplace quiet where I can think and maybe ask myself if you're worth any loyalty from me."

Peebo turned and walked toward the barn. He walked with a slow pace that seemed deliberate and calm.

"You son of a bitch," Anson huffed. But Peebo kept walking. He did not wince or tense up, but seemed almost casual about getting away from the seething Anson.

Anson turned to Ken, who was regarding him with avuncular patience, his arms folded across his chest, his mouth pushed upward on one side as if he had swallowed a handful of carpet tacks.

"You got somethin' to say, Ken?"

"Maybe."

"Then spit it out. I ain't got all damned day."

"Peebo was right, you know. You're not mad at him, or me. I think you've got a burr under your saddle about your father leaving you again."

Anson huffed in a breath, batted his eyes closed for a moment.

"I don't much care what my daddy does anymore, Ken. He comes and goes, just like that wind out of west Texas."

"I think you do care, but it's none of my business."

"That's right. It's none of your business."

"I do have one thing to say to you, though, Anson. As a friend. As a friend to both you and Martin."

"Go on ahead." Anson's rage simmered just below the surface and his lips tightened together in a sullen frown.

"You're just about to run out of friends," Ken said. "You might want to consider that. I think Peebo there is just about the only one you have left, besides me. If you let him walk away like that, you just might lose him. And if you don't have any friends, you don't have much of anything."

"Peebo's just a damned nuisance sometimes."

"Most friends are, now and then. That's a funny thing about friendship. It doesn't care much about a person's faults."

"I think you're leaving out something, Ken. What I was talking about before."

"Oh, what's that?"

"Friends are loyal to each other. No matter what."

"You mean they don't fight with one another? They don't disagree? They don't question each other?"

"Something like that." Anson dropped his gaze to his feet and started worrying the dirt with the toe of his boot. Then he looked over toward the barn. There was no sign of Peebo. He had gone inside.

"You want your friends to be obedient, then, I guess," Ken said.

"No, you know that's not what I mean."

"You want a friend to follow you blindly. Anywhere you go. Right or wrong."

"You're twisting my words, Ken."

"They're your words. What's loyalty, anyway? Do you know what it is?"

"I know it means you stick with someone when the chips are down."

"No it doesn't, Anson." Ken's voice dropped into a lower register, just above a whisper.

"What do you think it means, then?"

"Oh, it means that, all right, Anson. But it means much more than that. Loyalty is a matter of honor, too. And you can't have one without the other."

"Two different things, Ken."

"Maybe, but the two go together. You can be loyal to someone without honoring that person. Loyalty has all kinds of strings attached to it. Honor is unfettered. It shines like a lamp in the darkness. It burns through fog and doubt like a torch. If you lose honor, you lose everything worth having. You lose your soul, Anson. Loyalty can be bought. Honor cannot."

"Well, Peebo will get over his fret."

"You wounded him, Anson. He was trying to get you to do what he's doing right now."

"What's that?"

"He wanted you to think about firing your hands. He wanted you to find out what you're really mad about and not lash out at everybody close to you."

"None of his business."

"If it isn't, then you don't value him as a friend."

"Maybe he isn't. If he's disloyal, then I don't want him as no friend."

Ken smiled and shrugged.

"That's something you're going to have to work out for yourself, Anson. This whole question of loyalty and disloyalty. I see it different."

The sun was falling away in the afternoon sky, slanting the light and making the shadows long across the earth. Anson looked at the ruins of his home and across the fields beyond the orchard. The place seemed so empty, so quiet, so bereft of people all of a sudden.

"I'll think about it," Anson said finally. "But I'm not backing down on letting those hands go. They had no right to buck me just because I got something to do that they don't understand the first thing about."

"Good," Ken said. "That's a start. You're losing some good people."

"I know it. They were the ones who wanted to leave, though. I didn't force them."

"It was entirely their decision." There was a tinge of sarcasm in Ken's voice.

"Pretty much."

"Then your conscience is clear."

"Clear enough."

"Fine. Then you'll sleep sound tonight. Speaking of which, I'd better head back to town. I want to bring some workers out tomorrow and get started on rebuilding your house. You still going after that white bull?"

"My mind is set on that. Roy Killian can handle the ranch while I'm gone."

"Peebo going with you?"

"I reckon. If he wants to."

Ken smiled a paternal smile of forbearance and indulgence.

"I hope he does, Anson. Otherwise, you'll go it alone, I imagine."

"Damned right."

"I'll see you when you get back. I wish you luck."

Ken turned away, and walked over to where Socrates still sat, doodling in the dirt with a stick. Anson kicked the dirt one last time with the toe of his boot and started walking toward the barn. The sun began lighting the clouds on the western horizon, turning their bottoms to gold and bronze and pink as if they were sculptures firing in a kiln.

"Damned day is wasted," Anson muttered.

Then he stopped and watched the procession of men, women, and children stream onto the south road beyond the barn, their *carretas* laden with furniture and clothes, pulled by burros, the wheels creaking in the stillness of late afternoon.

Peebo emerged from the barn and stood there, too, watching the Box B empty itself like water running down into a sinkhole. None of the people turned around or waved goodbye; they just plodded on like refugees fleeing a war, silent and homeless.

Anson felt his stomach roil with bile and turn queasy as if he were sick from bad food. He wanted to cry out and ask them to come back, but before he could utter a word, even to himself, they were gone, vanished beyond the trees and the mesquite, headed for the Rocking A or Mexico, and he knew he couldn't beg or change what had already happened.

The sun slid below the far horizon and the salmon clouds this side of the sunset began to darken and lose their golden edges until they turned to ashes in the sky.

Anson felt very alone, just then, and he was struggling not to cry.

Peebo was walking back to the barn without looking at Anson.

Anson called out. "Peebo. Hey, wait up."

Peebo stopped. And he waited, his figure swallowed up in shadow, his face and its expression invisible to Anson as he hurried toward his friend.

15

LUZ AGUILAR SHIVERED in the cold of the dawn and scooted closer to the fire Fidel Rios had built to roast the rabbit he had killed with his bare hands. He had skinned it with his knife, gutted it and run a sharpened stick through its breast to hold it over the blaze.

Luz cradled her son, Julio, in her arms, keeping him warm under her shawl, next to the heat of her body. The boy was asleep, but his mouth was moving and she knew he was hungry. They had ridden through the night, she, Julio, and Fidel, to get as far away from the Rocking A as they could, in case Mickey Bone intended to follow her and bring her back. She had been bewildered at all the zigzaggings and turns, and she was bewildered now. The land was lighting up with the rising sun, illuminating the brush and the mesquite trees, the live oaks and the endless wilderness country, but she did not know where they were. She only knew that she had never been in this part of the Rio Grande Valley before. She had to stretch her neck to see that much of the country, and when she eased her head back down, all she saw were the small hillocks that surrounded them, as if they were sitting in a small bowl of the earth.

"Fidel," she said, "do you know where we are? Are we yet on the rancho?"

"Do you not hear the creek?"

She turned her head and listened. The soft sound had escaped her hearing before then, but now she heard the low murmur of running water. But she could not see the creek because they were in a shallow depression.

"I hear it," she said. "So?"

"It is the little creek called Bandera and this part is on the rancho. Another part flows onto the Baron rancho."

"Where are we going, Fidel?"

"Where do you wish to go?"

In her haste to get away from Mickey Bone and his lust, she had not thought about a destination. She had been so distraught to learn that her husband was a prisoner of the Texas Rangers and that Bone meant to violate her, and perhaps harm little Julio, that she had just fled, with little more than the clothes on her back, seeking out Fidel to help her escape, knowing that she could trust him, and perhaps only him, to help her flee Bone.

"I want to find my husband," she said. "Matteo. My Miguelito."

"I do not know where he is."

There was a sadness to her elfin features in the early morning light, yet there was a flash in her dark brown eyes that caught Fidel's attention and made him sorry he had said such a thing to the wife of his *patrón*. He felt as if he was looking at a Madonna with child, the way she was holding little Julio against her breasts, with her hands so graceful, like sleeping doves, and her black hair falling over her shoulders like a silken shawl. He saw the Indian blood in her delicate high cheekbones tinged with the rouge of that blood, and he saw the aristocracy of her Spanish lineage in the straight and majestic line of her nose and on the pale pewter of her lips.

"We must find Matteo," she said. "He will tell us what to do."

"He would want us to kill Bone," Rios said. "I want to kill him myself. He is *sin vergüenza,* a truly shameless man with no conscience."

"Yes. Matteo wants Bone dead. And so do I, Fidel. He makes my skin feel as if maggots were crawling over me. I hate that filth of a man, that bastard son of bad milk. *Aquel cabron, hijo de mala leche.*"

Fidel had never heard Luz swear like that. Not even his own wife had ever used such language in his presence. He took the gourd that was hanging from his neck with a cord and handed it to Luz. The water inside it sloshed.

"Take yourself a drink of water," he said.

"It will not cool the burning inside me," Luz said, but she took the gourd and pulled the top of it off and drank the cool water. She wiped her lips, capped the spout, and handed the gourd back to Fidel. "I burn with a hatred for Bone. I flame with the hatred for the white men who have taken our land and taken my husband away."

"It is a bad thing," Fidel said, taking the gourd and slinging it around his neck once again. He twisted the stick in his hand and turned the jackrabbit over so that the backside of it began to crackle and sputter from the flames. The rabbit was slowly turning brown in the dawn light, the meat cooking through over the fire.

She was tired and sleepy and hungry. The aroma of the cooking meat filled her nostrils and the hollow in her belly grew larger, more vacant. She looked down at the sleeping Julio, knowing his belly was full of her milk. She was grateful that she could still feed him, for a tooth was breaking through his little gums and she knew she could not nurse him much longer.

"Why do we ride to the north?" she asked Fidel.

"That is where the Rangers will take Don Matteo. He was captured at the Baron rancho. Dagoberto says they will hang him. I have sorrow."

"The gringos will never hang Matteo," she said, with a bitterness in her voice that stung Fidel's ears.

"That is true. Don Matteo is *muy sabio*. He is too wise to let them do that to him."

"We will go south. I will go south, with Julio. Back to Mexico to wait for Matteo. You will tell him I have returned home."

"I will take you there. Where do you go? Where is your home?"

She thought of that place, so long gone from her mind, but never from her heart. It was a place of bleak beauty, a poor place of flowers and guitars and the doleful strains of the *son huastecos*, a place in the shadows of the dark and somber mountains where Matteo had come and had found her, when he was hiding from his family and his heart was troubled.

"It is a town called Valle. It is south of Matamoros."

"I have never heard of this *pueblo*," Fidel said. "I am from Monterey. But I do not remember it well."

"Valle is east and north of Monterey. It is near Camargo, but it is a very small place and the people who live there are very poor. But they are proud and they are of the earth. They cut wood in the mountains and they raise the sheep and the goats and every house blooms with flowers and every house has a small garden."

"My family left Monterey when I was a small boy and they took the journey to Matamoros where we lived until I was grown into a man. Then they left and went back to Monterey and I have not heard from them in many years."

His words made her long for home, for her own family, for her sister and brother, her aging mother. Her father was dead, killed by a knife in a fight with a man over a goat. He had been a good man, but born with a hot temper and a fondness for mezcal. His blood had soaked the land like so many others, and her brother had killed the man who had killed their father, but she had wept over his death for many nights and days when she missed his gruff voice and the smell of tobacco and mezcal on his breath, the scent of goat in his clothes, the dark earth under his fingernails that came from the soil of their garden.

A pair of mourning doves whistled by, their gray bodies tinged with a reddish hue from the rising sun, their bodies twisting as they knifed through the air, and she heard a meadowlark trill in the distance. An answering call from a mockingbird in a nearby tree seemed to announce the morning to all who could hear, and Luz felt it was a good sign, a sign that there was life everywhere, and in that life, a little joy following the darkest of nights, the deepest of fears.

"Let us go to the place my husband calls El Rincon, where I will wait until you can bring me food and clothing for my journey back to Valle," Luz said, letting out a sigh of finality, as if she had thought of a reasonable plan, finally, and come to a decision.

"You do not want to go there," Fidel said. "It is a place of snakes and wild pigs and scorpions, a place where the mesquite grows thick and the water is bad."

"Matteo has taken me there. He showed me the old adobes that crumble like dried bread. There is shelter there for me and Julio until we can take the good journey to the south."

"Bone knows that place, too. He might come to look for you."

"You must take care. You must not let him follow you. Talk to Dagoberto. Tell him I need food for my journey and clothes for Julio."

"You will go to Mexico alone? Only you and your baby?"

"Yes. I know the way. And I have the shotgun that Bone threw at me when he came into my house. Can you get me more cartridges? I will shoot birds and rabbits and cook them for my meat along the way."

"Yes. I can bring you the cartridges and clothing."

"And cloth. I will make a sling to carry Julio on my back in the old way of my people so that my arms do not grow tired from carrying him."

"Yes. My wife can make you one."

"Do not take too much time, Fidel. No more than two days. There may be a puma in the *brasada* at El Rincón and when Julio cries, the lion may come and try to get him."

Fidel made a face that wrinkled his leathery features, as if he had dredged up memories of stories told by his people of the puma coming into a house and carrying off a child in the middle of the night.

"We will eat," Fidel said, turning the rabbit one more time. Its juices no longer dripped onto the flames sending sparks hissing into the air. The meat was cooked.

"Let the meat cool for a few minutes or we will burn our tongues."

Fidel laughed, and drew his knife from its scabbard. He pulled the stick away from the fire and poked the knife into the chest meat. He held the rabbit close to his mouth and blew on the roasted carcass to cool it.

A quail piped nearby and more doves flew past, darting and weaving through the air like shuttles through a loom. The sun topped the horizon and splashed golden light through the mesquite and onto the oak leaves, threading through the brush and spangling the nopal and the cholla blossoms.

A light breeze lifted from the land and blew across the creek and into her hair like a soft caress and the meat cooled and the two began to eat. Julio stirred in his mother's arms. Fidel cut off a tender chunk of breast with his knife and held it flat against the blade with his thumb. He handed her the meat and she took it, began to chew it.

But she did not swallow. When it was well masticated, she removed it from her mouth and stuck the end of it into Julio's mouth. His eyes, bright as agate buttons, widened as he tasted the meat. He began to move his jaw, his gums treading back and forth across the cooked flesh. He made smacking sounds with his lips and Luz smiled down at him.

"This will make his teeth grow," she said. "Soon, he will be able to chew the soft meat and he will grow strong."

"You have a fine son, Luz. He will grow into a strong man."

"I will have another," she said. "So that Julio has a companion. When Matteo returns, we will make another baby, another boy."

Fidel nodded as he chewed on the rabbit in his mouth. He cut off another piece of meat and gave it to Luz. She chewed it and swallowed and gestured for Fidel to hand her the gourd. Julio kept masticating the chewed meat in his mouth, sucking on it to draw out the remaining juices. He made noises as if he was dining on a feast although he had no teeth large enough to cut through the meat.

Luz looked over at the horses standing hipshot and hobbled near the creek. She could only see their heads and chests, but they were shining in the sun, their coats sleek as if saturated with a fine thin oil. Matteo had given her that mare she rode, and as she looked at her, she missed Matteo even more.

While she ate, Luz began to pray for Matteo in her mind. She recited the Ave Maria to herself and then she said an act of contrition for herself and for Julio, just in case something happened to them on their journey. She crossed herself and bowed her head as she prayed the Paternoster in Spanish, hearing the words even though her voice was silent.

She would wait for Matteo in Valle. And he would come for her one day and they would return to the rancho and live there until the end of their days. Her husband would kill Bone and she would say an act of contrition for him when he did. She knew God would not punish him for such a deed, for Bone had broken the Commandments and deserved the harshest punishment.

"Are you saying grace?" Fidel asked.

"No," she said. "I am praying for Julio and the safe return of my husband."

"I will pray for Don Matteo, myself," Fidel said. "I will pray for his return and that he does not hang."

"You are a good man, Fidel. I will pray for you, too."

Fidel drew in a breath and dropped his head in reverence. He stopped chewing and crossed himself.

Luz smiled with approval. She knew in her heart that she and Julio would be safe and that Matteo would come to Valle and take them back home where they belonged and they would make more babies and live the good life.

Faith, she told herself, could move mountains. And people, as well.

16

DARNELL AND SHEPLEY approached the settlement of Bandana with caution, but did not halt their horses.

"Let's water 'em," Shepley said, pointing to the trough just outside of town.

"We'll wait here for Al and Baron to come up," Darnell said.

"Town's quiet." Shepley kicked his heels into his horse's flanks.

"It's always quiet here."

"Quieter than usual."

"Siesta time, Dan. Even the damned dogs are asleep."

Shepley laughed. " 'At's a custom we gringos ought to adopt."

"You ever sleep in the saddle? We already have adopted the custom."

Shepley pulled up to the trough, loosened the reins. His horse bent its neck and began to drink. Darnell came up a second later and let his horse take in water. The horses slurped and worried the bits in their mouths as they drank, their rubbery noses flexing, their lips moving to splash the water so that they could suck it in.

"Here they come," Shepley said, looking back down the road.

"I don't see 'em."

"I hear 'em, Ken. They won't be long."

The rifle cracked and Shepley saw Darnell twist in his saddle, turn to look at him with a surprised expression on his face. For a few seconds he didn't realize what had happened. Then Darnell opened his mouth as if to say something and blood bubbled up from it and ran down his chin. He reached for the rifle in his boot as his horse swung around away from the trough, but he never made it.

Another rifle report burst the silence and Shepley felt a hammer slam into his side. He doubled over in pain as Darnell pitched from his saddle and hit the ground with a resounding thud. Pain surged through Shepley's chest as one lung collapsed. He felt a burning and a blackness begin to descend on him.

Two more shots rang out. Darnell's body twitched as a .50-caliber lead ball ripped into him, flattening to a deadly mushroom shape, smashing into bone, tearing through flesh and sinew, veins, and capillaries. Shepley felt another blow to his neck and the darkness increased. He turned his horse toward the town and raised a hand to his neck. Blood spurted from his throat and drenched his hand. Blood flooded into his undamaged lung. He choked and then dove into the blackness as he felt his life slipping away. Then he was falling and he heard shouts that sounded as if they came from mouths stuffed with cotton and he wondered, for a moment, if he was ever going to hit the ground, but the blackness beat him to it and suddenly there was no more memory, no more sound, no more feeling.

Oltman drew his rifle from its boot and then heard the sizzle of a bullet frying the air next to his ear. He ducked, with his caplock rifle halfway out of its sheath. Then he felt a stinging in his hand and the rifle vibrated like a tuning fork as a lead bullet slammed into the receiver, snatching it out of his grip.

Martin saw Shepley fall from his saddle and hit the ground. He also saw a bright orange flash from one of the windows in an adobe beyond the watering trough.

Out of the corner of his eye, he saw Matteo's arm shoot out. Aguilar snatched the rifle from Oltman's grasp. He grabbed the barrel with both hands and shoved the butt hard into Oltman's side, knocking him from his horse. Then he turned and swung the rifle at Baron.

Martin threw up an arm to ward off the blow. He felt a crashing shock as the butt of the rifle struck the underside of his forearm.

The shock waves penetrated to the bone, crushed blood vessels until his arm blossomed a purple bruise. He felt himself slipping from the saddle, and then Matteo was on him, lashing out with his fist, smashing him in the jaw. A black cloud exploded in Martin's brain, then filled with a shower of silver sparks that cascaded like a host of falling stars.

Another rifle shot boomed and Martin felt his horse stagger, then begin to topple as its forelegs collapsed. He braced himself for the fall, reaching out into thin air. The horse's rear legs gave way and Martin was thrown from the saddle. He rolled as he hit the ground to avoid being crushed by the weight of the animal. He heard his rifle máke a sound as the horse's full weight fell on it.

Matteo spurred his horse and galloped toward Bandana, hunching low over the saddle, Oltman's rifle pressed against the pommel. He raced for an opening between two buildings, then glanced behind him.

Martin drew his pistol, cocked it. He sat up and drew a bead on the fleeing Aguilar. He fired, trying to knock down the fugitive's horse.

Another rifle shot cracked and the ball tore a furrow a foot from where Martin sat. He ducked his head, scooted away and crawled behind his horse, using the animal's body for protection.

Oltman struggled to rise, let out a groan of pain a few yards away. His horse had wandered off the road, confused.

"Get down, Al," Martin said.

"Huh?"

"Matteo got away and somebody's trying to kill us. Stay down."

"Christ," Oltman swore as a rifle barked and the ball pushed air past Oltman's ear. He flattened himself to the ground and turned to look in the direction from where the shot had come.

"Crawl over here."

"Your horse dead?"

"Yeah, and I think they got Shepley and Darnell."

"Damn. Aguilar grabbed my rifle."

"And rode into Bandana. So we've got at least three guns in there."

"Did you get a look at who's shooting at us?"

"No."

Oltman hugged the ground like a legless lizard and started

inching toward Martin and the fallen horse. Another ball whistled over his head and struck the road several yards behind him. Oltman pulled himself toward Martin on his elbows and soon reached the safety of the equine bulwark. He panted, out of breath, and drew his Colt .44. He checked the cylinder, spinning it to see if all the percussion caps were seated. The grease had melted out of the cartridge cylinders and he dug into his possibles pouch for the tin of lard. He pushed the thick lard into the front of each cylinder, covering each lead ball to prevent flash firing when he shot the pistol.

"This damned heat," Oltman said.

Martin said nothing. He peered over the top of the saddle, looking at the adobes lined up beyond the watering trough. He saw the snout of a rifle jutting from a window to the right, and then movement inside another window of an adobe to his left.

"They've got us braced," Martin said. "And they are well hidden behind adobe walls."

"That damned Aguilar."

"This was no accident, Al."

"No. For damned sure." He scooted up and peered over the horse's rump. A rifle cracked and the ball thumped into the dead horse's belly. Oltman ducked back down behind the horse's rump.

"I saw that rifle shot," he said. "Off to the left."

"That's one of them. Other shooter is off to the right. I don't know where in hell Matteo is. He's only got one shot, though, with your rifle, unless someone gives him ball and powder."

"I reckon someone will."

Martin thought about it. They were at a standoff, but were pinned down. His own horse was dead; Oltman's had wandered off back down the road. They were facing at least three rifles, and whoever was in those adobes were pretty good shots.

Beyond Martin's dead horse, there was no cover. He and Oltman could not rush the adobes. That would mean certain death, he knew. Meanwhile, he and Al were at the mercy of the sun and the heat. If they showed themselves, they would become perfect targets. All he could hope for was that whoever was shooting at them would grow impatient, or make a mistake and expose themselves. But he could not watch those two windows all the time. Sooner or later, one of the shooters would surely pick him off with a head shot.

"What are you thinking, Martin?" Oltman slipped off the bandana around his neck and wiped the sweat from his forehead and eyebrows.

"I'm thinking we're in a pretty bad spot."

"The worst. Only way out, I see, is if we flank 'em. Get behind 'em."

"And how do we do that, Al? We can't even flank my dead horse."

"I don't know. We could wait for nightfall, I reckon."

Flies buzzed around them, their wings creating a threnodic drone as if they were miniature vultures waiting to gorge on sweat and blood. Some landed on their faces and others settled on the dead horse, while others circled in acrobatic maneuvers seeking landing places where they could feed and defecate.

"I think my canteen's underneath the horse," Martin said.

"And mine's on my horse. We could suck on pebbles, maybe."

"What if they flank us?" Baron asked.

Oltman seemed to puzzle over that question for a moment. He scanned both sides of their position and licked dry lips. His shirt was soaked through with sweat and he dabbed at his eyebrows again with the bandana.

"At least they'd be out in the open. And we'd know who in hell ambushed us."

"That's a great comfort, Al."

"What do you suggest, Martin? Ever face a situation like this before?"

Martin shook his head. "I've had some squeaks, but this beats all."

The rifles were silent and the loudness of the flies seemed deafening in the hush of the afternoon. Beneath the hum of the insects, Martin thought he could hear the ticking of a clock. There seemed to be an urgency pervading the quiet, as if the silence was building to a crescendo until someone fired another shot.

"There's no cover between us and the town," Baron said. "I guess we'll just have to wait it out. Be a long afternoon."

"You got plenty of powder and ball?" Oltman asked.

Martin felt his possibles pouch, shook one of his powder horns, hefted it. He nodded to Oltman. "Maybe forty or fifty rifle balls, a couple of dozen for my pistol. Plenty of powder and caps."

"About the same for me, but I only have this pistol. Worthless at this range."

"Maybe they'll rush us," Martin said, without conviction.

"Maybe your horse will rise from the dead and carry us the hell out of here."

Martin leered at Oltman, who winked.

"Now I know how those men at the Alamo felt," Martin said. "Waiting for Santa Ana's next attack."

"Let's see if we can't dig that canteen of yours out from under your horse," Oltman said. "I'm dry as desert sand."

Both men lay flat on their bellies and pushed their hands underneath the dead horse, feeling for the wooden canteen. Martin groped in the place where he thought it would be. He felt dampness, and then his hand touched a splinter of wood. He worked it out from under his horse and looked over at Oltman.

"Busted," Martin said. "This is a chunk of the wood and it's damned near soaking wet."

Oltman worked his hands over to where Martin had found the splinter. He withdrew his hand. Wet sand clung to his fingers.

"That's a fine kettle of fish, Martin."

"I generally carry two canteens."

"But you didn't this time."

"Nope."

"Shit."

"Looks like we wait for nightfall."

"I wonder how long it takes a man to die of thirst."

"About a week, maybe," Martin said.

"That's a comfort."

They waited. Martin shaded his eyes and glanced up at the sun, marking its track across the sky. Then he slumped back down, his shoulders nudged against the dead horse's spine. There was a lot of day left, he thought, and the horse was starting to swell up. The flies were thick around them and the silence from Bandana hovered in the background of the buzzing, as loud as a deserted graveyard. And two good men lay out there by the watering trough, their bodies turning ripe in the sun.

And all he could think of just then were those men at the Alamo, waiting, just waiting for the death they knew would come.

H ATTIE, HER SLEEVES rolled up and her hair tied in back of her head with a scarf, lifted the pot of boiled turnips off the stove with her hands protected by wadded-up towels.

"Make way," she said to her daughter, Wanda, who was standing next to her, stirring the gravy still simmering on the stove.

"Gravy's ready, too," Wanda said, stepping aside.

"Then bring it." Hattie walked briskly into the next room where the men were seated at the dining table: Roy, Forrest, Pluto, and Socrates. She walked past the table to the door, set the pot down on the floor and opened it. She picked it up again and, squatting, poured the water onto the ground outside, trying to avoid the scalding steam that rushed upward in a vaporous cloud.

She then returned to the table and set the pot on a trivet and removed the lid. More steam issued from the pot and rose upward until it evaporated. Wanda entered the room and set the gravy, which she had transferred to a large porcelain bowl, on top of a knitted potholder, a ladle jutting from it at an angle.

"You get the taters, Wanda, and I'll fetch the meat. Peaches on?"

"Yes'm," Wanda said, and the two women left the room. The men looked at their empty plates, waiting until the rest of the food was served.

Moments later, Wanda and her mother sat down, hot food gracing the table in plates and bowls.

"Ma, you left the back door open," Wanda said.

"Shut it."

"Yes'm." Wanda rose from the table and closed the back door while everyone watched and waited. She sat down, shooting her mother a look of resentment. Hattie ignored her daughter and looked at her prospective son-in-law.

"Roy, will you say grace," Hattie said.

"Aw, Hattie."

"You're the head of the household and it's your place to ask blessings for the food."

"Perhaps we should let our guest say grace," Wanda said, enjoying the needle she was sticking into her mother. "Forrest, would you like to offer grace this evening?" Her voice was so sweet it made her mother frown.

"Yes, Forrest," Hattie said quickly, "do say grace for us, please. You're our guest and it's only proper that you be granted that honor."

Forrest cleared his throat. He squirmed in his chair, his discomfort showing in the glance he shot to Roy. Roy nodded. The two lamps on the table burned with a magnetic brightness, throwing those at the table into stark relief, as if they had sat for a painting, and every eye was now fixed on Redmond, who sat between the two ex-slaves, Pluto and Socrates, as if he had been relegated to their company according to Hattie's design.

"I'll be happy to oblige, Hattie," Redmond said, and bowed his head. He brought his hands up and clasped them together. He cleared his throat again, as if he was clearing his mind.

"Do go on, please," Hattie interjected into the silence. All heads were bowed, except hers.

"Heavenly Father," Forrest intoned, "we ask that you bless those at your table and bless the food which we are about to eat. Amen."

"That was very good, Forrest," Hattie said, a silken thread in her voice as she looked at Roy. "Now, let us eat and enjoy the meal Wanda and I have cooked."

Hattie and Wanda passed plates of food, and the men forked them onto their own plates, as the soft din of clattering utensils and pewter plates filled the room in the vacuum of speechless activity. When they were all eating, concentrating on their food, Hattie took to her nightly pulpit like a preacher-woman with messages to deliver to her flock.

"You boys stay out of town from here on out," she said. "There's talk of an army recruiter being sent down from Austin."

"Where'd you hear that?" Roy asked.

"It was in the town paper. You need to stay to home, Roy, and Forrest, you left Arkansas because you didn't want to get caught up in this insane conflict."

Forrest nodded.

"Governor Clark is issuing orders right and left," she said, "calling for more militia to clean out the Federals and prepare to do battle all over the place."

"I ought to serve," Roy said, which brought a withering look from Hattie.

"You're needed here, Roy. Anson needs you and Wanda and I need you."

"Anson and Peebo done pulled out, and they's not a Mexican hand left on the Box B," Roy said.

"Where did Anson go at such a time?"

"Him and Peebo went off after some old white bull Anson wants for his seed, I reckon. He's plumb crazy, if you ask me."

"Martin joined up with the Texas Rangers," Forrest said. "He's gone, too."

"Anson wants me to run his ranch while he's gone," Roy said. "I told you that, I think."

"Then that's why you have to stay and not go off fighting over slavery. Besides, we don't hold to slavery, do we?" She looked sharply at Pluto and Socrates. Both men dipped their heads to avoid being in her spotlight.

"No, ma'am," Roy said. "But Texas is a Confederate state."

"Not this part of Texas," Hattie said. "You're not joining up."

"Yes'm."

"Besides," Hattie said, "talk in town is that all of the fighting will be way over in Virginia and in the north. There's talk of the Texas militia being disbanded now that General Twigg gave up his arms and soldiers in San Antonio. And most of the Federals have either left Texas or surrendered."

"That so?" Roy asked, his mind on other matters. "Well, maybe they won't send recruiters down to Baronsville."

"No, they're coming, all right. Texas is going to act like a Confederate state even if it isn't. None of the Mexicans give a hoot nor a holler about the damned war and they aren't going to join any army."

"Ma, can't we talk about something else?" Wanda said. "It makes me fearful to even think of war."

"I heard something else in town, too," Hattie said. "And I view this news as an opportunity for all of us."

No one wanted to know what Hattie had heard so no one asked her a question. This annoyed Hattie, and she forked a chunk of beef into her mouth and chewed it with exaggerated ferocity, sipping from her water glass to wash the masticated meat down her throat.

"Cotton," Hattie said, and she looked directly at Pluto and Socrates.

"Cotton?" Roy asked.

"The Rio Grande," Hattie added enigmatically.

"Ma, whatever are you talking about?" Wanda asked.

"The South needs cotton for uniforms. Lots of it. Some of the ranchers in Baronsville are going to plant the crop and freight it down to Brownsville to load on boats and take back to the clothing factories where they'll make uniforms for the Confederate troops. We're going to plant a crop. This is a golden opportunity."

"I don't know nothing about no cotton," Roy said.

"No, but these boys here do, don't you, Socrates?"

"No'm. I just picks it."

"Pluto?"

"Me, neither, ma'am. I just plucks it and puts it in a tote sack."

"Well, I've heard there's nothing to it," Hattie said.

"I need Pluto and Socrates to help with the Baron house," Roy said. "And there's cattle to tend, Anson's and ours."

"I brought some plants back from town," Hattie said, "and tomorrow, my daughter and I, along with Pluto and Socrates, are going to start plowing and planting cotton. You can have the boys in the afternoons. Mornings, we'll be plowing and planting."

Roy frowned. He looked at Socrates and Pluto. They looked dumbfounded, but they had stopped eating as their fate was being decided by the strange white woman who talked like a hellfire preacher.

"It's going to slow the work on the Baron house," Roy said.

"What difference does it make?" Hattie said. "Martin's off with those Rangers and Anson's not here, either. Besides, I think both those men are a little crazy."

"I gave my word," Roy said.

"And you'll keep it, Roy. But here's our chance to make a great deal of money, and help the South without hurting anyone or getting hurt ourselves."

"Ma," Wanda said, "none of us knows anything about raising cotton. We're trying to build our own ranch here. Roy's too busy and I certainly don't want to pick cotton in the hot sun."

Hattie waved a fork in the air as if to swat down all objections from those seated at her table.

"Nevertheless," Hattie said, "we're going to plant cotton, acres and acres of it, and we're going to make a fortune to build a ranch even bigger than the Box B."

Forrest's eyes rolled in their sockets. He looked as if he wanted to flee before he became ensnared in Hattie's scheme. She skewered him with a look.

"Forrest, you're designing the Baron house, I know, but surely that doesn't take up all your time. You can help in the mornings, too."

"Well, I—" Forrest started to say.

"I knew you would help," Hattie said, a benevolent and indulgent smile on her face. "We'll start plowing in the morning. Now, everyone enjoy this good food."

Wanda sighed and looked helplessly at Roy. He pushed his plate away, his meal half-finished. Wanda reached over and put a hand on his arm as if to stay him from leaving the table.

"It seems," Roy said, "like I don't have no say-so in how I run my own ranch. I came here to raise cattle, not grow cotton. Hattie, with all due respect, I think you're the one who's a little bit crazy."

"No, Roy," she said, "I'm just smart, and you wouldn't even have a ranch if it weren't for me. I hope you don't disremember that fact when you go to sleep tonight. And I think you do mean disrespect. I'm your elder, and I know what's good for you and for our ranch."

"Our ranch?" Roy said, his jaw dropping.

"Yes," Hattie said. "We most certainly have a stake in this ranch, and when you marry my daughter, I'll be right by your sides, helping you to make a success of it."

Roy didn't leave the table. He just sat there, staring down at his plate, wondering how he had let himself be taken over by these two women. He realized the hold they both had on him and that he had allowed it to happen.

"Forrest," Roy said, after a few seconds, "in the morning, pack up all you have. We're going to set up a tent and live in it while we build Anson a new house. That all right with you?"

"Sure," Forrest said, with so much eagerness, he startled himself, not to mention Hattie. "That will work out fine. There's a lot of work to be done."

Roy turned his gaze to Hattie. She glared back at him.

"I want Pluto and Socrates on the Box B by noon," he said. "I mean to put up that house in jig time. You and Wanda can plant all the damned cotton you want, Hattie. And you can, by God, pick it, too."

"Well, I never—" Hattie started to say, but Wanda fixed her with a look and shook her head.

"That's enough," Wanda said. "Roy is the master here and he'll do what is best. Isn't that right, Mother dear?"

Hattie huffed and sat there glowering, her eyes glittering like those of a hunting serpent temporarily robbed of its prey. Then, as if nothing had happened, she began to attack her food once again, and a blessed silence settled over the small assemblage. Once again, the clink and clatter of utensils striking pewter plates filled the air.

Roy pulled his plate back in front of him as Wanda removed her hand from his arm. He looked at her, smiled wanly, then began to eat. Socrates suppressed a knowing grin and Forrest looked as if he had been granted a reprieve from a death sentence. Pluto, bewildered, ate very quietly, careful not to make a sound that would draw attention to himself.

No one looked over at Hattie, who sat there at the head of the table in regal haughtiness, her very silence creating a commanding presence. They did not look at her, but they all knew that her mind was working as furiously as a millrace. They were sure they had not heard the last from her on the subject of cotton. Nor on the war that loomed over them and was now surely at their table like some spectral presence that, while invisible, would not vanish for a long time to come.

18

JULIO SIFUENTES KNEW they were going in the wrong direction. The road south, toward the Rocking A Ranch, had disappeared over an hour before. He said so to his wife, Carmen, no more than an hour after he and the other Mexicans who worked for Anson Baron had left the ranch headquarters.

They were herding their milk cow and their cart, pulled by a burro, clanking with the clatter of empty pails, lulled them both into a kind of stupor that had dulled their senses. But now, as the mesquite and prickly pear shadows thinned and stretched behind them, and as the sun sank slowly to eye level in front of them, they felt disoriented, as if they had been wandering in circles inside a labyrinth.

"You should ask Carlos Quintana why he goes this way, my husband."

"I will ask him."

"This is not the way to Mexico," she said. "See where the sun is going."

"I see it. We are not going to the south. We are going to the west."

"*Verdad.* That is not the way, Julio. Carlos has lost his way. Perhaps he has been drinking the mezcal."

"No. Carlos is not drunk. But I am thinking why does he go this way."

"You must ask Carlos. I am already tired. My legs have pain. I have hunger, as well."

The Mexicans, walking in procession, were strung out over an eighth of a mile of distance, the straw hats of the men bobbing like corks upon a sea. The women, in their harlequin dresses made from cloth scraps of many colors and patterns, along with their children in more drab clothing, trailed the men, carrying their few goods on their backs or driving carts hitched to burros. There was little talking and no laughter, and the faces of the people were dark grim masks hammered of old bronze, as if they were marching to some un-known prison beyond the horizon. Here was land they had lived and worked on, spilled their blood on, and it was now their desolation and their sadness, retreating under the tread of their sandals as they passed in mourning.

Julio could feel the sadness of his people, and he knew they felt his own sadness, as well. They were all suddenly homeless, with very little money and very little food, and they were going back to a land that was even poorer than they.

"Go speak to Carlos, Julio," Carmen said. "I want to know where he is taking us. Find out if the man is blind, or loco from the burn-ing sun."

"Carlos will stop soon. The sun is going away already, and we will have to make camp. I will speak to him then."

"Why do you know he will stop soon? Maybe he is crazy and will make us walk past the setting sun and into the night. The man is crazy. Or he is lost."

"Shut your mouth, woman. Carlos will stop because we come to the little creek and he will want the horses and burros to drink. See the row of trees that grow in a line? That is where the little creek we call Aguadulce runs."

They passed Box B cattle grazing on sparse grasses, the long-horns lifting their Viking heads to look at the caravan, some lowing as if conversing with their brethren. The cattle bore the Box B brand and Julio remembered the branding of them, and this too filled him with another kind of sadness that could not be explained in words.

Ahead of them, they heard Carlos giving orders and they saw the people break from ranks and fan out along the treeline that bordered the little sweet-water creek. Carmen let out a long sigh of relief and clicked her teeth together as she tapped the cow in front of her with a willow switch.

"You will harm the milk if you make the cow run," Julio said.

"The milk will go sour anyway."

The sun sank from the dusk sky shortly after the Mexicans made camp and started their cookfires. It left a crimson glow on the western horizon as the clouds turned ashen on the rim of the world. Shadowy figures moved behind the orange firelight, hobbling burros and cows and goats, fetching water from the stream, filling pots as the boys rolled barrel hoops and the girls helped their mothers.

Julio found Carlos after Carmen chased him away from their fire, urging him to talk to Quintana before supper. Carlos squatted beneath a mesquite tree, pulling smoke through his pipe and gazing westward at the darkening sky, the first stutters of stars winking on as if lighted by some unseen force.

"You do not take us to Mexico," Julio said, as he squatted down beside Quintana.

Quintana adjusted the battered straw hat on his head so that the sweat on his forehead gleamed dully in the fading light. He drew on the pipe and breathed in the harsh smoke, then let the smoke ease out between his lips before he spoke.

"I will talk to the others, Julio, when I have finished the smoking of my pipe and made my thoughts clear in my mind. You have reason, however. We are walking to the west on this land without pity and tomorrow we will turn right and walk to the north."

"You are leading us back to the Baron rancho, Carlos?"

Quintana smiled without showing his teeth. It was just a wrinkling of his lips that made the smile but Julio could see it in the soft light from the cookfires.

"No, Julio. We do not go back to the Baron rancho. We go to another place where I believe that we will be given work to do and money to put in our pockets and food to place on our tables."

"Where is this place, my friend?"

"I will tell you when I tell the others. Have you not seen me talking to the *curandero* this day?"

"No. Are you speaking of *el loco,* Bendigo Vargas, *el anciano?*"

"Bendigo is not crazy. He is a true *curandero* and he does not have the years that show on his face. He is very strong. I think he has no more than thirty years and his hands can heal the sick and he has powers. I believe that he talks with the saints."

"I do not believe this, Carlos."

"Did you not witness the healing of the little daughter of Augusto and Lucia Montecito, when she had the yellow fever?"

"I have heard of this. Did Bendigo truly heal the little girl? That was a long time ago."

"The girl plays and dances with her friends. She smiles. She laughs. Those he did not touch are now in heaven."

The smells of cooking beef and lard and corn tortillas drifted to the nostrils of the two men and they both could hear the innocent laughter of the children playing in the darkness by firelight now that their chores were done. And they could hear the clanking of pots and pans and eating utensils and the low talk of the women to their men.

"Come, Julio," Quintana said. "We will take food and then I will speak to our people. Bendigo is a very wise man, *muy sabio,* and he can foretell the future. This I know. This I believe."

"I will eat and I will listen. But I hope that you are not crazy, too. Like Bendigo, the old man who talks to himself all the time and walks with a limp."

Quintana laughed.

"You must look beyond what you see on the outside of a man, Julio, and see what is truly inside. Bendigo does limp, but he walks in a straight line, and who is to say that he is not talking to someone other than himself? Perhaps to the saints themselves. Perhaps to God."

Julio snorted, but he rose when Quintana got up and the two men walked to their camps, separating without speaking further to each other. Julio walked through fiery sparks to where his wife was preparing their supper and he felt the warmth of their fire on his face while his sweat-damp shirt rippled in the cool breeze that caressed it.

"Did you speak with Carlos?" Carmen asked.

"Yes. He did not tell me why he takes us in a circle."

"You are a fool, Julio. You should make him tell you why we go this way."

"He will tell us after we have taken the meal."

Carmen lifted the sizzling tortilla from the pan of boiling hot lard with a fork and placed it on a clay plate that she handed her husband. He sat down, feeling the glare from his wife's eyes.

"You are not worth nothing," she spat. "Where is your backbone? Where is your pride? You let this man take us into the wilderness and you do not ask why. You have no balls, Julio. You are *sin cojones*."

"I asked Carlos why he takes us this way and not to Mexico. He said he would tell us later, my sweet Carmen. He said that he had been talking to Bendigo this day."

"Bendigo? The *curandero*?"

"Yes. But Bendigo is no *curandero*. He is a crippled old man."

"Ah, sacrilege, Julio. Sacrilege."

And then Carmen Sifuentes crossed herself and lowered her head. Julio could see her lips moving and knew that she was praying. Perhaps, he thought, she was praying for his soul.

Perhaps Bendigo was a holy man, a healer.

But he had his own thoughts, Julio did, and he was very hungry. He began to ladle meat onto his tortilla and then he took some beans and chilies and put them on his plate.

The breeze that sprang up was not cool enough to soften his wife's temper and the two ate in silence. Carmen glowered at Julio and she crossed herself often as they both waited to hear what Carlos Quintana had to say that night.

Julio wished he had never heard the man's name.

19

MATTEO AGUILAR GROWLED low in his throat as if he had reverted to some primitive form of animal and was confined to a cage. He stood inside the adobe with Jules Reynaud, looking out the window from back in the shadows where they both could not be seen from the road. He looked again at the two dead Rangers, the swarm of flies attacking their eyes, drinking their blood as it dried in the sun.

"You sweat, Jules," Matteo said. "From the heat. Or from fear. Martin is out there. He is alive. I want him dead."

Reynaud drew the back of his hand across his forehead. His rifle, where he held it, glistened with a sheen of sweat. The air in the room was close, unmoving.

"It is like an oven in here, Matteo. I have no fear. With Baron, right now, it is a standoff."

"A Mexican standoff?"

Reynaud would not be baited.

"A standoff," he said. "Martin will be killed. I want him dead as much as you do."

"And you want the money I will pay you."

"Of course, my Mexican friend. Blood money is sweeter than the sugar in your pay."

Matteo laughed harshly, the laughter hollow in the cavern of the bare room.

"Go and get Cullie. I need powder and ball, some patches, and the percussion caps for this rifle I took from the Ranger, Oltman. See if you can find Oltman's horse. If so, bring me his saddlebags when you come back. He probably has a spare powder horn in there, as well as caps and balls. I am thinking of a plan. But we must be ready to ride, as well."

"Why? Are you afraid, Matteo?" Reynaud's eyes glittered with an unspoken accusation, as if he was looking for any sign of weakness in his Mexican employer. Weakness in a man was Reynaud's stock-in-trade. He had used this tool in many a fight back in New Orleans. For he was a predator and he preyed on the weakest of humans, drew satisfaction from taking human life with such ease.

"I do not like being a prisoner. I heard Martin and the Ranger talking about meeting another Ranger. A man named Casebolt."

"Coming here?"

Aguilar shrugged. "Maybe. They were taking me to San Antonio. This Casebolt could meet them here or on the way to San Antonio."

"One man."

"One Ranger."

"Yes, there is a difference, eh Matteo? I will go and bring Cullie here. You watch the dead horse. I do not trust Martin. He is smart. But if he or Oltman leave that hiding place, you can pick them off. You will still have to pay me even if you are the one to kill Martin."

"You love the money, eh, Jules? The love of money is the root of all evil, it is said. But you are right. Martin and Oltman may grow tired of waiting and smelling the stink of that dead horse. They may rise up and come after us, shooting their guns. That is why we must be careful. If not, the snake might wiggle away and bite us in the ass."

"I have an extra powder horn and caps for that rifle, and plenty of powder and ball." Reynaud dug into his possibles pouch and placed balls, patches, and percussion caps on the windowsill. "This will hold you until I come back with Cullie, Matteo."

Matteo nodded and stepped up closer to the window. "But bring me the saddlebags from Oltman's horse." He looked out the window at Martin's dead horse. He knew Oltman and Baron were lying behind the dead animal. Oltman's horse had disappeared down the road and was no longer visible.

He looked up into the sky and saw the buzzards, a pair of them, circling overhead, their pinions quivering in the air currents. Then another buzzard joined the invisible carousel and another, and Matteo knew there would be more before the sun set. Even he could smell the ripeness of the dead men lying near the watering trough, the sickly sweet smell of death that reminded him of the war he had waged, and lost, on Martin Baron.

Martin was so close. His death was so near. Yet he was still alive behind that dead horse. What was he waiting for? For night to fall? Yes, perhaps. Or perhaps, Matteo thought, he was thinking of a way to come at them, he and Oltman, and yet there was only open ground between them and the little pueblo. It would be suicide for those men to get up and try to make a charge.

Martin, he knew, was a brave man, but he was not foolish. He did not know Oltman, but he was not so smart as Martin. Yet he was a fighter, too, or he would not be a Texas Ranger. No doubt he had fought the Apache and the Comanche and had outwitted them in battle. So there were two formidable opponents out there and they, like he, were thinking of a plan, of some way to get out of their predicament and emerge as victors.

A skeletal tumbleweed rolled past the window, propelled by the hot western zephyrs that dried the blood of the dead and carried their carrion stench to Matteo's nostrils. Cullie and Reynaud had picked a good place for the ambush.

By the time Cullie and Jules came back to the empty adobe, Matteo had made up his mind. He knew what they had to do and he knew it would take great courage, but it offered great rewards, as well as an end to this interminable waiting while the buzzards circled overhead hoping to feed on the dead.

"Ain't nobody movin' out there," Cullie said. "Here's them saddlebags, Matteo. I didn't look in 'em, but they're heavy."

Cullie held out the saddlebags and Matteo stepped away from the window and took them. He squatted down on the dirt floor and lifted their flaps. He took out the items on top, hardtack and bacon wrapped in cloth, a tool to pull horseshoe nails and trim the hooves, a straight razor, a piece of lye soap, an iron toothpick, fork, knife, and spoon, a small can that smelled of coffee and showed burn smears along its bottom and sides, a sack of coffee beans. In the other saddlebag there was a brass powder flask that felt full, a box of percussion caps, a small sack of .50-caliber lead balls, a bullet mold for both .50- and .36-caliber bullets. He stuffed his pockets with the flask, balls, and caps, and then found a .36-caliber pistol at the bottom of the bag, fully loaded and capped. It was a Colt Navy and when he spun the cylinder he knew it had been well kept by its owner. Instead of grease in the chambers of the cylinders, one of which was empty under the hammer, Oltman had pressed small greased patches made of heavy striped cloth.

"Now you're set, Matteo," Cullie said when Aguilar stood up.

"Do you have a plan, Matteo?" Reynaud asked. His tone was almost mocking, but Matteo stared him down as he slipped the .36-caliber Navy into his waistband, and picked up Oltman's rifle and clicked the hammer back to half cock.

"I have the plan," Matteo said. "It must be, *cómo se dice*, of the exact time."

"Perfect timing," Cullie offered.

"Yes, the timing must be perfect. Cullie, you and Jules will mount your horses. Cullie, you will ride to the right, behind the adobes that are between you and Martin. Jules, you will ride to the left. Both of you ride far enough so that you cannot be seen. Then, you will ride in on their flanks. You make your horses run to the gallop. I will hear, and they will hear, the horses. When you see them, you will start shooting."

"Where will you be?" Jules asked.

Matteo smiled. "I will be right here at this window. I will put the pistol up there and cock it. If either Martin or Oltman stands up, I will shoot them dead with the rifle. And if one is still standing, I will shoot him with the pistol."

"That's a good hunnert yards to where they're at," Cullie said.

"I am the excellent shot, Cullie. Do not worry. They will be caught in the crossfire. I may even kill them both myself from here."

"I don't like it much," Cullie said. "Seems that Reynaud and me are takin' all the chances."

"You will catch them by surprise," Matteo said. "We cannot miss. There is no escape."

"It might work," Jules said, the frown on his face fading as he thought about it. "The trick is to get to their flanks before they know we're coming straight at them."

"That is so," Matteo said. *"Vámanos."*

Jules started for the door. Cullie lingered a moment, trying to read Matteo's face. He finally shrugged and followed Reynaud out the door. A moment later, Matteo heard them mount their horses and then he saw Jules ride past his doorway. The hoofbeats of both men's horses soon faded from his hearing.

Matteo reached down and lifted the saddlebags, slung them over his shoulder. He picked up the rifle, walked to the window and took the balls and patches off the sill and put them in his pockets. Then Matteo walked out of the adobe. He draped the saddlebags behind the cantle of Oltman's saddle, stuck the rifle in its boot, and untied the reins from the hitchrail. He mounted the horse and rode in a straight line away from the adobe, keeping it between him and the road on the other side of the town where Martin and the Ranger lay behind the dead horse.

People peered at Matteo from doorways and windows, but none called out to him. He avoided the chickens, ducks, and dogs until he was clear of the town.

"Let the damned gringos fight with each other," he said to no one. "Maybe they will all kill each other."

Matteo drew in air and smiled. He had money in his boot, a good horse, weapons, and he knew the way back home to the Rocking A. If Reynaud and Cullie showed up and said that Martin Baron was dead, he would not pay them, not even with proof. If they survived the fight with Baron and Oltman, it did not matter. In Matteo's mind, they were both dead men. Now, or later.

20

A NSON DID NOT look at Peebo for a long time after they rode away from the Box B headquarters. Peebo kept his horse a few paces behind Anson's. They rode away from the falling sun, eastward, following the game trail they had ridden so many times before, one that had been widened over the years since Martin had bought the land and driven cattle along it to New Orleans. Anson kept studying the ground as they rode, and Peebo did the same. Anson was reading sign because it was now habit, and a necessity in a land that was still wild, still fraught with peril, still thick with Apache and other marauding tribes.

Anson thought of all that had happened so recently. He bore old scars and fresh wounds and he hoped that riding through the land once again would begin to heal him inside and outside.

The war with Aguilar had shattered his faith in men more than any other single act. And his father's leaving once again not only opened that old wound, but filled it with hot sand and cockleburs that festered in his mind like an open sore. The defection of the men who had worked with him left an emptiness inside him that could probably never be filled, a hurt that was so tangled up with old dreams, hopes, and expectations that he could not unravel the

twisting clot of snakes that poisoned him, made him sick in heart
and mind, made him want to lash out at everyone he had once
trusted or grab each one by the throat and ask them the questions
that burned in his mind, questions about loyalty and honor and ba-
sic human values.

The air was thick with the reek of creosote and cedar dust and
the cloying scent of rotting weathered wood, of live things and dead
things baking in the heat. The long wide valley that spread from the
Rio Grande never failed to fascinate and hypnotize Anson and the
smells brought him all the way inside the deep mystery of the land,
wiped out the taint of civilization on zephyrs that wafted northward
from the sea, tangy with the taste of Gulf salt and the musk of seagulls and shorebirds that somehow left their spoor on the vagrant
wandering breezes like oils seeping through a lamp wick.

"Want to stop for a smoke?" Anson said. "Maybe give the horses
some rest?"

Peebo breathed a sigh that might have been of relief. He cracked
that winsome smile of his and caught up to Anson, looked at him as
if meeting for the first time.

"Thought you'd never ask," Peebo said, reaching into his pocket
for the makings.

"There's a water oak over yonder with some shade."

"I see it."

The two men rode over into the puddle of shade beneath a lone
tree and dismounted with a creak of leather and the huff of horses
suddenly relieved of their loads. Peebo handed a thin scrim of paper
to Anson, took one for himself, making a trough with two fingers.
He shook tobacco into Anson's curled paper and then into his own.
He pulled the drawstring tight on the sack of tobacco and slid it back
into his shirt pocket. He rolled the quirly with two fingers, tightened
the wrap with a third, and licked the paper to seal it. Anson fished
out a lucifer and struck the match that lit both their cigarettes. He
drew smoke into his mouth and lungs like a man breathing on a
high mountain and he held the smoke inside and let it flow slowly
back out past his pursed lips.

"You notice the tracks on the hill above the barn, Peebo?"

"Couldn't miss 'em, son. 'Pears we had visitors."

"Damned Apaches were up there watching the whole fight."

"I marked Culebra and his bunch."

Anson nodded, sucking more smoke into his mouth. He turned away from the breeze that had sprung up and was blowing on his face. He looked toward the east, in the direction they were headed.

"Less than a day out in front of us."

"I don't reckon they're after that white bull," Peebo said. "But looks to me like they're going the same way we are."

"Culebra can save us a lot of trouble, you know."

"How's that?" Peebo turned away from the stiffening breeze, as well. His shirt, like Anson's, was blotched and stained with sweat even though the sun was dropping away fast in the western sky. He looked down at their elongated shadows stretching out in front of them.

"Seems like the Apache are headed the same way we are. Maybe going up to the Nueces."

"Maybe going where that white bull has staked out grazing rights," Anson said.

Peebo slid his hat back, his face lit with amazement.

"Huh? What'd you say?"

"Culebra was watching, and listening, maybe. He knows where we're going, I think. Maybe he aims to lie in wait for us when we come after Diablo Blanco."

"You got a head on your shoulders, Anson. Sure enough."

"There's nothing else over there for the Apache. No settlements, no squatters. Just a lot more undeveloped Box B land. And that white bull."

Peebo let out a low whistle. He pulled his hat back down after wiping his forehead with a swipe of his hand. He flipped sweat off his hand and pulled on his smoke.

"Well, maybe we'll have a fight on our hands when we get over yonder. And I don't mean with that bull."

"It's something to think about," Anson said, finishing his smoke.

They rode until their shadows melted into the shadows of the mesquite and the trail ahead dimmed. They came to a small creek that wound through the trees, the water a pale pewter in the twilight. Anson rode into a dense clump of mesquite, well off their path, and slid out of the saddle, his legs starting to ache from tiredness.

He and Peebo unsaddled their horses, hobbled them where the grass grew, and laid out their bedrolls.

"No fire?" Peebo said.

"No fire. Nothing much to cook anyway."

Peebo grinned. "You like it out here, don't you, son? Sleepin' on the hard ground, gnawin' on hardtack, and dippin' your gourd into branch water."

"It seems more like home to me than the house we lived in, Peebo. It's always here and you can't burn it down. You don't have to open windows or a privy door, or get water from a cistern. You don't have to dust it or sweep it or clean the chimney or worry about trackin' in mud in wet weather."

Peebo laughed and nodded.

"You take one end of the creek, Peebo," Anson said, "and I'll take the other. Let's see if we have company or if Culebra stopped by here to water his ponies."

"I'll take the south fork. Watch out for sidewinders, Anson."

The two men took their rifles with them and walked along the creek while there was still some light. Anson walked north, his eyes scanning the ground for tracks. When he crossed the trail they had taken, he noticed a moil of unshod hoof marks. He bent down and saw that they were a mix of ponies going in both directions at different times.

The lingering light played in the brook, its pale silver foil caught in the tiny wavelets, then washed away in dark ink only to reappear again, fleeting daubs of light and dark glancing off a ribbon of iron and velvet like a magical painting that constantly changed and, like the creek itself, was never the same from one moment to the next.

Farther on, Anson almost missed it. The small depression, a bowl in the earth set a few yards away from the creek. The smell drew him to it and he saw where the Apache had squatted and peed, and there were quail feathers clinging to brush and clods of dirt. The fire they had made was buried under dirt and sand, but he dug down into it and felt its coldness, the scrape of charcoal on his fingertips. He saw the tiny bones of the quail scattered around and put together a picture in his mind of the Apache band making fire to cook, sitting down around it and eating, then leaving that place to ride on. The fire was hours cold, the smell of urine faint, the tang of feces blended with the aroma of dirt and blood and ash.

Anson walked back along the darkened creek, the twilight almost gone, the shadows taking on odd shapes, both human and beastly, and the night coming on as the pale sky to the west shrank to a thin line across the horizon, a faint glow that would soon be extinguished.

Peebo had beat him back to their camp and was hunkered next to a small mesquite, the tip of his quirly an orange flicker in his hand, a streaking spark when he brought the cigarette to his lips.

"They were here," Anson said. "Up the creek a ways. Killed them some quail and cooked them over a fire. Long gone, I think."

"That's a mighty comforting thought," Peebo said.

"You hungry?"

"I could eat the southbound end of a northbound horse."

Anson laughed as he always did at the same old joke. But his own belly was growling and he sat down and hefted his saddlebags. They clanked when he lugged them to a spot in front of his crossed legs.

"What's that you got sticking out of them bags, son? Cookin' irons?"

"Box B irons. For that bull."

"Well, we got plenty of rope." He pointed to the coils of rope attached to their saddles.

Anson set aside the two branding irons, one a box, the other a B that was burned inside the square of the other. He dug out jerky and hardtack.

"Got an airtight of peaches," Anson said, "but thought I'd save it for later when we get tired of rabbit."

"Jerky's fine with me."

Peebo put out his cigarette and the two men ate quietly, listening to the night sounds, a whip-poor-will calling from somewhere downcreek, its lonesome trill flapping like a loose piece of leather being stropped, the melodic notes rippling up and down the scale in a peculiar key.

After they had eaten, Peebo wanted to talk and they rolled smokes and lit them as the stars seemed to come down close in the clear night air and the moon rose like some gibbous god's eye spilling dull melted silver on the leaves, splashing pale pewter on their hands and faces.

"I wonder where the Mexicans are tonight," Peebo said.

Anson did not reply to a question that could not be answered.

"Reckon they'll change their minds and come back?"

"If they did, I'd send them packing again."

"Why? They was good hands."

"Julio and Carlos made their beds. They don't like the way I run the ranch, so they turned tail and ran."

"I think they were tryin' to tell you somethin', Anson."

"I heard what they had to say."

"I mean underneath."

"Underneath?"

"Underneath their words. They didn't want to leave. But they didn't want you to leave, neither."

"Well, I can't have hands telling me what to do."

"No, I reckon not. Still, Quintana and Sifuentes were pretty fair vaqueros, don't you think?"

"They were good hands. I'll get others just as good. You want a man to stick with you, Peebo, through thick and thin. Julio hit me when I was down, dealing with what Aguilar did to my house and all the killing and dead men. A damned poor time to talk about quitting and just walk off like that."

"Where do you figure to find good hands like that, with a war breakin' out and all?"

"Ye gods, Peebo, use your brain, tiny as it is. There's a whole country down south full of vaqueros willing to work. It's called Mexico."

Peebo laughed. "You aim to go down there?"

"I do."

"When?"

"After we catch that white bull and pasture him with fresh cows, that's when."

"Too bad your pa had to up and leave, too."

The minute he said it, Peebo knew he had struck a sore spot. Even in the darkness he could feel the glare from Anson's eyes, and the silence was so thick he could have cut it with a knife.

"The less you talk about my daddy, Peebo, the less likely you'll catch a fist right square on your jaw."

Peebo held up his hands in mock surrender.

"I'll never speak your old pa's name again, son. I swear."

Then he grinned and Anson slapped him on the back, grinning, too.

They walked back to camp.

"I'll take first watch," Peebo said. "You get some shut-eye, son."

"Suit yourself. Wake me in three, four hours."

"I'll roust you out when my eyelids start turning to galena."

Both men laughed and Anson lay down on his bedroll and made himself a pillow with one of his saddlebags. He put his pistol close at hand, alongside his rifle and possibles pouch. He closed his eyes and heard Peebo walk upstream toward the trail, and the soft crunch of his boots lulled him to sleep as the whip-poor-wills called to each other across the dark, like the lost souls of men gone to perdition.

21

I N THE LAZY insect drone of afternoon, Martin suddenly heard a sound that didn't fit. He looked over at Oltman to see if he had moved, but Al was stock-still, in the same position he had been in before, leaning against the rump of the dead horse, his hat brim roofed over his face for shade.

Martin reached over and tapped Oltman on the arm, then held a straight finger over his lips. He cocked his head toward the town and then cupped his ear, urging Oltman to listen.

Oltman listened for a moment. Then he started to shake his head. Martin held up a hand, flat, palm out, as if to stay him from making any quick decision just yet.

Martin cupped his ear and turned his head to pick up that same sound he had heard. He nodded, pointed back toward the town.

It wasn't much of a sound, one that would be without meaning most of the time. But now that they were isolated out there behind a dead horse, facing three deadly rifles, the sound took on weight. It was just a scraping sound, very faint, then a soft thunk. Thunk, scrape, thunk, scrape.

Martin looked over at Oltman, who nodded this time and cocked a thumb back toward town. The insect sounds drifted into the background as the other sounds took prominence in their minds and ears.

"They're moving," Oltman whispered.

The sounds grew fainter, then disappeared.

"Could be just townfolk goin' about their business," Oltman said, without much conviction in his voice.

"The townfolk haven't stirred since we've been here. They're probably all hiding until this business is over."

"You figure Reynaud is coming after us?" Oltman's forehead stitched up with worry furrows.

"They're going to flank us," Martin said. "Reynaud has the patience of a starving man at a table full of food."

"Jesus."

"You keep an eye on your side," Martin said. "Better have your pistol ready and cocked." He slipped his own pistol from its holster and set it beside him as he rolled over to watch their right flank. He crawled a foot or two up to the horse's head and, hugging the ground, peered around it toward the line of adobes, looking for any movement.

He saw nothing out of the ordinary. Just a rifle snout poking out of one window. As he watched, the barrel slipped back inside and disappeared.

Strange, he thought. What in hell was going on?

The two men waited, listening.

The silence built up again, but Martin could hear the insects sawing their off-key tunes. Bluebottles and horseflies buzzed all around the horse. Some were sipping at the eyes; others were sucking at the dried blood or crawling over the animal's hide, sniffing every hair and pore.

It was dead quiet for a time. Oltman fidgeted with his six-gun, putting it on half cock, then full cock, testing the cylinder to see that the cartridge was lined up with the barrel.

"Where in hell are they?" Oltman asked.

"Just be quiet. If they're sneaking up on us, we'll soon know," Martin said.

"Oh, shit," Oltman cried out as he saw a horse racing his way at full gallop. There didn't appear to be any rider on it.

Martin glanced over his shoulder, and saw that the horse did indeed have a rider, one who was hugging the north side like an Apache.

"Shoot the horse when it gets close enough," Martin said, and turned back to look to his flank. He heard the pounding of hooves before he saw the horse emerge through shimmers of heat. The rider was leaning over the pommel, a rifle barrel jutting out parallel to the horse's neck. He picked up his rifle and held it to his shoulder. Mentally, he counted off the yards as he lined up the rear buckhorn with the blade front sight. He cocked the rifle and set the main trigger with the set trigger. A hundred yards, ninety yards, eighty, the horse galloped toward him and he leveled the rifle's sights on the animal's chest, the biggest target, the best place to bring him down with a lung shot.

Behind him, he heard Oltman's pistol bark. But the sound of hoofbeats on his side did not cease, and a split second later, he heard Oltman fire his pistol again.

"Got him," Oltman said.

"Horse or man?" Martin said.

"Horse."

"Now, shoot the man quick," Martin said, and then he saw the rider approaching him rise up and swing his rifle toward him. Martin lined up on the horse's plump chest, led it a few feet and touched the trigger. His rifle belched flame and white smoke and he felt it buck against his shoulder as ninety grains of powder exploded in the chamber and expelled the 180-grain lead ball from the muzzle.

As if time had shifted to slow motion, he saw the horse take the ball in its chest. Dust puffed up from where the ball struck. The horse ran on a few yards, then began to stagger just before its forelegs collapsed and its front end struck the ground. The horse skidded a few feet, carried by its forward momentum, and the rider flew out of the saddle and tumbled end over end backward, still clutching the rifle.

Martin slammed his own rifle down and picked up his pistol, got to his feet. He glanced to his left to see if anyone in town was going to shoot, and hunched over, he raced toward the fallen man. He knew who it was, Jules Reynaud, and he felt a clock ticking in his head as he ran a zigzag pattern toward the assassin, who was rising to his feet and swinging the barrel of his rifle around like the snout of some metal beast seeking prey.

Martin brought his pistol up level with Reynaud and squeezed off a shot from the single-action six-gun. The pistol bucked in his hand, belching smoke and fire. Martin felt his hand sting with the blowback of hot powder and the sound of the explosion deafened him for a few seconds. He thumbed back the hammer for a second shot as Reynaud cracked off a shot in his direction. But the Frenchman was already twisting with the impact of the lead ball that had struck him low in the right side of his chest, smashing the bottom rib, just missing the lung as it traveled through and tore a hole the size of a fist in his back.

The shot from Reynaud's rifle sizzled past Martin's ear and he felt the hairs rise on the back of his neck as if he had been electrocuted. Reynaud dropped the rifle and clawed for his sidearm, drawing his pistol from its holster even as he fought to stay on his feet. Blood oozed from his chest and soaked through his torn shirt.

Martin saw Reynaud's pistol snake out of its holster, then shifted his gaze to Reynaud's face, which had drained of color, tightened up in a squinch of pain into a frozen mask. Martin stopped dead in his tracks and took careful aim, all in an instant, and squeezed the trigger of the Colt .44. He judged his range to be ten yards, so close to Reynaud he could hear the ball smack into his gut, see the wind go out of the man's chest, double him over with the impact.

"Damn you, Martin," Reynaud gasped and sank to his knees, his pistol dangling from a hand gone suddenly limp. The pistol was uncocked, useless to the wounded man.

Martin strode up to Reynaud and kicked the pistol from his hand. It sailed a yard or two and skidded into the dirt. Blood poured from the hole in Reynaud's abdomen, spreading a crimson stain across his midsection. Martin cocked his pistol once more and placed the muzzle square against Reynaud's forehead, forcing him back on his haunches.

"You just couldn't leave well enough alone, could you, Jules?"

"*Cochon*," Reynaud gasped, struggling not to go down on his back. He stared up at the black snout of Martin's pistol and then into his face.

Reynaud's eyes glazed over with the dull frost of pain and his breathing began to come hard, every breath seeming to bring on more agony from the two bullet wounds.

"You know damned well I never sullied your sister, Jules. You can take your lies with you to your grave."

"You finish me, Martin. I curse you with my last breath."

"That's about all you're good for, you bastard. You'll burn in hell, still cursing, you son of a bitch."

Reynaud's eyes cleared for a moment as if the pain had been snatched away suddenly and his lips curled upward in a twisted smile.

"A curse on you and your son, Martin."

Then Reynaud's hand moved. He tried to lift it and aim the pistol at Martin. His smile faded into a tight grimace with the effort.

Martin straightened his arm and aimed his pistol at Reynaud's forehead. He squeezed the trigger with a smooth pull of his finger and the pistol exploded with a roar. Reynaud's head snapped back as the lead ball smashed into his forehead, then blew the back of his head out, spewing chunks of skull and clumps of brain outward in a rosy spray that peppered the ground. Reynaud's mouth opened and then his eyes flapped shut as his body slammed into the ground. He twitched once, and then his lifeless body lay still, contorted into a grotesque position. He fouled the air with the stench of his bowels releasing and Martin's nose crinkled up with the odor in his nostrils.

Martin fought down the bile that rose in his throat. His stomach convulsed and he drew in a breath to keep from being sick all over the dead body. He turned away and walked away from the smell of death and foul voidance.

Martin was shaking inside, but he cocked his pistol again and walked back to where his horse lay dead. He saw Oltman grappling with a man some yards away. Both men were smeared with blood.

That's when Martin recognized Cullie, a man he had not expected to see again. Cullie seemed to have the most blood on him, and when Martin looked closer, he saw that Cullie's belly was soaked and still spurting.

Oltman forced Cullie down to his knees, then drove a fist straight into his jaw. Cullie bent backward and Oltman dove on top of him. As Martin watched, Oltman lowered his head and turned it sideways. Cullie tried to fight back, but Oltman's teeth were on his neck. Martin heard a crunch as Oltman bit into Cullie's Adam's apple.

Cullie stiffened and Martin heard a rattling sound in his throat as he tried to breathe. Oltman leaned back and turned his head, spat out the chunk of bloody flesh between his teeth. Blood gushed from the ragged wound in Cullie's throat. Cullie shivered twice as his body convulsed in the final spasms of death, and then his torso went limp. Blood spurted from the hole in his throat and then stopped as his heart went still.

"That sumbitch," Oltman said, rising from the dead body. He spat out more blood and staggered away from the man he had killed. "Kicked me in the nuts."

"Where's your pistol, Al?"

"Damn, it's lyin' around here someplace. I thought the sumbitch was done for. Played possum on me."

"You're lucky."

"I won't never make that mistake again."

Martin looked around, then over at the row of adobes. He stared at the two dead Rangers lying near the watering trough, and at their horses, which were both standing stock-still, their reins trailing to the ground.

"Question is," Martin said, "where in hell is Aguilar?"

There was a long silence between them. Oltman walked a few paces and reached down, picked up his pistol. It was covered with dust and he brushed it off with his hand, then rubbed it on his trousers, flipping it from one side to the other.

"You hurt?" Oltman asked.

"No. You?"

"Nary a scratch. Just a ball ache where that bastard kicked me."

"I think Matteo lit a shuck," Martin said. "Else he'd have shot us both dead by now."

"You think so?"

"I damn sure think so. Aquilar's long gone. You can bet on it."

"I'm going to find my horse," Oltman said. "Why don't you pick out one of those by the trough and we'll track that Mex son of a bitch. I want to see him hang."

Martin thought about it. He needed a horse and he would have a time of it getting his saddle off his own horse, along with his bags and bedroll. The saddle fit him and he wasn't going to leave it behind. As for Matteo, no telling where he was, or where he would go just then. But eventually, he'd make his way back to his ranch.

"We won't catch him," Martin said, as Oltman was walking back down the road to look for his horse.

"Huh?"

"Matteo. He outsmarted these two and he'll outsmart us. If you want to waste days tracking him, fine with me. Let him go to ground, back to his ranch. We'll catch up with him there one day."

"Yeah, I think you're right. The war's more important than his sorry ass. We'll go on to San Antonio, hook up with Ford, and leave Aguilar for another time."

Martin sighed. Matteo had outsmarted them all. Now, he was running with the jackrabbits and the wind. There would come a day, he knew, when he'd have to finish this business with Aguilar, but that could wait.

He turned to say something else to Oltman, but the ranger was gone, back down the road to look for his horse.

It didn't matter, Martin thought. He wanted a horse under him. He wanted to get away from this place of death. He braced himself to look at Kenny Darnell one last time and say goodbye. Kenny, who was his brother-in-law, was the last member of his dead wife's family. Now, Caroline and all of her kin were dead.

Suddenly, Martin felt very old.

22

HATTIE WAS A determined woman. She had left early the previous afternoon with Socrates driving the buckboard into Baronsville. She and Socks arrived back the next day at the Lazy K around noon, the wagon filled with cotton seeds she had bought in town from a traveling merchant who was spreading the good news about growing cotton, making money, and supporting the South in its war of independence.

She had told Wanda to take Pluto out to an eighty-acre pasture, where she had already planted the plants she had bought earlier. Hattie had designated the area to be their first field, with instructions to measure out as many one-acre plots as they could that morning and to meet her and Socks back at the house by noon.

When Socks and Hattie pulled up to the house, Wanda was standing outside with Pluto, an exasperated look on her face. Hattie could tell that her daughter was distraught, and as she looked around the yard and out back, she thought she knew why.

There were Mexicans everywhere she looked, women, children, and grown men, with their goats and cows and burros, carts laden with household goods. The men were lolling in a bunch on the shady side of the house, while the women were lazing beneath the carts and the children were rolling barrel hoops around, yelling and dancing like city urchins at play.

"Well, I swan," Hattie said, as Socks set the handbrake and she climbed down from the wagon. "Whatever do we have here, Wanda, darling?"

"They just showed up about a half hour ago," Wanda said. "Just after Pluto and I got back from the field."

Hattie sniffed the air.

"What do I smell?" she asked. "Are you cookin' our lunch?"

"I was going to, but some of the Mexican women asked if they could cook for all of us. Three of them are in the kitchen now. I just didn't know what to do. Those men over there, I think their names are Carlos and Julio, want to talk to you, Ma."

"Who are they?"

"Don't you recognize them? They're from the Box B. They said they quit and want to come to work for Roy."

"Well, I swan," Hattie said, and walked over to the two men her daughter had pointed out. Wanda followed her mother, leaving Pluto and Socrates to talk to each other. Socrates started showing Pluto the cotton seeds in the wagon, explaining what he had learned about the plant in town. They had both seen cotton seeds before, of course, but neither man had ever planted the seeds. But when Pluto was a boy he had tagged along with his father, who had planted seeds. They had only picked cotton on a Louisiana plantation.

"*Buenas tardes,*" Quintana said when Hattie walked up. Julio murmured the same greeting. Both men removed their hats.

"What do you want?" Hattie asked.

"*Con permiso,*" Quintana said, "we have come here to work. We are very fine vaqueros, señora."

"You quit the Box B. Why?"

"Because there was much trouble," Julio said. "There was fighting and killing."

"I know," Hattie said. "It was just terrible."

"Then the old *patrón*, Martin, he went away. The young *patrón*, Anson, he go away, too."

Hattie looked at the women standing beyond the two men. One

or two held infants in their arms. Some wore shawls over their heads. All looked mournful and sad. They stood there like statues, their dark faces wooden, without expression. But their eyes glittered as if they were filled with tears, although none of them were weeping. Something about them, the way they stood there, tugged at Hattie's heart.

"Did Anson or Martin tell you to go away?" Hattie asked.

Quintana and Sifuentes shook their heads.

Carlos spoke. "They did not tell us to go away. They left us. They went away."

"I don't understand. Couldn't you have worked the ranch in their absence?"

Quintana turned and made a gesture toward the women and children standing some yards behind him.

"My people are like children," he said. "They must have a *patrón.* They feel as if their father has left them."

"Abandoned them," Hattie said.

"Yes. Abandoned," Julio said.

"So why do you come here, to this poor place?"

"We know you do not have money to pay us," Quintana said. "But if you let us work and grow food in our gardens, we will help you build the rancho. We are vaqueros and we can manage the cattle, and we can work at other things."

"We will be able to pay you one day," Hattie said. "You will have to be patient."

"Oh, we have the patience," Sifuentes said. "We are a patient people. And we work very hard."

"What are your names?" Hattie asked.

Carlos and Julio told her.

"Do you know how to plant and grow cotton?" she asked.

Both men looked sad and shook their heads. They clutched their hat brims in desperation.

"No matter, Julio, Carlos. We will learn together. I brought cotton seeds in that wagon over yonder and we will need the ground plowed and the seeds planted. The cotton grows very fast and it will make clothing for the Confederate soldiers. It will earn us money."

Both men smiled and nodded, showing that they understood.

"We will plant the cotton," Quintana said. "We will make it grow."

"Then it must be picked and taken to the boats on the Rio Grande and they will take the cotton to a gin."

"What is this 'gin'?" Sifuentes asked.

"It is a place that processes the cotton so that it can be spun into clothing that people can wear."

The two men spoke in rapid Spanish, too fast for Hattie to follow or comprehend. Then they turned to her.

"Our women will make the adobe for our houses while we work the cattle and plant the cotton," Quintana said. "The women will make the gardens and grow the food and we can hunt. And if you let us have some cows now and then, we will cook the meat for our food. We will grow corn and beans and chilies and tomatoes."

"You can tend our garden, as well," Hattie said, beaming. "I will show you where you can build your adobes. You will need water and straw and there is a creek over yonder and a good place for you to put up your homes. Is that all right?"

Both men nodded and grinned. Julio turned and translated what Hattie had said to the women and they all clucked to one another and smiled and patted their babies' backs.

"Ma, don't you think we better ask Roy about this before we let all these people move here?" Wanda looked perplexed, even exasperated. She was wringing her hands and fidgeting with a dangling apron string as if it was a string of worry beads.

"Nonsense, daughter. Roy will be pleased. We can sure use the extra workers. Things have been happening far too slow on the Lazy K to suit me."

"But it's Roy's ranch, Ma."

"Let's not talk about this now, Wanda dear. It's our ranch. Lord knows we have a sure enough investment in it. Now, you run along and help the women in the kitchen. I'm going to show these two gentlemen the cotton seeds I brought from town."

With that, Hattie beckoned to Quintana and Sifuentes, who followed her over to the wagon. In a while, Wanda rang the dinner bell and soon the yard was spread with cloths and food. Hattie sat and ate outside with the Mexicans while Wanda sulked inside the house. Hattie's laughter made the Mexicans smile and feel right at home.

And so it was that the former Baronenos came to Roy Killian's

Lazy K ranch and became Killianos. They built their adobe houses and made chicken coops and pens for their goats. They plowed the fields and planted cotton under Hattie's supervision, and they began to organize the cattle and set them on pastures where they could thrive and fatten.

And none of them thought about the war that was swirling around them at a distance, and Roy never did go into Baronsville to talk to the army recruiter, who soon went away, thinking that he had been to another country where people spoke a different language and had their own customs.

All of the ranchers began to grow cotton, while the Box B remained neglected and untended as Roy and Forrest, along with Ken Richman, watched the new Baron house go up, rising like a phoenix from the ashes, bigger, prouder, and as empty as an old abandoned barn.

Ed Wales published the war news in the Baronsville newspaper and people talked about it in the Longhorn, but they all had a sense of being in a place where time stood still and life went on as if set on a different course and the war was far away, back somewhere in Virginia, or over in Mississippi or up in Arkansas or Missouri.

Yet some, like Lorene Sisler and her friends, Millie Collins and Nancy Grant, the self-proclaimed bitches of Baronsville, felt the war more keenly than most, because they knew Martin Baron was somewhere in the thick of it, perhaps fighting on foreign, even Yankee, soil, and they wondered if he would ever come back to Baronsville and the Box B. And Lorene pined for Anson Baron, who had not been heard from in weeks; the only word she'd had was from Ken Richman who said the ranch was in sad shape and was still untended.

No soldiers from either side had come to Baronsville, but Ed Wales, in his editorials in the newspaper, warned that there would be a lot of fighting along the Rio Grande before the war was over and that Texas would soon be invaded by Union troops.

Wales urged that Baronsville form a militia, but none heeded his call, and he continued to be a lone voice in the wilderness, crying wolf to those who would not hear and did not believe.

And the summer wore on slowly in that part of Texas where the rattle of muskets and the roar of cannon were not heard. Yet none could deny the sense of doom that began to settle over Baronsville as Ed Wales printed both rumors and facts about the war between the States, warning that the South was going to lose the war and that all their lives would be changed forever.

And no one listened.

23

▬

MARTIN TOOK AN instant dislike to Colonel John Salmon Ford of the Texas Rangers. Ford, he thought, was a pompous ass with a foul mouth, who thought he was Napoleon.

"Just give him time," Oltman told Martin. "Old Rip grows on you."

"Rip?"

"When he writes letters to the families of dead soldiers, he always writes on the letters the initials R.I.P., 'Rest in Peace,' you know. So we call him Rip."

"Jesus," Martin said.

"Well, some of the men think Rip can walk on water, Martin."

They had arrived at the barracks in San Antonio the day before, and the first thing Ford had wanted to do was inspect their horses. He wasn't the least interested in the fight at Bandana, nor the subsequent escape of Matteo Aguilar. Martin did give him credit for being concerned about the deaths of Dan Shepley and Kenneth Darnell.

"At least he liked our horses," Martin said.

"He liked you, too," Oltman said. "He wants to see you again, now that you're officially a Texas Ranger. He's called us all up for a talk."

"He looks like a politician to me," Martin said.

"Well, he was. He was a lot of other things, too. He's a doctor, a newspaperman, and he fought admirably under Coffee Jack Hays, in the Mexican War."

"All I've seen of Colonel Ford is him strutting around looking at our horses and cussing the Confederate Army, the politicians in Austin, and the Union."

"Well, the army doesn't like the Rangers much, Martin. And Rip had to fight like hell to keep his Rangers from being conscripted by the army, and he had to buck the politicians in Austin, as well. He's one smart man and a hell of a soldier."

"He's old as hell. He's a graybeard and his hair is as gray as Louisiana moss."

"Well, the colonel's near fifty, I grant you that. He was born in 1815 somewheres in South Carolina, moved to Texas in 1836. He was a lieutenant in the army under Hays until '44. He was made captain of the Rangers in '49, I think."

"And now he's a struttin' colonel."

"He's military. Straight back and all. He was commended in the Mexican War by General Joe Lane hisself. For bravery."

"Well, I don't see much to him," Martin said as they walked to the headquarters of the newly founded Cavalry of the West. The horses in the corral were fine, he admitted. Ford had an eye for horseflesh. That was in his favor. But so far, Martin didn't know how well the man judged men. He hadn't met any of the other Rangers and had only seen Ford briefly the day before when he and Oltman had ridden in, dog tired, hungry, covered with dust, their clothes sodden with sweat and their tempers as short as a two-second fuse.

They had buried Darnell and Shepley themselves, and paid the townsfolk in Bandana to bury Cullie and Reynaud. He had hated like hell to put Ken Darnell in the ground. Ken was the last of the Darnell family as far as Martin knew, and he had once dearly loved his sister, Caroline, who had died far too young and whose life had been one of sadness.

"That stallion over there by himself is one of Colonel Ford's favorite mounts," Oltman said. He pointed to a black horse in a separate corral.

"Looks like he's got some Arab in him," Martin said.

"Sixteen hands high, mixed Arabian and purebred, I hear tell. Runs like a deer, that 'un."

"Ford knows his horses, I admit."

The two men walked toward a row of small buildings that were badly weathered and in disrepair. They passed by the old Spanish mission called the Alamo and paused there to reflect for a moment.

"It's hard to imagine," Martin said.

"I know. I get a funny feelin' ever' time I go by here."

"You can almost feel the ghosts."

Oltman nodded, his throat constricted.

"Crockett, Travis, Dickinson, Bowie."

"They sure as hell died with their boots on," Oltman said, his voice scratchy with emotion.

There was a sadness about the old, crumbling building that Martin felt in his heart as he thought about the brave men who had fought off Santa Ana for so long, and had died there, for a cause, for the republic, for Texas. It stood so silent now, like a giant gravestone towering over the field of battle where so many men, on both sides, died, thus giving life to a dream. It was enough to make a grown man cry, he thought, as he fought back the tears threatening to well up in his eyes.

It was hard to imagine what the old crumbling mission had looked like when Santa Ana had attacked it back in '36, but Martin could almost see the defenders standing on the walls, their cannons aimed at the advancing Mexican troops, their rifles primed and pointed, their hearts pounding, their stomachs fluttering with butterflies. The men in the Alamo had known they were going to die and they just wanted to make the cost of their lives as high as they could.

"We better get on over to the barracks," Oltman said, jarring Martin from his reverie. He nodded and took his eyes off the ruins of the old mission. "Rip is a stickler for promptness."

"I think he's a stickler for a lot of things," Martin said.

"You shouldn't judge the colonel just yet, Martin."

"I'm trying real hard, Al."

They passed a number of buildings all joined together, shops that were in sad shape, with their gypsum chipped away by weather, the adobe bricks smoothed from wind and rain, the lettering on their fronts—*cantina, abarrotes, mercado, ropa, cocina*—faded from green and red and yellow paint. There were a lot of buildings sprawled all over San Antonio de Bexar, but still, the place seemed almost like a ghost town, despite the people, the dogs and cats, who roamed the streets like sleepwalkers in no hurry.

"You know, Ford and a man named Neighbors rode from San Antonio to El Paso and mapped it back in '49," Oltman said. "Rip said it was almost like a desert, five hundred miles or so, as bleak and harsh as any land he'd ever traversed."

"Well, Texas can be like that in some places."

"They call it the Ford and Neighbors Trail."

"You don't say." Martin was still looking at the town and the people and wasn't really interested in hearing about Ford and his exploits. He had been sworn in as a Ranger the day before by the colonel, but now he was wondering if he hadn't made a big mistake by listening to Allen Oltman and joining up.

"There's the barracks," Oltman said. "Where the flag's flappin' on that pole."

"I see it. Two flags, though."

"Yeah, that one says '1824' on it and was the one flying over the mission when Santa Ana came here. Top one is the Confederate flag."

"First one I've seen, I reckon."

"It gets my heart to beating real fast."

"I suppose I'll get used to it," Martin said.

They joined the other men milling outside on the parade ground in front of Ford's headquarters. Many were young and looked just as lost and confused as he. Some were older and their faces bore the signs that they had seen much of the harder side of life, men who lived in the saddle and lived by the gun. Martin didn't know any of them, but Oltman spoke to several and then beckoned to one who broke away and walked over to them.

"Jimmy Joe," Oltman said to the man, "shake hands with Martin Baron. Martin, this is Jim Joe Casebolt."

"Welcome to San Antone," Casebolt said to Martin, squeezing his hand with a hard solid grip. "Heard Al talk about you. Sorry I didn't get down to meet you boys, but I had a bunch of hardcases to round up and put in the *juzgado*."

"Casebolt," Martin said, sizing the man up. He was short, stocky, with a chiseled face sporting a handlebar moustache and wide side-burns. His blue eyes were flint-hard and piercing, and his tanned face revealed that he was another of those who spent much of his time in the saddle.

"I saw that you brought in Dan's and Ken's guns and horses," Casebolt said. "We lost two good men there."

"They didn't have a chance," Oltman said. "They were ambushed and gunned down by cowards."

"Heard you took 'em down for good, Al."

"One got away."

"Aguilar? He'll keep. We got more important fish to fry with this war goin' on."

"What's Rip got in mind for us, Jim Joe?"

"I dunno. Got some new blood he wants to blow wind at today and then I reckon he'll put us in training. He don't want the regular army ragging at his heels."

"You mean criticizing him," Al said.

"Oh, they'll do that, all right. The generals don't like us Rangers much."

Oltman nodded.

Martin was getting the feeling that he had joined an outfit that didn't have much support out of Austin. The Rangers, he knew, had made a reputation, though, for fighting Indians and tracking down criminals that was second to none.

There was a commotion beyond the crowd of men and when Martin looked over at the headquarters building, he saw Ford and two other men emerge and stand in front of the assemblage. Ford held some papers in his hand and stood stock-still, looking over all the men with one slow sweeping glance.

"Attention," one of the other men called. "Gather round, gentlemen. Colonel Ford wishes to speak to you."

There was a murmur from the crowd of some sixty or so men and then they grew silent as they formed a semicircle around Ford and his aides.

The colonel was wearing a black frock coat with his insignia on the shoulders. He wore a pistol, too, a big one that Martin thought was possibly a Colt Dragoon. More than a handful for any man, he knew.

Martin walked up close with Casebolt and Oltman to hear what Ford had to say. There was a light breeze blowing that made the flags flap. Hatless, Ford stood there, his hair unruffled, his beard and hair neatly trimmed. He looked every inch the military man.

"Gentlemen," Ford began, "most of you have just been sworn in as Texas Rangers and I have not gotten to know you yet."

He looked down at the paper in his hand and held it up closer to his face.

"You came in response to this notice, which I will read, in part, so that you all know why each man who read it volunteered to become part of the newly formed Cavalry of the West.

" 'Persons who desire to go into service with the Texas Rangers will report to me at San Antonio,' " Ford read, " 'without delay, where they will be subsisted and their horses foraged.' "

Ford paused and smiled. "Well, you reported, and you're being subsisted and your horses are foraging."

There was a ripple of laughter from the men assembled before their commanding officer.

"You are all men of the West," Ford continued, "and you have been invited to turn out and come here. I want you to know you will all be defending your own homes. As I said in my notice to you, shall it be said that a mongrel force of abolitionists, Negroes, plundering Mexicans, and perfidious renegades have been allowed to murder and rob us with impunity? Shall the pages of history record the disgraceful fact that Texans have tamely and basely submitted to these outrages and suffered the terrible brand of dishonor?

"I do not think so, men. You were called here and you came. That alone proves to me that you are good men all, and that you will make Texas proud. I know this, for the honor of the state, for the sake of the glorious memories of the past, the hopes of the future, you are all called upon to rally to the standard and to wash out the stains of invasion by the blood of your goddamned ruthless enemies. Welcome to the Cavalry of the West."

A huge cheer rose up as Ford finished his speech. Men threw hats in the air and one fired off his rifle to add to the jubilation.

Martin felt the excitement and the stirring words still resounded in his ears. He had never read Ford's notice, but if he had, he knew he would have ridden to San Antonio on his own, and now, he was glad he had come.

With his speech, Colonel John S. Ford had risen several notches in Martin's estimation.

"Well, Martin, what do you think?" Oltman asked as the noise subsided and the men waited for orders from their commander.

"I think Colonel Ford has blood in his eye, Al. He's a man I damned sure want to fight for."

Oltman and Casebolt slapped Martin soundly on the back. They both grinned with approval.

"By the gods, Martin," Casebolt said, "I'm damned glad you're one of us. Now come on. Rip wants to give you a commission."

"Huh?"

"That's right, Martin," Oltman said. "Didn't I tell you? You're going to be a lieutenant. Rip likes you."

"Well, I'll be damned," Martin said. "I'll be double damned."

Oltman and Casebolt laughed and they grabbed his arms on either side and started hauling him up to the headquarters building while some men started barking orders and the new recruits started forming up in orderly columns.

Martin looked up at the flags whipping in the wind and he felt a surge of pride. Yes, he thought, he would fight for Texas, and if he could, he would bring honor to his service as a Texas Ranger.

24

MICKEY BONE STARED into the twilight's ashes floating over the far horizon in the dusk sky. He saw more than just another sunset that day, for he truly looked into the fading light and knew he was glimpsing his future. He could feel it in his heart because he had reflected long on the images that had populated his mind ever since he had come back to the Rocking A seeking a home for himself, for his wife and small son.

He sat on the back steps of the Aguilar house, the big house as his wife, Dawn, and the vaqueros called it, a home he had wanted to inhabit now that Matteo was gone. But after staying only one night, Dawn had refused to live in it. She had taken their son and moved back into the little adobe hut where they had lived before Matteo declared war on the Baron rancho and had ordered his men to kill him, Mickey Bone, who had always been loyal to Matteo.

The scent of honeysuckle wafted to Bone's nostrils and as the breeze flowed against his face, he could smell the lespedeza and the clover blooming in the hay fields beyond. He could smell the earth itself and see its dark complexion in the sky, as if the two were connected for a few moments at twilight, a reminder of both his living spirit and his mortality.

Out of the corner of his eye, Bone saw his wife walking toward him. She was not carrying their son, Juan, so he knew the baby was asleep and probably being watched by one of the Mexican women. She seemed in no hurry, but her steps were deliberate. She wore a shawl around her shoulders and was barefoot, her form slender again after giving birth, sensuous, inviting.

"Madrugada," he said, using her Spanish name. "Why do you come here? Where is Juanito?"

"The baby is sleeping. Avril is with him. Why do you sit here all alone outside a house that is not yours, my husband?"

"We should be living here, inside this house."

She stopped and looked up at him, her face in shadow. But he could see her eyes, could feel them scouring his own face, probing, digging, accusing.

"No. This is not our house. It will never be our house."

"It is empty. No one lives here. It is a nice house. It is big."

"It belongs to Matteo and Luz."

"They are gone."

"You chased Luz away. I think she was afraid of you."

"I do not know why she ran away. I would not harm her."

"A woman runs from a man because she is afraid of him."

"That is a silly notion you have, Dawn. She had no reason to be afraid of me."

"Oh? You did not desire her? You did not want her? She is very pretty and her husband was gone."

Bone squirmed inside his skin. She stepped closer to him and he felt skewered on the seething intensity of her gaze. How did she know these things? How did a woman always know when a man desired another woman?

"Her husband is dead. Maybe that is why she ran away," he said.

"No, that is not why. You came into her house. You wanted her and she had fear, Miguel."

"Do not accuse me of something I did not do, my precious."

"I want you to come home. I do not want you to sit at this house and dream of being inside it. I do not like this house. I will not live in it. Ever."

He stood up and walked down the steps. He touched her and her body stiffened. The sky had turned dark all of a sudden and she was a shadow next to him, a shadow with eyes that glittered strangely, even so.

"Do not push me away, Dawn."

"Come with me to our house. I wish to talk to you about staying here in this place."

"I was promised a home here. For as long as I lived."

"Matteo has two faces. He does not want you here."

"The Rangers took him away. They will hang him for what he has done to Martin Baron."

"Maybe Matteo will die," she said. "Maybe he is dead already. But we do not belong here. I do not like this place. We are not wanted here."

She turned away from him and started walking back the way she had come, toward their small adobe dwelling that stood with the adobes of the vaqueros. He followed her, then caught up to her. He tried to put an arm around her waist, but she twisted away and pulled the shawl up over her head as if to hide from him.

The frogs began their crepuscular throat booms and the crickets struck up their orchestras around the pond as bullbats sliced through the air on silent wings, flashing their silver-dollar-sized markings as they dove and pirouetted on the track of mosquitoes.

"You are cold, Dawn," Bone said as they reached their home. "You accuse me of bad things, without proof."

She wheeled on her husband before she reached out to push open the door. Yellow lamplight flickered around the sacks covering the open windows from inside and now he could see her eyes flashing like ebony agates.

"Proof, Mickey? Did you think that you could keep it secret that you tried to put a fuck into Luz? Ha, everyone on this rancho knows it."

He stepped back, as if blown by a stormwind emanating from his wife.

"I do not know what you have heard—" he began, holding up both hands, palms out, in a sign of innocence.

"I talked to Fidel. Luz told him that you were going to put the fuck in her and that is why she ran away."

"Fidel? Fidel Rios?"

"Yes."

"I do not know of this. But he does not speak the truth. He is a liar."

"Did you know that Fidel helped Luz to run away from you and your big fat cock?"

Bone shook his head.

"Ha. Well, he did take her away because she begged him to help her escape from you."

"That is a lie, my precious."

"Do not say 'precious' to me, Mickey Bone, you filth. Fidel does not lie."

"Where did he take Luz?"

"Far away. She is going back to her people until her husband comes home. When she tells Matteo what you tried to do, he will kill you."

"Matteo is not coming back," he said, his voice weak, just above a rasping whisper.

"Go away," Dawn said. "I do not want you in my house. Go spill your seed somewhere else."

"What?"

She held up a tightly clenched fist as if to strike him.

"I do not want to see your ugly face, Mickey. I do not want to sleep with you. I am hurt that you would try to put the fuck into Luz."

"Where will I go?" he asked. "This is my home."

"Go after Luz. Go to Mexico. Go to the mountains. Just you go."

"No. I will not go."

"If you come inside, then you will not have to wait for Matteo to kill you. I will kill you."

Bone knew that Dawn meant it, too. He knew the fire of her temper and the scorch of her wrath. When her blood ran hot, he always tried to get away from her. She would throw lethal things at him or try to stab him with a knife or a pair of scissors. She threw pots and pans with amazing force and speed. She might kill him in his sleep, or cut off his manhood. She had threatened to do that before, and once, he had awakened to see her sitting on the bed next to him, a pair of scissors in her hand.

"I will go to the big house," he said.

Dawn's eyes narrowed and flashed as they reopened.

"If you do, you can never come back here. I will take Juan and go back to my people."

"Your people are all dead, just as mine are all dead, Madrugada."

"I will go to the Mescalero people. They do not lie as you do."

"I will not go to the big house, then," he said. "I will sleep on the ground."

"Will you not admit that you tried to put the fuck into Luz? Will you not beg for my forgiveness?"

Bone felt the rage rise up in him as he stared at the small woman who had suddenly become a stranger. His heart began to pound so loud he could hear it in his eardrums. His neck swelled and the veins stood out like blue worms.

"You *puerca*," he snarled, and as Dawn started to step back, Bone balled up his fists and lashed out with his right hand. He caught her on the jaw and Dawn's head snapped to one side. She staggered under the force of the blow. She screamed and brought her hands up to her face. Bone waded into her and snatched her hair up close to the scalp. He twisted the locks until her head turned back around. Then he slapped her hard across the mouth. Blood oozed from her smashed lips and she screamed again.

The door burst open behind her and Avril stood there, her eyes wide, her face contorted in horror. She was a young Mexican girl, no more than fourteen, with long raven hair, big brown eyes, and high cheekbones. Her face darkened as blood rushed to her skin. She screamed and took a step backward.

Bone shoved Dawn through the open door and into the adobe. She kept screaming and he slapped her hard across the face, again and again, until blood spurted from her nose. Avril tried to pull him away and Bone drove a fist straight into her mouth, squashing it like a ripe tomato. Avril whimpered in pain and crumpled up, dropping to the floor as if she had been poleaxed.

"Bitch," Bone snarled, and jerked Dawn around so hard that he heard a bone in her arm snap like a dry twig. Dawn screamed and cursed in Spanish, English, and Apache, but Bone was impervious to her invective and drove his fists into her again and again, boxing her ears and smashing the veins in her cheeks.

In another room, baby Juan woke up and began to cry. Avril tried to get up and Bone kicked her in the side, knocking her back down. Dawn tried to slip free of Bone's grip, her arm dangling like something on a broken hinge, and he jerked the arm until she folded up and fell to her knees.

Bone kicked her hard in the face and blood spurted from her forehead where he had broken the skin. She collapsed in a heap, moaned once, and then was still. Bone drove a moccasined foot into her rump, but there was no response. Then he turned on Avril and kicked her in the back as she groaned and squirmed to escape the blows. Finally, Bone began to wreck the furniture, staggering through the front room and into the next until he came to his son lying in his crib. The infant was bawling loudly, tears streaming down his cheeks.

Bone snatched up Juan by both feet and dragged him, screaming, into the front room. Dawn heard the baby crying and roused herself. She tried to sit up. She tried to stretch her arms out to grab Juan. As she looked on, Bone swung the boy up over his head and then dashed him down to the dirt floor. The boy's head made a whumping sound as it struck the ground and blood spurted from his ears and nose and mouth.

Dawn screamed and Bone threw the lifeless body of their son at her, striking her in the chest.

The baby had stopped screaming and its little body just quivered. It made a soft sound in its throat and then turned limp in Dawn's arms. She bent down and kissed the dead child on the cheek.

"Now, see what your mouth has done, Madrugada," Bone spat.

Bone walked over to a peg on the wall and took down his gun belt and strapped it on. His eyes blazed with the fury that was raging inside him.

A silence filled the room as Dawn slowly rocked back and forth, her broken arm dangling, her other one holding on to her dead child.

Bone took one last look at her and then walked out into the night. He turned toward the casita of Fidel Rios, Matteo's former house, his heart still pumping, his rage still growing. Clouds scudded over the moon and the night turned even darker than it had been. Somewhere in the distance a coyote yapped and the air was empty of bullbats, as if all life had vanished. Then, all he heard was the crunch of his feet on the earth and the terrible pounding of his heart sounding like an Apache war drum he had heard long ago, when he lived in a different time, in a different world.

25

R OY KILLIAN LOOKED at the row of tents standing between the orchard and the new house he was constructing.

"It's beginning to look like a little town here, Ken," he said.

"A town composed of the old and feeble. But they all wanted work and the Confederate Army won't take them."

"They've been a big help."

"House is looking good, Roy."

"It won't take as long as I thought. Forrest's plans are good, and as long as you bring the lumber and nails we need, we can finish in jig time."

"I'll take the wagons in tomorrow, bring back what you need tomorrow night."

"Forrest give you the list?"

"He did. He's very efficient. By the way, where is he?"

"He went on back to our tent. Him and Socrates and Pluto. The Three Musketeers."

Ken Richman laughed. "More like the Three Mosquiters," he joked.

"They get along, all right."

"Socks is fascinated with Mr. Redmond, I think. And Pluto worships him."

"Why?"

"I don't know. Because Forrest talks to them. You know. Not like the others from town do."

"Oh, I know what you mean, I think. We have some bitter people in town. Bitter about the war, bitter about the slavery issue. Bitter about states' rights."

"Well, they're old men and I guess they're entitled to their opinions."

The two walked away from the house, which was almost all framed and some parts already boarded. Some of the tents glowed with freshly lit lanterns and they could smell cooking at some of the campfires.

"This place reeks of death," Richman said. "So much blood spilled here."

"I know," Killian said. "It gives a man pause sometimes."

"Maybe that's why Martin lit out and joined the Rangers."

"I don't think death bothers either of the Barons much, Ken. They're pretty used to it by now, what with Apaches and that fight with Aguilar."

"I could never get used to it. You were in that last fracas with Aguilar. Doesn't it make you sick?"

"None of it was pretty. I don't think of it much."

"No, it's not a good thing to think about."

"You want to eat some grub with us, Ken?"

"I can. You have plenty of food to last until I get back tomorrow night?"

"Plenty. The old men don't eat a hell of a lot and they all like beans."

Both men laughed.

They walked to the trough and washed their hands, then strolled over to the cookfire outside Killian's tent. Socrates and Pluto had the pots boiling and the beef cooking, the beans sending up their own aromas in the steam. There was a table set up, one Roy and Forrest had built out of scrap lumber.

"You gonna eat supper with us, Mr. Richman?" Socrates asked, as he stirred one of the pots with a wooden stick that had been whittled to resemble a large spoon.

"Yes, Socks. Smells good. Say, where's Forrest?"

"Oh, he inside the tent, Mr. Richman. He studyin' like he always do."

"He readin' that old rock," Pluto said, a big grin cracking his face. "Mr. Redmond, he plenty smart."

Richman turned to Roy. "What old rock is he talking about?"

"Oh, it was something Mickey Bone had. It's got some scratchings on it from ancient times, Forrest says. He's been puzzlin' over it near ever' night."

"Hmm," Richman said, then walked up to the large square tent and ducked down, stepped inside.

Redmond was sitting on a blanket under a lantern hanging from a small tripod set up in one corner. He had some books open and spread around him and held a flat stone in his lap. He was looking at the markings on it with a magnifying glass. He didn't look up when Richman entered.

Ken walked over and sat down. That's when Forrest looked up.

"Oh, Ken. Didn't see you come in," Forrest said.

Richman sat on an empty nail keg and looked down at the open books and the stone. One of the books was a notebook and bore Redmond's scrawled notes, which were incomprehensible to Richman.

"What have you got there, Forrest?"

Before Redmond could answer, Roy Killian entered the tent. His face was still wet from washing it at the trough and he was drying the palms of his hands on his trousers. He nodded to Redmond and sat down on his pallet. He began to dry his face by wiping his shirtsleeve across it.

"You two go on and talk, Ken. I'll just listen."

"I was asking Forrest about what he was doing. Looks mighty interesting."

"These markings on this chunk of rock are similar to some I've seen before. Do you know what cuneiform is, Ken?"

"Nope."

"It was a form of writing used many thousands of years ago by the Sumerians."

"Never heard of them."

"They lived in Sumer, where the first civilization on earth was founded."

"How do you know all this?"

Forrest smiled. "I've been studying languages and history for years. All my life."

"How come? What good is it to learn a language that nobody talks anymore?"

"Well, nobody's been able to figure out what all those cuneiform signs mean, but I think I've learned some of the language just from studying the pictures. Nobody speaks the language, but you might find out how people lived five thousand or more years ago."

While Forrest was talking in his soft voice, Pluto and Socrates both entered the tent and sat down. They made no noise, as if they were entering a chapel. They looked at Redmond with rapt expressions on their faces. Killian, too, seemed fascinated by what his new-found friend Forrest was saying.

"This cuneiform," Richman said, "is like an alphabet?"

"I think so. At least some of it, from what I've been able to decipher. I think some of the signs, which are like pictures done with wedges and lines scratched into soft clay with a kind of pencil, a stylus they call it, are drawings of ordinary things, like trees, birds, sky, water, but I also think that some of the wedges have been combined into words."

"But you can't read the words."

"I think I can read some of them. I think maybe I, or someone, will one day figure out the language, just as was done with Egyptian hieroglyphics."

"Hiero what?"

Forrest laughed. "Hieroglyphics, a written language the Egyptians used. Scholars are still wrestling with that, but they've made great progress. I think I may be able to do the same with Sumerian. I brought back several clay tablets I dug up in Persia."

"You were in Persia?"

"And Egypt, Syria. I was part of an archaeological team digging up ancient sites, picking up relics, bones, and the like."

Richman let out a low whistle of wonderment.

"Forrest has a bunch of fascinating stories," Killian said.

"What have you learned from that chunk of rock so far?" Richman asked.

Forrest looked down at it and then leaned over, displaying it in
his hands.

"I saw markings, pictographs, like these in the Tigris-Euphrates
valley where the Sumerians once lived. And there appears to be
some cuneiform signs on them. One, I've translated as man. Another as god."

Pluto and Socrates leaned closer to hear what Redmond had to say.

"Oh?" Ken's eyebrows elevated and arched like a pair of aroused
caterpillars.

"And there are symbols on here that I recognize from other arti-
facts we found in Persia. Like planets and the sun. But there are too
many of them, so right now it doesn't make much sense."

"Too many what?"

"Too many planets. For our solar system. The old pictures show
twelve and we have only ten."

"What do you make of that?"

"I don't know. It's just one of the puzzles I'm working on. I hope
to publish a paper on my findings one day."

"I wish you luck," Richman said.

Redmond grinned and drew the rock back into his lap. He closed
all of his books and his notebook and put them all, along with the
stone, back in his knapsack. Pluto and Socrates looked disappointed.

"Thanks, Ken," Redmond said. "I've got a long way to go."

Killian looked at Socks and Pluto. "How's the grub doing?"

Both men's faces lit up with surprise and they rose. "We ready to
eat," Pluto said.

"If you didn't burn everything to a crisp," Killian said, grinning.
"Come on, Ken and Forrest. Let's get us some grub before it's
plumb dark."

The sun was setting when the three men emerged from the tent.
Already, some of the old men had hung lanterns from tripods outside their tents and were sitting down to supper.

This was the time of day Roy liked best, although it was also a
time when he sometimes wished he was back home with Wanda,
even if her mother was there, barking orders, dispensing advice, and
urging him to do one thing or another. But the work was done for

the day and his muscles were sore and that made him feel good at the end of a day.

Pluto handed out pewter plates and forks while Socrates ladled the stew and poured coffee into their cups. Pluto served shortening bread after the others had all sat down and were starting to eat.

"You make this, Pluto?" Killian asked.

"Yes, sir, I makes it just like my mama done."

"Well, it's good."

"Yes, sir, I knows it's good."

When they were finishing their supper, Pluto looked at Redmond and began trying to form words with his lips. Finally, he was able to say what had evidently been on his mind all during the meal.

"Mr. Redmond, can you tell us again about that big stone they done found in Egypt land? The Rosey stone?"

Forrest laughed. "The Rosetta stone, you mean."

"Yes, sir, that's the one."

"Well, I think it was one of Napoleon's lieutenants who found the stone. It was broken, but there was enough writing on it to tell us that it was written in two languages, but in two different scripts. One language was Egyptian and the other Greek."

"Never heard of it," Ken said.

"Well," Forrest said, "it's true. I've seen the stone myself. It's in the British Museum in London."

"Boy, you been everywhere," Roy said.

"What was the other script?" Richman asked.

Pluto and Socrates were hanging on every word.

"The scripts were hieroglyphic, demotic, and Greek," Forrest said. "People back then could read Greek and some scholars could read demotic, an older form of that language. But nobody could read hieroglyphics, which were symbols of birds and ships and pyramids and gods. For years nobody could decipher the hieroglyphics. Until one man started fiddling with the demotic script and started looking for likely words in the same places as the Greek and the demotic."

"And that did it?" Richman asked.

"Pretty much. Oh, it took a long time to decipher and we probably don't know all that we could know about the Egyptian language, but scholars continue to pore over that stuff."

"So you have a knack for languages," Richman said.

Forrest blushed slightly and dipped his head.

"I really liked history, but learned that knowing languages was the best way to get at history. If we could figure out all the languages, we would know how people lived, what they thought, and how they managed their livelihoods. I guess I like to study old languages and try to figure out what the words mean."

Ken grunted and got up. Pluto took his plate and fork. "Well, I've had enough history for one night, Forrest."

Roy got up too and handed his plate and fork to Pluto. "Me, too," Roy said. "Pluto, maybe you better go to school before you get too old if you want to learn all this stuff."

"Yes, sir, I surely would like to go to school someday," Pluto said with a shy grin.

"Well, maybe you will," Roy said. "Thank you, Mr. Redmond. For telling us about that Rosey stone again."

"Maybe I'll draw you a picture of it sometime, Pluto," Forrest said, rising from the ground and handing him his plate with the fork on it.

Roy shook his head and walked away to relieve himself.

"I'm going to turn in," Ken said. "I'll see you in the morning before I leave, Roy. You let me know what you need from town."

"Yeah. I will."

Forrest lifted a hand in farewell as Ken walked down to his tent. Then he went back inside his and Roy's tent. Pluto and Socrates began to talk in low tones to each other.

Roy looked out at the land beyond the orchard. He could see the dim shapes of cattle grazing, their backs lit by the moon that had risen during supper. The sky was filled with winking stars and all seemed in order.

But the night sky gave him no comfort. That talk about ancient peoples and old civilizations had stirred up something in him. He wished now that Bone had not given him that stone and that he had not given it to Forrest. He did not like to think of people who had once populated the earth and had since vanished. It made civilization seem so fragile, to know these things had happened. From what he had heard, Bone's tribe no longer existed, and even the tribe of his wife had been extinguished. And now, this war between the North and South, this terrible war between kinfolk. What would happen to all of them now living?

Would he, too, and all of those he cared about, simply die out in wars or famine, then maybe someone like Forrest, hundreds or thousands of years from now, would come across his bones and wonder who he was, who he had been? When he looked up at the stars now, he knew they had been there a long time, longer than any tribe or people on earth. He knew too that he was looking into the past, into darkness, and only the stars remained, blinking, watching, while foolish men wiped each other out and left others to come along and try and figure out what had happened.

He walked farther away from the glowing tent walls and out into the empty field where it was even darker, and he wondered about Wanda and Hattie, wondered what they were doing, what the Mexicans who had run away from the Box B were doing now that they had found another home. And what of those remnants of Aguilar's men who had carted the bodies of their dead back to the Rocking A? What were they doing this night? Were they wondering, like he, if any of their tribe would outlive this war and future wars?

Probably not. He wouldn't be thinking of such things, either, if Forrest hadn't started talking about that damned chunk of rock again, that stone with the strange markings on it that made no sense. But someone, long ago, had taken a piece of flint, or a knife, and carved out a message on that stone, had made a record so someone someday would know they had been here, had lived here on this same patch of earth, and then had died, every one of them, leaving nothing behind but a homely piece of rock with some unknown scribblings on it to show that they had once existed, had once breathed the same air and looked up at the same stars and the same wise old moon.

He and Forrest were building a house where another once had stood. Was this what civilization was about? Roy wondered. Something is burned down, you rebuild it. A tribe is killed off. You replace that tribe with others who know nothing of the trials and tribulations of the previous inhabitants. Just as no one would know that the new house was standing atop the ashes of the old house.

It all seemed so purposeless just then. How long would this new house last? What if a gaggle of Union troops rode up and burned this one to the ground?

Roy felt the anger rising in him, but he knew it was more than that. It was a sense of futility, too. He felt so small at that moment, so insignificant under the majestic canopy of stars that he knew to be millions of miles away. Was anything decent or permanent within mankind's reach? Not the stars, certainly. Not the planets. Not even the relatively close moon. All was futile. And senseless.

What was the sense in getting married and raising a family if, one by one, all of his seed would one day be wiped out, would vanish, and only disease and death awaited him and his loved ones? Anson's mother, Caroline. Dead. His own father, Jack. Dead. And what of them remained? All that was Caroline had been in that house that Matteo Aguilar had burned to the ground. All that had been his father were his worn-out boots, a pistol, and gun belt, and even these would one day disintegrate and be no more.

"Shit," Roy cried out, and his voice died in the night. He turned to see if anyone had heard him, and he was ashamed for his outburst. Then he saw a lone figure walking toward him. He could not make out who it was.

"Are you all right, Mr. Killian?"

Socrates. His deep resonant voice. His African voice, so fitting out there in the darkness under a sky that might have been African as well as Texan.

"Yes, Socks. What are you doing out here?"

"I was worried about you, sir."

"No need to worry about me."

"No sir, I reckon not. But I worries just the same."

"You're a good man, Socrates. Don't you miss your home?"

"My home, sir?"

"Africa. Wherever you're from."

"No, sir. I don't remember it much. And home is where I's at, I reckon. This place be home to me now."

"I guess I'm feeling the same way right now."

"But you has a home, sir. You can just ride on over to your ranch and be right there at home with your lady."

"I hope you have a place of your own someday, Socks. And a family."

Socrates laughed. His grin flashed white in the darkness. Even when the grin vanished the afterimage seemed to remain, like the smile of a jack-o'-lantern.

"Yes, sir, I hopes so, too."

"Let's get on back, Socks. Thanks for walking out to check on me."

"It was no trouble, sir."

As they walked back, Roy was silent, still thinking those dark thoughts, made even darker as he thought about Socrates, once a slave and now a person whose race might be dying out, a man with no family, no roots, no perceptible future.

"Shit," Roy muttered under his breath.

"Sir?"

"Nothing, Socks," Roy said. "Nothing at all."

And the night followed him into the tent and lay down with him on his pallet. He let the darkness close over him and wipe out his black thoughts. But an afterimage remained for a long time, a piece of white cloth with writings and pictures on it that he could not decipher in his dreams and would not remember when he awakened.

26

——■——

ED WALES WAS surprised that the door to Doc Purvis's home and office was latched and barred so that he could not just walk inside, as usual. He knocked, softly at first, then more loudly, until he heard footsteps on the hardwood flooring. The door opened and Lorene Sisler stood there, her face drawn and blanched, the sleeves of her blouse rolled up to her elbows, and her apron soiled and stained, reeking with the acrid smell of alcohol and some kind of liniment.

"Ed," she said. "My uncle's busy. Can you come back later?"

"I'm sick, Lorene. Sick as a dog."

"The doctor can't see you now," she said, her voice tight and crisp, delivered at a level just short of rudeness.

"Will he be long? I saw the wagon come up a while ago, that one parked outside. I didn't see who was in it."

"Is it your stomach again, Ed?"

"Yes, but I've got a lot of pain. Like a knife in my side. I can hardly stand up straight."

It was true. Wales was bent forward as if favoring his side. His face was scraggly with beard, unshaven for at least three days. Jutting out of a pocket of his rumpled suit coat was a copy of the *Bugle*. His blue eyes were bloodshot and his cheeks flared with a crimson glow as if he were running a high fever. Lorene reached out and touched his forehead with her fingers, then she placed her palm on one cheek.

"Well, come in, then," she said. "You can sit in the anteroom with the others. Dr. Purvis will see you when he's finished, I suppose."

Wales followed Lorene into the outer parlor where she showed him to a seat along the wall. There was a young Mexican woman, or girl, sitting in a corner. Her face was swollen and one eye closed and puffy. Also, sitting near the girl was a young Mexican man who appeared to be uninjured. The room was sparsely appointed. A small ficus tree stood in a pot against one wall. The doctor's certificate in a modest frame adorned another. There was a table littered with pamphlets in front of the divan. A sign proclaimed "All Physician's Fees Payable in Advance," which Wales knew to be laughable. Some people who sought the doctor's help could not pay anything at all, in advance or otherwise.

Lorene disappeared as Wales sat there, holding his side. The flesh of his face had a faint yellowish cast to it. In the low light of the room, his visage appeared ghastly and the young Mexican man, after looking at him once, averted his eyes.

"What happened to you, miss?" Wales asked the young woman.

"*Yo no hablo inglés,*" she said. "*Un poquito, nada mas.*"

She replied in Spanish that she did not speak English. A moment later, she stiffened.

They all heard a scream from the doctor's office in the back. A woman's scream that rose up the scale and ended in a screech. Wales knew that had been a scream of pain. Severe pain. He looked at the young woman and saw her eyes widen and her lower lip tremble and quiver. The Mexican man crossed himself very quickly and looked up at the ceiling.

She began speaking rapidly to the young man in Spanish. Wales could not follow any of it. When they were finished, he turned his attention to the Mexican youth.

"Where are you from?" Wales asked the young man in Spanish.

"We are from a rancho," the Mexican replied. He also spoke in his native tongue.

"Which rancho?"

"From the rancho of Matteo Miguelito Aguilar."

"Ah. Then you are far from home. Is that your sister who is with Dr. Purvis?"

The young man shook his head. The girl was listening intently to the sounds from the back room, wringing her hands as if she was washing them without any water. Her eyes were still wide open and she looked very frightened.

"No, it is the wife of another man."

Wales winced as a sharp pain shot through his side. He grimaced, then moved his feet, which were also hurting him. He stretched out both legs and looked down at the shoes he wore. They were not laced up tightly because his feet and ankles were swollen. His entire body appeared bloated, which, in fact, it was, much to his discomfort and chagrin.

He had lost weight, he knew, but he also knew that it didn't show because of the bloating. And he knew why he was in this condition. Doc Purvis had warned him that he had to stop drinking. "Stop consuming liquor, or any alcohol," Purvis had said. "It's poison for you. Your liver can't handle the poison."

And he had tried to stop drinking, but the pressure of the war, the writing he did for the newspaper, the long hours, all worked on him so that he had to have some relief, some way to sleep, to relax. But he knew the drinking had gotten out of control, and now he was so sick, he wanted to die. But he didn't really want to die. Not this way. Not now.

He heard more muffled screams from the doctor's examining room and noises that sounded like someone thrashing around. He heard Lorene's voice rising above the din as she tried to calm the patient.

The young woman's eyes grew even wider and she turned to the Mexican man and spoke to him in a stream of Spanish. Then she got up and started running toward the door that led outside. The man leaped to his feet and grabbed her, tried to pull her back away from the door. He turned toward Wales and pleaded for help with his eyes.

Wales got up, but the pain in his legs slowed him down. It felt as if he was walking on his eyeballs. Still, he managed to reach the girl and help lead her back to her chair. She was obviously frightened and on the verge of hysteria.

"*Calmate, calmate,*" the young man said in a soothing voice. "*Esperate.*"

Up close, Wales could see the deep bruises on the young woman's face and on her arms, the blackish-blue splotches on her flesh. Looking at her almost made him forget his own pain.

He walked slowly and gingerly back to his chair and sat down, exhausted from the effort of helping the young woman. His stomach churned and swirled with gases and he had to fight to keep from vomiting.

More thrashing from the examining room. More muffled cries but they were softer now, and it sounded as if the patient was pleading with the doctor. He could not hear Lorene or Doc Purvis, but he knew they must be saying something to calm the woman down.

Wales was curious about the patient in the back and the two people in the anteroom. But his Spanish was limited to only a few words and he hadn't the strength to question the young man further.

Just then, the door to the anteroom burst open and Lorene rushed in. She looked, Ed thought, terrified, or at the very least, agitated. Her face was drained of color and her eyes were owlishly large as she rushed over to the young man.

"Jorge, come with me. Quick."

Then she looked at the girl, who bore that same frightened look on her face.

"You can come, too," Lorene said, beckoning to the young woman. "Hurry."

Wales opened his mouth to speak, but before any words could come out, Lorene and the two Mexicans were gone, leaving the door to the examining rooms wide open. He sat there for a moment, his own pain forgotten for a few seconds. He heard voices and then crying, presumably from the young woman.

Wales stood up and limped over to the doorway.

"Pray for her," Wales heard Doc Purvis say. "I may lose her."

He heard the young man repeat the supplication in Spanish. Then he heard the girl praying to the Virgin Mary. The young man was murmuring a prayer, as well.

Wales walked through the door and down the hallway. He came

to the room where Purvis and the others were and slipped inside. He leaned against the wall, his forehead sleek with sweat from the effort.

On a table lay a young woman who appeared to be struggling for breath. One of her arms was encased in plaster of Paris. She was nearly naked and there were ugly bruises all over her body where the flesh showed.

Purvis stood by the injured woman's side, holding one wrist. He wore a stethoscope and, with the other hand, was holding one end in the center of the woman's chest.

"Her heart is still beating," Purvis said to Lorene. "But her pulse is very weak."

"What should I do?" Lorene asked.

"Just do what they're doing. Pray."

All at the table were intent on the injured woman's condition and none looked up as Wales watched from a place just inside the door. Lamps blazed against a mirror, which reflected light onto the woman atop the table. The room reeked of disinfectant and salve and a host of other medicants. There was a bureau with trays atop it, a porcelain pitcher and bowl on a table where also lay several instruments, scissors, bandages, gauze, and bottles filled with dark fluids. The room was warm and Wales began to sweat even more profusely until perspiration ran down from his sideburns and streaked his face.

The young woman was sobbing and the young man looked grim. His lips moved as if he was praying and he bore a worried look on his face. Lorene was massaging the bandaged woman's left arm, rubbing it up and down as if urging the blood to circulate through her veins. The injured woman's eyes were closed and her face was more badly battered than that of the young woman who stood by her side, praying.

Soiled towels lay strewn on the floor around the table and Wales noticed a bundle over on a corner table that appeared to be a blanket soaked in blood, a blanket wrapped around something that he could not see.

"Her pulse is weakening further," Purvis said. "Her heartbeat is slowing down."

"Oh, dear," Lorene said, and continued to massage the woman's arm.

Finally, Purvis removed the bell of the stethoscope from the woman's chest and let the cord dangle as he stepped back away from the table. He leaned down and put his ear close to the woman's mouth. He then pushed a finger into her mouth and opened it. Wales heard the woman make a rattling sound in her throat. And then she expelled a breath and did not draw in another one.

"She's gone, Lorene," Purvis said, a solemn tone to his voice. "I fear she's bled internally to the point of extinction."

"You did everything you could, Uncle Pat."

"Only God could have done more," he said, with finality.

Then Purvis looked up and saw Wales.

"Ed, what in hell are you doing in here?"

"I heard the commotion and I walked in. Who's the patient?"

Purvis walked over to Wales, looked at him closely and shook his head in exasperation.

"You don't look long for this world yourself, Ed."

"I'm feeling poorly, Doc."

"Well, as you can plainly see, we've got our hands full here. You'll have to wait before I can talk to you."

"What happened to these women, Doc? I am a reporter, you know."

"Do we have a constable in Baronsville?" Purvis asked.

"Yes. Sort of. Roberto San Juan is acting constable. The one we had up and volunteered for the Second Texas and is off to war."

"When we get finished, you send the constable by here, Ed. I want to prefer charges against the man who injured that young woman there and murdered the one on my table."

"Do you know who the man was?"

"Yes, I believe so. Both the young woman and the man said they were beaten by someone named Mickey Bone."

"Christ," Wales said.

"Do you know the man?"

"I've seen him. Heard about him. A Yaqui Indian, I think."

"Well, that's his wife who just expired. And the young woman was her companion or something. Her name is Avril Conseco."

"And who is the young man?"

"His name is Jorge Rios. This man, this Indian savage, Bone, shot his brother to death. I guess Bone went on a rampage down at the Rocking A Ranch."

"Christ Almighty."

"I hope to hell that's a prayer, Ed. Now, excuse me while I tend to business."

Avril wailed as she realized that Dawn was dead. She threw her upper body over the dead woman and wept, tore at her hair. Jorge stepped back, a look of confusion on his face. He swore in Spanish, and Wales understood what he was saying when he called Bone a bastard.

Lorene put her arms around Avril and drew her up and away from Dawn's body. Purvis pulled a sheet over Dawn and covered her entire body and her face. Avril wept more loudly as Lorene led her from the room, not even glancing at Wales.

"Jorge," Purvis said, "take these powders for Avril. Mix a small spoonful in water and make her drink it. Every four or five hours. Do you understand?"

Jorge nodded.

"You go now. Take care of Avril. You can both put up at the hotel. I'll take care of it. Understand?"

"Yes. The hotel. We will stay."

Jorge left the room. Purvis heaved a heavy sigh and motioned Wales to a stool beside one of the cabinets. He pulled a chair away from the wall and sat in it.

"I feel stupid," Ed said. "Coming here with my little problems when you've been up to your armpits in this mess."

"You are stupid, Ed. Because there's nothing I can do for you. You're dying. Whiskey is your poison. Look at your skin, it's as yellow as a banana."

"I—I've tried, Doc, really."

"Unless you never take another drink, I don't give you two more weeks to live. Your liver can't handle the poison anymore. I imagine it looks like a sieve about now."

"Isn't there anything you can give me? I hurt all over. My feet and ankles are swollen and I'm real sick to my stomach."

"You've got to get that poison out of your system. Just drink a lot of water and pee a lot. Water, Ed. Just water. I can give you something for the pain, but you've got to get through this by yourself. You're beyond medical help. Stay away from the liquor. Period."

Wales nodded. "I'll try."

"No, you have to quit. Right now. Forever. When you start feeling better, if you ever do, you'll want another drink of that poison. If you take even one swallow, you're a dead man. I can't put it any plainer than that, Ed."

"I appreciate your honesty, Doc. I'll quit. I swear."

Purvis rose from his chair and walked over to a cabinet. He opened a drawer and pulled out some pills. He shook some out into the palm of his hand, then put them in a small envelope. He gave the envelope to Wales. "One of these every six hours for the pain. Come see me tomorrow, if you want, but it's going to take three or four days, maybe a week, for you to get that edema down, that swelling. You've got jaundice and that means your liver is not doing its job. You're at death's doorway, Ed."

Wales took the envelope and stuck it in the inside pocket of his suit coat.

"What's in that bundle over on that corner table, Doc?"

Purvis turned around and looked at the bloody blanket. He beckoned to Ed and the two walked over to it.

"Brace yourself," Purvis said.

He picked up the folded blanket and unwrapped it with delicate hands. Then he set it back down and pulled away the last fold.

Wales stared down at the young boy, naked, stiff, his head smashed in, blood smeared all over his crumpled face and chest, his lips black, his eyes closed.

"Jesus Christ," Wales said. "Who?"

"That's Mr. Bone's little boy. He picked him up by his feet and dashed his head to the ground, crushing the skull."

Wales doubled over then, and began to vomit on the floor.

Purvis wrapped little Juan back up in the blanket. He went over to the bureau and poured a glass of water, then took it to Wales.

"When you finish puking, Ed, drink this water. Then get the hell out and send that constable over here."

Wales nodded dumbly as tears flooded his eyes.

When he stood up, the room spun around. He reached out one

arm as if to balance himself. Purvis didn't come to his assistance, but turned on his heel and left the room.

Wales took in a deep breath and lifted the glass of water to his lips. But he couldn't drink. He was all alone in the room and the room smelled of death.

It was enough, he thought, to make a man swear off drinking— for life.

27

THERE WERE TIMES when Anson wanted to give up and just trust to luck and Providence. The tracking was hard, but after two days, he began to make sense of the Apache spoor. He'd had a strong hunch that he should follow Culebra's tracks, and now he was certain that he had been right. But that didn't take away the ominous feeling that he was venturing into their world, a place where it was dangerous, and might prove fatal. And perhaps, he thought, Culebra wanted him to do this, to follow him to some destination where Anson and Peebo would be fair game.

"I still don't know why we're follerin' these damned tracks," Peebo said, on the third day after they left the creek that first night.

His shirt, like Anson's, was soaked with sweat and the air was so hot it was like breathing from an open furnace. The horses, also, were sleek with sweat and they could not travel fast. The tracks were at least two days old and led through a bewildering maze of mesquite and cactus and brush. But the Apaches knew the land better than they, and they always found water and forage for their mounts.

"Because that bastard Culebra is going where we're going, Peebo. Can't you see it?"

"For the past two days, I been thinkin' we're just lookin' for trouble. Hellfire, Anson, you can't see fifty yards in front of us and my stomach's in knots thinkin' there's a passel of Apaches just waitin' to jump all over us, them all hidin' up in the next clump of damned mesquite."

"That could be. But if we don't follow Culebra, he'd still be waiting for us somewhere up ahead and we wouldn't know where."

"You think that?"

"I do. Now. Can't you see it?"

"See what? Hardest tracks to foller I ever seen, and they don't seem to be goin' anyplace but far away."

"I think good ol' Culebra's stalkin' that white bull same as us."

"Huh? What I hear is them Injuns and the Mexicans are scared shitless of Diablo Blanco. 'N, come to think on it, I don't exactly cotton to that big-ass bull myself."

"You better keep your eyes open, Peebo. 'Stead of sawing wood all day in the saddle."

"Who in hell can sleep in this godawful heat? Not me, son."

"Those Apaches are trackin' wild cattle, same as us, and they're not vaqueros," Anson said. "They know where we're goin', sure as hell."

"They might know where you're goin', son, but I sure as hell don't. Seems to me we been wanderin' around in a maze the past couple of days."

Anson snorted. "Sometimes, Peebo, you're a real pain in the ass."

"And you, your royal highness, are always a pleasure on these long rides through Apache country."

Anson laughed despite himself, and was rewarded with Peebo's flashing grin. It would be many hours before either man laughed again or Peebo's face broke open in a grin.

They began to see wild cattle, bunches of them with great long horns, that eyed them with suspicion before fading into the trees and brush. Most were too far away to bring down with a rifle shot, but even the closer ones were as skittish as deer.

The Apache tracks led them ever southward, paralleling the Gulf Coast. Anson and Peebo passed the place where they had last seen the huge white bull and Anson noticed that Culebra and his band had scoured the area for fresh tracks and cowpies. But apparently the place held bad memories for Diablo Blanco, for the cowpies were old and dried and musty.

For days, the two men tracked the Apaches, who moved ever slower but remained at least two days ahead of them, and their own days stretched into weeks where they lost the spoor and the wild bunches of cattle grew more numerous, leaving tracks that seemed to lead everywhere and nowhere.

They rode long days through ever-changing land, weathering the squalls and storms that raged off the Gulf, erasing hoofprints, wiping out sign as an eraser scuffs chalk from a blackboard. And never any sign of the elusive white bull.

"I'm beginning to think there ain't no white bull," Peebo said, one noon when they ate and rested at a small salty creek.

Anson was checking his black horse's hooves, noting the wear on the iron shoes, cleaning the frogs.

"He'll run out of country out here, same as us, Peebo. He's not going to go swimming in the Gulf."

"Hell, he might."

"We're on the bull's track right now," Anson said. "Have been since mid-morning."

"We are?"

"If you get up and walk fifty paces to the north, you'll see his hoofmarks, Peebo. I'm surprised you missed them."

"Son, I've seen so many tracks in the past weeks, they've all done blurred out in my mind."

Not concealing his sullenness, which was unusual for Peebo, since he was generally so full of congeniality, he rose and walked in the direction Anson had pointed. He bent down after taking half a hundred steps and traced a hoofmark with his finger. Anson heard him let out a breath.

"Be damned," Peebo said. "If that ain't the beast hisself, it's damned sure his twin brother."

"Oh, it's Diablo, all right."

Peebo returned and leaned against a tree, pushed his hat back on his head. He looked hard at Anson, that same sullen expression on his face that he had worn for days.

"That track's not half a day old," Peebo said.

"He's mighty close, and in no hurry. And neither will we be."

"You got something in mind? Like maybe getting back to the Box B and tending to your ranch?"

"Let's have a smoke and I'll tell you what we're going to do."

"The inside of my mouth is dry as a corn husk. I don't fancy dryin' it out no more with tobacco."

"You are a contrary son of a bitch, Peebo."

"Did you happen to see any more 'Pache tracks, son? I haven't seen any the past three days."

"No, but they're around here. Somewhere."

"And how do you know that?"

"I can smell 'em, Peebo."

Peebo snorted in disbelief. He dug out a sack of tobacco and tossed it to Anson. Anson fished a packet of papers from his pocket and made a trough of the paper with his fingers. He sprinkled tobacco along the depression, pulled the string on the tobacco sack, closing it. Then he folded the paper over the tobacco into a tight roll. He put the quirly in his mouth and flung the sack back to Peebo.

"Lucifer," Anson said.

"Hell, son. You want me to smoke it for you?" Peebo handed Anson a match, which he struck on his boot, cracking the head into flame. He lit his cigarette and tossed the match down, ground it under the heel of his boot.

"Now what?" Peebo asked.

"Now we're going to walk a ways on foot. Real quiet."

"So what are these horses for? Decoration?"

"I think we might just get close to that old bull, Peebo. But before we do, I want to build a little corral."

"And how do we do that? We've got plenty of rope, but then how do we catch el Diablo? With our bare hands?"

"You got your machete, don't you?"

"Hell, yes."

"And I've got mine. When we get to the spot I pick, I'll show you how we're going to build us a little corral."

"And what about Culebra?"

"I reckon he'll let us know when he wants to pay us a visit."

Peebo cursed a blue streak, draining his vocabulary. The two started walking, following the distinctive tracks of the white bull, leading their horses behind them as if they were only out for a short stroll.

Anson tried to picture the white bull in his mind. The last time he had seen him, the bull was big enough. But now, the animal had grown even larger and had assumed mythical proportions. The tracks bore out the longhorn's enormous size. For when a cow following the bull stepped in the big tracks, Diablo's still stood out.

Both Anson and Peebo walked slowly, stopping often to listen, careful when they approached any sizable stand of trees. Neither wanted to walk into an Apache ambush. They made little noise, and when they stopped, they heard only faint birdcalls, the piping of a quail, the rustle of leaves in the Gulf breeze that had sprung up mercifully in the baking heat of afternoon.

Anson examined the droppings along the way, opening the pies with a stick to expose the innermost layer, looking for steam to rise. The cow pies were not very fresh, but he figured they were no more than half a day old. He wondered where the big bull was leading his herd, and why he was taking the path they were following. For the tracks wound through the mesquite and did not follow a straight line, as they would have done if the bull were leading his herd to a predetermined destination.

They passed open places, small savannahs of grassland where the cattle had grazed for a time, and eventually the cowpies grew fresher and more prevalent. Other cattle had joined the herd, he determined from the thickening maze of tracks, and they were wary, veering radically in their course at times, as if fleeing some pursuing force.

Late in the afternoon of that day, when fluffy white clouds were beginning to fill the sky, blown to the blue spaces by the Gulf winds, Anson saw the pattern of the tracks change dramatically. Farther on, he saw evidence that the cattle had started running. They had scattered as if frightened. Following the white bull's tracks, he noticed that the herd around the bull had thinned considerably.

"Watch yourself, Peebo," Anson whispered. "Something sure as hell scared these cattle."

"I reckon you're right, son. They lit a shuck, for sure."

Anson and Peebo came to an open place amid the thicket of mesquite and, in the center, they saw a freshly killed cow. And a few steps later, Anson pointed to the ground.

Pony tracks. Unshod.

A silence grew around them as they gazed at the dead cow lying in the open. They stood there in the shade of the trees and could hear the flies buzzing as they attacked the fresh meat. Anson sniffed. He could smell the blood and, when he looked closer, he saw that the dead cow had left a short blood trail, and around it, more blood, as if it had been cut open, and only the organs removed.

Anson listened and could hear only the drum of his heart. Even in the heat, a cold chill rose up inside him and he felt something crawling up his spine.

And not a sound. Not a single, blessed sound in all that emptiness where the dead cow lay as if inviting them to view it and die there themselves where it lay.

28

———■———

ROBERTO SAN JUAN stood by the Rocking A buckboard talking to Jorge Rios and Avril Conseco, who were seated, ready to leave Baronsville. San Juan was a stocky man with a beard riddled with silver flecks of graying hair. His eyes twinkled with light even under the brim of his hat, light that seemed reflected off his silver badge fastened to his vest.

The wagon stood in front of the general store, brimming with provisions given by the townsfolk who had attended the burial of Madrugada Bone and her son, Juan. Out of kindness and sympathy, many had responded to the urging of Millie Collins, Lorene Sisler, and Ken Richman, to bring foodstuffs and money to Doc Purvis's office before the young people left town. After the burial, Nancy Grant put the idea into Ken's head and he gladly became the first contributor, pressing a ten-dollar bill into Jorge's hand, and giving five dollars to Avril, "to buy anything you want."

"Jorge," San Juan said, in Spanish, "if this Bone is still at the rancho when you return, I want you to send back a message for me. I will come and arrest him."

"I do not think Bone is still there."

"Why?"

Jorge shrugged. Avril opened her mouth, then closed it quickly. San Juan's eyes narrowed.

"The more you can tell me about this man, the better," San Juan said. "If we can catch him, he will be punished. He will not be able to hurt anyone else."

Jorge thought about the two crosses in the Baronsville cemetery. They were wooden and had been painted white. Someone, he did not know who, had painted the names on the crosses, Dawn Bone and Juan Bone. He thought of his brother, Fidel, buried in the cemetery plot on the Rocking A, with only a homely rock to mark his grave. He vowed to himself that when he returned he would make a cross and put Fidel's name on it, just like the ones for Madrugada and little Juan.

"Mickey Bone is a very bad man," Jorge said. "I do not think you will catch him easily."

"I will not leave town to chase this man," San Juan said. "But if he is still there on the rancho, I will bring a posse to catch him. If we catch him, we will bring him back to the pueblo and he will have a trial before a judge and a jury. If he is found guilty, we will hang him."

Avril choked back a sob.

San Juan looked at her, his brown eyes glinting from the reflection off his badge.

"You do not have to return to the rancho, Avril," San Juan said. "If you are afraid of this Bone, this coward, you can stay here."

"I will return," she said. Her bruises were healing, but their discolorations remained on her face like little splotchy shadows. "I am not afraid of Bone. I will carry a knife and I will kill him if he touches me again."

"You are very brave," San Juan said.

"I am not brave, sir. I hate that man. I hate any man who kills a baby as he killed little Juan."

"I think we should leave," Jorge said. "It is very far to the rancho and the mule is very stubborn on such a hot day as this."

"Go with God," San Juan said. "You have good luck, you know? In a few weeks, there will be no doctor here in Baronsville. The doctor is joining the Army of the Confederacy. He is going to be an army surgeon. His niece, that pretty gringo girl who calls herself Lorene, is to go with him, and the woman who brought you food, Millie she is called, she will go, too. They will be nurses. Maybe some others. We will have no doctor here in this pueblo until the war is no more."

"We have gratitude," Avril said.

The sun was a blazing disk in the sky and the air was close and breezeless, fetid with the smells of the town's garbage and the stench of the privies in back of the many houses and businesses. Mingled with the scent was the acrid aroma of lime that stung the nostrils like nettles or urine.

"Yes. You go now," San Juan said. "Remember what I told you. If Bone is still there, send someone to tell me. I will come, with a posse."

"I will do this," Jorge said. He rattled the reins over the mule's back and the mule stepped out, taking up the slack of the harness. From the porch of the Longhorn Saloon, Millie waved to them as Jorge turned the wagon and passed by. Seated nearby, Ken Wales lifted a hand as if it were an effort. His bloated face was yellow even in the shade.

"Go with God," San Jose said again.

"Until then," Jorge said. "Until then," Avril murmured, then lowered her head. Nancy Grant had given her a bonnet to wear, for which she was grateful. She had never owned a bonnet before, and this one, blue and white checked, made her feel protected, not only from the sun, but from the stares of the white people who lined the street or paused to look at them as they passed. San Juan did not wave, but watched them go, and then walked back up to the boardwalk and entered a door marked TOWN CONSTABLE.

Jorge looked back as the wagon reached the end of the street. Then he turned the mule toward the fork that would lead them southward. He heaved a sigh and clucked to the mule.

"Gringos," he said, and spat.

"The gringos were very nice to me," Avril said.

"I do not like gringos. They are not *simpático*. They look down on us like we are bugs or lizards. You can see it in their eyes."

"I saw only the kindness, Jorge."

"Pah! You are only a girl, Avril. You do not see behind things. Matteo, now, he knows the gringos. He could tell you something, eh?"

"I do not know the *patrón*. You do not know him, either."

"Matteo and I are like this," he said, holding up his right hand and pressing two fingers together. "Like this."

"I do not want to talk about the *patrón* any more, nor of the gringos. I want to go home."

"Maybe you want to stay with the gringos. They give you money and that stupid *sombrero*. It makes you look like a droopy flower."

"How cruel, Jorge."

"I did not mean to be cruel. It is that I do not like the gringos. I do not like the clothes they wear. I do not like the things they make."

"I have no lice. They make good soap, the strong soap."

Jorge laughed. "Yes, they make good strong soap."

The wagon bounced over the rough road that wound through brush and trees, a road not much traveled. It was not the shortest road back to the Rocking A, but it skirted the white men's ranches, crossing over Box B land but not going near the headquarters or any of the buildings. There were streams along the way and places to stop and rest that were safe, and places to spend the night. It was the way they had come to Baronsville, the road used by Matteo and those who worked for him when they had to come to town.

"You are an orphan," Jorge said, after a long silence between them, when they both were looking at the small white clouds in the blue sky and watching meadowlarks flit across the road, and gray mourning doves slice through the air in pairs with whistling wings.

"Yes."

"You live with Lupe Ortiz and her husband, Renaldo."

"Yes. They are from my little village in the mountains of Mexico, a place called Alta Vista."

"That is near where Matteo once lived and made the ranch, with cattle."

"Yes. Renaldo and Lupe, they worked for him and I lived with them."

"What happened to your father and mother?"

"I do not like to talk about that," she said.

"I am just curious, that is all."

"Everyone is curious. I have much pain when I think of my father and mother. My father was young, as was my mother. He had long black hair like you have, and it was thick and shiny like a black crow's wing. And my mother had long hair, too, and she was very beautiful."

"It was the disease then, that took them away from you?"

"No," she said, and dipped her head so that it was hidden beneath the cowl of her bonnet. "They were killed when the government paid a bounty on Apache scalps. Some men came to our village and they waited by the well and killed people with their machetes. Then they took their scalps and said they were Apache scalps and they got money for the hair they cut from the heads of those they killed."

"I am sorry, Avril. Were the killers of your parents gringos?"

"No. They were of our blood. They were very bad men."

"I have heard of this money paid for Apache scalps. Does not the government know the difference between an Apache and a Mexican?"

"I do not know, Jorge. Please, let us not talk of these sad things. I cry every night thinking of what happened to my mother and father. What happened to some of my friends."

"Yes. We will not talk of these things. The world is a cruel place. There is no justice in this world."

"There is no justice," she said, and he heard her sniffling as if she was trying not to cry.

In the afternoon, there were dark skies to the west and they could see the rain like a dark curtain shading out a large part of the horizon. The wind had begun to blow and they felt it push against them with an invisible force. The mule picked up its pace as if it smelled water, but Jorge knew it was only the wind and the rain that was coming.

Suddenly, Avril gasped and pointed off to the left. Jorge turned his head to look in that direction.

"There is someone there, on a horse," she said

"I see him. He is waiting for us."

"Who is it?"

"I do not know," he said, and licked dry lips, fear inside him making his stomach swirl with flying moths.

The rider waited for them. He sat very straight in the saddle and he had a rifle across the pommel. He lifted the rifle and gestured for them to stop.

Jorge pulled on the reins, halting the mule. The wind died down for a second as the rider approached.

"Is that you, Jorge?" Matteo said.

"*Mi patrón.*" Jorge gasped. "It is you, Don Matteo."

Matteo grinned and rode up close. He looked down at Jorge and Avril.

"And who is that with you, Jorge? Avril Conseco? She is too young for you to steal. What are you doing here?"

Avril looked up at him from under her bonnet. *"Mi patrón,"* she said, in a shy whisper. "We are returning to the rancho."

"You are not dead, as they have said you were, Don Matteo," Jorge said.

"No. I am returning home, too. Do you have things to tell me? How is my wife and son? Does the rancho do well?"

Jorge told him about Bone, and about his brother Fidel, and the death of Bone's wife, Madrugada, and how he had slain his son and beat Avril, all in one terrible night. And, at the last, he told him about Luz and their son, Julio.

"Where did she go?" Matteo asked.

"To Mexico, Fidel he told me. She said she would return to her people in Valle."

"That is good. And what of Bone, that son of bad milk?"

"I think he is gone, Don Matteo," Jorge said.

"To where has he gone?"

"I do not know."

Matteo Aguilar's face darkened like the sky to the west and Jorge shrank away from his anger. Avril dipped her head like a drooping flower, for she too could feel the wrath building in Don Matteo at all this bad news from them.

"I know where he is going," Matteo said, after a moment.

"Where is he going?" Jorge asked.

"To hell when I find him," Aguilar said, his voice so soft they could barely hear him above the whip of the wind in the rattling mesquite leaves. And dust sprang up around them in a swirling dance that stung their eyes and faces and clogged their noses, as if that door to hell had opened just for a fleeting moment.

29

H ATTIE, HER FACE shaded by the large-brimmed straw hat she wore, stared down a row of growing cotton, then turned her head to look at all the other rows, all straight as a string, geometric and symmetric, fanning out as far as the eye could see.

"What God hath wrought," she murmured on a breath of wonder.

"What Hattie hath wrought," Richman said. He stood beside her, next to the wagon she had driven to the fields along with all her new hands, the ex-slaves from town he had brought out two weeks before. They had all wanted to come and work the fields, to be with Pluto and Socrates and sing their praise-the-Lord songs on Sunday with others of their own kind.

"I never saw anything grow so fast," she said. "In less than a week, those buds started to form. The cotton is supposed to be ready to pick in three, three and a half months on the first crop. I started with eighty acres, like I told you, then we plowed and planted eighty more."

"So now you're up to a hundred and sixty acres. Are you sure you can manage so much cotton?"

"You told the man, didn't you? And he said he'd buy."

"I told him. He'll buy."

"What's his name again?"

"Robichaux. He's from New Iberia, Louisiana. He saw your fields. He said they were good."

"I know. I was so excited because he brought me more seeds and told me what he would pay for my crop when it came in."

Richman laughed. "He said you drove a hard bargain, Hattie. Wouldn't take Confederate money or even greenbacks."

"No, I told him he had to pay me in gold or silver."

"Louis must have choked on that."

"Yes, that was his name. Now I remember. Louis. He pronounced it 'Looey.'" She chuckled. "He said he'd pay me in silver."

"Which is as good as gold."

"Nothing's as good as gold," Hattie said, smiling.

"Well, you've got pickers now."

All of the ex-slaves, freed from Aguilar and Reynaud by Martin Baron, were scattered throughout the rows, swinging their hoes high, murdering the weeds with skill. They could hear them singing spirituals, hoeing to the rhythm of their songs, calling out to each other between phrases.

"They are a wonder," Hattie said. "They're living in those tents you brought, but the Mexicans are going to build them little adobe houses and they're all excited about that."

"Where's Wanda?" Ken asked.

Hattie turned to him and looked up into his eyes. She pushed her hat brim up with one hand and held it there, folded back. Strands of her russet hair dangled next to her face in curly tendrils.

"A woman gets lonely, Ken," she said. "Wanda's staying with Roy over at the Box B."

Richman's eyebrows arched and his mouth twisted into a wry smile.

"I suppose you get lonely, too, Hattie."

"I haven't been with a man in a long while, Ken. I don't know if you get used to it, but you make do. I have longings."

"You ought to get into town more."

"All the young men have joined the army. I like them young. Energetic."

Ken's face took on a slightly rosy cast and his neck swelled like a bull in rut.

"There's not much to pick from, that's for sure. The cook at the Longhorn and the waiter."

"Worthless trash," she said. "And I suppose you're taken by that pretty schoolmarm."

"Nancy? Not taken, exactly. But I do see her."

"Court her, you mean."

Ken's face turned ruddier and the color traveled down his neck to his chest.

"I may ask her to marry me," he said. "Soon."

Hattie slipped her arm inside of his and led him away from the wagon. She walked down the rows, toward a thick stand of mesquite that bordered the field.

"Georgia Cotton," she said.

"Huh?"

"That's the kind of cotton we planted. Supposed to be good for this climate."

She squatted down by one of the plants, touched the stem with caressing fingers.

"Come on," she said. "I want to show you something."

"Where are we going?"

"You'll see." There was a lilt to her voice and a smile on her face as she squeezed his arm. With her other hand she waved at a pair of blacks working several rows away.

"Fidelius and his wife Petunia are hard workers and they've sort of adopted young Claude since they came out here."

"Claude did some work for me in town," Ken said. "I thought he was Beulah's boy."

"No. Beulah is Fancy's mother, but Fancy is only thirteen, a year younger than Claude. I think Claude was getting ideas so her mother asked Petunia to take the boy in at her place."

"Seems to me that you're a mother to them all."

"They do need guidance, Ken. And they look up to me, sure enough."

"I can see why. The way you've raised Wanda. Very admirable."

"Oh, Ken, don't patronize me. Wanda's got my wild blood in her and sometimes I wonder if I'm raising her, or she's raising me."

"What do you mean?" he asked, as they drew closer to the mesquite thicket, and left the row of cotton to follow a small path leading into the trees.

"I learn so much from her, from watching her life unfold. I not only learn about her, but I learn about myself. I can see my blood in her blood, if you know what I mean."

"I think so. She is from your seed, and you see your own characteristics in her."

"I couldn't have put it better, Ken. Not only that, but I see the generations in Wanda. I see my own mother, and my own father, and my grandmother and grandfather. And maybe I see all of my ancestors, and hers, too, of course."

"I never thought of it that way. But you're right."

"I've been thinking about that a lot lately, as I grow older and watch my daughter grow and fall in love."

"You see your own traits."

"More than that. I see in her, and in myself, everyone I've ever loved, ever known. That's why I want to show you something and tell you why I'm talking about these things just now. My loneliness comes not so much from being without a husband, but being without a companion, someone to confide in, to trust, to honor."

"You have Wanda, and Roy, and those who work for you, Hattie."

"Oh, I know. But I also have someone else. A lot of people, really. Come. We don't have far to go. Just through these damned mesquite trees."

Richman laughed as Hattie bent her neck and ducked to go under a leafy branch that blocked her way. She held the limb back so that it did not strike Ken as he followed her.

They walked past more trees and then the mesquite thinned and they stepped into a huge open meadow with a high-banked pond in the middle of it. There was a lot of scrap lumber lying about along with shovels and picks under a canvas canopy, which had been strung between some trees at the edge of the clearing.

"The Mexicans who are working here are on another job, but they'll be back in the morning. Come up to the top of the bank with me and I'll show you what they're doing."

Ken followed Hattie up a path to the top of the bank. They gazed upon a huge pond, glinting like a mirror in the sunlight, flashing with little silver chips of reflected light, a faint ripple on the surface.

The pond covered almost five acres and stretched from their end to surrounding patches of mesquite and oak trees.

"I'm astounded to see a pond this size here," Ken said. "I had no idea."

"Look over there," Hattie said, pointing to a place off to the right where the bank was wide and flat. There, he saw what appeared to be a number of long boxes nailed together with fresh wood, but a closer look revealed that they were three-sided and framed like miniature watering troughs.

"What are those?"

"Flumes," she said, glowing with pride.

"Flumes?"

"Like ancient Roman aqueducts, only they're constructed of wood. Forrest Redmond's idea, and his design. They will run from gates in the pond that we can open and close, and they'll be attached to the mesquite trees in a gradually descending line, straight out to the cotton fields. We'll dig ditches all along the edge of the field and then smaller ones along the rows of cotton plants. Irrigation, Ken. Making the parched land bloom."

"Ingenious," he said.

"What I wanted you to see and know is that this is only one of five ponds that border all the cotton fields, and you know who's responsible for them?"

"I have no idea. Forrest?"

"David Wilhoit."

"The surveyor who was killed in the Baron war?"

"Yes. He surveyed everything for miles around here and he discovered a number of natural springs. He told me I could have ponds and stock them with fish, use them to water our cattle. But at the time, I never dreamed we'd be growing cotton. I showed the ponds to Forrest after we dug them out. Most of the springs were near some gullies and we only had to bank one end. That too was designed by Forrest, who's quite a brilliant man."

"I'll say."

"It was Forrest who told us about the aqueducts and suggested how we could make the water flow to the fields and get the water to the plants."

"Amazing," Ken said.

"The coming of the Mexicans was an added blessing for us. If they hadn't left the Box B when they did, none of this would have happened. Divine Providence? Maybe. But I'm thinking that we owe it to David and Forrest and whatever prompted those Mexican families to come to our small ranch looking for work."

"I'm beginning to understand what you're been trying to tell me, Hattie."

"This is a most beautiful country. And with people like you and Roy and Forrest in it, it's going to be a wonderful place to live. It already is, don't you agree?"

"Yes, I do. I think you owe Martin Baron's vision a great deal of credit, too. He was the man who first saw the land, who first realized its potential. I saw it when I came here and met him, talked to him. He's a dreamer, and he saw cattle on land that was desolate, wild and savage."

"But Martin is unreliable," she said.

"Oh, he drifts off now and then, but he always comes back. He still holds the dream in his mind."

"I give him credit. And I give Roy credit for settling here, too, getting land from Martin and Anson."

She drew in a deep breath and looked out over the pond shimmering in the sunlight and at the mesquite forest below them, and beyond to the cotton fields stretching out to the horizon.

"When I look at all this, Ken," she said, "I'm not lonely. I feel part of the land and the sky and the water here that can do so much for us, the precious water that no one knew was here. No one except Dave Wilhoit, poor man, God rest his soul. I feel full and complete when I think of all the possibilities, of a future bright and promising for us all."

"When this war is over," Ken said, a sober tone to his voice.

"When this damned war is over," she breathed and took Ken's arm in her hand and squeezed. "I pray that it won't last long."

"You'd better pray it lasts long enough to provide a market for your cotton."

"No, I don't care about that. I'd gladly plow it all under and plant alfalfa if the war would end before lives are lost."

"Amen," Ken said, and looked at Hattie with renewed respect.

"You are truly one of those dreamers, like Martin Baron," he said. "You belong here. And I'm glad you are here."

"So am I," she breathed. "I'm glad we're all here, in this lovely place at this time. This is, I truly believe, the promised land."

Her chest swelled with pride as she drank in the air and the majesty of the land that surrounded her on that high place by the shining waters. Her face became radiant and her eyes shone with a fervent light that seemed born of the sky and the pond. She took off her hat and shook her head to loosen her hair and it shone like copper and gold, like some essence of sun come to earth from across the far reaches of limitless space.

30

HE RODE DOWN through the night, like a vaporous wraith in the ghost-pale light of the quarter moon. He crossed the Rio Bravo with a slosh of hooves and the lapping murmur of the current and stepped his horse onto the dank and fetid shore of Mexico where the landscape loomed like a shapeless mass of unwanted universe. And down he rode into the desolate land he knew so well, land that reeked with blood and memories and lay stark and deserted under the scourged remnant of moon that glided like a luminous fingernail across the blackened slate of the sky.

He rode alone and cursed, with a raging heart that had filled with hatred instead of remorse, a heart that thrummed a savage tattoo in his ears like the threnodic beat of ancient war drums. He rode until he smelled the smoke and the cooking odors; until he heard the faint yapping of dogs and the curdled cries of children and the sharp voices of Mexican women calling to their thin and bony offspring across the widening light of morning. He came to the old town, but he did not enter it, nor did he even see it, except in his mind.

Bone watched the town for three days. He camped in different places where he slept unobserved. He was a shadow when he moved, an invisible sentinel with no silhouette, no distinct form, when he stood still, watching the road that came from the north.

He lived on lizards and snakes that he killed and skinned with his knife. He made no fire and ate his food raw. Sometimes, at night, he walked into the town on silent moccasins and listened to the sleepers snoring, or looked in windows where the moonlight shone in and he could see those who were abed and oblivious to his presence. On the third night, he slipped up on a sleeping dog and opened its throat with the blade of his knife and held the quivering body to him, drinking the blood that flowed from the gaping wound beneath the mangy fur. He took the dog to his sleeping place among the rocks and cactus and skinned it, then sliced the meat into strips which he chewed and swallowed, like the heart he had eaten first, to give him strength for the rest of the ritual.

On the fourth day, he saw her coming from a long way off. He knew it was Luz for he recognized the horse she rode, the horse she had taken with her when Fidel had helped her escape. He knelt among the rocks and yucca and cactus, and waited until she was close enough so that he could see her face, so that he could be sure it was Luz Aguilar, and no other.

To his surprise, she was alone. She did not have her son, Julio, with her and he wondered what she had done with him. Had the boy died on the ride south? Perhaps he had drowned in the Rio Bravo, or been bitten by a rattlesnake or a scorpion. That was disappointing, because he meant to kill Julio as he had killed his own son, Juan. He wanted Luz to pay for her denial of him and for her escape.

He had wanted her to watch her son die by his own hand before he bedded her and planted his seed in her. But she had robbed him of that pleasure, too, it seemed. Either Julio had died, or she had left him with someone before returning to her people. Fidel had said she might do that just before Bone had slashed his throat with his knife, nearly severing his head from his body.

Bone knew where Luz's family lived, for he had been there with Matteo when Matteo was in exile, hiding out in Mexico on a little ranch waiting to return and claim the Rocking A for himself. He knew her father, Nuncio Montenegro, a crippled old man in ill health, and her mother, Caridad, also old and consumptive, her little brother, Sergio, and her pretty twin sister, Lucinda. Once or twice he had thought about marrying Lucinda, but he was already with Madrugada at the time, and he had thought to be faithful to his woman. But then, the Lipan were in the mountains and the tribe was together. Now, they were all surely dead and he belonged to no one.

He was in no hurry. He would watch the town a while longer and let Luz become accustomed to being back with her people. She would not be expecting him. She would be waiting for her husband, Matteo Miguelito, and he would never come. He was still curious about what had happened to her son, Julio, and had begun to think that he might have died on her journey to Valle.

Bone watched the town in the daytime for the next two days. In particular, he watched the Montenegro house, a crumbling adobe at the edge of the small village. He watched as Nuncio was helped outside in the late morning to sit in the sun, while his wife sat on the ground in the shade, coughing as she puffed on cigarettes. Luz wore mourning clothes when she went to market with her sister, Lucinda. Sometimes their brother would tag along, pushing an old rusted barrel hoop with a stick. He was only twelve and as filthy as the other children in the pueblo who seldom bathed. Lucinda seemed content to have her sister there, but Luz kept her head bowed and avoided talking to people in the street or in the market.

He crawled to those places where he could observe the town and not be seen. He made himself part of the landscape, and when dogs came near, he retreated, hissing like a snake and using his teeth and tongue to imitate the clicking of a rattlesnake's tail. He knew he could not stay unseen much longer, though. Already, people were looking his way, with suspicion in their eyes.

Bone had watched the woodcutters come and go with their burro-driven *carretas* for days, and now he saw Luz's brother chopping up kindling for their stove. When the boy was finished, he leaned the axe up against the wall of the house and carried the wood inside. His parents emerged a short time later to sit outside. Luz and Lucinda made them comfortable and then went back inside for a time. When he next saw Luz, she was no longer dressed in black and she spoke to her parents for some time, gesturing and pointing to the north. Bone had the distinct feeling that Luz was going to leave the pueblo very soon, perhaps the next day.

That night, Bone waited near the Montenegro dwelling, watching it as a wolf eyes a grazing deer in a meadow. Gradually, the lamps in the town dimmed and went out. The Montenegro adobe was plunged into darkness. And still, Bone waited, watching the half moon rise and bathe the land in a dull silver luminescence. He waited and then slinked closer. Finally, he stole up to the window where he knew the family slept just inside. He was very quiet and very calm. He listened to the sounds of breathing, the rattling snore of the old woman, the snuffled gasp of the old man.

Bone picked up the axe the boy had left leaning against the house and then walked around to the front door. It was not latched, and he carefully pushed it open, then slipped inside. He stopped and listened, sorting out the sounds. He walked to the single room where all slept and stood just inside, looking at all the shapes, defining, in his mind, who was sleeping where. In the dim light of the moon, his eyes gradually became accustomed to the darkness.

He padded over to the pallet where the old man and his wife slept. He raised the axe, then brought it down hard, crushing the man's skull. Quickly, he raised it again and smashed the old woman's head into two pulpy halves. The sounds awoke the boy, and Bone swung the axe as the boy half-rose from his pallet. The blade sliced into his head right at the ear and he slumped over, gushing blood.

Lucinda let out a startled cry and started to sit up. Bone stepped up to her and hit her hard with his fist. She dropped back down on her side, unconscious.

"Lucinda," Luz called out in a sleepy voice.

Bone dropped the axe to the dirt floor and fell on top of Luz. He clamped a hand over her mouth. She struggled and fought, trying to free herself from his grip.

"If you scream, I will break your neck," he said in Spanish.

She made muffled sounds, and these turned to sobs as Bone began ripping her nightgown from her body.

"I will kill you, Luz, if you cry out," he said, forcing her legs apart. He could see her breasts and her slender form as he opened the fly on his trousers and released the hard bone of his sex. He forced himself into her as she squirmed and tried to fight him off with a pummeling of tiny fists.

Bone slaked his lust on her, exploding his seed inside her with a grunt that sounded more like relief than pleasure. Then he hammered a fist into her face again and again until she fell unconscious.

He rose up from Luz, then stared down at her sister. Without hesitation, he grabbed Lucinda's wrists and pulled her up. She began to awaken, and he closed a hand over her mouth and whispered into her ear.

"Do not make a sound," he said huskily.

He carried Lucinda from the house and walked toward his camp with her slung over his shoulder like the carcass of some animal he had slain. When she began to struggle, Bone set her down and then beat her senseless, without rage or feeling, then carried her unconscious body the rest of the way.

In moments, Bone was astride his horse and riding away, with Lucinda held in his lap, his arm around her waist. She was slumped over, a dead weight, in a deep swoon. He rode through the night to the old ranch where Matteo Aguilar had once lived, and where he knew it would be deserted and going to ruin.

He smiled, knowing that his seed was inside Luz Aguilar and that his vengeance was complete. Luz, he knew, would remember this night for as long as she lived. And he would take her sister, Lucinda, for his wife and make another son to carry on his name. From this, he vowed, Lucinda would never escape and would bear him many children.

He felt as though he had been reborn as a man, and as an Apache. He felt as if he was once again fulfilling his destiny, knowing his tribe would go on like raindrops falling into a stream that flowed down to the everlasting sea.

31

Anson and Peebo stared at the dead longhorn, neither moving nor speaking. The hot sun burned down on the dead animal and a light breeze fingered its hide with faint ripples in the longer tufts of hair. Something fluttered and made a sound like a stick racked along a picket fence. A whirring sound, so faint they could barely hear it. But it was there, and it was a sound that should not have been.

"What in the hell is that?" Peebo whispered.

"Look what's sticking out of the cow's neck, Peebo." Anson's voice was measured, low in his throat. His eyes were narrowed to dark slits as he peered at the object just barely visible. The object was striped, black and gray, very hard to see.

"Looks like a piece of turkey feather," Peebo said. "What the hell . . ."

"It's the top of an arrow stuck in that dead cow's neck," Anson said.

Another silence, as the seconds ticked by and the breeze stiffened, made the feathers whir like a miniature buzz saw.

There was something else, too, that Anson noticed. He studied it for a long time before he began to figure it out. Peebo looked at him, wondering at Anson's long silence, but he waited him out, knowing that Anson was intent on something important.

"Culebra wanted us to find that dead cow," Anson said, finally. "Notice anything else about that arrow sticking out of its neck?"

Peebo shaded his eyes, even though he was standing in the trees and needed no extra shade. He looked at the arrow for a long time. Then he saw something else move.

"That cow ain't dead, or it's got something sure as hell movin' on its neck or head," Peebo said.

"I don't think Culebra's waiting in ambush for us. He left this sign to get under our skins. He's waiting somewhere around that white bull, sure enough, Peebo. Let's walk up and see what that Apache left for us to read."

"Maybe I better cover you. Or you cover me."

"All right." Anson gulped in a lungful of air, handed Peebo the reins to his horse, hunched over and ran a zigzag pattern to where the dead cow lay, its body swelling in the heat of the sun.

Nobody shot at him, and he pulled up short, his hand on the pistol in his holster, ready to draw at the first sign of an ambush. He looked down at the arrow, then beckoned for Peebo to come up with the horses.

The whirring sound wasn't only from the fletching on the Apache arrow. The loudest noise came from a rattlesnake impaled by the arrow. It was still alive, and writhing in spiraled arabesques, trying to escape. Peebo walked up warily, his ears full of the rattling sound. The horses balked and would not come close, but he jerked on the reins and pulled them up to the dead cow. Peebo stared down at the twisting snake skewered on the arrow that stuck out of the cow's neck.

"God Almighty," Peebo breathed with an air of wonderment. "If that don't beat all."

"A little message from Culebra."

"I reckon so."

"That's not all," Anson said. "Looky here at the brand. This isn't a wild cow, but one of ours."

Anson pointed and Peebo's gaze followed in the direction of Anson's extended finger. There, on the rump of the dead cow, a two-year old heifer, was a box with a capital B inside it.

"I branded that calf myself," Anson said. "A year ago."

"So Culebra's sent you more than one message, it looks like."

"The bastard."

Peebo sucked in a breath, looked around. Anson did too for he felt as Peebo did, that they were being watched. All they saw were scattered mesquite trees and a couple of scrub oak, some brush and prickly pear cactus dotting the plain.

Yet Anson knew that an Apache could lie in the dirt right out in the open and be like a quail in brush, invisible. After a few moments, though, he knew that Culebra and his bunch were not there. He and Peebo were alone, which made him feel even more uncomfortable.

"Culebra's pretty sure of himself, you ask me," Peebo said.

"Yeah. He knows we're going after that white bull and he's tracking it. I think he wants to jump us when we're busy roping that big old longhorn."

"Maybe we ought to give it up. Go on back to the ranch and wait for another day."

"You can go on back if you want to. I'm going to catch Diablo and burn the Box B into his hide."

"Then what?"

"Then I'm going to drag his ass back to the ranch and put him in with some white-faced cows and let him hump to his heart's content."

Peebo grinned.

"I wouldn't miss any of this for nothin', Anson, son. I think you ought to ride him back to the ranch, in fact. Make a mighty pretty sight."

"Well, we haven't got him yet. I might ride him. Right over your sorry ass, Peebo."

Peebo laughed. The rattlesnake's tail rattled with a fury, and the arrow feathers hummed and whined in the breeze in a staccato counterpoint.

"Let's get the hell out of here, son. I don't like those noises. Whatcha gonna do with that rattler?"

"Leave everything be. Like Culebra left it. If he wants to come back and get his damned arrow, he can have it. And I hope he gets bit. Right in the balls."

Anson took his reins from Peebo and walked away from the dead cow, which was beginning to smell. Overhead, two or three buzzards had picked up the scent and were circling in the sky, their pinions extended, riding the currents, their heads and beaks pointed down.

Peebo followed Anson and looked up at the sky.

"Should be right interestin' when them buzzards land and start pickin' at that cow meat."

"They'll kill the rattler, straight off," Anson said. "They don't just eat carrion, you know. They're predators. They kill for food, too."

"I didn't know that. I thought they only ate dead things."

"Didn't you ever hear that old joke about the starving buzzard sitting on a fencepost?"

"Nope. But I'll bet two bits you're going to tell me."

"The buzzard says, 'Patience, my ass, I'm goin' out and kill something.'"

"Pretty funny, son. And we're still afoot, with buzzards circlin' over us, probably hungry as hell, and a pack of damned Apaches somewhere up ahead just waiting to feed them suckers with our carcasses."

"Don't get morbid, Peebo. Keep your eyes on Diablo's tracks and look for unshod pony marks in the damned dust."

"Yes, sir, son. I surely will, but my feet are beginning to swell, walkin' in these boots."

"The horses can give us cover if we're on the ground. If you're in the saddle, you make an easy target for an arrow or a lead ball."

Peebo snorted and began to exaggerate his walk, then faking a limp, and doubling over like an old man bent from age. Anson didn't laugh. He was figuring out how far ahead of them the white bull was. When they came across a fresh cow pie, he stooped to examine it.

"Still two or three hours ahead of us," Anson said, after his last look at a cow pile.

"Unless the old he-bull stopped to graze. He could be right over the next rise. Along with about a dozen 'Paches."

"I count eight."

"Eight, then."

They were following a wide trail, and had been for some time. A half hour later, the trail led onto an old road that still showed wagon ruts.

"You notice something about Diablo, Peebo?" Anson asked, stopping for a moment.

"About what?"

Anson took off his hat and walked back to his saddlebags. He reached in and pulled out a sack of grain, poured some in his hat. He put the sack back inside the bag and walked up to his horse's head, held the hat down. The horse nibbled through the bit in its mouth.

"That bull is following old game trails and roads, just like that time we found him before."

"So?"

"And he's not just roaming around, visiting his old haunts. At least not willingly."

The horse continued to tackle the grain, making loud noises with its rubbery lips. Peebo's horse whickered and he filled his hat with corn and oats, let the animal feed while they were stopped.

"So?"

"Culebra's driving that bull and his herd," Anson said. "Haven't you been studying the tracks?"

"Well, yeah, son, but I thought Culebra was just follerin'. Like us."

"No, he's driving Diablo somewhere."

"Where?"

"I've been thinking about that for the last half hour, Peebo. Thinking real hard about it."

"Well, I've been thinking about a cool beer and a nice soft bed and maybe a good woman lyin' next to me in a big old hotel room in some fancy town."

"I reckon you like to torture yourself, Peebo. I've been thinking about that bull and the Apaches, and where they're headed. They're damned sure headed someplace, someplace we both know. Think about it."

Peebo studied the sun in the sky, looking upward, not directly at it, but to one side, a hand shading his eyes.

"Looks to me like they're headed west and south."

"That's right, but this is a wagon road we've been on before, one my father put through here a long time ago, when he went to Corpus Christi and drove cattle over to New Orleans."

"Well, that bull ain't goin' to either place," Peebo said.

Anson smiled.

"No, you're right. Up ahead, right off this road, there's an old spring, and a little creek that runs all year, and something else I remember."

"Yeah? What's that, son?"

"Kind of a gully, or a ravine. Sometimes we put cattle in there and roped 'em in overnight. There's grass in that little box gully and plenty of hiding places all around it. If a man was to go in there after that bull, Apaches could crawl over the top and shoot him like a fish in a rain barrel."

"I remember that place. There's a whole lot of mesquite around it, too. The road winds right through it, passes right by that little canyon, or gully, whatever it is."

"That's where Culebra is driving Diablo," Anson said, taking his hat away from his horse's muzzle and shaking it out before he placed it back on his head. He patted Nero on the neck and the horse nodded and switched its tail. It whickered for more grain, and twisted its neck to look back at the saddlebags.

"An ambush," Peebo said. "That's where Culebra's waitin' for us, you think."

"Damned sure he is."

"What do you aim to do, then, son?" Peebo asked as Anson climbed up into the saddle. "Ride right into it?"

"Mount up, Peebo. We're going to ride around it and come in from the south side, through all that mesquite. Two can play this game."

"Oh, it's a damned game, is it? I think you're full of that well-known brown stuff."

"Maybe," Anson said, as Peebo shook out his empty hat and then climbed into his saddle with one fluid motion. He put his hat back on his head. Both men had thick beards by now and looked like refugees from some foreign country. They looked like strangers to each other at that moment of decision. They looked older, if not wiser, and their clothes were clogged with dust and reeking of sweat, their stained shirts plastered to their bodies. They no longer noticed the smell because it was like horse and sand and crawling lizards and rattlesnakes and cooked rabbit meat.

Anson clucked to his black horse and prodded its flanks with his knobby spurs. Nero stepped out, still shaking its head as if in protest.

"How far do you reckon that there gully is from here?" Peebo asked, as he caught up to Anson.

"I mean to make it by nightfall."

"Them Apaches will hear us coming a mile away."

"No they won't, Peebo. Tonight, we're going to be Apaches our-selves. We're going to be so quiet, you'll hear your own heart beating."

Peebo snorted. Anson kicked his horse and broke into a gallop, leaving Peebo behind.

He hoped his hunch was right, and that they could get the drop on Culebra and his band.

By the time he slowed his horse, he was going over the terrain around the gully, the spring, and the creek in his mind. He and Peebo would be outnumbered, but perhaps they would not be out-smarted. As he rode, his skin tingled with excitement. But in his belly, the first swirls of fear began to roil and tiny spiders crawled up and down his spine with hairy feet that were as cold as ice.

32

Doc purvis had read the letter several times. This morning, he read it again as he sat at his kitchen table with his niece, Lorene. It was early and they were both fully dressed, their coffee cups steaming. Neither wanted to eat breakfast. They were too excited. The soft fragrance of honeysuckle wafted in through the open window, mingled with the aroma of boiled coffee.

"They should be here before noon," Purvis said.

"Let me see the letter again, Uncle Pat." She smelled of crushed lilacs and ground coffee beans, and her dark hair glistened from a hundred brushings that morning. Her mouth was delicately tinged with a pale crimson that gave it definition and her cheeks seemed to glow with the faint rouge she had rubbed gently into her skin.

Purvis slid the letter across the table. It had come a week ago, and now a sign hung outside on his door, saying that his office was closed until after the war. There would be no patients to see today, except for Ed Wales, who was stopping by shortly, at the doctor's request.

Lorene read the letter again. It was from Colonel John S. Ford, Colonel Commanding, Cavalry of the West, and it had come from San Antonio.

"The letter is endorsed by our new governor," she said. "See? Francis R. Lubbock, Governor of Texas."

"I know. Ed Wales told me he won by 124 votes."

"And Colonel Ford will be here today. At noon."

"I wonder how punctual the colonel is."

"I wonder where we'll be going. All the fighting now seems to be on the eastern side of the Mississippi."

"I don't know. He just says that he is bringing an ambulance with him and I am to be ready with my own medical kit and a list of needed supplies that may not be in the ambulance."

"It's very impressive, Uncle Pat."

"Rip Ford, that's what they call him. Rip has quite a reputation. He's done just about everything and done it all well. He's even a doctor, like me."

"A doctor?"

"That's what they say."

"It's hard to imagine a doctor leading an army. Fighting and killing."

"I surmise that Colonel Ford is a bit of a paradox."

"Do you admire him, Uncle?"

"I don't know him at all. I think all the stories I've heard keep me from knowing the man. I will soon meet him, however. And I'm looking forward to the pleasure."

Lorene shook her head and sipped her coffee. She looked into her uncle's eyes, then reached over and touched the back of his hand.

"You could never be like him, Uncle Pat. You're too kind. You have a good heart. This Colonel Ford evidently kills people."

Purvis smiled at his niece. "Who knows what is in any man's heart, my dear? I have pledged to save lives, not take them, that is true. But who is not to say that Colonel Ford heard a different drummer, somewhere along his path through life? And who can tell whether or not he will hear that same drummer at one time or another?"

"You sound so somber, Uncle. I don't think you would ever listen to the same drummer as a man like Ford."

Purvis shrugged, and lifted his cup to his lips. He blew on the surface, then drank, sipping the warm liquid, letting it cool in his mouth before he swallowed it.

They heard footsteps on the front porch stairs and then on the porch boards. Someone rapped sharply on the front door.

"Come in," Purvis called. "That's Ed, most likely. I'm amazed at his improvement since he stopped drinking."

"Yes, he does seem to have some of his natural color back."

They heard the door open, and a moment later, Ed Wales appeared in the kitchen. He was carrying a fresh edition of the weekly newspaper and, from the looks of it, the ink was still wet. He had a paunch now, a distension of his belly that looked as if he had tucked a small throw pillow under his belt.

"Ed, good morning," Purvis said. "Sit down. Will you have some coffee with us?"

"If that's the strongest you have. . . ."

Lorene clucked at him and rose from her chair as Wales sat down.

"That's the strongest I'll serve," Lorene said.

"Ouch." But Wales grinned at her, taking no offense at her remark. "Generally, I like a little whiskey in my coffee."

"You'll have to settle for a little chicory, Ed." Lorene lifted the pot from the stove and poured a tin cup nearly full. "Everything's packed," she said, as she carried the cup over to the table and set it in front of Wales. "So pardon the tin cup."

"Before you drink any of that, Ed, let me take a look at you," Purvis said, rising from his chair.

"I'm feeling some better, Doc."

"Hmm, well, let's see here. Tip your head back." Purvis pressed a thumb on one of Ed's lower lids and pulled it down. He bent over and looked at the inside of Ed's eye. Then he pried up the eyelid. He released the lid and stepped back.

"See anything in there?" Wales asked, spreading the paper on the table in front of his tin cup.

"Most of the jaundice seems to be gone. The liver can heal itself if it's not too damaged. You keep off the whiskey, Ed, and you might just have a chance. How do you feel?"

"I hurt. Food tastes like old wood. I get sick a lot if I eat too much."

Lorene sat down and pulled the newspaper toward her, turned it around so she could read the headlines.

"Don't eat too much," Purvis said. "You'll get over the nausea in time. Your body still wants whiskey, even though it's poison for you. Cramps?"

"Sometimes, yes."

"Get lots of rest. Drink lots of water. No whiskey, no beer, no wine. No alcohol of any kind."

Ed snorted and lifted his cup, pursed his lips and blew little dark waves on the surface of the liquid to cool it. He slurped coffee into his mouth by sucking air over the top of the rim.

"You're still a little jaundiced," Purvis said as he sat back down. "But I'm generally pleased with your progress, Ed."

"If you call dying of thirst progress . . ."

"That kind of dying may very well save your life, Mr. Wales."

Ed groaned. But he also smiled.

"Uncle, listen to this," Lorene said. She read one of the headlines: " 'Texans Capture Three Federal Forts.' "

"Old news, I'm afraid," Wales said. "But all the news is old by the time I get it."

"It's new to us," Purvis said. "Where were these forts? In Virginia?"

Wales laughed. "Up in Indian Territory. Bill Young, who used to be a U.S. Marshal here and the biggest slave holder in the state, led a couple of thousand volunteers over the Red and captured those forts."

"It's very exciting," Lorene said. "Ed, you write well."

"Thanks. I think the forts he captured were pretty much abandoned. But the real story is that Mr. William Cooke Young made treaties with some Indian tribes up there, so we won't have redskins pouring over the border and taking advantage of us down here."

"Were any of the tribes Apaches?" Purvis asked.

"No. 'Fraid not. They were Caddo, Comanche, Wichita, and Chickasaw."

"Well, that won't do us much good down here," Purvis said. "We're a long way from the Red River."

"At least the state is clear of Federals," Purvis said.

"Wasn't Young against secession?" Lorene asked.

"He was. Definitely," Wales said. "How times do change."

Lorene continued to read. "Uncle, he has a story here about you, too. About Colonel Ford coming to Baronsville today."

"Hmm," Purvis said, mildly interested.

"Ford's already here. And guess who's with him," Wales said.

"Here? Now?"

"He just pulled in with his cavalry not ten minutes ago. They're all up at the Longhorn, drat it."

"Who came with him?" Lorene asked.

"Martin Baron, that's who," Wales said.

Lorene's face brightened at mention of the name.

"Only Martin?" she said.

"There's been no word of Anson, if that's what you mean," Wales said. "Last I heard, he was still off hunting a mythical white longhorn bull. Ken said his house is just about finished."

"Well, if Ford's in town, I guess we'd better walk over to the Long-horn so I can introduce myself," Purvis said.

"I'll wash out these cups and take them with us, Uncle." Lorene finished her coffee and stood up. Both Purvis and Wales drank the rest of theirs and handed her their cups. In a few minutes, the three of them were walking toward the Longhorn Saloon, Lorene and Purvis each carrying satchels, the doctor his medical kit, as well.

Main Street was thronged with people, gawkers, drifters, shop-keepers, bank workers, clerks, maids, curious Mexicans, farmers, ranchers, waiters, a drummer or two, and children of all ages, let out of school.

"I didn't know Baronsville had this many people," Lorene said, obviously excited.

"It doesn't," Wales said. "People have known about this for weeks, thanks to the *Bugle*. They all want to get a look at the famous Rip Ford."

"Look, Uncle Pat, there's the ambulance. I think." Lorene pointed up the street, which was lined with horses at the hitchrails, and people talking to some of the Rangers who had stayed outside, presumably on guard duty.

"Yep, that surely looks like it," Purvis said. "It's not new, but it looks well cared for."

"Hard to miss with that big red cross on the canvas," Wales said, a trace of sarcasm in his voice. "A bloody cross. The universal sign of illness and death."

"Ed, you're both bitter and a cynic," Purvis said.

"I'm a realist, Doc. And I've looked death in the face."

"No, Ed, you haven't. You've only heard it whisper to you and maybe seen its reflection in the bottom of a whiskey glass."

"Now, who's the cynic, Doc?"

Both men laughed.

Some of the storefronts boasted makeshift bunting, and here and there, people waved small Confederate flags, the stars and bars that were like the one that flew on the flagpole in the center of town.

"I keep thinking there's going to be a parade at any minute," Lorene said, looking all around.

"Well, all we need is a band," her uncle said, and then pointed to a group of musicians setting up in front of the Longhorn. "And there they are." A moment later, the small band, consisting of a banjo, a fiddle, a couple of guitars, a bass drum, and a squeezebox, struck up "Old Joe Clark," and people began to gather in front of the saloon.

"Sounds like Saturday night," Wales said, "and this is only Monday."

The three walked up to the ambulance. Lorene was the first to peer inside, standing on tiptoes to gaze over the tailgate. Purvis came up beside her and looked inside, as well.

"Very neat," he said. "Stretchers, linens, an operating table on the floor, boxes of bandages, and trunks that probably contain medicines and nostrums."

"It looks like Colonel Ford thought of everything," Lorene said.

Wales did not look in, but stood there, counting the newspapers he saw stacked in the saloon window. He smiled with satisfaction.

A man in uniform approached the wagon. He wore gray, had a beard, and sported colonel's insignia on the shoulder boards of his frock coat.

"Dr. Purvis, I presume," Ford said, extending a hand. "I'm John Ford."

"Dr. Ford," Purvis said.

Ford chuckled. "Colonel now, sir. I gave up medicine, the law, newspapering, and loose women a long time ago. Begging your pardon, ma'am." He nodded to Lorene.

"This is my niece, Lorene Sisler, Colonel. She is also my nurse."

"Well, you won't have the luxury of a female nurse, Doctor," Ford said. "Sorry."

Purvis opened his mouth, but before he could speak, Lorene

stepped up to Ford and looked him in the eyes with a boldness that raised Ford's eyebrows.

"My uncle Pat needs me," she said. "I'm going with him. As his nurse."

"If she doesn't go," Purvis said. "Neither do I."

"Well, I'll be damned," Ford said. "It looks like I've got a mutiny on my hands before we even get acquainted. I haven't heard this much goddamned sass since I left South Carolina."

Lorene glared at Ford, stood there defiantly, her feet spread apart and her hands on her hips.

Ford snapped his fingers and an orderly appeared, carrying a leather case. The corporal stood at attention, holding the case under one arm. Ford slipped the case from his grasp and held it out to Purvis.

"My surgical instruments, Dr. Purvis," Ford said. "I know you have your own, but I thought you might accept this as a gift for serving in my regiment."

Purvis did not take the case.

Ford looked at Lorene, then back to Purvis.

"Oh, go ahead, Doctor," Ford said. "I don't mind a little sass now and then. Bring your damned niece if you like. Just so she knows it's going to be hot, bloody, and she'll hear one hell of a lot of cussin' in my outfit. And most of the cussin' will be mine."

Ford thrust the instrument case into Purvis's hands. Purvis took it and opened it. The sun struck the instruments with a glaring blaze of silver that blinded Purvis. He shut his eyes, then closed the case.

"I'm honored, Colonel Ford."

"So am I, Doctor. Welcome to the Cavalry of the West."

Wales had taken a sheaf of notepaper from his pocket and was scribbling very fast with the stub of a pencil. He saw the two men shake hands, and then he saw Lorene stretch her neck and give the hard-bitten Ford a kiss on his cheek.

Ford blushed. And then he smiled.

"I'll be a son of a bitch," Ford said.

Purvis smiled. "Oh, I think you already are, Colonel."

Ed Wales scribbled furiously on his notepaper.

33

—■—

MATTEO WALKED THROUGH the empty house like a somnambulist, like a man in a daze. The sound of his boots striking the hardwood floors echoed in the hollow rooms, imbuing him with a deep sense of loss. He ached for the sound of Luz's voice, the tiny laughter and gurgles of his son, Julio. His hair was wet from the bath he had taken after arriving back at the ranch with Avril and Jorge. His body had been covered with dust like sugar sprinkled on flattened dough, his pores were clogged with the detritus of windblown days on horseback.

Back home, he thought. Back to emptiness and a profound loneliness, and an abiding hatred for Mickey Bone. Many of his men were no longer there, some killed in the war at the Baron rancho, some murdered by Bone. But it was good to know that those of his hands still alive and remaining on the Rocking A bore him no grudge, laid on him no blame for their thinned ranks. He had their sympathy for the loss of his wife and son because of the murder of Dawn, Bone's wife, and their son, Juan, a tragedy that none could explain or discuss with enough outrage.

In the bedroom he and Luz had shared, there was an almost spectral hush that sounded like the roar of a seashell in his ears. He looked at their bed, the crib where Julio had slept. As if in a spell, or because of some unknown compulsion, Matteo walked over to Luz's dressing table. There, he looked down at her combs and her hairbrush, the little pins and clasps she used in her hair. He closed his eyes and pictured her sitting there in front of the small mirror framed in ornate wood that he had bought for her in Galveston. He could see her brushing her hair and combing it out, placing the little combs strategically to hold her hair up just right so that the light would catch it and make it shine like the back of a crow's wing. It seemed as if Luz had been there only moments before, but the room was musty and there was dust on the sills and every other surface, including the floor. He walked away from his wife's dressing table and out of the room, unable to think the unthinkable, a deep longing inside his heart for his wife and son.

Matteo felt a growing sense of suffocation as he walked through the rest of the house. In the front room, he opened a humidor and took out three cigars, smelled them. They smelled fresh. The scent of the tobacco was good in his nostrils. He put them in his shirt pocket, where he had matches, and was glad that Bone had not stolen his cigars.

He knew that Bone had been in the house and that angered him. Jorge had told him that Bone had wanted to live in the house, but that Dawn refused. For that, perhaps, Bone had killed her. He hated Bone, not for the murders, but for his ambition. How long had Bone harbored his dream to take over the Rocking A? Who could know what was in the black heart of a man like Bone? Who could know the lengths such a man would go to steal what belonged to another? Matteo smiled. He knew, for he had harbored the same blood thoughts, and had slain his own family to realize his ambitions. Perhaps he and Bone were not so different, after all. Perhaps that was why he hated Bone so much.

Matteo shook off his thoughts and heard his own labored breathing as he walked to the front room and looked out the window before going to the door. There was much to do and he could not breathe the stale air any longer. He had sent word to Nuncio Alicante and Tomas Lucero to come to the house at dusk and the sun was just brimming the far horizon before it sank from sight in one last burst of shimmering gold.

He walked out onto the porch and took in a deep breath, a breath

scented with the fading blossoms of honeysuckle and the mint growing beneath the cistern, the pungent aroma of the barn and corrals. It
was good to be home, but he could not live there until he had his Luz
back, and his son, Julio. He knew where they had gone and he would
ride to Valle and bring them back.

But back to what? The bad memories? Luz had told him something once that he had almost forgotten, until now. It was while he was
training his men to be soldiers, and before they attacked the Baron
ranch. He had been angry at his parents for selling off their land to
the gringo, Martin Baron.

"You must not have anger all the time, Matteo," she had said to
him. "Some things you cannot change."

"I want the Aguilar land back," he had said. "All of it."

"No," she said. "You want to change what cannot be changed."

"Yes, I want to change the way things are now. I will change
things."

"Do you know how to change your life?" she asked.

"Change my life? What are you talking about, woman?"

"You are unhappy, my husband," Luz had said. "I do not like this.
I do not like to see you have sorrow."

"I do not have sorrow."

"Yes. You believe you have been cheated out of land. You are
sorry that you do not have those hectares that Martin Baron bought
from your family."

"That is true."

"That makes you have sorrow, for what you believe you have lost."

"Yes. If you say it that way."

"The only way you can change anything, Miguelito, is if you
change yourself," she said.

"I do not want to change myself."

"Ah, but you must change yourself before anything in your life
will change. Before you can have that which you wish, you must
change who you are."

"Ha, you talk like a silly old woman."

"No. I know this to be true. My old father told me this when he
became very ill."

"Your father does not know much. Look at him. The way he is.
He is old and frail and very sick."

"But he has no sorrow. At first, when he became ill, he blamed my mother. He blamed my sister, Lucinda, he blamed my brother, Sergio, and, finally, he blamed God."

"Perhaps he was right. Perhaps he put the blame where it belonged," Matteo said.

"No. One day, he awoke from a dream he had and he said that he would no longer put blame on others, on God. He said he would change the way he looked at life. And he did."

"Did he become well?"

"No, he did not become well, but he became happy. He had no sorrow for his fate, for his sickness. He said that those were outside things that made him sick and that in his mind, he thought of himself as being well. He changed himself, and he changed all of us around him."

"Pah, that is stupid, Luz. Your father did not change anything. He was still sick."

"His body was sick, my husband, but not his mind."

"Well, I cannot change. I will not change. I do not have to change."

"Then nothing will change for you, Matteo Miguelito. You will not get the land back. You will have only sorrow in your heart."

He leaned against a post holding up the porch roof and looked at the steaming land stretched out for as far as he could see. He felt a fullness from the sight of the cattle grazing in the last rays of sunlight, good stock that would grow his wealth and give him the power he sought.

He saw two horsemen silhouetted in the fragile light of late afternoon, riding toward the house along the edge of a grazing field, their white shirts glazed with bronze on one side, their straw hats bobbing like gulls upon a wavy sea. Their faces were in darkness, but he knew who they were: Nuncio and Tomas. Riding some distance behind them was Alessandro Gomez, whom he had sent to find the other two, a young man who had been one of his soldiers when he waged war on the Barons, months ago. He was glad that these men had not been killed and he was sorry that Martin and Anson Baron were still alive.

He'd had the chance to kill Martin Baron, in Bandana. So had Reynaud. He put no blame on himself, though, for having escaped the town without facing up to Martin and killing him. He doubted if Reynaud had killed him, either. Or that Cullie had. He wished he knew whether Martin was dead or alive, but he figured that if Reynaud had done his job and killed Martin, he would have shown up at the Rocking A by now to collect the rest of his reward. No, it was almost certain that Reynaud and Cullie had both failed, and Martin Baron was still alive. If so, someday Martin would show up and either try to arrest him or kill him. "I surrounded myself with imbeciles," Matteo said to himself. "It will not happen again."

As Matteo watched, Alessandro turned off and rode toward his house, while Nuncio and Tomas headed his way, passing by the barn and turning their horses at the corner of one of the corrals. The sun was now just a fingernail glimmering on the horizon and the shadows around the house were deepening, resembling black snow. The fields beyond his gaze turned to ashes and would soon disappear.

The two men rode up to the hitchrail and dismounted. They wrapped their reins around the cross pole and stood there for a moment, as if uncertain where they should go.

"Come," Matteo said. "I wish to talk to you."

Both men said, "Yes, *patrón*," and walked up the steps. They removed their straw hats out of respect.

"Sit on the bench, there, Nuncio. You, too, Tomas."

Matteo sat in his rocking chair to one side, facing the men. As the sun sank over the horizon, a whip-poor-will began calling from far away, somewhere deep in the mesquite forest, which had turned dark, along with the land around it. He reached into his pocket and withdrew the three cigars. He handed one to each man, bit off the end of his own and stuck it in his mouth. Then he struck a match and lit the cigars.

"You have surprise to see me," Aguilar said to the two men.

"*No, patrón,*" Nuncio said.

"*Sí', patrón,*" from Tomas.

"Alessandro told you the things that happened to me, eh?"

Both men nodded as they puffed on their cigars. Aguilar blew a thin stream of smoke from his mouth and pointed to the west.

"The sun sets," he said. "Tomorrow, I am going to Mexico to get my wife and son. Nuncio, you and Tomas will accompany me. Do you wish to come with me?"

"Yes," Nuncio said. Tomas nodded in agreement.

"You were both good soldiers. You fought well."

The men said nothing. They smoked and they listened to Don Matteo.

"Do you want to know why I am taking you with me?" Aguilar asked.

"It is of no import," Nuncio said.

"It is nothing," Tomas said.

"Neither of you are married. We go to Valle, a little pueblo not far from the Rio Bravo. That is where my wife has lived and where she has gone with our son. Luz has a twin sister, Lucinda, who is unmarried. So you know her beauty before you ever see her, is that not right, Nuncio?"

"Yes, that is true."

"Perhaps Lucinda will wish to marry you, Nuncio."

"Perhaps."

"Do you want to get married?"

"I do not know, Don Matteo."

"Tomas, do you want to get married?"

"I have thought about it. But I am poor and I am only a vaquero."

"When we go to Mexico to bring back my wife and son, that is not all we will bring back. And you will share in that."

"What do we bring back, Don Matteo?" Tomas asked.

"Many horses and cattle, Tomas. There is a big war on and we can sell the horses to the army. No matter which army, we will make money. And you both will share equally with me."

"Is that true?" Nuncio asked.

"Truth. Now, we will leave in the morning. Pack what you need. Bring powder and ball for your pistols and rifles and food to eat, water to drink. It is going to be a long ride and we must do it in a hurry."

"We will do it, Don Matteo," Nuncio said. "We will be ready."

"We will hunt on the way?" Tomas asked.

Aguilar smiled. He took a deep puff of his cigar and let the smoke linger in his lungs. Then he let the smoke out slowly between his smiling lips.

In the darkness, he saw several horsemen ride back into the barn. They did not make much noise. When someone lit a lantern, Aguilar could see their dark figures and he knew Alessandro was waiting for them, waiting to give them instructions for the time Don Matteo would be gone to the south.

"Yes, we will hunt," Aguilar said. "We will hunt for some of our food, the rabbits and the quail and the deer, the turkey. But we will also hunt something else when we are in Mexico."

"What is that, *mi patrón?*" Tomas asked.

"Bone," Matteo said. "When Bone runs, he runs to Mexico. We will hunt Bone and I will give two hundred dollars to anyone who kills him."

"That is a lot of money," Nuncio said.

"It is more than Bone is worth," Aguilar said. "Go and sleep. We will leave at dawn."

The two men said good night to Aguilar and he watched them ride their horses to the barn. The orange glow from inside gave him comfort as he finished smoking his cigar. Soon, he knew, Avril would come and cook for him, and perhaps she would warm his bed this night. She was loyal to him and she was grateful to him. She would be happy to do anything he asked of her.

More important, she was young. And she was a virgin. It was his right, as Don Matteo, to take his pleasure with her. For that, she would be even more grateful.

34

PEEBO SAW IT coming. Anson smelled it. Both knew they were in for trouble as they looked to the west and saw that something was devouring the blue sky from the ground up. The horizon had disappeared and was now a murky haze of yellow, ocher, burnt umber, and sienna, as if a painter had smeared the canvas with a mixture of these colors.

"It looks like hell comin' our way, son," Peebo said.

"Smells like an old moth-eaten blanket," Anson said, sniffing the suddenly still air.

That was what had first alerted them as they tracked the white bull. The breeze had vanished as if it had been sucked up by some invisible vortex, and the air had turned stifling, close, smothering.

"That's a damned dust storm," Peebo said. "Blowin' half of New Mexico right at us."

"Or Mexico, maybe," Anson said, looking around to get his bearings. It was hard to tell with the sky so blotched and out of kilter, but the sun had been falling toward the west for the past couple of hours.

"This will wipe out all the tracks, Anson."

"No matter. I can still find that gully."

"Not if you can't see."

"We'd better hole up somewhere until it passes. Get the horses under cover. I've seen sandstorms like this before. A man can choke to death in 'em."

"Is that what that is? I don't hear nothin'."

"Not yet, you don't. But when it hits us, the wind will fair howl like a cow with its teat caught under its hind foot."

Suddenly, Peebo let out a cry. "Whoooee," he shouted. "Will you looky yonder." He pointed to a large swirling mass somewhere in the midst of all the flying sand in the distance.

"That's a damned dust devil," Anson said. "You get in one of those and it'll whip you to death."

"Christ. It looks just like a twister."

"It is a twister, but a little itty-bitty one."

"You get twisters down here in these parts, son?"

"You're damned right we do, but mostly along the coast. They come out of the water and play hob with everything and everybody on shore."

Peebo swore again, and remained mesmerized by the growing cloud of dust that seemed to be eating up the sky to the west.

"Let's get to shelter, quick," Anson said, slapping the tips of his reins against his horse's rump. He put the spurs to the black's flanks and the horse surged under him like the rolling crest of an ocean wave.

Riding well off the road, Anson looked for a large stand of mesquite trees, the thicker the better. He didn't know how much time they had before the dust storm hit them, but he knew they were going to be blasted by wind and sand very soon.

Peebo was right on his heels, as Anson wove a path through the trees, giving the horse its head when it was safe, otherwise guiding him so that he wouldn't get brushed off by tree limbs. Finally, he reined up in a clump of mesquite that was broad and wide. There were some oaks mixed in, too. He slipped out of the saddle as Peebo rode up.

Then Anson looked back out over the plain toward the road. The road was still there, but beyond it the sky was nearly obliterated by dust. It seemed to hang there like an ominous shroud with a yellowish cast. The dust devil had worn itself out and he could no longer see it swirling toward them.

"How much time?" Peebo asked as he reined in his horse and jumped from the saddle.

"I don't know," Anson said. "Not long. Ten minutes, maybe. I just know there's a hell of a wind behind that cloud of dust. Look at it. It stretches clear across the horizon."

"What do we do now?"

Anson didn't answer right away. He hadn't seen a dust storm like this one in a long time, and during the last one he had been inside. His mother and father and their maid had all scrambled to hang wet blankets and towels, anything that would hold water, over all the windows so that they could keep some of the dust out. The wind had rattled the house and peppered its wood with dust and grit. The blankets and towels had helped, but the howling wind had nearly driven them all mad. It had blinded some of their cattle and scared hell out of the chickens. They had not been hit by a twister, but the windblown grit had scoured the paint off the house and blown part of their roof off, had taken some things left outside and flown them to other parts.

"Let's wet down a couple of bandanas for the horses, tie them to the bridle rings, and put a couple over our own faces. Then we'll hunker down under our soogans."

Peebo nodded and started fishing for the spare bandanas in his saddlebag. Anson tied his horse to a sturdy mesquite trunk. He picked a tree that lined up with others in a fairly straight row facing the oncoming dust cloud.

Peebo tied his horse behind Anson's, giving it further protection if the blowing dust continued on its present course. Then they both wet their own bandanas and tied them over their noses and mouths. They hunkered down behind the horses, and behind another mesquite tree with thick leafy branches.

"Still a long ways off, son," Peebo said.

"It'll be here soon enough. Look at that damned sky."

Peebo craned his neck to look. From where he squatted, he could not see all of the sky, but enough to know the cloud of dust was rising ever higher. Soon, it would blot out the sun if the dust continued to thicken and rise into the air.

"Is it going to get dark?" Peebo asked.

"Not dark, maybe, but that dust is going to damned sure cover the sun."

"Maybe it'll rain."

"Oh, there's probably rain behind it, all right. Way the hell behind it."

Peebo forced a grin, but it was lost on Anson, who continued to stare toward the west. The part of the western sky he could still see had turned to a sickly yellow color with blotches of brown and umber. Around him it was dead calm and he strained his ears for the howl of the wind. But the storm was still too far off. He had never seen an uglier sky and in that silence he had the eerie feeling that the land was holding its breath and that there was nothing alive out there in the range of his vision. He felt as if he was caught somewhere out of time, that all life beyond his immediate area had ceased to exist. The thoughts made his skin crawl, and deep in the pit of his stomach, he could feel the tentacles of fear squirming around like a cluster of cold, wet earthworms.

Anson and Peebo watched in silence as the dust cloud moved closer and the sky began to disappear even faster. In a few minutes, the sun appeared as a pale yellow ghost shimmering through the pall of dust, and then they were in shadow as the high winds stretched the cloud over them.

"Here comes the blow," Anson said, ducking his head instinctively. "Hold on."

"Can't see much," Peebo said, and then the wind sprayed grit against his face and he let out a sharp yell. The horses whickered and turned around so that their rumps faced the wind.

In seconds, Peebo and Anson were enveloped in dust. It seemed to float in ahead of the brunt of the wind, peppering their faces and exposed skin. Then the first hard gust struck them and they heard the high-pitched keening of the wind behind the cloud. Within a split second, they felt the full force of the wind as it struck them, hurling curtains of sand and grit at them, whistling past their ears, rattling the leaves on the trees, ripping through them, shredding them on their branches, tearing holes through them until they resembled punched green tickets.

A blown limb smashed into Anson's nose. Blood spurted from one nostril. He doubled over and felt the wind blowing against the crown and brim of his hat. Peebo was already bent over to protect his face and to keep his hat from flying off. The trees around them rattled as pebbles and twigs hurtled through the air like projectiles.

Anson pulled his slicker over his head and drew its sides down and under his chest. The back of it began to flap with merciless regularity. He stole a glance at Peebo, who was wrestling with his own soogan. It was like trying to put up a tent in a windstorm, except there was no anchor for their slickers and they whipped noisily and threatened to fly out of their hands.

The wind increased in its ferocity, the sun was completely blotted out, with only a faint pale light that swirled with flying debris. The horses fought to hold their footing as the wind blasted their rumps, stinging their hides with sand and grit, occasionally pelting them with small sharp stones and broken branches and twigs. The animals staggered and weaved in place, struggling to breathe through nostrils clogged with fine dirt.

Anson breathed through the wet bandana covering his face. It was turning stiff with clogged grit and his lungs seemed unable to take in enough oxygen. His chest burned with fire, as if he was breathing in air from a blast furnace. But he knew it would be folly to panic. He had to keep his head and hold on to his soogan. His hands stung with blown sand and his knuckles throbbed with pain from the wood particles that struck them with blinding force.

Peebo cried out as a rock struck him in the head, square in the center of his skull, ripping a small hole in his flapping slicker. Blood flowed from the wound and he tried to turn around as the horses had done and present his rear to the onslaught of fierce winds. But the force was too great and he huddled up into a tight ball, pulling the slicker down underneath him to protect his hands and keep the soogan from being jerked from his grasp.

Anson knew he had never been in a blow this powerful. The light grew more dim and he wondered how long he could hold on. The noise of the wind was deafening, a maddening howl in his ears. It seemed as if the entire world had erupted from some volcanic upheaval and was being rained down on them like grapeshot and cannonfire. He hurt in a dozen places and the backs of his hands felt as if they had been blasted with shotgun pellets. They stung and throbbed and bled, and soon he lost all feeling except for pain.

Then the wind began to swirl around him and he heard a roaring noise that sounded like a herd of cattle stampeding toward them. He knew the sound. A twister was building and possibly headed their way. If it struck them full force, he knew they would be blown from the ground, and possibly would die.

"Brace yourself," Anson yelled to Peebo, but the wind snatched away his words like torn pieces of paper and the roar of the storm swallowed up all sound that issued from him, Peebo, and the screaming horses.

Anson felt his body scooting backward as the force of the wind increased and he tried to dig in the toes of his boots. He felt that, at any moment, he would be blown back into the trees and smashed like a wooden doll against the trunks.

He was no longer able to think, to reason. The wind whipped and ragged at his clothing and dust sprayed him with incredible force, stinging him through his clothes, tearing holes in the soogan and puncturing his hat until his scalp tingled as if stung by nettles or drenched in boiling oil.

He could no longer see Peebo, or the horses. He could not see the ground beneath him.

All he could hear was the roar of an approaching cyclone that seemed certain to strike them. Suddenly, his mind cleared for a moment, and he was possessed with a momentary calm and clarity that made him realize his time on earth was up. Surely, he thought, he was going to die.

And there wasn't a damned thing he could do about it.

35

—■—

MARTIN BREATHED IN the heady, almost dizzying scent of Millie's musk as they lay naked together on her bed, torturing each other with wet kisses and exploring hands. Her mouth was steaming, her tongue a laving caress inside his mouth, sensuous against his own ravenous, twining, tangling, tongue. Caroline had never done this to him, no woman had; and his senses raged with a fire that coursed through his entire body like a volcanic lava flow.

One of her hands massaged his chest, kneading the tiny nipples, swirling through his hairs like blind animals nibbling, nuzzling—like pups at a mother's teats. And her other hand flowed so gently at his loins and over his rock-hard manhood, stroking his shaft, then sliding down to his scrotum, holding him there until her warmth penetrated every fold of his skin, down deep to where his seeds boiled like a milky soup over lashing tongues of flame.

Her mouth tasted of crushed mint and cloves, and her skin gave off the faint scent of blooming lilacs. He gazed into her eyes and saw the shine of a woman in season, full of a veiled lust that excited him, the boldness of a woman sure of what she wanted and a confidence in how to get it. When she took her hands away from his loins, she grabbed his buttocks and slid them up his back, and he felt the tips of her fingernails rake his skin like a cat's paw with the claws re-tracted nearly all the way.

The wind raged at the shutters of her house, setting up random squeaks through all the rooms, pressing to get in and cover every-thing with fine sand. The wind had come up that afternoon and they were in the midst of a full-blown dust storm flung at them with furi-ous intensity from the southwest. He had helped her tack wet sheets and blankets over all the windows, but still the grit came through, leaving a patina of silt over virtually every surface.

"I want you, Marty," she breathed, and there was a huskiness in her voice that sent shivers of electricity through his loins and hard-ened him even more.

He wanted her, too. He slid on top of her and heard the bed-springs give and creak. He straightened his arms and rose above her. He looked down at her and thought of Caroline, the image nearly choking him. But Millie was not his dead wife and she looked noth-ing like her. But seeing Millie naked beneath him brought back long-forgotten memories of the wife he had once loved and had lost long before she died.

Martin took a quick breath and hesitated, trying to shake off his thoughts of Caroline. A puzzled look crossed Millie's face.

"What are you waiting for?" she whispered.

"I, uh, nothing. I just—just wanted to look at you for a moment."

She sighed and pushed, lifting her hips off the bed and toward him.

He drank her in, all of her, and the memories of Caroline faded. The sheen of sweat on her skin, the pursing of her lips, so inviting, so sensuous, made him forget the woman he had once loved. There was no comparison. Millie was young and soft and he liked the way she smelled, the way she touched him, with just enough boldness to make her alluring, not so much as to make her seem aggressive.

Martin dipped his loins downward and touched her with his swollen manhood. She pushed up and he impaled her, sank through the velvet folds of her sex, and then she bucked up, ever so gently and subtly, and he sank deep into her steaming sheath, lost to her charms, oblivious to all else in the world. Her warmth flooded through him and he stroked her slowly, enjoying the movement and her reaction. Every time he was on the point of breaking free of her, she pulled his hips back down and he rocked into her and onto her, caught up in the ageless rhythm of love, of mating. Her sighs excited him and her kisses drew him deeper into her spell, sent shots of electricity through his veins.

"It's so good, Marty," she breathed. "You're so good."

"You, too, Millie," he said huskily, and the bedsprings sang in soft lyrical counterpoint to the blasting wind outside, a wind that ruffled the house and scoured it with dirt and sand as if trying to intrude on their lovemaking, sniffing like some prowling wolf at every window, every door.

He touched her soft breasts and kneaded the nipples with his fingers until they became hard nubbins. Her aureola flared with the pale colors of wild berries and she purred with pleasure in his ear as he bent to kiss her swollen breasts. He was lost inside her, lost to her gentle movements and her sighs, lost to the warmth of her, warmer than a buffalo robe or a woolen blanket.

She smiled up at him and raked his back with her fingernails to indicate her pleasure. She did not break the skin, but he felt the tingle from her nails and it sent ripples of pleasure through his veins.

Then all of his hunger caught up with him and he raced to the climax as Millie gasped and held on. She moaned deep in her chest as he plumbed her depths and then she bucked and quivered against his loins, holding him fast inside her as he trembled, spilling his seed. She screamed with delight as they floated down from the dizzying heights where they had been, like two feathers from an eagle's nest.

"Yes," she breathed in contentment, her face glistening with a patina of sweat.

"Beautiful, Millie."

"Yes. Very beautiful, Marty. I'm very happy."

He gave her a last squeeze and then rolled from her body, sated, out of breath from that last effort.

She lay next to him as he gazed around her bedroom. He had never been to her house before. It was small, and still smelled of new wood. There was a fireplace in the front room that had not been used much, but there was a smell of burned wood in the house that bespoke her loneliness on cool evenings when perhaps she had lit a fire for comfort. For some reason, the thought made him homesick for his own home, for times gone by, but he quickly erased such thoughts in the wonder of the moment. He was still suspended out of time, floating just above the earth, his body still tingling as if he had run a mile or two in the rain.

"What are you thinking?" she asked.

"Nothing."

"Really?"

"I was just looking at your room, Millie."

"It's not much. But it's home. I helped build it."

"You did?"

She nodded and lazed a hand across his midsection, moving it back and forth idly, but with a hint of possession that did not escape him.

The walls of the room were knotty pine and he knew the lumber had been shipped in, probably from east Texas. The room had a nice smell to it, and part of it, he knew, was her, her own musky scent, the faint aroma of honeysuckle or lilacs. There was a small bureau set with brush and comb and other women things, little vials and bottles like those Caroline had possessed. He put his hand on her tummy and it felt soft and yielding, as though, if he moved his hand lower, she would open up to him like a flower and take him into that mysterious world of pleasure once again.

The wind sawed at the shutters, not as strong as before, but still sniffing like a prowling wolf, ebbing and flowing, gusting and wafting, as if it had a prying sentience, wishing to intrude on their world where all was calm and peaceful, all was perfectly symmetrical.

"It's odd," he said, staring up at the ceiling.

"What's odd?"

"That most beautiful moment of release, that wonderful feeling, and then you can hardly remember it. It's like being with God for that one instant and then it's gone."

"It's like being God," she said.

"Yes."

"But you remember the experience."

"Yes. I will always remember that. It's just that one moment. It can never be recaptured."

"Except to do it again," she said, a coy lilt in her voice.

"But it's different every time and you swear to yourself you will hold the moment forever in your mind. And it just floats away, never to return."

"You sound so sad, Martin."

"It is a sadness. You know what the Mexicans call that moment?"

"No."

"They call it the 'little death.' To them, it's like dying just a little."

"Maybe they are talking about something else dying."

"I don't think so."

"Well, it felt wonderful to me, Martin."

"But do you remember that moment, that one splendid moment when I filled you with seed?"

"Yes, I remember it." She touched his hand with hers. "And I always will."

"This is not your first time."

"No. A boy did it to me when I was young. It was awkward and sudden and I don't really remember it. I felt dirty afterward. Ashamed. I went to church and prayed for my soul. But I've had a couple of beaus since then."

"You have never been married, Millie?"

"No." She sighed. "It's funny you would mention that."

"Why?"

"Most men run when the word 'marriage' comes up."

"You must have brought up the subject before," he said.

"No, I never have. And I never will. It's the man's place to ask."

"Yes, it is."

There was a silence between them, then.

She squeezed his hand.

"I know this," she said. "I want to be with you. A lot."

"I'm leaving," he said. "Not because of you. But because I'm in the army now. The cavalry."

"Yes. I hate to see you go, though. I wish I could go with you."

"Well, you can't."

"Why can't I?"

"Colonel Ford wouldn't allow it. No womenfolk."

"Lorene is going."

"That's different. She's a nurse, helping her uncle."

"I worked as a nurse once."

"Ford doesn't want nurses. He doesn't want Lorene, really. He's just doing Doc Purvis a favor."

"Two nurses are better than one, Martin."

He laughed.

"Not with Ford. He's a bastard, really. I don't think he wants any truck with women, on or off the battlefield."

Martin started to rise from the bed.

"Must you go so soon?" she said.

"I have to check in at headquarters. Officers' call is at sundown."

Millie pouted. "I hate this wind," she said incongruously.

"This is only the edge of it. It must be blowing hard along the Gulf. You can taste the salt in this one."

He rose up and scooted off the bed. He walked to where his clothes hung over the back of a chair. He started dressing. Millie watched him, then got up, wrapping a sheet around her naked body like a Roman toga.

She padded over to him and started to help him dress.

"I can do this," he said. "Been dressing myself for a long while now."

"I know. Maybe it's about time you had a woman help you with some things. Your house is finished now, you know."

"It's mostly Anson's house. And no, I didn't know."

"Anson isn't there, however. He's off chasing some wild long-horn bull."

"He has his heart set on catching that white bull. I guess you know more about it than I do, Millie." He finished pulling on his boots and was strapping on his gun belt. He buckled it and adjusted the sidearm to suit him.

"I could manage your home for you while you're gone," she said, stepping back to admire him. The sheet slipped slightly off her shoulder.

"We have Mexican women to do that."

"Do the Mexican women do everything for you, Marty?"

He blushed. "Not everything, no."

Martin became aware of the tension that was building up in the room. He looked at Millie and tried to fathom the look in her eyes, realizing that she was as much a mystery to him as Caroline had been. He did not know women and admitted it, at least to himself.

But he knew Millie wanted something from him, something more than what he had given her this afternoon. Perhaps the offer to look after his house was genuine, but he also knew that once he let her inside, it would be very difficult to get her out. And he wasn't sure that he wanted to settle down with a woman. Certainly not now, not while there was a war on and he wasn't home to take care of her.

He was beginning to feel uncomfortable with Millie and he didn't want that. They had been good friends and now that he had bedded her, he wanted more of her company. Occasionally, though. Not all the time. He didn't know if he could handle another wife at his age. After Caroline.

When Millie had invited him over to her house for a drink, for "refreshments," as she had put it, he never imagined that he would go to bed with her. But one thing had led to another and they had done the deed. Now, it seemed, she wanted more, and perhaps had wanted more for as long as he had known her.

"Did your wife ever go sailing with you, Martin?" Millie's question caught Martin by surprise.

"No."

"I would," she said. "I'd love to sail with you."

"I probably will never go back to sea."

She looked sad and wistful just then.

"I guess what I'm trying to say is that I would go anywhere with you."

"Well, you can't do that, you know." He felt awkward talking like that. She wasn't exactly pushing him, but he sensed her need, her need to clutch him, to hold on to him. And he was not ready for that yet. Maybe someday, he thought.

"Before you leave, I want to read you something. It won't take long. Will you listen?"

"I really should be getting back to the hotel."

"A minute?"

"All right, Millie."

He followed her into the front room, the sheet wrapped around her trailing on the floor. She walked to the bookshelf and pulled out a book. It looked very worn and the pages seemed to have loosened from the binding.

"What's that?" he asked.

"Lorene loaned me this. Her uncle got it from New York."

"It's not a Bible."

"No. It's a book of poetry by a man named Walt Whitman. It's called *Leaves of Grass*. Maybe you'll think of me while you're gone and maybe you'll remember the words I'm going to read you."

"I'll try," he said.

She leafed through the pages until she found what she was looking for.

"Here it is," she said. "It's from a long poem called 'Starting from Paumanok.'" She began to read:

> I depart as air, shake my locks at the runaway sun,
> I effuse my flesh in eddies, and drift it in lazy jags.
> I bequeath myself to the dirt to grow from the grass I love,
> If you want me again look for me under your boot soles.
> You will hardly know who I am or what I mean,
> But I shall be good health to you nevertheless.
> And filter and fibre your blood
> Failing to fetch me at first keep encouraged,
> Missing me one place search another,
> I stop somewhere waiting for you.

She closed the book and looked at Martin.

He sighed, not knowing what to say. But the words had a powerful effect on him.

She walked up to him and kissed him. Then she pushed him toward the door and he could see that her eyes were filling with tears.

"I'll be waiting for you, Martin," she said, as he walked out the door and into the wind. He held on to his hat and waved goodbye.

And the blowing dust swallowed him up and he was gone.

Millie stood there in the doorway for a long time, as though wondering if he would change his mind and return.

Finally, she closed the door and put the book of Whitman's poems back on the shelf. Then she sat down and began to weep. She listened to the wind shake the house and rattle the shutters, and the house echoed with a deep emptiness as the sun sank in the dusty sky and the dark came on.

36

ANSON SAW THE twister waggle and weave, changing directions like some maddened beast, rising from the land and whirling ever larger as if it were a djinni sprouting from a magic lamp. He crawled over to Peebo, rose up and slammed him facedown into the ground.

"Stay flat," Anson yelled above the roar of the wind.

Peebo said something that Anson couldn't understand, but he thought it was probably an oath. They both lay flat, hugging the ground as if they were on the deck of a pitching ship in the midst of a storm at sea.

"If you ever prayed, son," Peebo yelled right into Anson's ear, "now is the goddamned time."

Something hurtled toward them, sailed over their heads and smashed into one of the trees behind them. Anson saw the gray fur and knew it must have been a rabbit, hurled by the wind. He heard its bones crunch as it struck the tree, but he knew the animal had been dead before he ever saw it. More debris flew through the air. Branches and twigs and pebbles struck and stung them. They covered their heads and their hands became pocked with sand and grit, ached where small stones ripped into their flesh before glancing off like bullets shot from a gun.

Anson could not see. He opened his eyes to slits once, and they filled with dirt. He closed them quickly against a world of whirling wind that tore at his clothing and sucked at his breath and pulled at his feet and body like a wraith trying to tear him off the face of the earth. He sensed Peebo next to him, like him, hanging on for dear life in the howling maelstrom of wind and detritus that spun over and around them like a vengeful banshee from another world.

Then Anson felt himself being lifted from the ground. He stretched out his arms and dug his fingernails into the dirt, trying to keep from being snatched up into the vortex of the twister. But he kept sliding and falling, rising again, and then he felt a hard smack on his leg as he was twirled around, striking the trunk of a tree. He opened his mouth to scream and he knew he did scream, but the wind tore the sound from his mouth and swallowed it up and he choked on the dirt that flew into his mouth and throat.

Underneath the roar of the wind, Anson heard the horses scream and then he felt himself being whirled away, twisting through the air, helpless, his arms and legs flailing. He became dizzy and sick to his stomach, and then he felt himself falling, not slowly but fast, and then he flew into a silence and hit something hard with his head. Bright stars flashed in the darkness of his mind and he blacked out, oblivious to the maelstrom around him.

Anson dreamed of wild horses trampling rabbits and birds falling broken-necked from a dark sky over an eerie landscape of sandy hillocks and rivers running with thick mud. He chased after the horses and they turned into Apaches painted like hideous dolls, and then they, too, changed, into fierce longhorns with long white beards that thundered toward him in a ground-pounding stampede. He felt their hooves slashing into his flesh and the dust they raised filled his lungs and he gasped for air, struggling to rise and run away. But he was trapped there in the dream, trying to scream, and the longhorns faded away and left their hides covering him like thick blankets, suffocating him, smothering him in the infernal, back-blistering blackness.

Anson had no idea how long he had lain unconscious, but when he awoke it was night, and although the wind still blew, it was not as strong, and by turning his head away from it, he could breathe. The air was still filled with sand. He could hear it sweeping across the earth like a whispering viper, and when he looked up, he could not see the stars. He had no idea where he was, but he knew that Peebo was nowhere near him, nor could he see the horses. His head hurt and his ribs were tender. When he touched the sore place on his chest, he nearly fainted with the pain. He surmised that he must have cracked a rib or two. When he sat up, the ribs were stabs of pain with every breath.

His clothes were infested with sand and grit. His shirt felt as if it weighed forty pounds and his trousers were stiff and heavy with embedded sand. His breathing was shallow, painful, and his mouth was dry. He wished now he had thought to sling a canteen around his neck, but he had left it dangling from his saddlehorn and his saddle was on his horse, Nero, wherever he might be.

He was hungry, too, but too sick inside to think of taking in food. His stomach was sour and his lips cracked and swollen slightly. His cheekbone hurt, too, as did his forehead, and when he touched it, pieces of tree bark flaked off. "I must have taken a hell of a whack," he thought.

Anson lay back down gingerly, his face to the ground where it was easier to breathe. The wind and sand coursed over his back and when he closed his eyes, he thought that if he went back to sleep he would surely be buried alive.

His bandana had slipped from his face and was yoked around his neck. He pulled it up and covered his nose and mouth. But the cloth was saturated with dust and dirt. Still, it helped keep him from breathing in more silt. He willed himself to stay calm, knowing he would have to ride out the sandstorm if he was going to survive. He felt a sinking sensation in his stomach, wondering if Peebo was still alive, and where he was. Was he, too, hurt? And where were the horses? Had they been injured, as well? So many questions crowded his mind, and he had to quell the fear that crawled in his belly and simmered up into his brain like broth boiling in an iron kettle.

Anson lay there listening to the wind whistle through the trees, hearing the rustle of leaves blasted by blowing sand, the creaking of mesquite limbs, the crash of debris slamming into trunks, and sand pelting him, covering him inch by inch.

He fell asleep, despite the pain, but drifted just under the surface of consciousness, the wind a long hum in his ears, the sound of blowing sand against the tree trunks and leaves a threnodic hum that kept him drugged with its monotonous tone. He felt a kind of detached annoyance at the sound, but could not rouse himself above a stupor that kept his ribs from hurting as long as he didn't move.

Anson awoke to a murky dawn, to a pale brown sky filled with blowing dust. His ears were clogged so that the wind was muffled. His nose, too, was filled with dirt and fine grains of sand and his mouth tasted of grit. He touched his face and it was rough and sandy under his beard. He dug in his pocket for another bandana and drew it out. He twirled one end to a point and spit on it. Then he began to clean his ears until he could hear the wind again. He switched bandanas, putting the fresh one over his face. He gazed around at his surroundings, trying to figure out where he was. He could see no more than a hundred yards in any direction, and what he saw was an eerie world of shadowy trees and clumps of matter that had no definable form that he could recognize. He felt bewildered and lost, with no bearings from the sky or the land.

He called out Peebo's name. He called out to Nero and Peebo's horse, Bucky, short for Buckaroo. His words came back to him in showery gusts of sand, dying as if they had never been spoken. The emptiness, the wordless silence only deepened Anson's sense of isolation, his dread of the unknown.

He stood up, pain spearing through his ribs, and looked up at the brown sky again, feeling the pressure of the wind. He looked at the ground, knowing he would see no tracks. But he knew he had to find Peebo and the horses. He tried to remember in which direction the twister had thrown him, but his mind was still addled from the experience and, in the gloom of dust, he could not get his bearings. He remembered what his father had told him about navigation at sea, especially about dead reckoning. Perhaps, he thought, he could figure out how far he had been thrown and in what direction. Perhaps he could retrace his course and return to where he and Peebo had been lying under the brunt of the sandstorm.

At the same time, Anson did not want to stray too far from this place. Peebo could be looking for him, if he was still alive. He took out his knife and walked to the largest mesquite tree. He cut a slash all around the trunk, peeling off the bark with his blade. He walked a few paces away and was satisfied that he could find that tree again, if he got close enough.

Then Anson started walking in the general direction of where he'd been when the wind picked him up and flung him into this grove. He knew he was walking blind, but he knew he had to do something. His mouth was dry with a powerful thirst, his belly empty and growling like a hungry lion.

As the sun rose in the sky, the light changed to a yellowish haze and the wind seemed to be losing some of its strength. It ebbed and flowed, giving Anson some small moments of relief as he walked a hundred yards in a straight line from the blazed tree, calling out Peebo's name every few feet.

When he had gone a couple of hundred yards, Anson began walking in a circle, holding the memory of the blazed tree in his mind, feeling that he was using a form of dead reckoning. He imagined where the tree was and kept looking in that direction while trying to walk in a circle.

He found the horses. They were both lying down, their legs folded under them, rumps to the wind. He walked up, speaking softly to them. The horses whickered in recognition. As far as he could see, after looking around, they were in the same place. He knelt down and saw that Nero's nostrils were clogged with sand. He took off his bandanna and cleaned the grit from his nose and ears. Then he did the same with Buckaroo. Neither horse made an attempt to get up, for the wind was still blowing in the murky yellow light.

"Peebo," Anson called as he sat between the horses, drinking from his canteen. The water tasted brackish, but he was able to rinse his mouth and wash the grime from his face.

He looked at his rifle and pistol. Both were saturated with sand and he began to wipe the dust and dirt away with one of his bandanas. Both, he knew, would get a good cleaning once the sandstorm abated or stopped.

He heard a noise and both horses lifted their heads and looked off in the direction of the sound, their ears twisting like sharp-pointed cones.

"Peebo? Is that you?"

A few moments later, Peebo walked into view. That is, he limped into Anson's line of sight. He was carrying two hats. One of them was Anson's. Both horses got to their feet when they saw Peebo. Both whinnied a greeting to him.

"You're alive," Anson said.

"That's your opinion, son."

Peebo's clothes were slashed as if he had just come from a knife fight and there were ugly bruises on his forehead and cheek. It was obvious to Anson that Peebo was walking with a great deal of pain.

"I found our hats stuck in a patch of cactus," Peebo said. "Christ, I got sucked up like a leaf when that fuckin' twister hit. Dragged through the brush, splattered into cactus. Then got knocked clean cold against a damned oak tree."

"It was pretty bad," Anson said.

"'Bad' ain't the word for it, son. It was plumb harrowing."

Peebo held out his arms and rolled up the sleeves of his shirt. His arms were peppered with small red dots as if he had been stuck with a hundred sharp needles.

"Cactus ain't friendly to human hide," Peebo said.

"Damn, you look like a pincushion, Peebo."

Peebo rolled his sleeves back down and walked over to his horse. He rubbed Bucky's nose in an affectionate gesture. Nero craned his neck and nudged Peebo's arm at the shoulder. Peebo patted Nero on the neck.

"I'm mighty glad to see these two boys," Peebo said. He took his canteen from the saddlehorn and washed out his mouth. Then he drank. And spit.

"Whooeee, that water's hotter'n piss."

Anson laughed, then winced at the pain in his ribs.

"You hurt, son?"

"I think I cracked a couple of ribs," Anson said.

"Want me to take a look?"

"You won't see anything. It hurts when I take a deep breath or move wrong."

"Well, don't take no deep breaths or move wrong, son."

"You can joke if you want. We're both lucky to be alive."

Peebo looked around and up at the dusty sky. He put on his hat and threw Anson's hat to him.

"How long do these sandstorms last?" Peebo asked.

"Too long. This one's lasted longer'n any I've ever seen."

Peebo drank some more water, then sat down opposite Anson. He began to dig at one ear with the little finger of his right hand.

"I cleaned mine with a bandana," Anson said.

"I've always wanted to own my own land."

Anson looked at his hat, at the holes made in it by prickly-pear spines. He tried to reshape it, then put it on his head. He dug out the makings and tried to roll a smoke. The wind blew the tobacco away and then snatched the paper from his fingers.

"Give it up, son."

Anson grinned sheepishly.

Wind blew combers of sand between them, leaving ripples on the earth's surface, like miniature dunes.

"Damn, is this wind ever going to stop?" Anson said.

"It's lightened up some, I think."

They sat there, hanging their heads. Peebo used Anson as a shield from the wind, but he was just as disconsolate.

"Maybe we ought to eat somethin'," Peebo said, after a while.

"I'm hungry, but the thought of food makes my stomach churn."

"Mine's pretty sour, too. It's just hell sittin' here like this, getting' blown all to hell with sand in your eyes and mouth and everywhere else."

But they sat there. Eventually Anson lifted his head. He held out a hand, palm up.

"Feel that?" he asked Peebo.

Peebo looked up at him.

"Feel what?"

"It's getting cooler."

"Yeah, some."

Anson sniffed the air, then looked up at the sky.

"It's getting darker, too," Anson said.

It was true. They could now see the sky through sheets of flying dust and there were dark clouds moving in.

"Rain," Peebo said.

"And more wind."

As if to underline Anson's words, they were struck with a sudden gust of wind that billowed out their shirts and blew their hats from their heads. Both snatched their hats before they could blow away.

The horses whickered and Nero started bobbing his head up and down and pawing the ground.

"I see you lost your slicker," Peebo said.

"I don't see yours anywhere, neither."

Both men laughed.

"Well, we're going to get wet," Anson said.

"And we're going to get mighty muddy, too."

The first sprinkles of rain began to fall. Ten minutes later, they were hammered by spitwad-sized hail that pelted them and the horses with wind-driven force. Both men crawled under their horses' bellies and watched the ground sprout white balls of ice.

A few minutes later, the hail stopped and turned to a heavy rain. It became very dark as the main thunderhead rolled over them, blotting out the sun. The rain melted the hail and the wind turned slightly warmer.

Anson looked over at Peebo, who was grinning that big wide grin of his. Peebo folded his hands in an attitude of prayer and looked upward, his eyes close to Bucky's belly.

"Thank you, sweet Lord," Peebo said, then winked at Anson.

Anson smiled. "Amen."

The rain swept through the trees in shimmering sheets and water puddled up beneath them. The horses shook their heads and then their bodies as if to rid themselves of all the sand in their coats.

"It's a damned sight better than sand," Anson yelled at Peebo.

"Long as we don't have to swim," Peebo said.

The two men hunkered down in the rain and watched it pelt the earth, grateful that the sand had stopped blowing and they could breathe clean fresh air. They shivered in the coolness, but both were smiling and stretching their necks as they stuck their heads outside and opened their mouths to the sky, letting the water spatter into their mouths.

Anson felt as if he had emerged from the desert into an oasis.

He didn't care if it rained all day and all night.

37

ROY AND FORREST were still asleep when Wanda and her mother, Hattie, began taking the heavy sand-blasted blankets down from the windows. Rain lashed against the house in a driving fury, but at least the sandstorm was over. The floors were covered with fine dust, and the house smelled musty. But Hattie wore a smile on her face.

They put the blankets in a galvanized-tin tub next to the back-door, stacking them up like cordwood.

"Thank goodness that sandstorm is over," Wanda said. "But, it'll take forever to get the dirt out of these blankets."

"I just hope that hail didn't ruin the cotton crop," Hattie said. Just before the rains, they had been struck by hail, which was melting fast in the downpour.

When they finished stacking the blankets, the two women sat at the kitchen table, sipping tea that Hattie had brewed. It was quiet in the house. Muffled thunder rumbled in the distance, and there was an occasional javelin of lightning rending the far-off elephantine clouds.

"Are you getting sweet on Forrest, Mama?" Wanda stirred sugar into her cup with a silver spoon.

Hattie flushed slightly.

"Whyever do you say such a thing, daughter?"

"I hear you talking to him at night. He reads to you from the *Decameron* by that Italian."

"Boccaccio."

"Yes, and he reads other books to you."

"Goethe, Shelley's poetry, and Lord Byron's."

"Yes, poetry."

"Forrest is a fascinating man. And well read."

"So are you, Mama. But with him, you act as if you were a dull little schoolgirl."

Hattie flushed again, and fingered aside a lock of hair that had fallen into her face.

"You shouldn't concern yourself with what I do, young lady. You're dragging your heels with Roy."

"Why, whatever do you mean, Mama?" Wanda wore a puckish look of innocence, although she knew very well what her mother meant.

"It's time you asked Roy to set a date for your nuptials, dear heart. You've been living in sin long enough."

"I've been meaning to bring it up, Mama. But Roy and Forrest are so wrapped up in work. Forrest wants Roy to build windmills to bring water up from the wells, water the crops and such. He's designed the pumps and everything. But it's going to cost money for the pipes and gears and windmill blades."

"That's why you have to marry Roy very soon. As his wife, you will have more say in how the money is spent. The cotton is going to make Roy very rich. The war is going to make him rich. And you must be his partner for life. Do you understand, my darling?"

Wanda nodded. "Yes. I understand. But I'm afraid if I nudge Roy too hard, he will run away."

"Nonsense. You have to make him think the marriage is his idea."

"How do I do that, Mama?"

"Roy is a passionate man, is he not?"

Wanda nodded, a look of curiosity in her eyes and in her facial expression.

"He is a persistent and amorous lover."

"Mother!"

"That which a young woman most treasures is uppermost in all men's minds, my dear. You know that and I know that."

"You told me it was natural. That it was nature's way of propagating the species."

"That is true, darling. It is natural. And, too, it is natural for a woman to use her, ah, her sex, as a weapon in the battle between the sexes."

"Whatever in the world are you driving at, Mother?"

"The next time Roy wants to partake of your flesh, you must tell him that you are no longer willing to offer yourself to him without a commitment."

"You mean, don't let him do it to me unless he marries me."

Hattie smiled knowingly. She sipped her tea, as if she was the wisest person in the world and had just made her point.

"That is what you must do. You must tell poor Roy that unless he marries you, there will be no more free loving in this house."

Wanda drew herself up straight and regarded her mother with an angry cast to her eyes. It was an attempt to show her indignation.

"Mother, that will make me sound like a common trollop."

"A whore, you mean."

"Yes, if you want to be crude about it."

Thunder murmured far off across the Rio Grande Valley. Rain beat a staccato tattoo against the nearby windowpane. Water streamed down the pane in vermicular rivulets like exposed veins of crystal-clear blood.

"Perhaps we women have a closer kinship with whores than most people would imagine," Hattie said.

"Mother! What if Roy were to hear you talk like this? Or Forrest?"

"I expect they both might agree with me."

Wanda shook her head and, as if in counterpoint, picked up her cup, swirling the tea inside it.

"Roy is very . . ." she started to say. Her mother waited. "He's very . . ."

"Amorous?" Hattie supplied.

"Yes, that, too. But when he wants it, wants me, I mean, he is . . . impatient."

"That's good, daughter. If he wants you that much, it means you have a hold over him. You can demand that he marry you, and if his ardor is not satisfied, he will succumb to your wishes."

"You make it all sound so . . . so heartless and cold, Mother."

"Roy has had plenty of time to make you an honest woman, dear Wanda. I think the man needs a little nudging in that direction. There is a great deal at stake here."

"Money, you mean."

"Money, and status. Texas is growing. There is great wealth to be made here. Roy must make his claim or someone will come along and take you away from him."

"Why, Mother, whatever goes on in that mind of yours? I swan. You think of the most devious things. I love Roy. I would not run off with another man. And certainly not for money, or station."

Hattie coolly sipped her tea, then turned her head to look out the window at the gray land scrimmed with sheets of rain. Lightning flashed the bulging, black clouds in the distance, backlighting them so that they looked like soundless explosions.

"There is another way you can force Roy to marry you, my dear," Hattie said. "But, only as a last resort."

"I dread hearing what that might be, Mama."

Hattie turned to look at her daughter. Her eyes flashed with a fervent radiance.

"If your efforts of persuasion fail to bring Master Killian to the altar, dear Wanda, then you must become pregnant."

Wanda recoiled as if she had been slapped. "But . . . but I've been so careful, and Roy, he . . ."

"See. Roy knows the consequences. I suggest you become less careful should he resist your pleas for marriage. Once you are carrying his child, he will do the honorable thing. He will marry you."

"Mother, that is so underhanded, so . . . so deceitful. I would be shamed."

Hattie finished her tea and stood up, walked to the window.

"I love the rain," she said. "It cleans the air, brings a freshness to the land. It waters our cotton crop and the hay growing in the fields, the vegetables in our lovely garden. The rain is so relaxing. And tomorrow when the sun comes out, and shines so bright, it will be like a new beginning. To everything."

"Mother . . ."

Hattie turned from the window and skewered her daughter with a look. Wanda froze as if she was a child again and had been caught doing something naughty. She knew that look of her mother's only too well.

"I want you and Roy married within the month," Hattie said. "I shall begin making plans."

"Mama, no, you . . . you can't," Wanda pleaded.

"Yes I can, Wanda dear. And so can you. Roy has been drinking free milk long enough. It's time for him to buy the cow."

Wanda looked stricken, her face frozen in a mask of utter horror. She brought a hand to her mouth as if to stifle a scream. Or a curse.

Hattie smiled and turned back to the window, shutting off all further conversation on the subject of marriage and Roy Killian.

38

—■—

MICKEY BONE DROVE the three scrawny longhorns over the rocky, cactus-dotted land that was as bleak as scorched earth, and much to his liking. The rancho had been an idea for Matteo Aguilar and it suited him, for the present. He had made improvements to the ramshackle place, but not many. He had cleaned the well, nailed up some loose boards on the house and barn. He had directed Lucinda to plant corn and beans with seed he had bought in Matamoros. He had planted alfalfa and sheared off the spines of nopal to feed the few head of cattle he had managed to find in the rugged country around the rancho.

He was not worried about Lucinda trying to run away. He had brought her there in the dead of night, and when he left the property, he told her he would kill her if she tried to escape. He brought her cloth and thread and needles from town so that she could sew and mend their clothing and make new dresses for herself. He told her he wanted her to be pretty for him and he gave her cheap jewelry and combs for her hair, even a mirror.

Matteo had chosen this rancho well. It was set in a large box canyon that had only one easy entrance. It was ringed by rocky foothills that rose sheer and steep to the sky, with treeless ridges that afforded a view of anyone coming over them. Matteo had been hiding out when he had lived here, as he, Bone, was hiding out now, not because he was afraid, but because his spirit needed healing and these were Apache hills, like the hills where he had grown up and lived much of his life. A creek ran through the land and an underground spring fed the well. So he had plenty of water, and grass grew between the hills in a wide, tapering valley. They did not get much rain here, but the spring flowed beneath the ground and the little tank caught all the water that drained off the hills. It, too, was fed by one of the underground springs that were so rare in this country. A man could live in such a place for a long time, Bone thought, but he would not stay long. One day, he would take Lucinda and ride back to Texas. Maybe when this war was over. He had seen a lot of soldiers in Matamoros and on both sides of the border, soldiers with different uniforms. There were Union soldiers, Confederate soldiers, along with Mexican, French, and German officers and troops.

He had seen the steamboats on the Rio Bravo, some heading upriver carrying military supplies, others leaving ports heavily laden with goods, and soldiers everywhere, blue coats and gray coats mostly, all oblivious to his presence. Prices were high along the river, but stealing what he needed and wanted was free. He now had a serape and had brought back a crate of chickens so that they had eggs. He had seen a woman with a boy that looked like Julio, but he could not be sure. When the woman stopped to talk to some Mexican soldiers, he could not get any closer and so had left Matamoros without knowing for sure if he had seen Matteo's son.

The longhorns were yearlings and had no brands on them. One had a cut ear, though, but that did not matter to him. Brands were scarce in that part of Mexico. Farther south, on the big ranchos, of course, all the cattle were branded, just like in Texas. He would have no use for a brand himself, because he knew he would not stay long at Matteo's abandoned ranch. It was just a place where he would remain for a time before he returned to Texas, after the war was over.

Lucinda had been tamed. He had made her into a wife, who, if not loving, was at least attentive. And she was bearing his child. The bleeding had stopped a month ago and he could see that her belly was rounding out slightly. He hoped she would give him a son, for he wanted some blood of his tribe to live on. They were not many, the

Lipans, and he knew he was among the last. And even he was not pure-blood. So it would be with his son, should Lucinda give birth to one.

The late morning sun rose above the ridge beyond the little adobe ranch house, lighting the valley. Bone urged the yearling longhorns on, cutting across the open end and into the hidden valley. Behind him, he felt as if a door had closed, for the entrance was difficult to see from any distance. It was just one of many arroyos that trenched that part of the country, some small, some large. The little mountains seemed to have been pushed up by some great force a long time ago, perhaps before humans came to live on the earth. The land was wrinkled from these thrusts, and scarred and wounded from countless centuries of wind and rain and earthly upheavals. The land suited him and it resembled him and it was his home.

Lucinda was hanging clothes on the line stretched between two trees on the side of the adobe. Bone saw her turn to look at him. He waved one arm in a gesture and shouted to her.

"*Abre la puerta. Andale, andale.*"

Lucinda understood. She dropped a wet shirt into her basket and started running toward the corral. She opened the gate and stood behind it, to one side, waiting for the cattle to be driven past her.

Bone kneed his horse to keep the three longhorns bunched up and headed for the corral. The horse worked the cattle well, knowing its job. The cattle started to veer, unwilling to be corralled, but Bone's horse cut them off and then swung to the other side. Bone yelled at the cattle and they leaped through the opening. Lucinda quickly swung the gate shut and lashed it tight with the looped rope. Bone reined up.

"You can go back to your washing now," he said.

Lucinda nodded obediently and traipsed back to the clothesline. Bone watched her go, her dress clinging to her rounded buttocks, her dress flapping against her lean legs. He was consumed with a wave of sudden lust, but he quelled the urge to go after her, drag her into the house and throw her onto the bed. Tonight would be soon enough, he thought. He had chores to attend to before she made his lunch. He had left early that morning, before the sun was up, knowing he would find the cattle he had been tracking the day before, until it turned too dark to see.

The cattle in the corral milled around until he gave them fodder. He saw to it that there was water in the drinking trough. He looked down the valley to the other fence and saw his other cattle grazing near the trees that bordered the creek. Soon, he thought, he would have a good fat herd to sell to the army in Matamoros. He felt rich.

It was late afternoon when Bone saw the man enter the valley riding a small burro. He did not recognize him. The man seemed in no hurry. Bone sat on the porch, his chair leaned back against the wall. He was smoking a cigarette and Lucinda was inside, preparing supper. The clothes had dried and she had put them all away. She was a neat person and he liked that about her.

Bone was not worried. He did not feel threatened. He was curious, though. Perhaps, he thought, the man is lost and merely wants to ask where he might be. Or he could be one of those *campesinos* who farmed a small patch of ground somewhere nearby. As the man drew closer, Bone noticed that his clothes were sewn from cheap cloth. His straw hat looked as if it had been worn for a long time because it had pieces missing from the brim and holes in the crown. The burro itself seemed to have seen better days and did not move fast or well.

"Lucinda, come here," Bone called into the house, when the burro rider was still some distance away.

Lucinda came outside.

"Yes, Mickey, what passes?" she said in Spanish.

"Look there," he said, without pointing. "That man. Do you know him?"

Lucinda looked and shook her head. "He is an old man. I have never seen him before. Why is he coming here?"

"I do not know. Go back inside the house. I will talk to this old man."

"Yes, I go," she said. "I will prepare more food for him."

"No. He will not stay for supper."

Lucinda hesitated, then disappeared inside the adobe.

Bone reached down and touched the butt of his pistol, loosened it in the holster. Just inside the door, he kept a rifle leaning against the wall. In case he had an unwelcome visitor. He did not expect any trouble from this old man, for he did not appear to be armed, but he had lived this long, he knew, because he was careful.

The old man approached. As he rode up, he looked into the corral and turned his burro toward the house.

"Good afternoon," the man said in Spanish.

"Good afternoon."

"I am surprised to see someone living here."

"Why?"

"Miquelito Aguilar once lived in this place. I sold him the land."

"I work for Miguelito," Bone said. "I call him Matteo."

"Ah, yes, he told me to call him Matteo, too. But I know he also calls himself Miquelito."

"That is true."

"How are you called?" the man asked.

"I am called Hueso. In English, they call me Bone."

"Miguelito spoke of you, I think."

"Why do you come here? And how are you called?"

"I am just called 'Viejo' because I am an old man. But I am baptized Fidelio Antonio de Lopez y Santiago." The old man cackled. "It is a long name. It is much too long for me."

Bone waited for the man to reply to his second question.

The *viejo* looked toward the corral.

"I see you have one of my little cows."

"True? I have one of your cows?"

"True."

The man was very old, but Bone could see that his eyes were still sharp.

"How do you know this, old man?"

"I know my cows. I made the cut in the left ear when that one was a small calf. I was going to brand him, but he was too wild for me. I did not think there was any hurry to put my brand on him."

"Those are wild cows that I found in the brush," Bone said.

"Oh, yes. They are all very wild. But that one with the cut in its ear is mine. True."

"I caught that little cow. Do you want him?" Bone asked.

"I have a rope." Bone watched as the old man unwrapped the rope from around his waist. Bone had thought it was to hold up Viejo's trousers. Viejo grinned. "I will take him to my house and put the brand on him." The old man then held up the short thin rope that was limp and black from use.

"You take the cow, then, old man."

The man grinned, but he had very few teeth, and the ones he had were carious, rotted to dark stumps.

"You are very kind, Bone."

"I will help you catch him."

Bone walked out to the corral. The old man rode his burro over, dismounted and walked to the gate, carrying the rope. He walked on bowed legs and rocked from side to side as if he were on the deck of a rolling ship. He seemed to be in pain, but he did not complain.

The cattle were wary and ran to a corner of the enclosure. Bone opened the gate. He and the old man stepped in.

"Can you catch him?" Bone asked.

"You walk on the right. I will walk on the left. I will catch him."

And that is what they did. The man roped the yearling easily after making a quick, deft loop. Viejo led the longhorn from the corral and Bone closed the gate.

"Until I see you, then," Viejo said, as he rode off on the burro, leading the yearling.

"Go with God," Bone said, his eyes narrowing to black slits, as the hatred welled up in him, floated at a deadly, dangerous level.

He stood there watching Viejo ride to the end of the valley and turn where the high ridge cut into the entrance. Then he walked to the barn, saddled his horse. Lucinda came out onto the porch, a grease-stained apron tied around her swelling middle.

"Where do you go?" she asked. "The meal is almost ready. It is time for your supper."

"I will be back soon," he said. "Give me the rifle by the door."

"You are going hunting?" she asked.

"Yes. I am going hunting. Now, quick. The rifle."

Moments later, Lucinda handed the rifle to Bone and he slid it into its scabbard. He rode off without saying anything more to Lucinda.

"It's that old man, isn't it?" she said, knowing Bone could not hear her. She shuddered and walked back inside the house, tears streaming down her face.

The old man was not traveling fast and it did not take Bone long to catch up to him. He rode up behind him and then overtook him.

The old man did not look surprised.

"You have lived long enough, Viejo," Bone said, drawing the rifle.

"That is true. I have lived a long time. Before you kill me, though, I have something to tell you. It is very important that I tell you this."

"Maybe you should pray to your Christ," Bone said.

"Oh, I have done that, and to the Virgin Mary, as well. This is important to you, Mickey Bone."

Bone was surprised. He had not told Viejo his full name, the name he was called by all who knew him.

"Oh, yes, I know who you are, Mickey Bone. I once lived in the village of Valle and I knew Matteo Aguilar well. And I know his wife, Luz, and her family. I know, too, that you have her twin sister at the rancho with you, for I have watched you for many days, trying to figure out why you were here and Matteo was not."

"This is not important to me, Viejo," Bone said.

"I have a son who lives in Valle. He rode away this morning because he had business in Matamoros that was very urgent and necessary. He told me not to come here and get my cow from you."

"Your son gave you good advice," Bone said.

"My son's name is Francisco Santiago. He is called Paco."

Bone leveled the rifle at Viejo and cocked the hammer back.

"I told Paco that if I did not come to Valle tomorrow, it would be because you had killed me. He said that if that happened, he would come here and kill you. My son is a very good hunter and he has a keen eye. He has killed many men and he has strong friends."

"You should not have taken that cow back," Bone said. "I caught it. It is mine."

"No, you stole this cow, and now it will have my blood on it if you kill me."

"Go with God," Bone said, his finger edging toward the trigger of his rifle.

"I put this curse on you, Mickey Bone. My son will hunt you down and kill you. For he was hoping one day to marry Lucinda. He did not know where you were until this morning when I told him. If he had not had urgent business in Matamoros, he would have come here and killed you. I curse you, you filth, you bastard, you—"

Bone squeezed the trigger and the rifle bucked in his hands. The lead ball smashed into Viejo's chest and knocked him from the burro. He fell to the ground, dead, a splash of blood on his chest, just over the heart that was no longer pumping. The rope slipped from his hand as the longhorn jerked away and started to run.

Bone rammed the rifle back in its sheath and caught up to the yearling. He snatched up the rope and jerked it taut. Then he started riding back to the rancho. He put the cow in the corral again and threw the rope on the ground.

When he entered the house he was hungry.

"Did you kill Viejo?" Lucinda asked.

"Why do you ask? I did not know you knew the man. What about his son, Paco? Do you know him?"

She turned away from him, tears welling up in her eyes.

He grabbed her arm and jerked her around to face him. Then he slapped her hard across the mouth.

"We will leave this place tomorrow," he said. "You will never see Paco Santiago again."

She began to cry and Bone struck her again, knocking her across the front room. She crumpled to the floor, whimpering.

"Get up," he said. "We will eat and then we will go to bed and I will show you what a real man is like, you whore."

Lucinda rose slowly and walked to the kitchen, Bone behind her. She wiped her tearstained face with the hem of her dress and began to serve the food as Bone sat down.

"All for a poor little cow," Lucinda said as she sat down, her voice barely above a whisper. She crossed herself. Bone scowled.

"It was my cow," he said.

Lucinda bowed her head and began eating. She never said another word.

And neither did Bone.

39

THE UNCERTAIN DAWN seemed long in coming the morning that Colonel John Salmon Ford led his Cavalry of the West out of Baronsville. After the rains, the ground was soaked and fog lingered in the bottoms like ghostly battens of gray wool. The town evaporated behind the cavalry column and faded into nothingness. Out of the fog around Baronsville, wagons emerged suddenly as if from nowhere, then disappeared again as they rumbled into huge banks of cloud-fog that clung to the ground like battlesmoke.

For a time, Ford's column followed the road to the Baron ranch, then veered off onto a secondary road that Martin pointed out to the colonel. Ford was full of ginger that morning. Sitting a horse seemed to drop years from his face and body. He sat straight-backed in the saddle, his uniform cleaned and pressed, as gray as the dawn itself. He seemed, Martin thought, ready to lead a charge at any moment, but he held his mount in check, observing the land they crossed, paying particular attention to the old road, which was faintly scarred with ruts that had been filled in by sand and then washed out again by rain.

"Major Baron, we have a fine goddamned road to ride."

Martin wondered if Ford was being sarcastic. The road was barely visible in the thick fog and it had not been used in years. He had hoped they might ride to his ranch and then veer to the east to avoid the brasada, but Ford had told him he wanted to head south on the oldest wagon trail there was, one not heavily traveled.

"I don't want to run into civilians or cattle that might hold us up," Ford had said. "And I don't want anyone to know where the hell we are going."

"Sir, nobody around here gives a damn where we're going," Martin had said.

"That's the goddamned idea, Major."

Martin had grudgingly begun to develop a deep respect for Colonel Ford over the days and months he had trained and served under him. He was, he decided, more than a little astounded by him, by his brilliance as a military thinker and a man of some culture. Deep down, though, Martin was suspicious of Ford because of his predilection for politics. He suspected that Ford had much higher aims, although he admitted that this was only a strong hunch.

At other times, Martin wondered if Ford had not squandered some of his abilities by having worn so many hats. The man was smart, and he was talented, but he had never followed through on any particular career or endeavor. Was Ford an opportunist? Or did he possess such a complex mind that he became bored easily once he had mastered an occupation? If so, Martin could understand that, since it was a tendency that matched his own at times. Beyond all the speculation, however, he found Ford to be a more than capable leader with not only a sincere appreciation and affection for his men, but a profound knowledge of human psychology. Ford seemed to be able to look through men and find out everything about them, and he was shrewd enough to exploit both their weaknesses and their strengths. Which was what made Ford such an outstanding leader. He knew men. He knew how to get them to do what he wanted them to do.

"Wonderful country," Ford said later, as the column wound its way through mesquite, open plain, crossed creeks and climbed low rises. "Wild. The way I like country to be."

"We're on Box B land," Martin said. "Have been ever since we left Baronsville."

Ford let out a low whistle. "All this belongs to you?"

"Over a million acres, Colonel."

"Well, Major, you're a rich man. A very rich man, indeed."

Martin could see the damage caused by the sandstorm and the way the land had come back to life after the rains that followed it. It was grand country, he thought, and someday it would be all grass and all the cattle would carry the Box B brand. That had been his dream and he still believed it could come true. But the work ahead was staggering to contemplate.

"Depends on what you mean by 'rich,' " Martin said.

"Resources, Major, resources. Land is the basis of all wealth, you know. That's why Texas is going to be the richest state in the South."

"Not the Union?"

"The South is going to win this war, Martin. But I fear it will lose anyway."

"What do you mean, Colonel?"

"The South is fighting for a lost cause. Oh, you'll hear that it's a matter of states' rights, but this war is really about slavery. And too many people are against it. The entire economy of the South is based on slavery, and that will never do. If we win the war, as I suspect we shall, we will never win the country. And if we break the country in half, we'd have two small countries, forever divided, forever enemies. So, war will beget war, and finally, each side will whittle the other down so that any country with half a mind can come in here and take us over."

"That's a pretty grim picture you paint, Colonel Ford. And if you say we will win the war, you're saying we haven't won anything."

"Oh, I was talking in a military sense. Lee is the best general in the entire nation. He's brilliant. But Jeff Davis is a weak president, a weak man. He's sickly and indecisive. Lincoln is strong, strong in his convictions and strong in his decisions. He just doesn't have the generals right now. But someday he will, I think, and so while we may win this little war, it will, in the final analysis, be only a battle, a skirmish, and the North, with its immense resources and superior numbers, will always be a rattlesnake in our house. It will strike back and recover its losses, the land, the Southern government, and everything. Yes, it's grim. But men will fight. And men will die. All for a lost cause. Slavery will vanish here as it has in England."

"I hope it does," Martin said. "I don't hold to slavery."

"Nor do I. But I do believe in the right of each state to determine where it stands on the issue. Let slavery die on its own. Washington should not impose its laws on the entire country. For Christ's sakes, man, George Washington himself was a slaveholder and so was Jefferson, for that matter."

"But if all men are created equal—"

"I believe that, God damn it. But all men do not wind up equal. Those with money can enslave their employees, their towns, their businesses. That's slavery, too, without any papers."

"Are you a bitter man, Colonel?"

"I'm sure as hell gettin' that way, Major Baron. There are no clear lines of battle drawn in this war. In fact, we're at war with a whole lot more than the Union. We're fighting the Mexicans, the Apaches, the Comanches, the French, maybe, and, hell, maybe even the Germans. I've got orders to go after a Mexican named Ochoa, the son of a bitch, and I want to be fighting with Lee in Virginia."

Martin sucked in a breath. Ford was even more complicated than he had thought, and he seemed to know more about the governments on both sides of the war than the average man. Of course, he was a politician, too, and that would certainly shade his thinking.

"Here comes one of the scouts," Ford said. "And he's wearing out the horse under him."

The scout riding back toward them was Pierre Debois, a corporal from Odessa, but the men called him Dubious, which contradicted his character, for Dubious was a self-assured young man, a hunter, tracker, whose mother was as Irish as a shillelagh, one Molly McGinty, from County Cork.

"Sir," Debois said, as he reined to a halt and saluted Colonel Ford.

"What is it, Dubious?"

"Sir, me'n Sergeant Reasoner done fixed on some pony tracks that just holler out Apache. Must be eight or ten of 'em, and that ain't all."

"Well, God damn it, Dubious, you better give me all of it. I haven't the time to indulge in a guessing game."

"Sir, they's another set of tracks, some fresher by a damned sight than them others, the Apache ones. And these tracks are from shod hooves."

"And what do you discern from those tracks, Dubious?"

"Sir, I discern quite plain that them two boys on the shod horses are trackin' them redskins, sure as shootin'."

"Anything else, Corporal?"

Debois squinted and shoved the brim of his hat back and scratched just above his temple. His blue eyes crackled like sapphires.

"I reckon, sir. They's a whole slew of cow tracks, longhorns I figger, and they're older'n any of the others. Me and James figgers it this way. Them red niggers is trackin' the cows, and them two dumb jaspers are trackin' either the 'Paches, the cows, or both."

"That's a pretty good report, Dubious. You and Sergeant Jim know your tracks, do you?"

"Yes, we sure do."

Ford sucked in air and his chest swelled against his uniform coat. The brass buttons glinted in the sun. He started to say something when he heard Martin clear his throat.

"Corporal," Martin said. "Was one of those cow tracks any different than the others?"

"What are you driving at, Major?" Ford asked, a sharp tone to his voice.

"Maybe nothing, but I'd like to hear what Dubious has to say about those cattle tracks."

"Well, shit, so would I, then," Ford said. "What about them, Dubious? Is one any different than the others?"

Again, Debois scratched his head, but he didn't seem confused or unsure of himself.

"You know, sir, Sergeant Reasoner, he mentioned that right off after we figgered out what all was what and who was who in that mess of sign. He showed me one cow track that was real huge like and made me look at it real close."

"And?" Ford asked, his eyebrows arching like a pair of inchworms.

"I never saw no cow tracks as big as them," Debois said. "Shit, they was more'n twice the size of any of them others. Just real big, sir. Big as pie plates, I reckon."

Martin said something under his breath, so low, Ford looked at him to see if he had actually spoken.

"You say something, Major?"

"Diablo Blanco, sir," Martin said.

"White devil?"

"It's a big longhorn. Kind of a legend in these parts. I think I know who's riding those two shod horses."

"Major, maybe you can enlighten me and Dubious here. I'm not much on secrets during wartime."

Martin laughed, despite himself.

"Colonel, I think that's my son Anson, tracking that big white longhorn bull. He rides with a man who works for him, Peebo Elves. And those Apaches just might be Culebra's bunch. He's been trying to kill off Anson for quite a while."

"Hell, why didn't you say so?" Ford exploded.

"I just did," Martin said.

"You don't have to get smart about it, Major. Corporal, you ride back up there and tell Sergeant Reasoner to hold up, study those tracks real well and wait for us to catch up."

"Yes, sir," Debois said, saluting. He rode off at a gallop and was soon out of sight.

"You're going after Culebra?" Martin said to Ford.

"Hell, this outfit's still part Ranger, you know. One of our jobs is to attack and destroy hostiles wherever we find them. You're damned right I'm going after that Apache. What I want to know is why your son and his man are going after a bunch like that, just the two of them? They're badly outnumbered."

"I think Anson is after that white bull, sir."

"Hell, that ain't no reason to commit suicide."

"He's had run-ins with Culebra before, and so have I."

Ford motioned for the column to pick up the pace and he put his horse into a trot. Martin kept up with him.

"I'd like to meet this son of yours, Martin. He sounds like my kind of man. Unless he's loco. Is he loco?"

"Not in the regular sense, sir."

"A hothead, eh?"

"I don't know if he's that. Determined, I'd say."

Ford grinned.

"Yes, sir, I want to meet this wild boy of yours, and the other fellow, what's his name?"

"Peebo."

"Odd name, that."

Martin made no comment. He was thinking about Anson and Peebo following that white bull. If Dubious had read the tracks right, Anson was riding right into trouble. Although they'd had their differences over the years, Martin loved his son. He had been unable to show it, and now he began to regret that he had been so distant from Anson. He had never figured that he and Anson had much in common, but now that his son was in danger, he felt an overwhelming sadness and a fear that something would happen to him. He did not like having to face these emotions in himself. Distance from Anson had always made him feel more comfortable, but now he wanted to rush to his son and help him. He had a sickening feeling in the pit of his stomach, as if it was suddenly too late for both of them.

"A penny, Major," Ford said after they had ridden nearly a mile without speaking.

"What?"

"For your thoughts. You seem preoccupied. Worried about your son?"

Martin drew in a breath and held it. He held the thought in his mind and turned it all around and held it up for examination.

"Yeah, Colonel, I guess I am."

"Perfectly understandable, Martin. But don't let your feelings affect your judgment in a fight. For you, Anson is just another civilian in trouble, and you're part of a cavalry unit coming to his defense."

"Yes, sir," Martin said, but Ford's words didn't help. He had a sudden dread that he would never see his son again, and he was gripped with a deep sadness, and a longing, too, a longing for a past that could never be retrieved, a longing for a closeness that he had denied his son and himself. What a pity, he thought, that I can't talk to Anson now and tell him . . .

Tell him what?

The thought screamed in Martin's mind, but he knew he could never form the words to tell Anson how he felt.

They just weren't in him, and that caused him an even deeper sadness, as they rode up on the two scouts, Dubious and Jim Reasoner, who had dismounted and were waiting for them with expressions on their faces that were as dark as the cloud forming in Martin's heart.

40

T HE AIR WAS thick with the smell of flowers and the smell of
death. The skies were gray as slate, sunless at mid-morning. The
funeral procession led down Calle Principal and emerged on the
other end of Ciudad Valle, then began the trudge up the hill to
the cemetery, six men carrying the unpainted wooden casket, behind the priest and the *alcalde*, and followed by Paco Santiago and
his family, the women dressed in black dresses, the men wearing
dark shirts. Altar boys in their cassocks bore a cross. The priest
swung a smoking pot that trailed the scent of incense. The women of
the town wept and the men's faces were stoic and stern.

Two boys carried a sign between them that said: VIEJO.

Matteo crossed himself as he dismounted and tied his horse to a
hitch tree in front of the Montenegro house. Jorge Rios did the
same. Both men fell in behind the procession and no one seemed to
notice.

"Do you know who it is that died?" Rios asked.

Matteo nodded and said no more.

"I saw your wife, I think. Luz, she is here?"

Matteo nodded then put fingers to his lips.

He and Rios stood at the edge of the crowd as the pallbearers lowered the casket into an open grave. They listened to the words of the priest in both Spanish and Latin and they heard the wailing of the women at graveside.

"God will bring the murderer of Viejo to justice," the priest said. "Vengeance is mine, sayeth the Lord."

A woman screamed, "No," and then there was a long silence. Finally the priest pronounced the final intonations and men began to shovel dirt over the casket. The crowd broke up and Matteo stood there waiting for Luz. When she saw him, her eyes widened, but she did not run to him. She kept her dignity and honored the solemnity of the occasion.

"Where is Julio?" Matteo asked, when she came near.

"In Matamoros with my cousin Lupe," she whispered, as she took his hand in hers. "I am so grateful that you are alive, my husband. I am happy that you are here."

"Why did you leave Julio with your cousin?" Matteo asked.

"I was afraid Bone would come and kill him."

She would not tell him that Bone had raped her. But she told him about her parents and her brother and sister and she wept as the words slipped from her mouth like the black ribbons on a mourning wreath.

A moment later, Paco Santiago appeared, his face rigid with grief, the tracks of his tears still visible on his cheeks, like faint scars.

"Matteo," Paco said.

"I am sorry about your father, Viejo."

"It was Bone."

"Bone killed him?"

"Yes. I am going after him. He is living with Lucinda at that old ranch of yours."

Matteo cursed.

"I will go with you, Paco. Come when you are ready to leave."

"I will come. I must be with my family now. We will go in the morning. Come to the house, please, and eat and drink with us. You know where I live."

Matteo nodded. He took Luz by the arm and they walked toward her home. Jorge walked away to get their horses. In a few minutes, he was following behind them.

"Did Bone hurt you?" Matteo asked Luz.

She shook her head quickly. Too quickly, Matteo thought.

"No. But I am sad that he took Lucinda. I did not know where he was, that he was at your old ranch."

"Maybe it is good that you did not know."

"I would like to kill that man."

"I will kill him."

She squeezed his arm, praying that he would not find out what Bone did to her, that he would never know that she was carrying Bone's child in her womb. She had tried to kill it with herbs that the *curandero* gave her, but the baby was still inside her and she wept every night after she prayed to the Virgin Mary and asked God to forgive her for her sins.

Luz had kept the house clean, but Matteo was struck once again by how poor her family was, how poor the people of the town were. He felt uncomfortable and self-conscious to be sitting there in squalor when he had a fine home and cattle, much land. He did not like all the religious icons in the main room of the adobe, the *bultos,* little statues of saints that were inset into the walls, the statues of Jesus and the Virgin Mary. These made him feel as if he were being watched by dozens of eyes, and criticized in statuary silence. There was a gloom that pervaded the house even by day, as if death still lingered in every cold shadow, and the spirits of those who had been murdered here were lurking in every dark corner. The smallness of the room, with its cheap, hand-made furniture and its dirt floor, made him feel as if he was sitting in a jail cell awaiting the tread of the hangman's feet just outside the rickety wooden door.

"Bone said you were dead, that you had been hanged, Miguelito *mío.*"

He told her about his escape from Martin Baron and the other Rangers.

"I have been betrayed by many," he said. "Bone, Reynaud, and other gringos. I will not let these things happen to me again."

"What will we do?" she asked, as she brought him a glass of *tepache.* She had made it with beer and bananas. It was sweet and very mild, but she had made some in the big clay *olla* every week, for visitors and just in case her husband returned one day.

"When I have killed that bastard Bone, we will return to our rancho. We will watch Julio grow big and strong. I stayed for a little while in Matamoros and talked to some people there and I listened. This war, this stupid war, will make us rich. There is much opportunity. There is much commerce along the Rio Bravo, which they are now calling the Rio Grande. We will grow cotton and perhaps I will make guns or ammunition. There is much need for these things. I will sell my cattle to the army and I will catch horses and sell those, too."

"To which army?"

"It makes no difference. To the one who will pay the highest price."

"You have much ambition, my husband. Will not the Texas Rangers come after you again?"

"I do not know. But if they do, I will be ready for them. I will have my own army again, I think."

He sipped the *tepache* and mused over his dreams, a faraway look in his dark brown eyes. Luz sat beside him, stroking his arm, feeling the strength there, wanting him, wanting him with her forever.

"I will go to Matamoros and bring Julio here," she said. "Now that you are here with me."

"No. When I come back from killing Bone, we will go to Matamoros together. I have money, money that I hid in our house. I will buy cotton seed and implements and we will take Julio back to the rancho with us."

"That is good, my husband. I will wait for you here."

"Yes."

"We should go to the house of Santiago to pay our respects."

"Yes, we will go when Jorge arrives. I want to know if Bone hurt you when he was here?"

"No," she lied. "He . . . he is crazy. He took my sister, Lucinda."

"He wanted you."

"You do not know that."

"I know. Bone is a bastard. I should have killed him long ago."

"Yes, you should have, Miguelito. You will kill him soon. I know this."

Matteo drew in a breath, held it. He looked deep into Luz's eyes, wondering if he could see the truth in them. He knew that Bone had come to Valle, not for Lucinda, but for Luz. That would have been his revenge for the order Matteo had given to have him killed. He trusted his wife, but he knew how women could lie to men. They did it as easily as breathing and no man could ever tell the difference. He accepted it, but he wondered why Luz would not tell him the whole story about Bone. He knew better than to question her too much, though. She would just become silent and not talk to him, then turn on him, accuse him of doubting her. These were a woman's weapons and he knew them well.

They heard a rap on the door.

"That is Jorge," Matteo said. "Let him in."

Luz rose and went to the door. Rios stood there, his hat in his hand.

"Don Matteo," Rios said, "you must come quick. There is something passing in the pueblo. It is very strange."

"Where?" Aguilar said, rising from his chair.

"At the house of Santiago. They are seeing something on the hill, up by the cemetery."

"Let us go," Matteo said. He and Luz followed Rios to the Santiago house, which was on the edge of the little town. A crowd of people stood outside, all looking up at the cemetery. Paco saw Matteo coming and beckoned to him.

The people gathered at the edge of the pueblo seemed fearful to Aguilar. Some shrank back as if terrified. Others gawked up at the cemetery with open mouths, their faces registering shock and awe.

"What passes, Paco?" Matteo asked.

"Something very strange, Matteo. Look up at the cemetery where my father is buried. What do you see there?"

The gray skies offered a sharp and uncluttered view of the hill and the cemetery with its jutting crosses and headstones. In the midst of it, something moved. Something brown and slow that was not a dog. The animal was too large.

"What is that?" Matteo asked. "A deer?"

"Ha. You see it." Paco rubbed his eyes as if to clear his vision. "I see it, too, Matteo. And so does everyone else."

"What is it?"

"A burro. Yes, that is my father's burro. It is a sign."

"A sign?"

"Yes. That burro was left at my father's place. He was riding it when Bone shot and killed him. The burro has come here at my father's bidding to seek justice for his master's death."

Matteo looked at Paco as if the man had suddenly lost his senses.

Then he heard the burro bray. Matteo looked back up the hill and saw the animal lift its head and bray again.

The people around them murmured and crossed themselves. Some of the children ran away and the women shrank behind their husbands. Paco's wife, Perla, looked frightened and edged toward their house, her lips moving in prayer. When she opened the door, the smell of food cooking rushed outside. But the aroma had no effect on the onlookers, who stared at the braying burro as if transfixed.

Someone murmured, *"Es un milagro."* It is a miracle.

"Hey, burro," Paco called, his voice carrying across the jumble of rocks and cactus, up the hill, to the top of the cemetery.

The burro stopped braying, lifted its head with a sudden jerk and looked straight down at Paco.

"See?" Paco said. "It is my father's burro."

"Yes, yes," the crowd chorused, along with words such as *"verdad,"* and *"claro."*

"I am going up there," Paco said, and before anyone could stop him, he started running toward the cemetery.

"Paco, no," Matteo called. Luz pulled on his arm to hold him back. Surprised, he looked down at her, saw the flashes of fear in her dark eyes, the mask of terror on her face.

"What passes with you, Luz?"

"I do not want you to go up there."

"Paco is a fool."

"Maybe the burro is a sign from God," she said.

"It is a sign of stupidity. That burro is as mindless as the stump of a tree," Matteo said.

Paco reached the cemetery. He dashed toward the burro, calling to it, calling to his dead father. The burro stood next to the fresh grave. There was a rope around its neck and the animal was tightly hobbled.

Paco stopped short when he saw the hobbles. He knew then that something was wrong. He looked around.

That's when he saw Bone and Lucinda sitting on a horse, out of sight of the town, on the far edge of the cemetery.

"Bone," Paco said huskily, his voice trapped in a throat tightening with fear.

Bone brought up the rifle and took aim.

Paco turned, started to run.

They all saw it. Those in the town below. Those standing outside of Paco's house. They heard the crack of a rifle and they saw Paco throw up his arms and pitch forward. The women screamed. The men growled and shouted.

Matteo cursed.

Luz began to cry, gripping her husband's arm so tightly it stopped the blood as surely as a tourniquet.

Matteo wrenched away from her and drew his pistol. He started running up to the cemetery, but he knew what he would find. He heard hoofbeats and knew that Bone had come back for the son who would avenge his father's death.

He knew he would find Paco dead and Bone gone. Still he ran, the blood lust in him surging into every muscle and sinew of his body, pounding in his temples. He wanted to kill.

He wanted to kill Mickey Bone.

41

I N THE INTRICATE and sublime calculus of dawn, the eastern sky
bloomed with faint pastel salmon hues that shifted gradually into
burnished brass and gold, clouds gilded with vermilion. The stars
faded into a hesitant monograph that turned as blue as litmus paper
soaking up the chemistry of creation. There was that soft gray hush
that precedes every dawning in the west, when all the nightbirds go
silent and the morning birds have not yet awakened to proclaim the
new day.

Forrest stood there, watching Roy splash his face over and over
with pump water. Roy must have washed his face that gray morning
half a dozen times. Now, he was rubbing the water into the flesh as if
it was some kind of healing oil.

"It won't wash off," Forrest said.

"Huh?"

"Whatever you're trying to wash off your face. Humiliation,
maybe. Fear. What did Wanda do? Slap you? Insult you?"

"Forrest, sometimes you get on a man's nerves real good."

"Just trying to help, Roy. Whatever's eating you isn't going to get
washed away with water."

Killian looked toward the house. The women were still sleeping, but he knew they would be stirring soon. Hattie and Forrest had planned to go into town today. Ken Richman had ordered the parts Forrest needed to build two windmills that would help them irrigate the cotton crop, which was coming along nicely, thanks to the irrigation work he'd already done.

"Wanda's driving me plumb loco," Roy said, his voice barely above a whisper. "But I think Hattie's behind it."

"Hattie's behind everything in your house, Roy."

"How true."

"Did you think your relationship with Wanda could go on forever this way? You can only keep a girl of marriageable age dangling for so long, you know."

"So you know what the problem is. Wanda wants to get married. Now."

"Oh, that's not the problem," Forrest said. "That's always been there."

Roy looked at Forrest with an abject expression on his face. "You know, then? What Wanda's doing to me?"

"The house has thin walls."

"Damned woman. Wants to get married before the next sunrise. And me up to my armpits in work."

"Well, the calving's over and the Killianos are picking cotton today. Kind of a lull, I'd say."

"What are 'Killianos'?"

"Oh, that's what the Mexicans are calling themselves now. I think they want to rid themselves of any ties to the Barons."

"I should be out there in the fields seeing to the cotton picking."

"The Mexicans know what to do, and you've got Socks and the other Negroes showing them how. They'll get it done."

"Are you on Wanda's side, Forrest?"

Forrest grinned and threw up his hands in mock surrender.

"I'm not taking sides, Roy. Just noting that your excuse doesn't hold water. Hattie and I are going into town this morning to pick up those windmill parts at the freight office. Might not be a bad time to come along with us, you and Wanda, and stand before the preacher."

Killian reached for a towel hanging from the bent tine of a hay fork and wiped his face dry.

"I won't be forced," Roy said. "Not by no woman."

"Is she forcing you?"

"She cut me off."

"Cut you off?"

"You know. She won't let me no more."

"Ah, I see," Forrest said, trying not to smile. "There is no power like that possessed by a woman who crosses her legs before a man."

"She done that, all right. And I ain't about to beg for it."

"That's her weapon, Roy. She's already won the battle. And will probably win the war."

"Not with me, she won't. I can take the dry spell as long as she can. What about you and Hattie?"

"What about us?"

"I mean, none of my business, but she seems pretty sweet on you."

"I've known Hattie and Wanda for a long time, Roy."

"But are you and Hattie . . . ?"

"Lovers?"

"Yeah, I guess that's what I mean."

"We spend time together."

"Does she want to marry you?"

"Maybe. I don't know."

"Would you marry her if she cut you off?"

"Not for that reason. Roy, this isn't getting you anywhere. Hattie and Wanda are two different people. I'm attracted to Hattie. She's got a lot of wonderful qualities. She's smart. She's very comely, and she's good company."

"Same with Wanda, but Wanda wants more than companionship. Doesn't Hattie?"

"I don't know what she wants, Roy. Let it be, will you? I don't feel comfortable discussing me and Hattie with anyone."

"But I'm discussing Wanda with you."

"You brought up the subject. Not I."

Roy frowned. He didn't know whether Forrest was an ally or in cahoots with Wanda and her mother. As he said, he had known them a long time. Maybe, he thought, he should be talking to Hattie, not Forrest. But he would feel uncomfortable doing that, just like Forrest was, talking about him and Hattie. Roy felt bewildered and outnumbered.

The sun rose above the horizon and light was spreading over the land. A bird piped in the nearby trees and, in the fields beyond, a meadowlark trilled a lyrical song. The two men still stood in shadow, but the grass and the vegetables in the garden sparkled with jewels as the sun struck the beads of dew on their leaves. Fresh scents rose up from the earth, filling the air with a heady perfume.

"I've got to go hook up the buggy," Forrest said as Roy hung the towel back on its hook. "What are you going to do? With Wanda, I mean."

"I don't know. Talk to her, I guess."

Forrest snickered. "When a woman has her mind made up, talking doesn't change it."

"Well, she can go take a flying fuck, for all I care."

"She might, Roy. But not with you."

With that, Forrest walked off toward the barn. Roy stared after him, feeling helpless. Forrest had not given him any advice he could use, and he was plainly not very sympathetic. Maybe, he thought, once Hattie was gone into town, he could reason with Wanda. He knew damned well that her mother was behind all this defiance and pressure. Maybe Wanda would not be so strong once her mother was away from her.

He vowed not to go back into the house until Hattie and Forrest had left for town. Let Wanda wonder where he was. He walked over to the houses where the Mexicans lived and sat down behind one of them and rolled a smoke. He watched the men all leave for the cotton fields as the sun rose high in the sky and burned off the morning dew.

When he heard the wagon creaking and heading for the house to pick up Hattie, he stood up and watched until he saw Forrest drive the wagon away, toward Baronsville. Then he slowly walked back to the house, resolving to confront Wanda and have it out with her one last time. He would tell her that he'd marry her when he was damned ready and not before, and if she wanted to stay in his house, she had better uncross her legs and stop being a stubborn old mule.

For Roy, it felt like the first time he had been thrown from a horse. One minute he was riding high in the saddle, and the next, the horse bucked and ran out from under him, leaving him high in the air for a moment before he came crashing down to the ground with a thud. That's how he was feeling as he watched Wanda in the bedroom, a carpetbag open on the bed, as she placed her folded panties inside it, right on top of her folded dresses.

"What are you doing?" he asked.

"I'm leaving you, Roy."

"Leaving me? Why?"

"You don't seem to respect me and I've decided that our relationship is not going anywhere."

"Well, you're right about that, Wanda. It seems to have reached a dead end."

She stopped packing for a moment and looked up at Roy. "It doesn't have to be like this, you know."

"I liked things the way they were."

She huffed in a breath.

"Oh, you. Roy, a woman needs more than just promises."

"I never promised you anything. You moved out here. You and your mother. I never asked you to."

Tears began to well up in her eyes. She clenched her jaw, as if determined not to give him the advantage of seeing her cry.

"It was for your benefit, Roy. My mother helped you. And so did I."

"That's true."

"Some things are just unspoken, that's all."

He walked over and sat on the edge of the bed, as if to close the gap between them. He looked sadly at the suitcase on the bed.

"I don't want you to go, Wanda. And I do want to marry you."

"You do?"

"Why, sure. That might have been unspoken just because so much has been happening around here. But I surely appreciate all you and your mother have done here for me and all. I don't always say what I'm thinking, I guess."

"And what are you thinking, Roy Killian?" She stood with her feet apart, taking a militant stance and folding her arms across her chest.

"I just like having you here all the time, hon. I'm happy with you."

"What about marriage, Roy?"

He looked up and saw her piercing gaze.

"I thought it was the man's place to ask."

She glared at him with even more intensity. Her fingers tapped on both elbows as if a clock was ticking in perfect tempo.

"I mean, can't you wait until I ask you? Formally?"

Still, Wanda said nothing. Outside, they heard the wagon roll up to the house.

"Wanda, are you coming?" Hattie's voice.

Wanda did not answer.

Roy squirmed on the edge of the bed like a man in torment.

"Wanda." Hattie's voice was louder this time.

"Coming, Mother. Just a minute."

Wanda went to the bureau and picked up some folded blouses. She started to put them in her suitcase. Roy shot out a hand and stopped her.

"Don't do that, Roy. I'm leaving. Mother's waiting."

Roy heaved a sigh. A faint trace of a smile played on Wanda's lips. Roy hung his head for a moment, then raised it, looked at her. He let his hand drop away from the blouses. She started to put them inside the suitcase.

"What if we wait until after roundup, huh? Could we get married then?" This was a man in defeat. This was a man surrendering.

"That would be just fine, Roy. Are you sure?"

Roy sighed again. "Yeah, I'm sure. After the fall roundup."

"Thanksgiving," she said.

He nodded.

"Wanda!"

"I'll be right back," Wanda said. She ran to the front door, opened it and shouted to her mother. "Go on. I've changed my mind. Talk to you when you get back."

"Well, I swan," Hattie said.

Wanda closed the door as the wagon rumbled off toward Baronsville.

When she entered the bedroom, Roy was lying atop their bed. Her suitcase was on the floor, closed.

"Roy . . ."

"I want you," he said, opening his arms to receive her.

"Just like that, huh?"

"It's been a spell, hon."

"You bastard," she said, and then laughed. She threw herself atop him and they embraced. He began to kiss her until her passion was a blushing rouge on her pale cheeks, spreading down to her neck and her chest. When he opened her blouse, her breasts were aflame with that same hue and soon it enveloped her entire body.

"Thanksgiving," she breathed into his ear.

"Thanksgiving," he echoed, and soon their thrashing on the bed blocked out all other sounds, and the morning flared into full bloom with the mathematics and magic of sun and sky and earth just outside their window, like a brightly lit image of paradise in all its splendor.

42

■

E D WALES WAS dying, not only physically, but spiritually. He had thought about dying a lot, and came to the realization that his spirit was dying faster than his physical body. It was a sobering thought, and somewhat disconcerting. He was more afraid of his spirit dying than he feared his body's slow, agonizing death. But he continued to put out the newspaper. He viewed the *Bugle* as his only physical link to life. He thought the newspaper was more alive than he was, and took pride in seeing it come to life every week. He enjoyed bringing news of the war to the Rio Grande Valley, even though most of the battles had been up in Arkansas and Missouri, and not always against Union forces. Many of the Confederates were engaged against Indian marauders, Kiowa and Comanche, up along the Red River. But he now knew that John S. Ford was to patrol the Rio Grande from Brownsville to El Paso, and he felt the war would soon sweep their way. There was life in the war; but there was death, too, and, with those attributes, he was utterly fascinated as he felt his own life and spark slowly ebb away, like sand trickling through an hourglass.

"I'm thinking of going down to Brownsville," Millie said. She and Ed were drinking coffee in the nearly empty Longhorn Saloon.

"Why?"

"To see Martin. And maybe I can help Doc Purvis and Lorene. Do my part in the war."

"That's going to be a dangerous place. If the Federals come down there, and they will, it will be damned bloody."

"I can't just sit here," she said. She had been pining for Martin ever since Ford's cavalry had ridden out. She missed him so much that she cried herself to sleep every night. He hadn't been gone for more than a few days, but to her, it seemed as if he had left Baronsville months ago.

"One thing for sure, Millie. You can't go traipsing off down south all by yourself. Too many Apaches, Comanches, who knows what all."

"I'm trying to talk Nancy Grant into going with me. She and Ken should be stopping by any minute now."

"Oh, two women riding alone through all that wild country. Sure. It would be suicide."

Millie forced a laugh. It was plain that she was nervous. She kept looking toward the door, as well as at the tables where people sat. She was, he knew, still at work, but was kind enough to spend some time with him. For the past half hour, he had been talking a blue streak, about the war, the paper, the fact that they no longer had a doctor in Baronsville since Doc Purvis had left to go with Colonel Ford and the Army of the West.

"No school today?" Wales said.

"Where have you been, Ed? It's summer, and school lets out until September. Next month. Nancy has been tutoring a couple of students, but not today. I think she and Ken are making wedding plans."

"Oh? I'll be sorry to miss that."

"I think they're talking about Thanksgiving. Or Christmas. You won't miss it."

He looked at her, his eyes sad, rheumy. His skin had that yellowish cast to it again. He did not look very well.

"Do you really think I'll be around that long, Millie?"

"Ed, please don't talk that way. If you follow Doc Purvis's orders and don't drink, you can live out your life. You aren't drinking anymore, are you?"

His short raspy laugh was his answer.

"You musn't," she said softly.

Ed looked away from her, into a distance only he could see, and there was a sadness in his eyes that almost made her shudder.

"Besides," she said. "There is your book."

"My book?" Ed looked bewildered and the sadness in his eyes turned to smoke.

"The history of Texas you're writing. The history of Baronsville. How's that coming along?" Her words were rushed, as if she was changing the subject quickly, as if that would keep him alive, give him a reason to live.

"I gave up on it, pretty much, dear Millie."

"Why? You were so enthusiastic when you began."

Again, Ed looked off into an impenetrable distance, the smoke in his eyes wafting away, leaving a dull blue glitter.

"I wrote a great deal," he said, in an almost disembodied voice. He looked down at his coffee in its cup as if trying to divine something from its darkness. "Then, I saw very clearly that history contained all the sad and broken dreams of mankind. Very depressing."

"Oh, you must not think that way, Ed." She reached over and placed her hand atop one of his. "You told me that the history of Texas was exciting. You said it was the greatest story in the world."

"It may be. But I'm not the one to write it. Texas is covered with blood, and so many flags have flown over it, I'm not sure I know what it is any more. Worse, I no longer know what it will be. I put my main stock in your man Martin Baron, but he seems to have lost track, too."

"No he hasn't," Millie said, defiance in her tone. "He still believes in Texas or he wouldn't be off fighting with Colonel Ford."

Someone at one of the tables beckoned to Millie. "Excuse me, Ed," she said, and got up. As she walked away, Wales reached into his back pocket and pulled out a flask. He opened it and poured whiskey into his coffee. He recapped it and put it back in his pocket. He sipped his coffee now, which had cooled, and smacked his lips as the whiskey burned its way down a familiar path.

He knew Millie would not serve him a drink, so he had come prepared. He had tried to give up the whiskey, but he just couldn't. He couldn't stand the nights of sweating until his sheets were soaked, the midnights of despair, and the dawns when he shook so hard he couldn't think until the first jolt of whiskey calmed his nerves, alleviated the palsy. So he had learned how to keep himself from falling over the edge. A few judicious sips every so often kept the shakes down and added some clarity to his mind. It wasn't enough to quell the yearning for alcohol, but it was the only way he could get through the day and the night.

There was fear behind that routine, too, because during his last dry spell he had seen things, terrible things, things that had not really been there. He knew, from talking to Doc Purvis, that he had been having deliriums, that the writhing snakes he saw and the large insects were not real, but they seemed real. And one night, he had lain in bed, sweating, and heard beautiful organ music, unearthly music that swelled through the house and seemed as if it was coming from heaven. And then, he saw the bugs and the snakes streaming down from the ceiling and crawling over his sheets and feeding on his brain. He had screamed at the top of his voice, but the visions only went away when the sun rose and took away the terrible night.

Millie returned to the table a few moments later and sat down.

"Warm up your coffee, Ed?"

"No, I'm fine," he said.

"I've had too much today. Goodness, where can Nancy and Ken be? I thought they'd be here by now."

Ed leaned back in his chair and sipped his whiskey-laced coffee. He wanted to be as far away from Millie as possible, so that she would not smell the fumes, either in his cup or on his breath. That was the part about the drinking; he couldn't help himself. Even though everyone knew he drank, he had to keep up the pretense that he was following doctor's orders.

"Oh, here they come," she said, her face brightening. She craned to look out the window. Ed turned and saw Ken and Nancy cross the street. Ken was carrying a sheaf of papers that Ed recognized. He had given them to Ken two months ago and had forgotten about them.

Ken and Millie came in, walked over to the table.

"Coffee?" Millie asked.

"Tea for me," Nancy said.

"Anything," Ken said, as he pulled back a chair for Nancy. Then he pulled up another chair and sat down.

"Eduardo," Ken said, smiling. "*¿Cómo está?*"

"*Bien, bien.*"

"I'll be right back," Millie said. "Don't talk about anything important while I'm gone."

They all laughed as Millie skipped away to bring tea and coffee,
and cups for Ken and Nancy.

Ken laid the sheaf of papers on the table and folded his hands
atop them. Ed took another swallow of his enhanced coffee, but did
not look at the papers. He knew Ken would bring up the subject as
soon as Millie sat down again.

"I hear you're getting married," Wales said to Nancy. "Ken will
make a fine husband."

"We want you at the wedding, Ed," she said. "It'll be small; just a
few friends."

"Millie wants to go down to Brownsville. By herself, or with you,
Nan."

"She asked me. Ken won't let me go down there. Besides, I'm too
busy, and so is he. Ken's thinking about making arms for the Confederates. Putting in a factory here in Baronsville."

Ed's eyebrows arched.

"That's not for publication, Ed," Richman said. "I'm just mulling
it over."

"Sure. Big mistake, though."

"Why?"

"This is going to be a short war. The South has no money. And
what it does have, isn't worth the paper it's printed on. And after the
war, with no call for military rifles, what will you do with a big old factory smack-dab in the middle of Baronsville?"

"Good point."

"You might do better, in the long run, if you built a cotton gin.
Cotton is here to stay. You know, Ken, Martin Baron was the man
with the vision of raising cattle in the Rio Grande Valley. Since he
came here, ranchers have sprung up all over and all around here.
And he saw cattle ranching as a business long before there was any
market for beef."

"What's your point about the cotton gin, Ed?"

"The same as it is with cattle. People have to eat and people need
to be clothed. If you're going to introduce industry to Baronsville, it
might be better to create something useful. Munitions have a limited
mercantile life. Cloth and beef are essentials."

"He's right, Ken, you know," Nancy said.

"More often than not," Ken said, and the three of them laughed.

Millie returned with a tray bearing cups, a pitcher of coffee and one of tea. She set the cups out and poured tea.

"More coffee, Ed?" she asked, poising the pitcher over his cup.

"Just a wee slosh," he said, smiling. His hands seemed to be guarding his cup, placed on either side of it like small curved walls. Millie poured his cup nearly to the brim. Ed frowned, but said nothing.

Richman glanced at Ed and started to shake his head. Nancy tapped him in the side with her elbow. Ken and Millie said nothing. Millie sat down.

"What's that, Ken?" Millie asked, pointing to the sheaf of foolscap under his hands. Ken shoved the papers toward Wales. Millie glanced at the words on the top sheet, written in large block letters, all capitals: "GENERAL SAM."

"Nice work, Ed," Ken said. "What are you going to do with it? Make a nice feature in your paper, or maybe—"

"Nothing," Wales said quickly. "Thanks for reading it."

"What is it?" Millie asked, looking straight at Wales.

"He interviewed Sam Houston in Galveston," Richman said. "Damned fine job."

"Why aren't you going to publish it?" Millie asked, persisting.

"It's too sad. General Sam didn't want Texas to secede from the Union, you know. He fought against it, but was beaten down in Austin. He's a shell of a man now. Broken, dying. I haven't got the heart. Besides, it wouldn't do any good now. The war is too far along."

"Isn't that playing politics, Ed?" Richman asked.

"That's a newspaper's job, Ken. To play politics. To shape the thinking of the public. To guide the sheep as they're being led to slaughter."

"Is that what you believe?"

"Whether I believe it or not, it's true. A newspaper, in theory, is supposed to hold an objective view. Not take sides, except in editorials. But all newspapers slant their stories. They publish those stories that either sell copies or promote some political aim. At times, a newspaper publisher wields his power for personal gain."

"Is that what you do?" Nancy asked, her brown eyes glittering with a fervent light.

"Luckily," Ed said, "I had a good teacher. I worked for a newspaper in East Texas when I was just a young lad. Owned by a man named Tim Pendleton and his wife, Sharon. This man used his newspaper like a weapon. He ran false stories about unsuitable land and was able to buy up property for pennies on the dollar. He manipulated elections, saw to it that his cronies sat on the city council. He elected the mayors, the sheriffs, the tax collectors. He lied, intimidated, coerced, and undermined government to suit his own purposes, for his own personal gain. He and his wife became very wealthy. It made me sick. Not because they were rich, but over how they used their newspaper to wield power. I guess I was an idealist. I guess I still am."

"So," Nancy said, "you think a newspaper has a public responsibility."

"I do," Wales said. "If someone pays a nickel or two cents to find out what's going on in his world, he deserves honesty and fairness. Freedom of the press is a sacred trust, not a license to steal or intimidate or create falsehoods for personal gain."

"But you still think a newspaper is political," Ken said.

"Absolutely. But life is political. War is political. Of the people, by the people, and for the people. The newspaper is the voice of the people, but it is also the conscience of the people."

Ed picked up his cup and drank half of it, as if renewing the energy he had expended on polemics. His forehead glistened with beads of sweat. He sighed deeply and braced himself against the pain that coursed through his body like an electric current.

"And I thought a newspaper was just a newspaper," Millie said. "News and paper, as it says."

"A newspaper is a vital part of civilized life," Wales said. "You know, the first business in every new town that springs up in the West is a newspaper. It represents vitality, growth, promise. A publisher must not betray that trust granted him by the people he serves. You can measure the character of a town by the character of its newspaper. Period." ·

Millie held up her hands in mock surrender. "You've convinced me, Ed. Maybe that's why I like Baronsville. It has an honest publisher and an honest newspaper."

"Hear, hear," Ken said, and they all laughed.

Ed finished his coffee in one gulp and then his eyes widened. He stiffened in his chair and his right hand flew to his chest. He knocked his cup away and it rolled toward Millie. He gasped for air, shuddered, and then slumped over. His head fell on top of the Houston manuscript. Blood squirted from his nose, slowed to a trickle, then stopped. The blood stained the top sheet of Ed's manuscript. Millie screamed. Nancy scooted her chair back and ran to the other side of the table. She leaned down and put her ear close to Ed's mouth. Richman got up and lifted Ed's head. It fell backward, lifeless.

Nancy straightened and stood up. She looked at Ken, tears brimming in her eyes. She shook her head.

"He's dead, Millie," Ken said.

Millie crumpled up and bowed her head. She began to sob and then she lifted her head, reached across the table and put her hand atop one of Ed's. She blinked, squeezing out tears.

"Goodbye, Ed," she breathed. She picked up Ed's cup, which lay on its side, and brought it up to her nose. She sniffed it and then gazed upward at the ceiling.

"Damn you, Ed," she said lovingly. "You dear, dear man."

Ken blinked back tears. Nancy put her arm around his waist and squeezed him.

Ken put his arm around Nancy, too choked up to speak.

He looked down and saw the bulge in Ed's back pocket. He winced and squinched his eyes shut as the tears spilled over his lids and coursed down his cheeks. The few patrons looked over and froze, shocked, and the room filled with a long deep silence as if time had ceased to be.

43

ANSON KNEW IT was a bad place the moment he saw it. He couldn't have defined his realization in concrete terms, nor even with any logic. It was just a feeling for the stark land, the emptiness of it, the big oak tree that had been struck by lightning and had burned down to a skeletal hulk that jutted up like something disfigured and dead. The tree stood at the edge of an open, grassy plain, and the cattle were gathered around it, feeding, as if this was a place where God had thundered and speared the earth with the magical lances of electricity, charging the very ground with an unseen energy, imbuing the earth with mystical powers.

Anson and Peebo lay on their bellies at the very edge of that place; their horses were tied to mesquite trees, out of sight some yards behind them, in a place where they could feed in the shade and warn them if anyone came up behind them.

Low hills surrounded the place on the western side and behind them, but they were more than a rifle shot distant from the open plain that stretched out before them.

"What do you think, Anson? Ain't that old Diablo Blanco yonder by that burned oak?"

"That's him, Peebo. But he might as well be out in the middle of the Gulf. We can't get anywhere near him. Can't rope him. Can't corner him."

"If we was on our steeds, we could brace him, run him down."

"I can smell 'em, Peebo. They're here. They're all around us, just waiting for us."

"The Apaches, you mean."

Anson nodded.

"Well, we did see a lot of tracks back yonder, but they petered out. No tellin' where them red bastards is."

"When you see something like that, you know."

"What in hell do you mean, son?"

"No tracks, where there ought to be tracks. Tracks where they shouldn't be tracks. Culebra is full of tricks, all right. He's watching that white bull as sure as we are."

Peebo's scalp prickled, as if hot peppers had been sprinkled on his brain. He swallowed a lump in his dry throat. Something like fear crawled around in his stomach and he drew in a breath to quell the shakes he felt were coming on like buck fever.

"You think so?" Peebo whispered. "That old Culebra is out here in the brush?"

Anson looked at Peebo, at the sheen of sweat glistening on his forehead, at his parched and cracked lips, at the perspiration stains on his shirt, the slight tremor that rippled on his throat.

"Are you as scared as I am, Peebo?"

"Plumb shitless, son. It's too damned quiet and that bull ain't spooked none. That just ain't natural."

Anson turned his body slightly and winced at the pain in his side. He knew now that the ribs weren't broken, but just badly bruised. Still, the pain was enough to slow him down. He looked at the trees over at the left. There was just a whisper of a breeze to jiggle the leaves. Most likely that was one of the places where the Apaches were concealed. They'd have clear lines of fire at anyone who ventured out in the open and moved toward the white bull. To the right, the land was rolling, creased by small furrows clear to the base of the ridge. Apaches could be lying just over the ridgeline, waiting to pop up and fire down at anyone trying to rope the bull. If he and Peebo were to venture up toward their quarry, they'd be caught in a merciless crossfire. They wouldn't stand a chance, he knew. They'd be dead before they ever shook out a rope.

"Peebo, let's get out of here."

Peebo looked over at Anson, a shocked expression on his face.

"You givin' up, son?"

"Follow me."

The two mounted their horses and rode back the way they had come. Anson rode into a grove of mesquite, where he hoped they could talk without their voices carrying back to the place where the white bull was grazing. He reined up, let out a long sigh.

Peebo opened his mouth to speak.

Anson put up a hand to stop him. "Don't start in, Peebo. I'm not giving up on Diablo Blanco. But I know Culebra's there with his red brothers, just waiting for us to make a move."

"You got good sense, after all," Peebo said.

"While we were there, I got to thinking. Sometimes the best decision is no decision at all."

"Well, that makes sense if you've been hit real hard on the head and are a mite addled."

"Don't make jokes. I'm serious. Mickey Bone told me something, a long time ago, that I just remembered a few minutes ago. It might help us."

"Bone? That renegade?"

"Yes, Bone. There was a time when I admired him. Looked up to him. I wanted to live his life as a wild man."

Peebo laughed.

"I got over it," Anson said. "But he told me something that stuck with me."

"And what was that?"

"He said the red man had patience. He said the white man did not have patience. He said that was the big difference between the white man and the red man."

"I got all kinds of patience, son. I just don't like waitin' around for something to happen."

"Well, Peebo, that's the goddamned point. If we try and move in on that bull, those patient Apaches up yonder will have outwitted the hell out of us."

"So what's your idea, Anson? Outpatience the Apaches?"

"I say we ride back there, keep watching that bull, and just wait. Let's see who has more patience, us or the damned Apaches."

"Hell, we could be there for years maybe." Peebo flashed his winning grin, but it splashed off Anson without any reaction.

"I'm dead serious, Peebo."

"I guess, by gum, you are. Good thing our canteens are full. We can make camp there, cook some grub, and just wait while our beards get even longer."

"Don't be such a smarty britches, Peebo. When that bull moves, the Apaches will move, unless I miss my guess. And when they do, we'll either hear 'em or see 'em and . . ."

"And what?"

"Maybe get into a fight where we have all the advantage. Check your pistols and make sure your rifle works. It might get pretty hot."

Peebo shook his head. "I dunno," he said. "A whole bunch of ifs in there, son."

"I know. Culebra will be expecting us to ride up and start building loops in our lariats. We're going to surprise him and just wait him out."

Peebo drew his cap-and-ball pistol from its holster, spun the cylinder. He nudged a loose cap back on the nipple when it stuck and then reholstered the weapon.

"I'm ready," Peebo said. "So are Mister Colt and Mister Long Rifle."

"We'll tie up our horses behind us. They should warn us if an Apache tries to sneak up on our rear. We'll crawl close and lay flat, at angles, so we can watch more ground on both sides of us. Got it?"

"Got it," Peebo said.

Anson checked his weapons and, satisfied, turned his horse. Slowly, they rode back to the place where they had been. The white bull was still grazing on the grass that grew around the lightning-struck tree, but had moved closer to the stand of mesquite on the left. A cow was acting as lookout for the small herd, but was gazing and sniffing in a different direction. The two men dismounted and ground-tied their horses to a pair of mesquite trees. Then they crawled closer, cradling their rifles. They moved only when the lookout cow was looking away from them.

Anson stopped, indicating that this was the place where they would wait. He placed his right index finger on his lips. Peebo nodded and made a pinching motion to signify that he would not talk as they waited.

Anson scanned the trees off to his left and looked for any movement. He knew that if a man lay perfectly still, he would be almost invisible. The hunter looked for movement. Animals that did not move often could not be seen. It was the same for humans. He knew Peebo was doing the same off to the right, looking in every direction, not moving his head, but only his eyes.

There was enough brush and cactus to hide the two men where they lay, virtually motionless. Flies landed on their foreheads and sucked sweat, or buzzed their ears. The sun bore down, the heat baking them and the ground around them. The minutes slid into hours and still there was only the soft breeze murmuring in the leaves and the sound of the cattle moving around. Just after noon, the white bull moved off into the shade and lay down. Others in the herd followed and soon all but one cow were bedded down during the heat of afternoon.

Anson fought off sleepiness. His eyelids drooped and he longed for shade. It was only the thought of Culebra, his enemy, that kept him from dozing off and losing sight of his goal, to catch the white bull and burn the Box B brand into its hide.

Then Nero whinnied, followed by a nicker from Buckaroo. Anson stiffened. He looked over at Peebo, who tried to shrug from his prone position. Nero whinnied again, a long ripple of sounds, followed by a snort.

Then they both heard it. Hoofbeats. Off in the distance.

"Somebody's wearin' out leather," Peebo whispered.

"Shhh." Anson held a finger to his lips. He cupped a hand behind his ear. Then, out of the corner of his eye, he saw movement off to the right, at the top of the ridge.

"Look," he said to Peebo, nodding toward the ridge.

Two riders broke the skyline with their silhouettes. They appeared to be wearing uniforms. Gray uniforms.

"What the hell . . ." Peebo muttered.

"Confederate cavalry," Anson said. "But those hoofbeats are coming from behind us, beyond where we left our horses."

"Yeah, I hear 'em. Gettin' louder by the second, son."

Then, more commotion up ahead of them.

Anson turned and saw the cows rise up from their dust wallows and start to move. The white bull rose up and snorted, began pawing the ground with his front hoof.

"Maybe we better wave to them soldiers," Peebo said.

"Wait a minute."

"They've stopped. They're lookin' thisaway."

"Wave your hat, Peebo."

Peebo lifted his hat from his head and waved it until the riders caught sight of it, then he plunked it back on his head and continued to hug the ground.

Anson saw the sparkling flashes from a signaling mirror.

"Here they come. Look at them fan out. And they're both carrying rifles like they mean business."

Anson saw the two riders part and ride away from each other while pressing down the slope of the ridge, heading straight for them.

"The bull's going to run," Anson said.

Peebo turned his head and looked up at the burned tree. The cattle were all looking toward the two riders. All except one. It was looking toward the mesquite grove. It bawled and all the cattle, including the white bull, turned their heads and looked toward the stand of trees. Then the bull whirled and dashed off in a straight line, away from the burned tree.

Something else moved.

"Peebo, watch yourself," Anson said.

Then he saw the Apache rise from the ground near the trees. Then another and still another appeared as if by magic. Their faces were painted for war. One of them began shooting at the cavalrymen, while others swarmed among the trees and began running in various directions, away from the open plain.

Then the Apaches began yipping and yelling, the sounds high-pitched and unnerving, enough to chill the blood of a white man.

Anson rose to his knees and put his rifle to his shoulder. He took aim at one Apache and led him a few inches, cocked the hammer back on his rifle, and squeezed the trigger. The rifle bucked against his shoulder as it sprouted orange flame and white smoke. The smoke obscured his vision.

Peebo jumped to his feet and took aim at another Apache, but the warrior disappeared in the trees.

Seconds seemed like hours, as the two cavalrymen rode closer and the thunder of hoofbeats behind them grew louder.

Then, to Anson's surprise, the herd of wild longhorns reemerged behind the tree and were stampeding straight toward him and Peebo. Behind the cows, he caught glimpses of Apaches chasing them. In the lead was the white bull, growing ever larger as he charged down on top of Anson and Peebo, running like the wind.

"Oh, shit," Peebo said.

Anson had not had time to reload his rifle. He set it down and drew his pistol.

Time seemed to stand still. Anson thought he must have dozed off and was now in the middle of a nightmare. A nightmare that made no sense.

His heart caught in his throat as he cocked the hammer of his pistol, wondering if he was going to be trampled to death or shot dead by one of the screeching Apaches bearing down on him from all sides.

44

━█━

SHE WAS BEGINNING to wind her way into his bleak heart, but he didn't know yet if he could trust her. He did not know if she was broken enough to heel after him like a dog. But she rode with him now, back to Matteo's old ranch and she had not tried to escape when they were so close to Valle they could hear the voices of the *poblanos* and smell the cookfires and the food. She had watched him shoot the man and she had not bolted, but waited for him to turn his horse and ride back to her.

Now they rode back to Matteo's old ranch for the last time as the long afternoon shadows stretched across the land and the mountains darkened on their eastern sides, rugged, brooding, rock-strewn, ancient mountains that rose from the land like the armored plating of prehistoric beasts. Like the graves of giants that had once walked the land.

"You do not talk much, Lucinda," Bone said, when they were well away from Valle.

"Why did you shoot Paco Santiago? Why did you kill him?"

"Because I killed his father, Viejo. I did not want the son coming after me."

"Why did you kill Paco's father?"

"He stole a cow from me. He brought trouble. Do you not see the trouble he brought?"

"I was to marry Paco."

"He was not a man for you. I am."

"He was a good man."

"He is now a dead man, Lucinda. I am alive."

"Must there always be the blood?" she said. There was no whining in her voice. It was just a question.

"The land drinks blood. The land always has thirst for the blood."

"Must the strong always kill the weak?"

"That is the way life is, do you not know this?"

"I know," she said, and her voice was heavy with a great sadness.

Bone thought of Dream Speaker and his wisdom. For some reason he wished that Lucinda could have known him when he was alive, could speak to him now; could listen to his wise words. He did not know why he wanted this, but he thought it might have something to do with himself, with the worries he had and the turns his life had taken.

Dream Speaker had told Bone that it was not possible to live in two worlds in this lifetime. "You cannot walk the white man's path while you are wearing that skin," Dream Speaker had said. "If you are a wolf, you cannot be a snake."

"What am I to do, Dream Speaker?" Bone had asked. "Our tribe is going the way of the Old Ones, disappearing like the fires of the sunset, like the raindrops falling into a stream. I do not want to walk the white man's path, I want to walk my own path. But it is a narrow path and is thick with brambles and blocked with big stones."

"Look at the Mexican," Dream Speaker said. "He is of two tribes. He is of the Spanish and of the Indio. Now, he is a Mexican and walks the land that is soaked with Spanish blood and the blood of the Indio. So he is himself, with his own spirit, and one day, he, too, will die out."

"We all die, Dream Speaker."

"The red man dies faster now that the white man has come with his thundersticks and plagues. You stay now with the last of your tribe, and soon you will be the last of the last. You must mark your path and leave your seed in the belly of a woman so that some of your blood lives on, like the worms that come to eat the flesh of the dead. If you do not do this, Bone, then you will have passed this way for nothing. I left my seed in a Mexican woman, when I was young, and I did this so that my tribe would not die out."

"But you do not have this Mexican woman. You do not have your child."

"That is true. I do not worry about these things. I have planted my seed and it has grown. I will always be alive somewhere even after my spirit has left this old body and journeyed to the stars that shine like ghost candles in the darkest night."

Bone wondered what Dream Speaker would say if he was alive now and knew that Bone had killed his wife and his son. Had killed his seed. He knew what Dream Speaker would say. He would say that Bone had broken with life, had wounded himself and had left no trail, that his tracks were like grains of sand that had blown away in the wind and would never be seen again.

The twilight came on as the sun passed over the mountains, changing the land, softening it, lending mysterious shapes to the rocks and the cactus, the creosote bushes, the sage. The earth gave up its scents as the land cooled, imbuing the air with the exotic perfume of sage and succulents. The soil itself with its many secrets was abandoned by lizards, birds, snakes, armadillos, and insects, all of which had left their marks and tracks and excrement behind them.

Bone listened to see if they were being followed, but he heard nothing except the whooshing sound of air displaced by the bats as they flapped overhead on silent leather wings, and the faraway yip of a lone coyote beginning its hunt. There was still enough light to see the road and the surrounding plain, the dark shapes of mountains that rose up on all sides. He saw a small owl float by, heading toward the ranch on noiseless pinions like some guiding spirit pointing the way through the gathering darkness. The owl floated off and disappeared behind the entrance to the small valley, winging over the place where Bone had shot and killed Viejo, who was no longer there, his blood lapped up by ants and beetles and crows as if he had never existed.

But Bone felt the presence of death all around him, shrouding him like the night itself. And he could smell the blood of Viejo, or thought he could, because at that time of day, he could smell everything and death was something he could smell, too, and he smelled it now and he had no feelings about it because it was just another smell of life and earth that was always present when he was awake.

"I am tired," Lucinda said, as they came to the foot of the ridge that led into the valley where the ranch lay in the softening darkness.

"We will not stay here tonight," Bone said. "You will have no rest this night."

"Why? I am very tired."

"We will take the cattle and the horses and drive them to Brownsville where I will sell them."

"But you will not see in the dark."

"I can see. They can see. There will be a moon."

Suddenly Bone reined up and stopped his horse. He held out an arm. Lucinda pulled her horse to a stop, too. They had not yet rounded the foot of the ridge and entered the valley where Aguilar's old ranch was.

"What passes?" Lucinda said.

"Do you not smell it?"

Lucinda sniffed the air.

"It smells like smoke," she said.

"Yes. It is the smell of smoke."

"Someone is cooking."

"No, that is not the smell of a cooking fire."

Bone waited. The smell was very strong. The smell of burned wood. Something stirred in his memory. Something clawed at the pool of darkness in his brain, seeking recognition. There was something he had missed when they rode away to Valle and passed the place where he had killed Viejo. Someone had watched him and Lucinda ride away and he had not seen them. He knew that Paco had come there and found the body of his father and taken it away, taken it to Valle for burial. He had wanted to kill Paco when he came for the body, but Paco had come when Bone was not there to see him take his father's corpse away.

Bone rounded the foot of the ridge and entered the valley. The smell of smoke was much stronger. He could see the bare outlines of the adobe house as he and Lucinda rode toward it.

"What has passed here?" Lucinda asked.

The adobe was still smoldering. All the sills and beams had been burned and the porch and door were just ashes.

"Stay here," Bone said, and rode toward the corrals and the lean-to that served as a barn. But the horses were no longer there. The horses were gone and so were his cattle. The corral and lean-to were just smoking ruins. Something hard twisted in Bone's gut, and he muttered a curse, then turned his horse and rode back to where Lucinda was still waiting.

"What passes?" she asked, her voice trembling with fear.

"My horses and my cattle are gone. Stolen by that bastard Paco. He came here and burned everything."

"What will you do?"

"We will ride to Brownsville. I do not want the horses. I do not want the cattle. They are gone and I will not look for them. I have some money. It is enough."

"I do not want to go to Brownsville. I am afraid of the gringos."

"We will not stay there a long time."

"We will come back to Mexico?"

Bone looked at her as if she was addled. There was nothing here for him. There never had been. It had never been his land, even though he had once thought that it was. The smoke was making him sick. He wanted to kill someone. But he had already killed Paco and he knew that the burning was Paco's doing. So too the stolen cattle and his horses. A man could die only once. Maybe someday he would come back and kill Paco's relatives.

"We will stay in Texas. I know a place where we can live."

"Please, Mickey, I beg you. Let me go back home. Back to Valle."

"Lucinda, you will never go back there. You are with me now and where I am is where your home is. Do not mention this to me again. Do you understand?"

A sob caught in her throat and she nodded.

"Come," he said. "We will leave this place. We will leave this place forever."

He turned his horse and as they rode back out of the valley he could hear her sobs. They had no effect on him. He was glad to be leaving Mexico and going back to Texas.

45

━■━

T HE EMPTY HOUSE began to breathe as it filled up with people and came alive. It breathed with a sense of purpose as Hattie, with the help of Lucinda Madera, Esperanza Cuevas, and Petunia, began to fill it with furniture, cooking utensils, curtains, tablecloths, bedroom linens, and other furnishings.

She had discussed all of this with Ken Richman and he agreed that it would be better for the Martin house if it was occupied. He also agreed to help furnish and supply it.

"It's still not much of a ranch yet," Hattie had said to Forrest when they were moving in after bringing Esperanza Cuevas, Lucinda Madera, and the ex-slaves, Fidelius and his wife, Petunia, from Baronsville a few days before. "It's all gone to weeds and nobody to work the cattle, which are probably turning wild as March hares. But you and Roy have built a sound house and we'll make do."

"Hattie, you do more than make do," Forrest said. "You're a wonder. What you've done already is truly astounding. It was just an empty house before, but now it's beginning to look like a home."

"Well, I thought it was time we let the two lovebirds make their own way. Wanda was getting on my nerves and Roy is busy with the cotton and such. I think it's better this way, and the Barons will have something to come home to when this blamed war is over."

They walked through the bottom floor of the house.

"This is the den I built for Anson or Martin," Forrest said. "And down the hall, there's a sewing room."

"I know," Hattie said. "Petunia's already working in there, making curtains for the upstairs bedroom."

"You can smell the kitchen," he said. "That Lucinda's already using it. And Esperanza, she's helping her. You don't have to cook any more, Hattie."

"I love to cook, and I'm going to help. Why don't you use this nice den for your studies? Did you bring that old rock with you?"

Forrest grinned.

"You know me too well, Hattie."

They walked into the den and Hattie surveyed it with a practiced eye. There was a desk there, an oil lamp, chairs, and Forrest's papers and books were already on the bookshelves. The rock with the strange glyphics on it was atop the desk, next to a tablet and a quill pen and inkwell.

Hattie walked over to the desk and picked up the stone. She looked at the drawings and shook her head.

"I've never seen anything like it," she said.

"Neither have I."

"Why do you study it so, Forrest?"

He laughed. She put down the stone and he picked it up.

"This is about who we are," he said. "Where we came from. Maybe, even, where we're going. Those are the questions each man, and woman, must ask of himself or herself before we die. The questions are in all great literature, in the most magnificent sculptures, in music."

"I've never heard them before. I've never asked them. I know where I'm from. I know who I am. And, I know where I'm going."

"You're so practical, Hattie. But, these questions are more cosmic than practical."

"Cosmic?"

"Some of these symbols on here have to do with astronomy, with the planets, our own galaxy, perhaps. They seem to be telling us that there is life beyond this old Earth, and more planets in our solar system than we now know of. And this cross, it radiates."

"Maybe it's Christian."

"No, it's earlier than that. I think it has to do with someone coming here to Earth and crossing some place out among the stars."

"How can this knowledge help any of us?" Hattie asked.

"I don't know, Hattie. But, I think we here on Earth are part of something bigger. Something we can't see. The Indians know this, but we don't listen to them. They believe in spirits, in long dead and nameless ancestors of which there is no record but their own memories. Somewhere in all that tangle, I believe that there's something we're supposed to find out, something we're supposed to know before we die."

"Forrest, what makes you think about these things, these ancient peoples, ancestors?"

"I've spoken to many of the Osages in Arkansas, to the Cherokee in Oklahoma, and, lately, to the Mexicans now working for Roy. There seems to be a common sadness among them, a longing, and very little, if any, happiness. It's as if they all feel they are temporary dwellers here on earth and that they are just waiting to go back home, to the stars, to some distant place in the heavens. When I look at myself, I realize that, deep down, I am just like they are. There is that sadness of something lost, something lost a long time ago, and a longing to find my true father, perhaps the Father of All, what the Indians call the Great Spirit; what we call God."

"Forrest, you're not like those people at all."

"Oh, I think, in our hearts, our souls, we are all the same people, Hattie. We just don't like to think about it. I'm talking to some of the freed slaves and I'm learning the same things I heard from the Osage and the Mexicans."

Hattie sat down and looked at Forrest. There was a radiance to her face, as if the sun was shining through the window on it, but the room was in shadow. Her eyes glinted with understanding and affection.

"I think this is why I love you, Forrest. Why I've always loved you. There's something to you, something that might seem strange to others, but which I find very appealing. You have a vision in you and you see beyond what the rest of us see. Like this house. It was a burned-out hulk of a thing and you saw a new house standing on burned ground. Nobody else could see it, but you saw it in your mind and lo and behold, here we are sitting in it, getting comfort from it."

"I believe that all things are created from thought," Forrest said.

"But someone has to, has to, you know, make the things we think of. Isn't that true?"

Forrest sat down behind the desk and laid the stone tablet back down. His deep brown eyes shone with an inner light.

"The Bible," he said, "in Genesis, the English translation, in the King James version, says that in the beginning was the word and the word was God. But in my studies, the Greek word, taken from the Hebrew, is *logos*. Which we translate as 'word.' But in my readings, I have found that *logos* is much deeper than that; it has a fuller meaning, which might not even be translatable. But I think it means something like 'deep thought.' Maybe even magical thought, but thought. So when I read Genesis I read it as 'In the beginning was the thought.' I think that everything created was created from thought and I think there's something like that on this tablet if I could only decipher it."

"I'm just awestruck by you, Forrest," she said. "I mean truly. You have a powerful mind."

"Well, I have thoughts on that, too, Hattie."

"I'm sure you do. I want to hear them."

"Maybe," he said, "there's only one mind in the universe. And maybe that mind belongs to what we call God. Every thought, every concept, every design, plan, object, thing, if you will, is in that one great mind, and we all dip into it, as if it was some giant pool."

"My," she said, "that is a big thought right there."

"Well, that's only my theory. But I think behind our thoughts, our human thoughts, there's that thing called faith, or belief. If we had a truly powerful mind and had belief, or faith, then we could just imagine something, like a house, and it would rise up before our very eyes and we wouldn't have to saw a single board or hammer a single nail."

Hattie sighed as if she was breathless, and her face continued to glow with that same radiance. She rose from her chair, walked over behind Forrest, and put her arms around him. She leaned down and kissed his cheek.

"I treasure you," she whispered into his ear. "I love you and I treasure you, sweet Forrest. You are divine."

He reached up and touched her hand with his.

"So are you, Hattie. So are we all."

She sighed again and stood up, releasing Forrest from her embrace.

"I must go out to the kitchen and help the girls, or none of us will have any lunch," she said. "Stay here and think your grand thoughts. Enjoy this room in the house you built. And when the Barons return, we'll build an even grander place, you and I, my love."

"I think I'll go outside and talk to Fidelius, get to know him. Talking about all these things has gotten me excited again. About my quest."

"Your quest, Forrest. My, my, you do say such beautiful things."

Hattie left the room and Forrest sat there for several moments, thinking about their conversation. Hattie stimulated him. He didn't know if he loved her or not, but he admired her and she gave him a sustenance that could not be measured in concrete terms. She fed his mind and she gave him love. He would try and give love back to her, but he suspected it would be mostly physical. He wondered about his feelings a great deal because he had always been more excited about ideas than sex. Not that Hattie didn't excite him at times, because she did, but sex was not always on his mind. That part of him had to be drawn out and Hattie was an expert at that.

"I am so happy that you have come to the Baron house to live until Anson and Martin return," Lucinda said to Hattie. She did not mention Forrest, who was also living in the house, because she knew that he and Hattie were not married. But they slept in the big bed in Martin's room and said they were going to marry each other in the month of November.

Lucinda Madera was happy to be working again, cooking for someone besides herself and Esperanza Cuevas in the nice new house that had been so empty since she and Esperanza had returned at Ken Richman's request. She knew that Esperanza was happy, too, for she missed Lazaro Aguilar, the blind boy who had been adopted by Caroline Martin before her death. Lazaro was with his adopted mother in heaven now, Lucinda believed, and she firmly believed that he could now see, for God would have healed him.

Esperanza had told Hattie about Lazaro and Caroline, how they both had loved each other as both were dying.

"What did Caroline die of?" Hattie asked, as she put a tray of biscuits into the oven.

Esperanza looked at Lucinda. Lucinda nodded.

"She died of the syphilis."

"Martin's wife had syphilis? How ever . . ."

Lucinda, who was at the stove, stirring a simmering pot of beef and vegetable stew, understood English better than Esperanza.

"She was raped, the *senora*," Lucinda said. "Lazaro, he died of the syphilis too."

"What did Martin say about all this?" Hattie asked.

"He did not say nothing," Lucinda said quickly.

"What about Anson?"

"He was friends with Lazaro," Esperanza said. "He loved his mother very much."

Petunia entered the kitchen. She was a shy black woman, slender as a willow.

"Miz Fancher," she said, "I done finished sewing the curtains. What do you want me to do now?"

Hattie laughed. "It's almost time for lunch, Petunia. You sit down here at the table and listen to this delicious talk. You might learn something."

"Yes, ma'am. I learns a lot here already." She looked suspiciously at the two Mexican women, but sat down and clasped her hands primly atop the table.

"That is a terrible disease," Hattie said. "Caroline must have died horribly. Lazaro, too."

Lucinda looked questioningly at Esperanza, translated what Hattie had said into Spanish.

"They went to sleep," Esperanza said. She pointed to her head. Then she turned to Lucinda and spoke to her in Spanish, shrugging because she could not think of the English words.

"Esperanza says that before Caroline and Lazaro died, God took their minds away from them."

At that, Hattie was shocked and drew herself up.

"My, my, how tragic," Hattie said. "It must have been very hard on Martin, and on Anson. To watch Caroline die."

"It was very hard on all of us," Lucinda said. "We were all very sad."

"No wonder the Baron men act so strangely," Hattie murmured.

The Mexican woman stared at her with looks of incomprehension.

"Oh," Hattie said, "I was just thinking about Martin and Anson, leaving their ranch to the weeds and going off like they did."

"They will come back," Lucinda said, almost with an air of defiance.

"Yes," Esperanza said. "They come back soon, I think."

There was a silence, then, and Petunia cleared her throat and spoke. "Massa Baron, he gave us our freedom," she said. "He is a good man."

The Mexican women both nodded.

"And Anson?" Hattie asked. "After all, he mistreated the Mexican workers here, drove them away. What do you all think of Anson Baron?"

At first, none of the other women spoke. Hattie looked at each of the Mexicans in turn.

"*Lealidad,*" Esperanza said softly. "*Honor.*"

"She says 'loyalty' and 'honor,'" Lucinda said. "We know why the vaqueros went away. They wanted to change Anson. But he is a man of honor and he did not wish them to stay if they did not have loyalty or honor."

"That is what one must have," Esperanza said.

The smell of fresh biscuits baking filled the air inside the kitchen. Hattie opened the oven door and looked inside. The table in the dining room was set and she knew the stew was ready. She closed the door and turned toward Petunia.

"You'd better go outside and fetch your husband and Forrest," she said. "Lunch is ready."

"Yes'm," Petunia said, and went out the back door.

"You will eat with us, Lucinda, you and Esperanza. I want to hear more about the Baron honor."

"We would work for Martin and Anson for no money," Lucinda said. "We have the loyalty. The vaqueros who went away, they did not have the loyalty."

"And honor?" Hattie asked.

Lucinda and Esperanza looked at each other.

"That is what the Baron family give to us," Lucinda said. "They give us the honor."

"And so will I, Lucinda," Hattie said, trying very hard not to cry.

46

———■———

MILLIE SAT NEXT to Ken on the seat of the lead wagon as it rumbled over country that was new and strange to her. She wore a
straw hat that was secured with a scarf under her chin. She wore
a light flowered dress that was comfortable for traveling. Her lace-up
boots were freshly shined but were already covered with a patina of
dust, as was her sparsely made-up face.

"Just where is the Rocking A, anyway, Ken?" she asked. "I don't
see any signs of habitation. This road looks as if it hasn't been used
in ages."

"Another couple of miles. This road isn't used much. It's just the
shortest. Roy generally goes through the Box B to come to town."

"I would have liked to have seen the new Baron house."

"You will. When you ride with Roy and his hands down to Corpus
Christi, you'll go right past it."

"That was a nice funeral for Ed. I liked what you said about him.
That poor man."

"I lied," Ken said.

"Lied? What ever do you mean, Ken?"

"I said the illness took him young and that he had a bright future."

"Well, he was very sick."

"Ed committed suicide. He could have lived. If he had done what Doc Purvis told him to do, stay off the whiskey, he could have had a long life. He loved the newspaper business. But he drank himself to death. Deliberately."

"Well, I guess I know that."

"He just couldn't get over his wife's leaving him, I guess. That's when he started drinking. I thought he would change. That he would find another woman, a good woman, and give up the liquor. But he didn't."

"That is sad. What was the trouble with his wife?"

"She took up with another man. A man that Ed considered inferior. A man with no education, no ambition, no money, no prospects."

"Why would she leave Ed for a man like that?"

Ken shook his head. "Ed never understood it. He adored that woman, but she was a tramp."

"Did she drink? Maybe that was why."

"No, she didn't drink. Neither did he until she left him. The man she took up with was a drinker, though. Maybe a couple of cuts above being an outlaw. Ed's wife supported this man, who drank up all she earned."

"That's horrible. No wonder Ed drank."

"Ed thought of himself as a failure, which is what he became, of course. A failure at life."

"But he started that newspaper. He wrote good stories. He was a success, I thought."

Ken laughed a dry, sardonic laugh.

"He knew his business. But he didn't know himself. He told me one time that he didn't even like to drink. But maybe he thought his ex-wife would have liked him better if he drank, so he drank."

"That doesn't make sense," Millie said.

"Life seldom does. In Ed's case, life didn't make any sense at all. So he left."

Millie sighed and drew in a deep breath of air. She had liked Wales, had enjoyed talking to him about books and writing and the newspaper business. He hadn't sounded like a cynical man at all.

"How little we really know about people," she said. "I would have thought Ed had more gumption than to drink himself to death like that."

"I think he was all right when he was working. He told me that he just couldn't stand the nights when he was all alone. He said he kept thinking of his wife, her name was Betty, I think, and of that other man she was with. He said that every night he felt like he was dying. He could hear his own heart pounding and he couldn't breathe and there was nobody to talk to, and if he hadn't been a coward and if he'd had a gun, he said there were many times when he would have just blown his own brains out."

"My heavens."

Ken began to chuckle under his breath as the wagon rocked over the rough terrain. At first, Millie thought the bumping was making him laugh, but then she realized he was still thinking about Ed Wales.

"Something funny?" she asked.

"Not really. I was just thinking about Ed's peculiar view of life. I guess, deep down, he was a kind of philosopher."

"At times, he did seem that way, but I thought he was just being cynical."

"Well, he was that, of course. But he had a way of looking at people in general, and life in general, and summing it all up in a newspaperman's terms."

"I guess I never heard any of that."

"Oh, that's when he was in his cups and expounding on the mysteries of life."

"What did he say?" she asked.

"He said most people's lives could be put into headlines, big or small, or picture captions—you know, those lines under a picture that gives some identification to them?"

"Yes, I know what you mean."

"Well, Ed would say that some people's lives would be in six- or eight-column headlines, like Sam Houston's or George Washington's. Others might have a single column headline and a paragraph or two of what he called 'copy.' Most people, though, he said, had lives that would be set in six-point agate, which is a very small type. Some, he said, would be in two-point agate. The so-called average person who never did anything. They were born, they lived, they died, and that was that. He reduced people's lives to headlines and so many column inches of copy."

"Interesting."

"Oh, he'd rail on and on about people in that way. One night I asked him how he viewed his own life. 'What kind of headline would you rate?' I asked him."

"And what did Ed say?"

"That was the funny part, I guess. He said he wouldn't even rate a headline. Just a brief notice in the obituary section of the newspaper. But then he said something that stuck with me."

"What was that, Ken?"

"He got a funny, faraway look in his eyes and he said that when he looked at his own life, all he could see was 'fragments of love falling in the distance.'"

"Did you ask him what he meant?"

"I did. But he never answered that question. He just started to cry."

"That's so very sad, Ken. Makes me want to cry, too."

"Well, he was a good man. He just lost his way, that's all. And anyway, my mother told me not to speak ill of the dead. So I laid it on pretty thick at Ed's funeral. But inside, I was fighting with myself over the injustice of his death. He did die too young, and he did have potential. Trouble was, all of his promises were broken. By him, or by Betty, or by the man Betty took up with."

"No, you couldn't say all that. It wouldn't have done any good."

"Not far now," Ken said. He looked back at the line of wagons following them. They all carried portions of supplies Roy would need on the trip to the cotton gin in Corpus Christi. His hands from the Lazy K Ranch drove the wagons, which trailed the horses they had ridden into town. Roy should have enough wagons to haul his cotton to the gin, counting those he was borrowing from the Box B.

"Why do you do all these things, Ken? I mean, you built Baronsville, yet you help out the ranchers, especially Martin and Anson."

"Because I'm part of Martin's dream. When I came out here, there was nothing but wildness. Martin had a vision of a town, ranches, a cattle empire. That dream is coming true."

"It's hard to imagine what it must have been like when you came here. But even since I've been in Baronsville, there's been a great deal of progress. Yet, I know it's out in the middle of nowhere. How do men like you and Martin see into the future as you do?"

Ken laughed. "It's a gift."

"I wish I had it."

"Maybe you do. You're going down to Brownsville to see Martin, aren't you? You want to marry him. So you'll marry into the same dream. His vision will become yours."

She began to see a change in the landscape. Here and there, she saw cattle grazing and then some well-groomed fields where grass grew.

"We must be getting very close now," she said.

"Just around the next bend. We're going straight to the cotton fields, but you'll see the road that leads to the house. First, I want to deliver these wagons so that they can be loaded. For weeks now, the Mexican women have been sewing together burlap into bags. I bought large bolts of burlap and brought them out here. Hattie knew how big the bags should be and showed the women how to cut the burlap and how to sew them. You'll see."

A few moments later, Millie did see. She saw rows and rows of spiky cotton stalks picked clean. And on the roads and rows, large burlap sacks lay bulging with cotton. Little tufts of white cotton clung to the stalks and were strewn everywhere.

Two wagons were already fully loaded with cotton sacks and men were filling a third as Ken rolled up at the head of the wagon train.

Ken reined up and set the brake.

Roy walked out to meet them, his face grimy with sweat.

"That ought to do it, Ken," he said.

"I see you got the wagons from the Box B."

"Yeah. Hattie and Forrest are living over there."

"I know," Ken said.

"That's right," Roy said. "You know just about everything that goes on in these here parts."

Ken looked around, then climbed down from the wagon. He turned and held out his hand to Millie. She stepped down.

"I understand you're going with us to Corpus Christi, Millie," Roy said. "Then on to Brownsville."

"Yes. If you'll have me."

"No trouble. Glad to have some company that speaks good English."

They all laughed. Then they walked over to the wagon that was being loaded.

"Think that cotton will make the trip, Ken?" Roy asked.

"I'd put a tarp over every wagon and tie it down tight. I brought plenty of tarp and your supplies."

"Wish you were comin' along."

"Can't get away. You find the gin and the cotton buyers will find you. Whoever buys it will either haul it overland to New Orleans or someplace or put it on a boat and head for the Carolinas."

"Money," Roy said.

"Uniforms," Ken said. "For the Confederate troops."

"All from a few damn seeds."

"Ken," Millie said, "whatever happened to that idea you had about building a munitions plant in Baronsville? Are you still going to do it?"

"Are you a mind reader? I gave that up. Too shortsighted."

"What are you going to do?"

"I'm thinking now of putting in a cotton gin. If enough ranchers grow cotton, that could become a big industry here in the Rio Grande Valley."

"Good idea," Roy said. "There's plenty of land here in Texas to do just about everything a man could want to do."

"That's right," Ken said.

"Sorry to hear about Ed Wales. Sorry I didn't make his funeral. But I didn't know him all that well."

"It was a nice funeral," Millie said.

She turned away, then, and took a deep breath. She couldn't get it out of her mind what Ken had told her about Ed's view of his own life. And then she remembered something Ken had said to her one day, about people's lives being mere fragments.

"You couldn't put it all together, if you had to sum up anybody's life," he'd said. "You could only set down pieces of it, and that's all a person has, at the end. Broken pieces of a life that never ran smoothly, never became a single, connected piece of anything. Just fragments. Just little things we do here and there and now and then."

And then, she felt the sadness of what Ed had told Ken about his own life when he looked back at it and thought she understood the poetry of it, as well as the meaning. He had lost his wife to another man and all he could see was "fragments of love falling in the distance." Like the bits of cotton that were blowing away from the fields and falling like snow back onto the ground, all so lost and forlorn. She was gripped with a deep sadness for Ed and all the people in the world, including herself.

47

■

THEY BURIED PACO Santiago next to his father. The two graves, with fresh dirt piled atop them, loomed large in the minds and hearts of the mourners. The priest spoke of two murdered men who were now with God in his Heaven, and he spoke of death and resurrection, of sin and penitence. He spoke of ashes and dust and tried to give comfort to the living as the dark-shawled women wept and wailed at the loss of still another son, gone as so many others before him.

Matteo listened to the sermon and looked at the faces of the young men, wondering what they were thinking, wondering if they were feeling mortal, and he saw their mothers and their sisters clinging to them, grasping their arms as if to prevent them from dying as Paco had died, or vanishing into death's dark chambers before their very eyes.

Luz stood next to him, her face impassive beneath the black veil that obscured her eyes, and she did not hold on to him, but stood tall and straight and strong in the face of still another death, and Matteo wondered what was in her mind, as well, for she had said little after Paco had died, but seemed to be brooding over something so private and personal she could not divulge it, even to him. But he knew she was thinking of their son, Julio, and of Paco, too, who had hoped to marry her twin sister, Lucinda. She had not spoken of this, either, and he knew she was deep in melancholy, gripped by the same sadness that gripped the town and its people.

When he and Luz returned home after the feasting at Paco's house, after listening to the stories his friends told about him, and after offering condolences to his sisters and cousins and uncles and aunts, Luz gave him a glass of *tepache* and he lit a *cigarro* she had placed on the small table beside his chair.

Luz sat down on a chair across from her husband. She had changed clothes, removed the veil, and now her face was visible to him. Her gaze was penetrating and he knew she had something on her mind, something she wanted to say to him. He sat there and smoked. He drank sips of his *tepache* and watched the fumes from the cigar slither like ghostly serpents above his head.

"Where is Jorge?" she asked. "He did not come back with us? And I saw you talking to some of the men in the house of Santiago. What were you talking to them about? You do not know them. And you spoke to el Sabio too."

"You ask so many questions, Luz, my precious."

"I ask them because I want answers. I want to know what you are going to do, Miguelito."

"You and I will get Julio and return to our ranch. I spoke to some of the men who live here. I want them to work for me as vaqueros."

"What did you tell these men?"

"I told them to bring their families. That I would feed them and pay them and they would have houses and work very hard."

"Did you tell them about the war you made with Martin?"

"No. I did not tell them that."

"I will not go back to the ranch with you, Miguelito, if you are going to keep killing people. If you are taking men with you to fight with Martin, I will not go."

"Martin is on Aguilar land."

"No he is not. He bought the land from your family. He paid for it with money and he has the papers."

"Maybe."

"There is no maybe, Matteo Miguelito. What I say is true."

"Very well. I will not fight with Martin."

"You promise."

"I promise."

"Why were you talking to El Sabio? Don Carlos Figueroa?"

"I was not talking with him. He was talking with me."

"What did he talk about?"

"He is coming here tonight, with Jorge. He said that he wishes to speak with me about the families that will work on our ranch."

"He is a very wise man."

"That is why they call him El Sabio."

"You make the joke."

"Yes, because you will not. I want to see my son. I want to work my ranch. I have lost men in the war with Martin Baron. I think we will make much money in this war the gringos are fighting."

"There has been talk of that. There is much money in Brownsville. There are also many soldiers there."

"True. Soldiers need horses. Soldiers need meat. We have the cattle and we have the horses. We will sell them to the army."

"Which army?"

"It makes no difference, Luz. Whoever will pay the most money."

Luz left him there and went to the kitchen where she began preparing food for El Sabio, for it would be impolite not to offer food to guests who came to the house. Matteo sat there, drinking his *tepache* and smoking until he had finished both his drink and cigar. By then, the sun was setting and he walked outside to look at the crimson sky. The pueblo was very quiet, except for the yapping of a dog a few doors away, and then it stopped and he stood in silence as dusk began to seep through the pueblo in a slow trickle of shadows.

Luz had changed, he thought. She was not the same woman he had left at the ranch when he attacked the Barons. She no longer seemed as subservient or obedient. It was as if she had fled Bone and the ranch and had discovered a stronger will, perhaps even courage. She had never spoken to him as she had this evening; had never demanded anything of him. Now, she seemed determined to change him. He did not like that. A woman had her place and Luz had always known that. Her position in life had been bred into her and reinforced by her mother and father. A good wife never questioned her husband's intentions or actions. No, something had happened to change Luz, to stiffen her backbone, and that was something he was going to have to deal with after they returned home. As he would treat a spirited horse, he would give her her head for now, but later, he would have to rein her in, or break her all over again.

He dropped the stub of the cigar and ground it out under his boot heel. The colors in the sky had turned to pale ashes and were disappearing as the darkness descended and the first stars began to appear in the highest regions of the sky. Voices sprouted from adobes down the street, and from another place, he heard the faint strains of a guitar, the strings vibrating in a minor key. A child laughed and then was silent.

In the darkness, he thought of those men who had worked for him, his soldiers, who now were dead. The men he wanted dead, Martin and Anson Baron, and Mickey Bone, were still alive, and this angered him, fueled his hatred for those three. And as for those who had died, they had died because they were stupid and he felt no sorrow for them, had no remorse. He regretted that he had been captured, but he had not died. He was still alive and the taste of war was still strong in his mouth. He had loved the fighting and he had felt more alive when one of his lead balls found the heart of an enemy and spilled blood upon the ground. He could relive those moments for the rest of his life and find satisfaction and pleasure.

He saw them coming down the dark street. Not two men, as he had expected, but three. One he knew was Jorge Rios. The other, from the way he walked stooped over, he took to be El Sabio. The third man, in the middle, seemed out of place, and when they drew close, Matteo knew why he had seemed that way. He was wearing a black robe and, at his throat, a flash of white.

Matteo wanted to strangle Jorge for bringing the priest.

"Good evening," the priest said. "I am Padre Cruz, Mr. Aguilar."

"I know who you are. Why do you come here?"

"I was invited by El Sabio."

"And who gives permission to El Sabio to invite a priest to my house?"

"Why, your wife, Luz, Mr. Aguilar," Cruz said, with an amiable tone to his voice. "Shall we go inside, or do you prefer to talk out here in the street?"

"You must be a Jesuit," Matteo said.

"I am of the Society of Jesus, yes."

"You are not welcome here."

Luz appeared in the doorway. She walked outside, bowing slightly to Father Cruz and El Sabio.

"Please enter," she said. "My husband does not know what he is saying. He is not in a good mood."

She ushered Cruz ahead of the others and entered the house.

Jorge and El Sabio stood there, looking at Matteo. Copper light from the lamp inside lit their faces.

"Do not stand there like fools," Matteo said to the two men. "Go inside and let us get this over with quickly."

"With your permission," El Sabio said and led the way, with Jorge following close behind. Matteo entered last, a scowl on his face.

Luz had set out chairs for everyone, which Matteo noticed. It ran-kled that she hadn't told him she had invited the priest. He sat down as Luz brought plates laden with cake and forks. She gave out nap-kins and served steaming coffee just like the perfect hostess of a gringo manor house.

Matteo sipped his coffee in silence, waiting to hear the reasons that the priest and El Sabio had come to the house. He looked at El Sabio, who returned his gaze, then at the priest, who was already star-ing at him.

"I understand," Father Cruz said, "that you are moving some families from Valle to your ranch in Texas, Mr. Aguilar."

"That is true."

"You offer them a better life."

"Yes. This is a poor pueblo. The people here are poor. They do not have work. They have become lazy."

"It is said that you made war on one of your fellow ranchers," Cruz said.

"Of what import is that to you, Padre?"

"The people want to know if they will have to fight in a war be-cause the *norteamericanos* are at war."

"The war is far away from the Rio Grande Valley," Matteo said.

The priest breathed a sigh of relief.

Then El Sabio set down his plate and spoke to Matteo.

"Don Matteo," he said, "did you win the war with your neighbor, the gringo rancher?"

"It is of no import to you."

"That is true. But it is of import to you, Don Matteo. If you look at the history of war, at those who have started wars, you will see that the leaders of those armies wanted to lose and many times they did lose."

"El Sabio has reason," Cruz said. "The man who wages war against another knows he will lose the war, one way or the other. Even if he thinks he has won."

"I am not waging war."

"Good," El Sabio said, seemingly relieved. "These are my people, and I do not want to see them die without reason."

"Nor do I," Cruz said.

Matteo glared at them. Luz sat primly in a corner, watching them all like a cat with its tail twitching.

"Do not worry yourselves, then," Matteo said. "The families who come with me will work. They will not have to fight with anyone."

Cruz stood up. So did El Sabio.

"Then we will go and I will bless those who go with you, Don Matteo."

"Don Matteo," El Sabio said, "if you will have me, I will accompany you to your ranch. I am a good worker. Very strong."

"You may come with me, El Sabio."

Luz smiled wanly, but said nothing.

Jorge Rios cleared his throat. It was his mouth, Matteo knew, that had spoken of the war and the dead, including his brother. He would be punished for being a chattering magpie.

"Thank you, Don Matteo," El Sabio said. "Good night."

"Go with God," Cruz said.

Luz rose from her chair and saw the two men out. Matteo glared at Jorge after they had left. When his wife returned, he changed expression and smiled at her.

"You are a good man, Matteo," she said. "I hope you will keep your promises."

"I always keep my promises, my dear one."

Matteo set his plate down and his coffee cup, so hard that they clattered on the table. He stood up, looked at his wife and Jorge.

"I do a good thing here," he said. "The past is over. It is no more. Do not speak of our family to strangers ever again, either of you. Do you understand me?"

"Clear," Jorge said.

"Clear," from Luz.

Matteo walked over to the little box on a table and took out a cigar. He walked outside and lit it. He smoked and looked at the starry night sky and the way the smoke rose in the air and made the stars twinkle as if behind a thin shawl.

Luz came out a few moments later and stood next to him.

"I am sorry if I made you uncomfortable, Matteo. It was necessary to reassure those who would come with us to the ranch."

"I would have reassured them."

"I know. I have sorrow that I made you angry."

"It is done. Do not worry."

"I am pregnant again," she said. "We will have another child. I want him or her to grow up and be happy."

"That is good to hear," he said. But he said no more and Luz finally went back inside the house.

One day, Matteo thought, *I will kill Martin Baron and his son, Anson. And neither a priest nor El Sabio will stop me. I will have the Aguilar land back that they have stolen.*

He looked up at the sky and smiled.

"And God will bless me," he said aloud.

48

—■—

T HE HIGH-PITCHED APACHE screams were meant to terrify and
confuse their enemies. The Mescaleros had perfected this battle technique over centuries and used it because it worked. Anson
knew this, but the screams were so loud, they had the desired effect
on him, sending chills up his spine, churning his stomach into a fluttering caldron of fear.

He shook off the fear as he realized that the charging Culebra
and his braves were not coming after him and Peebo, but were racing to flank the charging white bull, their bows nocked with arrows,
their hands already pulling back their bowstrings.

In that single moment of clarity, Anson knew what Culebra was
going to do, and at the same time, he felt as if the ground was falling
away from beneath him. But it was only the sensation of his heart
sinking that he felt when he clearly and truly realized the savage nature of not only Culebra but the Apache.

Culebra galloped his pony straight at the white bull. He pulled his
bowstring back and leaned down to one side, toward the bull. He did
not present a clear target in that position and Anson cursed under his
breath as he brought his pistol up to take aim. Another warrior, on

the opposite side of the bull, also drew his bowstring taut and took aim at Diablo Blanco.

Anson cocked his pistol.

"Peebo, shoot that son of a bitch on the right," Anson yelled, as he tried to line up the pistol sights on Culebra.

He did not know if Peebo heard him because the noise of cattle and horse hoofbeats grew louder. Before Anson could fire his pistol, he saw Culebra come up very close to the bull and release his arrow. To his horror, Anson saw the shaft of the arrow fly to a point just behind the bull's right shoulder and sink into its flesh. At the same time, the warrior on the bull's left shot his arrow into a point behind the opposite shoulder. The bull staggered and veered first left, then right, blood spurting from both wounds.

Anson drew a bead on Culebra, fired, just as Culebra heeled his horse hard over, putting the animal into a tight turn. The ball hit the horse in the side, smashing through ribs and lungs. The horse foundered and staggered downslope. Anson had to jump aside to keep from being struck as the animal collapsed and fell. The momentum caused the horse to skid as Culebra leaped off to escape being crushed.

A cloud of dust and smoke arose, obscuring Anson's vision for a moment. Then, out of the dust, he saw Culebra rushing toward him, drawing a knife from its beaded scabbard as he ran. Anson turned to meet the Apache's charge, but he was too late. Culebra lashed out and knocked the pistol from Anson's hand. The weapon flew off in a crazy series of spirals and landed on the ground with a thud. Anson clawed for his own knife, slid it from its scabbard on his right hip.

Culebra started chanting in Mescalero, then rushed him again, his legs bent in a half-squatting position. He held his knife out from his body, high, as if to strike with a downward thrust. Anson whirled and danced away, slashing at Culebra with the blade of his big bowie knife.

"*Voy a matarte,*" Culebra said in Spanish.

"*Pues, venga, tu cabrón,*" Anson said.

Around him, Anson heard shooting, rifle and pistol fire, but it was as if he was listening through cotton. A painted demon danced in front of him, something hideous and alien, and when the two men drew close to each other, Anson could smell Culebra's fetid breath and the rank animal oils of his body, a body that seemed not to sweat but yet gave off a heady scent of some wild beast. The two men danced, bowed, ducked, thrust, parried like a pair of prizefighters, or gladiators.

Ford deployed his troopers in a pincer movement, cutting off the fleeing Apaches and closing in on them. One by one, the cavalrymen picked them off. They all died well. They all died bravely. But they were outnumbered and outgunned. Anson heard only part of it as he fought for his life, hand-to-hand, with Culebra, the bravest and fiercest of all the Mescaleros.

More Apache screams. And hoofbeats. Rifle shots. The crack of a pistol. Dust everywhere. And then, a sudden silence and, out of the corner of his eye, Anson saw shadows emerge and he caught sight of horses and mounted men as if he were locked into some kind of strange dream.

Culebra ducked and charged bandy-legged, swiping his knife in a wide arc. The tip of the blade caught on Anson's shirt and ripped it open as it passed close to his flesh. Anson swept downward with his own blade and slashed Culebra's arm, parting the flesh until it ran crimson, droplets of blood falling to the ground. Culebra twisted around and grazed Anson's open chest, slicing a long thin cut just under his rib cage. Anson felt the searing blade, like a firebrand across his body, and he sucked in his gut and backpedaled to avoid being struck again.

Culebra followed up on his advantage and leaped after Anson, slashing back and forth, thrusting, varying his strokes with a surprising expertise. Anson was panting from the exertion and sweat streamed into his eyes, stinging them with salt, nearly blinding him. He wiped the sweat away, but his face swam in it, glistened in the hot sun.

Mounted troopers ringed the two combatants. Peebo stood between Colonel Ford and Martin Baron, watching the fight in rapt fascination. At first, none spoke, but as the fight progressed, some of the men began to murmur and then Ford yelled out: "Anson Baron, you cut that son of a bitch into mincemeat."

Then the crowd began to cheer and call out encouraging words to their favorite, Anson Baron. Peebo too became caught up in the excitement.

"Anson, gut that bastard. Gut him good, son."

Culebra circled Anson, then reversed himself. Anson tried to correct his motion and that's when the Apache stepped in and caught him, driving his blade into Anson's left arm, twisting it, gouging out a chunk of flesh that flew up in the air as Anson jerked away. Blood gushed from the open wound.

Anson felt a weakness in his knees as blood poured from his arm. He gulped in air to get his second wind and went after Culebra, who twisted and writhed like a dervish to escape the slashing blade.

"We can kill that savage for you, son," one of the troopers said. "One shot ought to do it."

Anson shook his head, and closed on Culebra, fighting nausea and dizziness.

Culebra attacked Anson from his vulnerable side, the left, well aware that he had wounded that arm of his opponent. Anson knew what the Mescalero was doing and he did not change his position. But when Culebra dashed toward him, his knife poised to strike his left arm, Anson let him come close, then sidestepped and twisted his body around. At the same time, he ducked low and rammed his knife straight at Culebra's exposed left side.

Anson felt the knife strike the soft flesh in Culebra's side. He drew the blade inward as Culebra's momentum carried him forward. He felt the knife glance off bone and slide free. Blood gushed over his hand. He whirled to follow up as Culebra faltered, grasping his wounded side.

As Anson waded back toward Culebra, the Apache turned and grappled with Anson, grasping the wrist of his knife hand and pushing Anson backward. With his other hand, Culebra tried to slide his knife underneath Anson's arm and stab him in the stomach. Anson grabbed Culebra's wrist and bent his arm backward. The two struggled to free their hands and strike knife blows.

Anson felt Culebra's hot breath on his face, and as he looked into his enemy's eyes, he saw that Culebra's spirit was still strong. He could almost feel the Apache's muscles straining and he held on, trying to force Culebra down to the ground where he could finish him off.

Culebra said something in his native tongue, his face a hideous mask of paint.

The two men twisted and turned, each fighting for an advantage. Anson summoned up all of his strength, then relaxed. Culebra's body slumped forward and Anson brought up a knee hard, smashing the Apache in the testicles. Culebra doubled up with the sudden pain and crumpled.

Anson wrenched his knife hand free and brought the knife down, ramming the blade into Culebra's shoulder. He turned the knife to widen the wound, jerked the knife free and slammed the blade into Culebra's side with all the force of a pile driver. Culebra staggered away, mortally wounded.

Anson stepped in quickly, unwilling to trust the Apache to die before striking back at him. He grabbed a handful of Culebra's hair and jerked his head backward. Then he slashed at Culebra's throat. The blade parted the flesh as easily as a hot knife cuts through soft butter and Culebra's throat opened like a flower, spewing blood all over Anson, soaking his hand and arm in a flood of bright red fluid.

Culebra's eyes glazed over with the frost of death and the light went out of them as he sank to his knees. He opened his mouth, but no sound came out and he looked at Anson with an expression of surprise and bitterness. Then the wounded man pitched over and fell facedown on the ground. Blood pooled beneath his severed neck and spread out in a puddle that was quickly soaked up by the dust.

Anson stepped away, gasping for air.

A huge cheer arose from the troopers surrounding the field of battle and Anson felt faint. He tried to smile, but was too fatigued to even move his lips.

He heard the rumble of a wagon and the jingle of traces as Doc Purvis drove up in the ambulance. Men dismounted and rushed to Anson's side. Peebo was the first to grab Anson and keep him from falling as Anson's knees turned to gelatin and his legs started to wobble.

"You done good, son," Peebo said huskily, his voice filled with emotion.

Anson looked up and saw his father standing there. It was the first time he had seen Martin in his Confederate uniform.

"Doc Purvis is here," Martin said. "He'll fix that arm up for you, Anson."

"You look pretty good in that uniform, Pa."

Martin laughed. "It itches like hell."

Purvis and Lorene wove their way through the crowd. Purvis was carrying a black leather satchel. Lorene had a blue bandana tied around her head to keep her hair from falling in her face. She was carrying a tray of bandages and a tourniquet. The crowd moved back as the doctor examined the hole in Anson's arm.

"Took quite a chunk of meat out of you, I see."

"Anson," Lorene said, "does it hurt much?"

"I didn't know you were with the cavalry, Lorene," Anson said.

"He's lost some blood." Doc Purvis looked at Lorene. "Let's get a tourniquet on that arm, just above the wound, and take him over to the ambulance."

A few minutes later, Anson was lying inside the ambulance and Doc Purvis was cleaning his wound. He applied salve and Lorene bandaged it with clean linen. She then slipped his arm into a sling after he sat up. Peebo stood just outside the ambulance looking in.

"Culebra killed that white bull," Peebo said.

"I know."

"At least none of them Mescaleros will bother us no more. The cavalry done killed 'em all, except for the two you and I dispatched."

"Dispatched?" Anson looked at Peebo as if his friend was addled.

Peebo grinned. "That's what these troopers call it."

"You take on more new words than a woman does pretty dresses, Peebo."

"You should lie quiet for a while, Anson," Purvis said, climbing out of the wagon. "Colonel Ford is going to bivouac here for the night. Lorene will cook you up some broth and you can eat when you're hungry. Nurse Sisler will give you some powders for the pain. You'll be as good as new in a month or so."

"I've got to get back to the ranch," Anson said.

"You're not going anywhere," Lorene said. "Peebo?"

"She's right, son. Colonel Ford is going to enlist us in his cavalry. We're goin' to Brownsville. We'll get sworn in tomorrow morning."

"Huh?"

"Ain't no ranch to tend. Your pa says you can recruit you some Mexican hands down there and get the Box B up and runnin' again. You and me will just be temporary like with this here outfit."

Purvis walked away, and after Peebo nodded, he departed, too, leaving Lorene and Anson alone inside the wagon.

"It's good to see you, Anson. I'm sorry you got hurt."

"I never expected to see you out here, Lorene. I'm mighty glad to see you, too. You're Doc's nurse, huh?"

She leaned down and kissed him on the forehead.

"I love you, Anson," she whispered. Then she began to stroke his forehead with soothing fingers. "I love you so much."

"I reckon I love you, too, Lorene. More than anything. I'm glad I'm here with you."

"Does it matter so much that you didn't get your white bull? I know you had your heart set on him for breeding."

He thought of a lot of things that had mattered very much to him. All of them were yesterday's matters. Now, most of them did not seem so important. Culebra had killed the white bull, Diablo Blanco. And he had killed Culebra. Was that the way of the world? One thing killed another, and it didn't seem to make much difference. He no longer had Culebra for an enemy, but the time had come to give up that enemy. Maybe it was the white bull's time to die, as well. Maybe the big old bull was never meant to be caught or tamed or pastured. Juanito would have had an answer for such mysteries.

Anson looked up into Lorene's eyes and felt as if time had shifted, as if he had come through a hard bad place and emerged in another dimension, where life flowed freely and without harness, a place where it was cool and quiet and peaceful. Where there was a woman you loved and who loved you. It was a good place to be just then and it was where he wanted to be.

"No," he said softly. "It doesn't matter much. There are other things more important than that white bull, I reckon. And I'll find them in due time."

"You will, Anson," she said. "You'll find everything you want and need."

She leaned down again and kissed him on the lips and her shadow over his face was cool and soothing. It felt as if he was lying under the shade of a tree in some ancient and holy paradise. He felt, as the pain in his arm faded away, as if he had been kissed by an angel.

He closed his eyes as a weariness settled into him, the tiredness like a drug that wafted away all pain and turmoil. He could almost feel himself healing and he knew that it was Lorene's gentle touch that was making him whole again.

49

I N LATER YEARS, when the Civil War was over, Anson Baron began to reflect on the strangeness and incomprehensibility of life. For in that late summer of 1861, he found himself beginning a journey that was full of parallels and paradoxes. Then, he knew only that Colonel John S. "Rip" Ford was going to Brownsville, Texas, on the Mexican border. He had no idea that his life would be forever bound to that place, along with the lives of so many others he knew. It seemed to him as if they were all bound by fate to go to Brownsville, which lay in such a remote part of Texas, he had never considered it as a destination.

Yet in Brownsville lay not only his own destiny but the destiny of those others from the Rio Grande Valley. What drew them all to that place at that time? Anson wondered. Had he known what lay ahead during those war years, he might have chosen to return to the Box B and never venture into that unknown world that was waiting for him, as well as many of those he knew, including his own father. However, he realized that he would never have learned anything about himself, the people he knew, and those final days of the war, when he fought men like himself who were wearing the blue uniforms of the Union.

Had he not gone with Ford's Cavalry of the West that day, he would never have known about true courage, and honor. He would never have fought with Ford in the last battle of the Civil War, a battle that was fought, in an ironic twist of fate, a month after the war was over, at a place on the Rio Grande called Palmito Hill.

But afterward, after that last bloody and terrible battle, Anson would remember something his friend Juanito Salazar, the Argentinean, told him before he died.

"Life is a journey," Juanito had said, "and we cannot see into the future. We can only live in this present moment, this Now. And the Now is eternal. If you live in the present with honor, the future will not hold terror for you, but only promise. Fate would have it no other way."

Anson would come to learn that each action in a man's life sets forces in motion over which he has no control. In Brownsville, he would begin to see that all roads lead to the same destination, but that each man's journey to that destination follows a different path.

As Anson told Peebo later, "You know, I think we're always at the right place at the right time, Peebo. As if something inside of us, or outside of us, is leading us to a particular place when we're ready to go there."

"Son, I think you're plumb loco," Peebo said. "I don't never know where in hell I'm goin' and there's some places I just never want to be."

But Anson knew better.